IF ONLY

A Sam Westin Mystery

With Characters from
The Neema Mysteries

Pamela Beason

WildWing Press

Bellingham, Washington, USA

This book is dedicated to everyone who searches for missing hikers in our public lands. This includes many civilian volunteers, as well as park and forest service rangers, police officers, and sometimes teenage Scout troops, volunteer pilots, and military personnel.

WILDWING PRESS
Bellingham, Washington

Note from the Author

This is a crossover novel that includes characters and settings from my Sam Westin Wilderness Mysteries and my Neema Mysteries. If you are familiar with only one of these series, I hope you'll check out the other one. Evansburg, Washington, the setting for all stories involving Neema's gorilla family, Detective Matthew Finn, Dr. Grace McKenna, and the gorilla caretakers, is a fictional town in the foothills of the Cascades. North Cascades National Park Complex is a real location with wonderful scenery, miles of wilderness, and amazing hiking trails, many of which I have explored. But I have played fast and loose with Sam's cross-country travel in this story. While I have explored off-trail in many parks, I have never strayed far from the popular hiking trails in this area. I am a writer of fiction. I make things up.

IF ONLY

1

Evansburg, Washington

A loud bang startled Blake out of his dream, where he was cutting hundreds of gerbera daisies for bouquets while fretting about how his greenhouse employer could possibly ship them all before the flowers wilted.

Had that been a clap of thunder? Now he heard horrific noises that could only be described as shrieks of terror. Shrieks that were not remotely human.

The gorillas! He was ape-sitting in Evansburg, hundreds of miles away from home in Bellingham.

Grace hadn't mentioned anything about the apes being afraid of storms, and while the sky had been overcast when Blake had gone to bed, no thunderclouds had been in sight. As he groggily lifted his head off the pillow, he heard another loud bang. Throwing himself out of bed, his foot caught in the sheet and he landed on the floor. He pushed himself up and rushed to the window to stare out into the dark yard, his heart pounding.

The moon was obscured by clouds, and all Blake could decipher were black hulks rocketing around inside the gorilla enclosure. Was that a dark creature racing to the edge of the forest? Had the gorillas been attacked by a wolf? Or a cougar?

He tugged on jeans over his jockey shorts, grabbed the

flashlight from the bedside table, and rushed outside, barefoot. This would have to happen, whatever *this* was, on *his* watch. He'd been ape-sitting here for more than two weeks without incident in this weird gig that had already morphed from a month to six weeks, and now the gorillas were in an uproar over something. The apes were often raucous when they chased each other in play or fought over food, but he hadn't yet heard a cacophony like this. The volume of their alarmed cries was earsplitting.

He stubbed his big toe on a rock and then, cursing, hop-stepped on a patch of damp ground just before he reached the pole that held the switch. He flicked it on, flooding the gorilla enclosure with light. Gumu, the giant silverback, immediately rushed the fence, pounding his chest, stopping only inches away to bare long sharp teeth in a threat display that made Blake gasp. Despite knowing the heavy steel-mesh barrier had always held the apes, he backed up a few steps.

Use the feeding portal, but never let Gumu get close enough to grab you. Just pass the food through and let it drop into the bin below. Never go into the enclosure with the gorillas. Neema and Kanoni would never intentionally hurt you, but Gumu could rip off your head.

The warnings of Dr. Grace McKenna, the gorillas' keeper and language researcher, had made a believer out of Blake. He stayed well clear of the small rectangular opening in the fencing and made sure his helpers, Maya and Z, did as well. Setting the flashlight down by his feet, Blake held up his hands to show they were empty. "It's okay, Gumu. Whatever it was, is gone. You're okay. You're safe."

The large female ape huddled, her long arms over her daughter, three-year-old Kanoni. Both mother and baby gorilla continued to loudly howl their distress.

"Neema, it's okay now." Blake tried to make his voice soothing. Could she even hear him in this din? "Calm down." He bounced his open palms downward to sign what he meant, one of the few gestures he'd mastered.

The gorillas refused to believe his reassurance. The cacophony continued. Gumu grabbed his favorite toy, a massive, threadbare tractor tire, and hurled it into the far corner of the yard. The heavy tire bounced off the fence with a loud clang and rolled into the outside wall of the barn before thudding onto its side.

Across the yard, a door banged open. Jonathan Zyrnek, Grace McKenna's part-time helper who called himself Z, and Maya, Blake's young, wayward associate, stumbled out of the staff trailer, their clothes in disarray, hair hanging loose and tangled. They joined Blake beside the fence, and the three of them watched in horrified fascination as the silverback continued to ricochet around the enclosure, snatching up blankets and toys and throwing them in a fury. Maya clapped her hands over her ears.

The skunky reek of marijuana wafted from the couple. Weed was legal in Washington now, so Blake wasn't surprised that the laid-back Z used. But Maya had recently weaned herself off some hard-core drugs, and Blake didn't like Z leading her back down that path. He eyed his young comrades uncertainly. "Help?"

Maya wouldn't have a clue what to do, but Z had worked there for years and was experienced in dealing with the apes. However, Grace had warned Blake that Z wasn't always dependable. She'd hired Blake because she wanted "an adult in charge" of her beloved gorillas.

At this moment, Blake didn't feel particularly adult, and he certainly wasn't in charge of the situation. Recently he'd wondered if anyone else had even applied for this crazy temp job.

"What's happening?" Z finally asked, blinking.

"I heard two loud bangs," Blake told them. "At least, I think I did."

"Neema," Z signed as he shouted. "What happened?"

He had to repeat the question multiple times before the mother gorilla finally stopped her distress hooting, detached herself from Kanoni, and then rubbed her long arms across her chest a few times. She briefly touched the tips of her fingers together before she wrapped her arms around her daughter again.

"'*Baby, baby, baby,*' I think," translated Z, frowning in concentration. "And then, maybe '*hurt.*'"

"Hurt?" Blake picked up the flashlight and switched it on, swept the beam toward the edge of the forest. "I was afraid I saw an animal run away toward the woods."

The shaft of light revealed only fir trees, standing thickly shoulder to shoulder around the perimeter of the property.

"Could something crawl in through the feeding port?" Blake moved the flashlight beam to the rectangular opening. No incriminating tufts of an intruder's fur were conveniently caught in the metal frame. Nothing seemed amiss except for the gorillas' tantrums.

Moving the beam back, he shone it into the gorilla enclosure. Neema blinked at the glare and hid her face in Kanoni's fur. The bright light enraged Gumu all over again, and the silverback charged the fence once more, slamming into the chain link so violently that Blake feared the fencing would rip loose from the steel poles.

He quickly redirected his flashlight, focusing the beam down by his bare foot. Why were his toes red?

"Wait." Z snatched the flashlight out of Blake's hand, and shone it back into the enclosure, illuminating a pool of darkness beneath the huddle of fur that was Neema and Kanoni.

"Oh, poor things. They're so scared they peed all over themselves," Maya moaned.

"I hope that's only pee." Z moved the flashlight beam back and forth.

Blake retrieved the flashlight from him and swept the beam back along the route he'd taken from his trailer. A couple of yards away was a pool of wet darkness, vaguely red in the dim light. Focusing the light on his foot again, he said, "I stepped in what looks like blood. I think someone was here, shooting at the gorillas. And it looks like whoever that was injured themselves at the same time." He'd heard tales from his housemate Sam's lover, FBI Agent Chase Perez, about inept criminals who caught their hand in the hammer of a revolver or accidentally shot themselves, thus providing convenient DNA evidence at the scene of a crime.

"Baby hurt." Z's eyes were on the mother gorilla. His fingers were curled into the wire mesh of the fence, his face tense. "Neema, come," he urged. Releasing the fencing, he signed as he spoke. "Kanoni, come here."

Blake redirected the flashlight beam back to the mother and baby gorilla, hoping that he wouldn't see what he feared.

When Neema let go of her daughter for a moment, Z groaned. A large wet stain darkened the baby gorilla's chest and abdomen. "Shit, looks like the shooter nailed Kanoni."

"Christ." Blake sucked in a breath and held it for a few seconds, trying to focus his thoughts. Gumu continued his frantic rushes and threat calls, and both mother and baby gorilla resumed their anguished hooting, only slightly softer now. The racket made it hard to think.

Turning to Z, Blake asked, "So let's assume the little gorilla was shot. What's the procedure?"

Scraping his shoulder-length hair back from his face with his hands, Z scrunched his face up in a frown. "Call the vet ASAP. Tell her to bring a tranq gun and supplies to knock out three gorillas. Then call the cops."

Blake turned to go back to his trailer. "I'm on it. You two see if there's any way to talk Gumu and Neema down."

Z snorted in reply. Maya pressed her hands against the wire mesh, murmuring, "Oh, poor babies."

"Step away from the feeding portal," Blake reminded her.

She rewarded him with an annoyed glare, but pulled her hands away from the fence and stepped back, folding her arms across her chest.

Blake trotted back to his trailer, his heart pounding and his brain firing in all directions like a Fourth of July sparkler. Why had he taken this weird gig, anyway? Instead of this detour from normal life patching his broken heart back together, it just might fracture his sanity.

He really didn't know much about animals except for Simon, his feline housemate back in Bellingham. And whatever his human housemate Sam had told him about her adventures with wildlife. If only she were here instead of hundreds of miles away in Bellingham, or maybe on her planned backpacking trip in the North Cascades by now.

But Summer "Sam" Westin spent her time in the American wilderness; she probably wouldn't know much about exotic species like gorillas, either. The only person who really knew these apes was in Hawaii right now, on a rare vacation: Dr. Grace McKenna, the scientist who had trusted Blake to keep her three signing gorillas safe and sound.

2

Kona, Big Island, Hawaii

Dawn had only begun to lighten the sky over Kona on the big island of Hawaii when Detective Matthew Finn heard his cell phone chime from the bedside table. Forcing his eyes open, he snatched it and slid out of bed in one quick motion, turning his back as he answered quietly. "Finn. What's up, Dawes?"

Behind him his lover, Dr. Grace McKenna, turned over. "Matt?" Her voice was blurred with sleep.

"It's for me," Finn said over his shoulder. "Go back to sleep, Grace." He padded away from the bedroom toward the small balcony, grabbing his robe from a chair back and shrugging it on one-handed as he went. Outside, the chorus of tropical birds that heralded daybreak was growing in volume. A scarlet bird he hadn't noticed before touched down briefly on the railing before taking flight into the surrounding trees.

"Sorry to bug you on vacation, Finn, but we got a situation here."

Finn checked the time on the phone. 5:12 a.m. So a little after eight in the morning back in Evansburg, Washington. His detective partner, Perry Dawes, would have just reached the end of his graveyard shift.

"Spit it out," Finn urged. "Why call me? You got a whole police force there." The Evansburg PD was small but should be able to handle anything short of a terrorist attack.

"The, uh, situation is at Grace's compound. Someone shot the little gorilla."

"The baby? Kanoni? Shit." Finn turned to face the bedroom. Grace remained an inert form under the sheets. He pulled the glass slider shut behind him. "Did you nail the shooter?"

"Nobody even saw whoever it was. Just disappeared into the woods, apparently. But it looks like he got hurt, maybe cut his hand or shot himself in the foot or something. There's blood on the outside of the pen as well as inside."

"How's the victim?" Finn asked, reluctant to say Kanoni's name aloud again with Grace only a glass panel away.

"Vet says serious condition, but she—it is a she, right?—will probably pull through. You want I should call Grace?"

"Oh God, no." His partner hadn't had a break from taking care of those gorillas in at least a decade. Plus, she'd recently suffered a miscarriage. He and Grace had another week to spend in this peaceful condo overlooking the beach, and then they were planning another two exploring the island of Kauai. He'd banked all his vacation days to join her on this trip. "Are all the staff safe?"

"For now," Dawes answered. "We got zilch to go on, not even footprints, so right now, we can only hope that the shooter doesn't come back. The fruit and the freak that Grace left in charge are taking turns keeping watch."

"Watch it," Finn warned.

"Alrighty, then let's be PC. Of course, I am referring to that guy Blake that Grace hired, who—or is it whom?—as far as I can deduce, usually works in a greenhouse and studies cooking for fun. And what's-his-name, the hippie type who's usually here, Zyrtek, Z—"

"Zyrnek."

"Whatever he's calling himself this week. I think they can keep an eye. And I'll get the uniforms to cruise through a coupla times each shift. But you know a lot more about this ape business than any of us around here do. Didn't something like this happen before?"

"No shootings. Another attack, back a long time ago." Grace had lost her previous male gorilla, Spencer—one of the gorillas who could "talk," as Grace had explained during a television interview about her interspecies communication project—to an outraged religious fanatic who had poisoned him because he believed the ape was an abomination. The man claimed he'd done the world a favor, because animals couldn't think and certainly didn't talk. God gave only humans souls and language.

It was a disturbing thought that the maniac, Frank Keyes, was already back in society. According to Washington State law, animals were property. Killing a captive gorilla was animal cruelty in the first degree, not murder, and the maniac had served four years of his five-year sentence and paid his $10,000 fine to the university that had actually owned Spencer.

Crimes involving humans and animals and the legal system were always complicated, and the results were rarely satisfying. Since he had met Grace and her gorillas, Finn had been tangled in several disquieting incidents that he didn't care to examine too carefully. But this was the first shooting. And the shooter was still at large? Keyes had been out of jail for years now, and Finn hadn't checked up on him for at least a couple of those. Had he returned to kill another "talking" gorilla?

Finn sighed. "I'll be back on the first plane I can catch out of here. Keep 'em safe at the compound. Preserve all the evidence you can find."

"You got it. See ya soon."

3

Evansburg

By the end of the day, Blake's head ached from lack of sleep, and his neck was stiff with anxiety. After the shooting, which would probably scar the gorillas for life, Dr. Stephanie Farin had rolled out of bed when he'd called at 3:00 a.m. and shown up forty-five minutes later in her mobile vet clinic, carrying a pistol configured to fire anesthetic darts. She had requested that they close the rolling door between the outdoor enclosure and the gorilla barn before she arrived, but with the gorilla hysterics still going on, none of the humans was brave enough to risk going inside the fenced pen to do so.

Blake supposed that most frightened or wounded animals would have raced to hide in their safe space, but the apes didn't disappear inside their barn. Gumu was determined to keep all humans outside the fence. Neema wouldn't leave Kanoni, who hadn't moved from her hunched position since she'd been shot.

Dr. Farin darted the silverback first. When the dart struck Gumu in the back of his shoulder, he roared like Godzilla and slammed into the fence, his long, sharp incisors bared in rage.

Next, Dr. Farin darted Neema, who immediately yanked the dart from her backside, but then succumbed to the anesthetic only a minute later, crumpling into a mound of black fur and leathery hands and feet. Emitting a mournful howl, Kanoni threw herself across her mother and clung to her, whimpering. She didn't even seem to notice when the tranquilizer dart embedded itself in her thigh. She, too, was unconscious within seconds.

Gumu rocketed around the cage once, then reached for the bottom of the climbing net before he collapsed to the ground in a massive heap. The cacophony ceased, leaving all the humans in stunned silence.

Blake had never harbored a desire to go hunting, and this—shooting intelligent animals in a cage—felt way too close to that, except even more brutal. What kind of madman wanted to shoot a captive gorilla?

After a few minutes, Dr. Farin judged it safe to go in. With the help of Z and a very nervous Blake, she repositioned the tranquilized adult gorillas so they couldn't suffocate on their own vomit. When Blake tugged on Neema's arm, he was astounded at how long it was. Her leathery black fingers had the same joints and ridged finger pads and nails as a person. So human-looking. He couldn't decide if that was more disturbing than seeing that her feet looked like hands. So nonhuman-looking.

Fortunately, the female gorilla was relatively easy to roll. Blake guessed Neema weighed about the same as he did. Gumu was a different story, and it took all the humans to shift the huge silverback from his back, where he'd fallen, to his side. "He weighs about 375," the vet told them.

The silverback's mouth was open. His canines, Blake estimated, were more than two inches long and razor-sharp. What the heck did a plant-eating primate need with fangs?

Dr. Farin noticed Blake staring at Gumu's teeth and

answered his unspoken question. "For defending the troop. You know, his family."

The baby gorilla had collapsed onto her side in a fetal position, but the vet rolled Kanoni onto her back. The little ape's mouth lolled open, and her eyes were slitted but not completely shut. The vet squeezed some ointment into her eyes and then, while Blake and Z anxiously stood guard over the adult gorillas, she and Maya grasped an arm and a leg each and carried the tranquilized little gorilla to a cot inside the veterinary van, where Dr. Farin strapped Kanoni down.

Dawn was breaking as two patrol cars pulled up alongside the vet's van. Blake spent a good hour explaining what had transpired. They had shone their flashlights on the two large heaps of fur inside the enclosure, but the cops insisted on staying outside the pen. Blake couldn't blame them, especially after the vet returned with the tranquilizer antidote in a couple of syringes.

"Stay outside the enclosure," Dr. Farin ordered Z and Blake. "I'm going to inject these animals to wake them up. That could happen fast, so stand by the gate and be ready to close it behind me."

Neema and Gumu slowly came back to consciousness and seemed disoriented. They both lumbered into the barn, staggering like drunks. The vet watched them make their way, and then nodded in Blake's direction.

"Kanoni needs immediate surgery," Dr. Farin told Blake. "I've got to take her back to the clinic. You'll keep an eye on the adults to make sure they recover completely, right?"

"Of course," Blake promised, while wondering how the hell he was supposed to do that. What he knew about gorilla physiology and psychology could be etched on the head of a pin.

"There's a camera inside," Z informed the vet. "If the gorillas haven't dismantled it again, I'll turn it on and we can keep watch that way."

Noting a look of surprise on Blake's face, Z added, "Grace didn't tell you about it? It's there so the staff can keep track of the gorillas' signing when they're out of our sight, but we don't turn it on too often. The monitor's in the staff trailer." He tilted his head in that direction. "Somehow Gumu notices when it's on, and if he does, he usually rips it off the wall."

"Watch 'em, but I think they'll be fine." Facing Blake, Dr. Farin said, "I'll report back about the little one's condition. Grace is probably having a stroke, isn't she?"

"She's in Hawaii." Blake didn't tell the vet that he hadn't had the guts to call the woman in the middle of the night.

"Good for her," the vet said. As if she'd read Blake's thoughts, she added, "Actually, I wouldn't tell her if I were you until we know what the prognosis is."

With a curt nod, Dr. Farin drove away with the baby gorilla.

After taking down Blake's story and everyone's name and phone numbers, the two uniformed cops examined the pool of blood outside the fence. Then they walked the perimeter, studying the ground.

"Call in forensics?" Blake heard the shorter one ask the other.

"For an animal case?" The bearded uniform scoffed. "The sarge would never spring for that. That monkey isn't like a prime head of livestock. And she isn't even dead. This is Dawes's headache."

After promising to file a report, the officers left.

The officers hadn't seem particularly concerned that an armed, trigger-happy intruder was on the loose. But this was ranch country, and Blake supposed guns were common out here. Another reason he'd been insane to take this job. What the hell had he been thinking?

Around 6:30 a.m., Perry Dawes, a plainclothes detective, arrived, and Blake, Z, and Maya had to tell their stories all over again. Blake, feeling punchy by then, wondered how much his story had varied from cop to cop and how that might reflect on him. He really hadn't seen much of anything.

"The shooter probably hightailed it for the forest service road back there." Dawes pointed to the woods.

Blake raised an eyebrow. "I didn't know there was one."

"If you walk in past the tree line about one hundred yards or so, you'd run into it."

Should he have explored the area more thoroughly before settling in here? Should Grace have told him? What else didn't he know?

"Seems coming in that way would be a lot more work than coming down the driveway," Blake observed.

"True, but a safer bet if you're planning to do something illegal, like shoot someone's pet." Dawes shoved his hands into his front pockets.

The three gorillas were not pets but valuable research subjects in an interspecies language project, Dr. McKenna had explained. But Blake didn't care to get into that with this detective.

Dawes seemed in a hurry to leave. "I'll see if the boss will spring for some forensic work," he told Blake. "No promises."

A few hours later, a lone man in a jacket with an EPD emblem, apparently the Evansburg forensics "team," appeared to collect a soil sample from the blood-darkened earth. After walking around the property, he remarked, "No casings? Damn."

Blake felt like he should apologize, but he wasn't sure what for.

"Likely a revolver, then," the man concluded. "I'll ask Doc Farin about the bullet."

Mr. Forensics vanished into the woods for forty-five minutes. When he returned, he said, "Yeah, there are all sorts of tracks on the road back there. I'll drive around and make a few casts in case we get lucky, but don't get your hopes up. Gravel roads don't give up many details."

The following hours had passed as if in slow motion, with Blake and Maya and Z taking turns keeping watch just in case someone with a loaded gun showed up. Z brought out a shotgun that made Blake wonder even more about the young man's background.

When he caught Blake staring at it, Z shrugged. "Bears," he said by way of explanation, tilting his head toward the surrounding forest.

Great. Something else Dr. McKenna hadn't told him about.

Blake focused on his gorilla-keeping duties, which consisted mainly of gathering and chopping massive quantities of cauliflower and broccoli and assorted fruits into gorilla-size pieces, then baking heavy loaves of whole-grain bread for the apes, which he loaded into two big plastic bins. The bread seemed a curious addition. What wild food did bread take the place of?

He had been grateful when Grace had explained the apes were trained to use a latrine inside the barn, so he was spared gorilla litter box duty, a chore he hadn't even thought about up to that point.

When he walked outside with the food, Z and Maya were strolling toward Z's battered pickup.

"The gorillas are inside the barn, and they seem calm for now, both just watching a spider build a web in the corner," Z said. "I turned the camera on for five minutes to be sure. When Gumu turned his head toward the camera, I switched it off. I think it must make some noise that only a gorilla can hear."

"Thanks for telling me." Blake shifted the bins he held, balancing one on his hip.

"Since it seems like not much else is going on now, Maya and I are going to go for a hike, okay?" Z glanced toward the pickup, where Maya was leaning in what she probably thought was a seductive pose against the dented fender.

Blake nodded. He wasn't so keen on being the only human left in the compound, but Z was correct—nothing was going on at the moment. Dr. Farin said she'd call periodically with reports on Kanoni. The police were . . . He wasn't sure what the police were doing right now, but he certainly had no control over their schedule.

Blake dumped the food through the portal into the metal bin below, then filled the gorillas' water bucket by threading a hose through the fence, keeping a wary eye out for irritated gorillas emerging from the barn.

4

Evansburg

Widelene's brain drifted in and out of a fog. Johan had tied a strip of sheet around her body, over the hole in her abdomen and the matching one in her back. But she could feel wetness seeping into the sheets beneath her. The painkillers he had given her had worn off hours ago.

How many hours had she been unconscious? Never had she wanted her husband so badly. After three tries and thousands of dollars, he still hadn't been able to come to the United States. She worried about him every minute, and she'd been worrying for years. His job at a small bank in Port-au-Prince was secure, but nearly every day the gang that had killed so many others stopped him in the street to demand more protection money. Just last year, her husband had witnessed a gang leader murder the mayor of their town. Many had been killed for seeing less. Her brother, a cab driver, had been murdered years ago when he refused to hand over the cash from his taxi fares, and her mother had died in a crossfire of bullets from rival gangs while she was hanging out laundry in her own backyard. Haiti ran red with blood every day.

In their last phone call, her husband had told her he had a lead on a new route. But that had been nine months ago, before

Johan had quit paying for her cell phone. At least then she'd managed to tell her husband that she was living and working in Washington State. She'd tried to call him once on an ancient public telephone, but his number was no longer good. How would he find her? She'd worked at several different jobs since that last conversation, and this dark, cold house was the third place she and Johan had lived in this year.

Every time she asked when she'd get legal papers and a better job, Johan told her not to be an imbecile, that these things took time. He'd reminded her if she told anyone where she lived or where she was from, the ICE thugs would come for her and send her back home. Along with her brat. That's what Johan called Rosaline: *her brat.*

Her love, her salvation—that's how Widelene thought of her daughter. Her little girl was beautiful and so smart, so mature for her age. Widelene taught her to be quiet, obedient, and resourceful. Independent, not clingy like so many children. She had to be, to live the life they had. Best of all, Rosaline was American. Surely ICE would never deport an American child. But would they deport that child's mother?

Her husband would be so amazed to see Rosaline. Widelene had been almost eight months pregnant when the overcrowded boat had landed on the coast of the United States. Sebastian, one of their many guides, had told her the ground under their feet was called Louisiana.

After that, there'd been blistering days in the backs of trucks, their jolting journeys making her belly and her head ache. Never enough water, never enough to eat, pissing and soiling themselves like pigs in a barnyard. More than once, she'd wondered if this United States might be worse than home.

She had a cousin here, Mirlande Delva, somewhere in Washington State, and so with the last of her money, she'd arranged for transport in another truck to a place called Spokane, where Sebastian said a man named Johan would meet her and give her a place to stay and a job until she met up with her cousin. The truck had crossed so many different states, it was farther than she could ever have imagined from her island nation.

Her few remaining relatives in Haiti had told her that Mirlande was doing well. Family would help her find her way here in a new country. Here, at least, she had hope for a better future for herself and for Rosaline. Hope was something that no longer existed in Haiti.

She questioned whether the other migrants on her journey felt the same way. Most of the others in the truck spoke Spanish, and one looked and sounded as if he was Chinese. Or maybe Korean, or Vietnamese. On a particularly scorching day, one fellow passenger, a boy of seven, died. His aunt passed soon afterward. Their bodies had been taken away in the middle of the night. The rest of them had said prayers for the souls of the departed.

Today, Widelene needed someone to pray for *her* soul. "You have to get a doctor for me, Johan," she begged him.

He sat on the bed beside her and leaned close. "You know I can't do that. They will put me in prison. You can't survive without me. They'll take Rosaline away. Haven't I been good to you?"

She groaned. The pain was agonizing, so bad that it was hard to absorb his words.

"I know it hurts now, Lene, but it will get better." He bathed her face with cold water. "You're strong. You gave birth without help. I cannot believe that monkey shot you. I will kill it."

"No killing, please." She'd seen more than enough of that.

Johan had brought the gun to kill the gorillas simply because they made too much noise during the day when he tried to sleep. Too much whiskey always made him want to kill something. A rabbit in the yard, a squirrel, a gorilla. Sometimes she thought he killed things to show her how easily he could kill her whenever he wanted.

She touched his arm now. "You must find my cousin. Mirlande will take care of me."

Johan scowled, annoyed. "I told you, and I keep telling you, I'm trying. She moved, left no forwarding address, some say to California, others say to Montana. And it seems that maybe she got married and changed her name. But know that every day I am checking out leads on your cousin, sweetheart."

Widelene's heart sank. The United States was an unbelievably big country. Such vast spaces in which to get lost. Even this one state of Washington was nearly seven times bigger than her home country.

She suspected Johan was lying. Widelene understood that women often had to pay their way with sex, men with physical labor. But Johan required her to do both. He wanted her to keep on cleaning rooms and doing laundry in that decrepit hotel, making money for him in a place where nobody spoke her language. Thank goodness that sometimes kind tourists left small amounts of cash in the rooms. When she had enough to get away, she would take Rosaline and strike out on her own.

What would the hotel manager think when she failed to show up today? All the man could do was call Johan. Only his cell phone worked here, and nobody knew they were living in this old house. Camping, really, not living, with no running water or electricity.

Johan shifted his weight to stand up. Widelene clutched at his arm. "Promise me you'll take care of Rosaline." Her little girl was not quite three. "There's hardly any food left."

He nodded. "Of course I'll take care of her. Right now, I'm going out to buy medicine."

In Haiti, she'd worked as a nursing assistant. Pills were not going to fix her wound. "I need a doctor! Take me to a hospital!"

He pretended that he hadn't heard her, rubbing her shoulder as he said, "I'll get plenty of food, too."

"It's so cold." She felt like she might never be warm again.

"I'll make a fire before I leave. I'll be back soon."

She remembered now that he'd told her that he might need to go away overnight. "Do you have a job somewhere distant?"

"Get some sleep. Things will look better tomorrow." She heard him rummaging through the suitcases of their possessions, and then his footsteps creaked across the worn plank floor and down the stairs.

5

The next day, the gorillas seemed lost, wandering in circles, toying with their food, searching for their missing family member until well after dark.

Blake could do nothing to help the situation. Claude called twice, and Blake thought about designating his former lover's number as spam, but he wasn't ready to do that yet, although he didn't really understand why he hesitated.

Detective Dawes sent a text saying that a Detective Matthew Finn was coming back from Hawaii to take charge of the case and would be contacting Blake tonight or tomorrow.

Dr. McKenna too? Blake texted back.

No. Don't contact her. Finn's order.

Understood, Blake replied, relieved that he wasn't expected to explain the situation to the woman who had hired him.

He hadn't had lunch. Or breakfast, now that he thought about it. White wine would go well with the spaghetti and clam sauce he had planned for dinner. The grocery store in Evansburg offered only canned clams, but he'd make do.

As he was pouring himself a glass, his cell buzzed with another incoming text. Claude had no doubt intended it to read I love you, but he had used a heart symbol to substitute for "love."

"I heart you," Blake read aloud as he took a sip of the

sauvignon blanc. "Yes, you certainly did heart me, Claude. Now leave me alone. I'm busy dealing with gorillas and gunshots here."

He laughed out loud at the absurdity of the situation, and then thought briefly of calling his former lover and telling him about the drama in Evansburg. *See what you've forced me to do, Claude.*

Then his lover could tell him the latest news involving his wife and kids in British Columbia. The wife and kids Blake had known nothing about six weeks ago.

After a quick glance out the window to assure himself that all was quiet, he finished the glass of wine and poured another, then set a pan of water on to boil and pulled a saucepan and the ingredients for his dinner from the cupboard.

He missed his own cookware from home. The best description of Grace McKenna's trailer was "utilitarian." The kitchen consisted of only steel counters, a double sink, and basic stainless-steel appliances. The room looked more like a laboratory than a place to create meals, and Dr. McKenna had only rudimentary utensils to work with. It was clear that, like his housemate Sam, Grace McKenna was not much interested in what she ate. She lived to cater to the gorillas. Sam lived to seek out adventures in the wilderness.

The rest of the trailer was also austere. The main bedroom held a queen-size bed, a chest of drawers, and an old rocker. The only concession to comfort and style was a bright tropical flower cover on the bed and four pillows of excellent quality. The other tiny bedroom was used as an office, with a large scarred wooden desk, an equally beat-up file cabinet and set of bookshelves, and a desktop computer and printer. A laptop was folded away on a shelf, sandwiched between notebooks and reference books.

Blake missed the homey log cabin he shared with Sam. The cabin wasn't fancy or fashionable, but it was comfortable and colorful, with woven rag rugs and quilts on the beds. The walls held photos of various beautiful places his housemate had explored, as well as a few of his best flower pictures.

This whole place was dedicated to gorilla study and care. The barn had been converted from livestock use and equipment storage to gorilla habitat, and the outdoor pen stretched up two stories from the ground, totally enclosed in wire, like an aviary. A third of the space was taken up by a loose rope net that stretched from a few feet off the ground all the way to the chain link ceiling.

The apes had more space than the humans who lived here. The staff trailer was similar to Grace's single wide, except its bedrooms held bunk beds instead of a queen and the volunteers and lone paid employee, Z, had added their own touches in the form of posters and a blackboard on the walls. Currently the top of the blackboard read "What's Up Today" in neon green. The space below was blank.

If Blake lived here full time, he'd be desperate for a lengthy vacation, too. The yard enclosed by the three buildings had some sparse grass but was mainly bare dirt under the trees with only a large picnic table between the most-trodden paths. The only attempt to make the place homey was a wooden planter at the end of the driveway, filled with red carnations and marigolds. Blake was watering nearly every day to keep the flowers alive until Grace got back.

At midnight, Blake observed that the gorillas had not gone to their sleeping nests as they had on recent evenings. The animals were still understandably upset by all the activities that had happened during the previous hours of darkness.

Neema continually asked where her baby was, signing to

anyone who was watching.

"Baby hurt," Blake had learned to sign, copying the signs that Z had shown him. *"Back soon."*

"Back soon. Back soon." He'd repeated the signs over a dozen times, but Neema just kept asking. Apparently, signing apes had little concept of time. He hoped he wasn't lying to the mother gorilla. Doctor Farin told him Kanoni was in serious condition. Touch-and-go. No way was he signing that to a giant mama ape.

Neema hadn't been interested in anything else since she'd woken up from the anesthetic and discovered Kanoni was gone. Over and over again, the mother gorilla returned to the bloodstain in the outdoor enclosure, dragging her fingers through the damp dirt and then holding them to her nose, even tasting them, all the while whimpering mournfully. Z told him that Neema's gesture of pulling a finger down her cheek meant, *"Sad, cry."*

Gumu had settled down considerably but continued making frequent rounds of the entire gorilla habitat, outside in the fenced area and probably inside the barn as well, searching for the missing member of his clan. Whenever Blake or Z or Maya approached the fence, the silverback would rush toward them, teeth bared. Blake couldn't blame him. He tried to imagine what he'd feel like if this had happened to his daughter, Hannah. But at least *he* could understand what doctors and police would tell him. He had no idea whether apes could imagine anything that transpired out of their sight.

6

Rosaline shook Mama's arm again and again. Mama made a tiny little noise, but she didn't even open her eyes. Rosaline touched her fingers to Mama's cheek. So cold. Everything in the house was cold. And dark. The fire had gone out long ago, and there was nobody to light the lamp, either. She wasn't supposed to touch the matches. Dangerous.

She'd curled up on the bed next to her mama under the covers for a few hours, but now she needed food.

"Mama," she pleaded again. "Mama, me so hungry! Mama!"

She'd already searched the kitchen and eaten the potato chips she found in the cabinet. She'd drunk the milk left in the cooler, although it was starting to smell bad.

Where was food? When would Johan come back? She was so hungry that her stomach was talking. Mama had stayed in bed all day long.

Last night, when they went to see the big black animals, those animals had food in a box next to the fence. And those animals had been sleeping in a net, not even eating that food. Until Johan fired his gun. Then they got very mad, and very loud. And then Mama got hurt.

Go-rillas, Mama called them. The go-rillas had food.

Her mama always said, *Don't let people see you.* Rosaline parted the dusty curtains and peered out the dirty window. Dark now. She was allowed to go outside when it was dark. Nobody could see her when it was dark. It was a long way to the go-rillas, but she could go there. For food.

"Mama," she murmured softly to her mother on the bed. "I bring food."

She poked a finger into her mother's arm. Mama groaned but didn't open her eyes.

Rosaline left the outside door a little bit open, because she wasn't sure she could open it again if it shut tight. The woods were very dark, but she could see some light between the trees. *Nothing to be scared of in the woods,* her mama had told her. *But don't let people see you. Stay in the dark.*

She tried to stay in the shadows, hopping over the splashes of bright that filtered through from the moon. It was a long way through the trees. Past the old rotting tree, where her mama had shown her there might be mushrooms. Mushrooms were food, but when she checked, she saw none, and she was never to eat mushrooms unless her mama said they were okay. Then over the little creek, jumping from rock to rock. The last rock tilted and she fell, hurting her knee. Her feet got wet, and she was glad she wasn't wearing shoes. Her mama didn't like her to get her shoes wet.

She kept her eyes on the light she could see in the distance. That was where the go-rillas lived.

At the edge of the clearing, she stopped to look. The big black animals were inside their cage, but they weren't sleeping now. Maybe not their bedtime. Did they have a mama who put them to bed?

Rosaline approached the cage as quietly as she could, walking carefully on the black stripes of shadows from the woods and buildings.

The go-rillas were scary animals to look at, not soft and small like bunnies or squirrels. She saw only two of them now, one big-big and one small-big. Had Johan's gun scared the littlest one away?

The go-rillas had food. In a box below an opening was a big heap of food. Bread. Green things. Orange things. The small-big go-rilla had a chunk of bread in one hand and a green thing in another. Rosaline watched, saliva filling her mouth, as the black animal bit off a piece of the green thing. She thrust her fingers through the fence, clutching the wire, watching.

She moved to the big hole in the fence. The food was below, and she tried to slide her hand through the fence to grab the food, but her arm wouldn't go in far enough. She couldn't reach. Something brushed against her bare calves, and she leaped away, jerking her hand out of the fence hole. A white cat stood on the ground beside her, looking at her with big eyes, waving its tail in the air. It rubbed against her legs again. That felt good. She liked cats. There was an orange-and-white-stripey one where her mama worked. Sometimes it visited her in the storeroom where she had to stay quiet while Mama cleaned rooms. *Don't let anyone see you.* But the cat was okay, Mama said, because he wouldn't tell any person.

This cat went to the fence and jumped up, catching itself on the opening there. It pulled itself up, then jumped down on the other side, over the food bin.

The cat walked to the go-rillas. It wasn't afraid. The big-big go-rilla picked up the cat and hugged it. The cat wasn't afraid. It looked happy. So maybe the big black animals were nice. To cats, anyway.

The small-big go-rilla turned its head and stared at her. It had reddish-brown eyes and a big flat, black nose. Scary. They watched each other for a minute. Then Rosaline put her fingers to her mouth the way her mother had taught her when she was a baby. That meant food. That meant hungry. That meant eat.

Both black animals came toward her, using their hands and their feet to walk. Too big. Rosaline backed away from the fence. The small-big go-rilla put its big black fingers to its big black lips. Was it asking if she wanted food? Rosaline touched her fingers to her own mouth again.

The go-rilla poked the green thing through the opening in the fence. Biting her lip for courage, Rosaline stepped forward and grabbed it quickly. A few steps back, she examined it carefully. She'd seen it before. Sometimes Johan and Mama ate it. She didn't think she liked it. But it was food. She took a bite. It didn't taste very good, but she chewed it anyway. *That's what we have to eat, Rosaline.*

The go-rilla pushed a big chunk of bread halfway through the hole. It hung here, dangling. Rosaline caught it just before it fell to the ground. The bread tasted much better than the green thing, and she sat down on the ground to finish it, watching the go-rillas as they walked on hands and feet to their food box. In a minute, the small-big go-rilla came back and pushed a piece of apple through the opening, and then another piece of bread.

Rosaline snatched up both offerings. *"Merci,"* she whispered.

A noise sounded from the trailer across the yard, and then a curtain moved and spilled light from the window. Rosaline raced for the woods.

7

When Blake checked out the window in the middle of the night, both adult gorillas were at the side of the enclosure, at the fence under the canopy of the net, staring across the clearing toward the forest. Looking toward the woods, again. Normally at nightfall, they retreated to make their bedtime "nests" in the net. Their routine had been totally shaken up. Had the shooter come out of those woods last night, as the police officer had suggested?

The gorillas continued to gaze toward the woods. When Neema noticed Blake watching from the window, she signed. *"Baby,"* he could recognize as a rocking motion, but then Neema scooped the air with both hands and then tapped her fingertips on her chest. *"Baby, me?"*

Gumu turned in Blake's direction and thumped one fist against his chest, which could have meant anything. Or nothing. Since the movement was not accompanied by a vocalization, the gesture didn't seem threatening.

Neema repeated her signs. No, not *me.* She was signing something else. *"Come? Baby come?"*

Now *that* was heartbreaking. And confusing. Kanoni had been shot by someone standing outside the gorilla enclosure. So why would Neema think her baby was lost in the woods? Maybe the gorillas were confused because they'd seen the intruder

vanish into the forest after shooting Kanoni, and then Neema
and Gumu had been unconscious when Kanoni was taken away
by Dr. Farin.

Or had Neema seen something close to the woods that she
thought might have taken her baby? A cougar? A wolf? A bear?
Blake held his breath and squinted, focusing on the line of trees,
but saw no sign of movement. He'd never be able to sleep if he
didn't investigate. Picking up the flashlight and a cannister of
pepper spray, just in case, he walked across the yard to knock
on the door of the staff trailer. No way was he heading out into
the dark woods by himself.

Z and Maya came with him, each armed with a flashlight.

"Neema and Gumu weren't acting scared?" Z asked.

"You saw them there at the side of the cage. Seemed like they
were just curious. Or like they were trying to figure something
out."

"They'd recognize the shooter." Maya seemed certain about
that.

"Yeah, they would," Z agreed. "And both Neema and Gumu
would raise holy hell if they saw him again. But he could have
had an accomplice observing from the edge of the woods.
Returning to the scene of the crime to watch what's happening,
and all that. He might even belong to a group." The bearded
young man shot Maya a significant look.

Dr. McKenna had told Blake about Z's animal liberation
escapades in the past. Another reason she wanted a "responsible
adult" in charge. *Shit.* Now he had to be on guard for multiple
attackers? But animal liberation groups wanted to free animals,
not kill them. What possible motivation could a group of armed
ape killers share? Frustrated big game hunters? Some kind of
wackadoodle act inspired by TikTok?

The footprints in the dirt of the yard most likely belonged to the cops who'd been here this morning. There were no visible indentations in soil through the woods. No path that led anywhere. Just trees and more trees.

"I see nothing." Z crossed his arms. "Because we can never see much of anything after dark out here."

"This is getting creepy." Maya moved her flashlight beam over the trunks of trees. "Let's go back."

When they emerged from the woods, both Neema and Gumu were still at the fence, watching. Blake couldn't be sure, but a swift crossed-arm gesture from the silverback looked close to the *baby* sign. Amazing.

"At least we know the shooter didn't come back. Gumu would be destroying the place if he had," Z observed.

"Baby come," Neema signed. *"Baby, baby."*

Blake's heart went out to the sad mother gorilla. "Clearly she wants to know about Kanoni."

"Again." Maya's tone was annoyed. "How long will she keep this up?"

"She's a gorilla, Maya, not a human," Blake told her. "Time is not the same for her. Neema doesn't know where her baby is." Facing the gorillas, Blake signed, *"Back soon. Baby back soon."*

Neema moved her hand next to her mouth and quickly opened and closed her fingers.

"That's the sign for Kanoni," Z explained. "Swahili for bird."

Blake imitated the sign, then added, *Back soon.*

Neema gestured, *"Baby here."*

"Kanoni is with Dr. Farin," Z signed as he said the words aloud. "She's sick, but she'll be back soon."

The mother gorilla made quick gestures toward her face, then repeated her crossed-arm sign.

"Sad, cry," Z interpreted. Then, *"Baby here."*

"Back soon," Blake told her again.

Maya groaned. "This could go on all night."

Neema used a hand to make a gesture on top of her leathery palm.

"Or not." Z snorted. "Neema just signed *'Cookie.'*" To the gorilla, he both signed and said, "No cookie tonight. Bed now." He turned toward the staff trailer. "That's where I'm going."

Maya, too, said good night and followed Z into the trailer. After a last stroll around the perimeter of the gorillas' enclosure, Blake returned to his trailer and slipped into bed. Then he got up, retrieved two of his large homemade cookies—old-fashioned oatmeal, walnuts, very little sugar—from the kitchen. Barefoot and clad in only his jeans, he walked to the gorilla enclosure.

Neema and Gumu still crouched beneath their sleeping net, their backs against the barn wall. Their eyes gleamed in the dim moonlight.

"Neema," he whispered.

The mother gorilla knuckle-walked to the fence in her typical rolling motion.

"Cookie," he said. Then he made the sign that Z had, stepped sideways to the opening, and held out the cookie. Black gorilla fingers clutched delicately at the treat, and Blake marveled once again at her digits. Gorilla thumbs were shorter than human thumbs, and their feet were more like hands than human feet, but all their digits had fingernails. The apes' similarities to man were both fascinating and disturbing. Even the people who denied evolution had to recognize that apes and humans were cousins.

Grace McKenna had told him that these gorillas even had a hobby—painting—and most amazing, they "owned" the two pet cats that inhabited the property. Neema claimed the calico cat, which she'd named Nest, and Gumu had picked the pure white one, Snow.

He'd been skeptical that apes would not only show affection for another animal but also choose names for them. The name Snow made logical sense, as the gorillas had probably seen snow at some point, but Nest? When he'd asked about that, Grace had pointed to the multicolored heap of blankets that the gorillas piled around themselves as their sleeping nests. Who knew that an ape could compare a calico cat's fur with a pile of blankets? It was mind-boggling. No wonder his housemate Sam was always exclaiming over the skills of wild animals.

As Neema moved the cookie to her mouth with her left hand, she touched her chin with her right. Blake recognized the sign for *"Thank you."*

His heart skipped a beat when he abruptly noticed that the silverback had crept close and now stood only a couple of feet behind the fence, balancing on his knuckles and staring into Blake's eyes. But for once, the big male ape was not showing his teeth, and then, to Blake's delight, Gumu sat back on his haunches and signed *cookie.*

While carefully watching the silverback, Blake balanced the remaining cookie on the edge of the opening. When Gumu leaned forward, Blake quickly took a step back, well out of the big ape's reach. But the male gorilla clasped the treat just as delicately as Neema had and then pushed it whole into his mouth. Instead of signing *"thank you"* like his mate, Gumu grunted as if to remind Blake of his place. The silverback then climbed into the rope net and headed for his tangle of blankets high up near the barn roof.

Still staring at Blake, Neema signed, *"Baby."* Blake held out his hands to show he had no answer. Seeming despondent, the mother gorilla crawled up the net to make her own nest of blankets in the webbing.

Blake slowly walked back to his trailer, thinking about animal whisperers who bonded with giant draft horses and elephants and tigers. Both Neema and Gumu had communicated with him. Both were clearly suffering from the shock of the shooting and the loss of Kanoni. How did you comfort a massive ape that could tear off your head if it felt like it?

8

With limited choice of available seats from Kona, the three-hour time difference between Hawaii and Washington State, the five-hour flight to Seattle, and then the two-hour drive across the mountains to Evansburg, Detective Matthew Finn didn't arrive back at his desk in the police station until nearly two in the morning. He needed to catch up on whatever was known about the incident before he headed out to Grace's compound.

After logging into his computer, he read the case notes. Unidentified shooter in the middle of the night, baby gorilla known as Kanoni shot, blood inside and outside the gorillas' enclosure. Samples taken of blood, path to forest service road investigated, but so far, no real clues as to who was responsible. Dr. Farin reported that surgery on the gorilla had gone well, but recovery wasn't yet certain. Finn was debating whether to call this Blake guy, or maybe Jon Zyrnek at this ungodly hour, to see whether there'd been any further developments, when his cell phone buzzed from his pocket, startling him.

Grace's face appeared on the screen. He pressed the answer button. "Sweetheart, what are you doing up?"

"Missing you," she murmured.

He could hear the melodic cadence of waves crashing on the beach and wished he hadn't had to leave her. "Me too. Just an old case rearing its ugly head," he lied. "I was the principal on that, so they want me here. One of the many joys of working in a small town."

"Want to talk about it?"

He cringed. "I would if I could. You know that."

"I wish you were here with me, Matt."

"Ditto. Just enjoy the tropics. You haven't taken more than a few days of vacation for more than a decade." She'd be pissed off at his deception later, but for now, he wanted her to relax. "I can hear the ocean."

"I'm sitting on our balcony right now. Today was a little windy, but still heaven. I went to that barbeque shack for lunch and got more of that grilled mahi. Went for a snorkel at the beach this afternoon. And then I had a mai tai while I watched the sunset."

He groaned. "How many of those beach bums tried pick you up?"

"They're all just boys, Matt. Well, most of them. If I can handle Gumu, I think I can handle these guys."

"I'll be back as soon as I can," he promised.

After ending the call, he wondered precisely whom Grace had been thinking of with that *Well, most of them* comment.

He decided to contact his former in-laws to let them know he was headed back to his house. He needed a few hours of sleep and a shower before he drove to Grace's compound.

"I'll be coming through the front door soon," he told his groggy ex-father-in-law. "Don't shoot me."

In the background, he heard his ex-mother-in-law say, "Scotty is a terrible shot."

"I'll be there in an hour or so."

"Cargo and the cats will be excited to see you. And they've been fed, so don't believe their lies. Dolores and I will head off now and go home early for some predawn recreation of our own."

"In your dreams." This came from his wife.

"You don't need to leave in the middle of the night," Finn told Scotty. They always slept in his guest bedroom when they house-sat for him.

"It's fine. We'll be glad to get back to our own bed."

"You're not off the hook yet," Finn told him. "I'm going back to Hawaii, and then I'd like you to continue to house-sit if you can. I'm only here for a few days, just to wrap up this case."

"Something going on with those gorillas?" Scotty guessed.

"You know I can't talk about police business."

"Okey dokey. Just be like that. Dolores made meatloaf for dinner yesterday. Help yourself to what's left in the fridge."

"Tell her thanks. I couldn't ask for better . . . " He hesitated, then added, "friends."

Scotty chuckled, then the phone clicked off. Finn was dead on his feet, so he shut down his computer and headed for his house. True to Scotty's word, he and Dolores had vacated the premises before his arrival; their car was gone from his driveway. The second he stepped onto his front porch, a cacophony erupted inside: a chorus of booming barks, interspersed with the sound of scrabbling claws and a few woeful meows.

"Down, Cargo!" he ordered before he pushed open the door. The command worked as well as it ever had. The giant Newfie-whatever mix was instantly on him, his paws on Finn's shoulders and his tongue swiping across the detective's chin.

"For Christ's sake, dog," Finn complained, kneeing the dog in the belly to back Cargo up so he could close the door. The dog dropped to all fours and did a fast twirl to demonstrate his excitement, whacking Finn in the thighs with his tail as he turned. Then he sat and let out an ear-splitting bark of welcome.

Finn quickly counted Cargo's feline associates, fearful that one had escaped through the open front door. Two sets of green eyes gave him a baleful glare, either remonstrating with him for his absence or communicating their disgust at the canine antics, or both. With Lok and Kee, it was hard to tell.

"No, no, and no," he told them as he trotted to the refrigerator. "You've all been fed." He pulled out the meatloaf and didn't even bother to heat it in the microwave, eating from the plate off the counter while three pairs of eyes hopefully scrutinized every bite.

"Shower," he announced, pulling off clothes as he headed for the bathroom.

When he slid into bed, he was quickly mobbed by the two cats. Cargo attempted to join the sleepover, but Finn pushed him to the floor with a foot, and with a mournful moan, the dog finally sank to the floor on his bed.

"Go to sleep. Now." Finn yawned as he turned off the lamp. He'd grown to love all three of these pets, but the menagerie his ex-wife had left behind kept his home life in chaos. Thank God he had his ex-in-laws to take care of them when he was gone, and at least his pets weren't gorillas.

9

North Cascades

When she pulled into the trailhead parking lot in the North Cascades National Park complex only an hour after daylight, Sam Westin was surprised to see the east side of the parking area was occupied by a giant pickup and an even larger horse trailer, a reminder that this trail was one of the few that allowed stock animals. A buckskin gelding still wearing sweaty saddle marks stood tied to one side. The back doors were open, and the loading ramp was down.

The parking lot was dusty, the ground crisscrossed with tire tracks and more footprints than she would have expected for this early in the season. Highway 20, the road through the North Cascades had been cleared of snow and rockslides for only five weeks. The mountain passes still carved through high banks of white.

The variety of prints on the ground showed visitors were wearing everything from sneakers and flip-flops to heavy-duty hiking boots. There were hoofprints as well, and a pile of manure near the rear wheels of the pickup. The horse trailer had to be nearly forty feet long, with eight high windows and an area up front for tack.

A lone wrangler, dressed like a television cowboy with a gray

Stetson pulled low, plaid shirt, blue jeans, and even a pistol in a hip holster, emerged from the rear door of the trailer. Striding quickly down the ramp, the man nearly collided with her.

He gasped and did a quick sidestep before coming to a standstill and pushing his hat back on his head to stare at her.

"Sorry," Sam apologized. "I didn't mean to scare you."

The man's gaze quickly swept the parking lot before returning to her. The irises of his eyes were a light hazel, green mixed with gold and brown rays and a rim of dark brown. Although he looked to be middle-aged, those beautiful eyes had to draw in a multitude of young women.

"No problem," he said. "I just thought I was the only one out and about this early."

The name on the brass pin on his shirt was Wiley. Pulling down the brim of his hat once again, he deftly untied the buckskin and led the horse up the ramp at the rear of the trailer.

Sam had never taken a horseback pack trip, but she and Chase were scheduled to join one in Alberta in September, and she could hardly wait to be on horseback again. When Wiley reappeared, she remarked, "That's the longest horse trailer I've ever seen."

"Eight horse, slant load," he responded over his shoulder as he lifted the loading ramp and locked it into place. Under his cowboy hat, he was sweating, although it was a very cool morning in the Cascades.

"Living quarters and tack space, too?" she asked. "Some of the rodeo guys I grew up with had trailers like that." She eyed the door near the front of the trailer. "I'd love to get a peek at the inside."

The wrangler's jaw tightened as he turned to regard her. "Well, ma'am, normally I'd be happy to show you, but we just finished a pack trip, so right now that's all stuffed full of camping gear. You wouldn't see a dang thing."

Served her right for being so nosy. "Oh, I guess that makes sense. You just came off the trail?"

"Yep." He shut the right back door of the trailer and reached for the left.

"You must have had a large group. Seems like a lot of work to do by yourself."

"Had a partner, but the lazy SOB already took off." He latched the back doors shut with a clank, rattling the handle to double check.

"So, Grafton Stables"—she read the name off the side of the trailer—"is a horseback pack outfit? Do you do a lot of trips here?"

The wrangler's expression was harried. "Yeah, a fair amount, all the eastside trails and through the Okanagan. This was a good trip." He yanked a bandana from his jeans pocket and removed his hat to reveal close-cut blond hair dented by the hat band. After swiping at the sweat on his forehead with the kerchief, he jammed the cowboy hat back on. "The riders were in a hurry to peel out. Back to hot showers and Starbucks, I expect. I'm ready for a cup of coffee myself."

"I'll bet." She focused on his belt. "You always carry a pistol?"

He glanced down at his sidearm. Rubbing his bandana across the back of his neck, he explained, "I got a rifle, too. The guns are just in case of a grizzly or a cougar. Boss's orders; I've never used either of them."

"See any wolves?"

Again, he looked startled. "Well, yeah, as a matter of fact, we did see one, a big black yellow-eyed monster."

That gave her a thrill of hope that maybe she'd see at least one wolf.

Pushing the kerchief back into his pocket, the wrangler

continued, "I woulda shot him, but a few of the guests were probably some of those eco-types."

Sam, an "eco-type" herself, was appalled. "Good thing you didn't, because shooting him would be against the law. Wolves are an endangered species."

Wiley ducked his chin and gave her an incredulous look, lowering his lids until his light-colored eyes were half-hidden. "No shit. Endangered species."

"I'm here to write about them. I'd love to see a whole pack."

He exhaled heavily through his nose, shrugged a shoulder, and focused on the pickup. "Well, to each his own, I guess. 'Scuse me; I gotta get a move on."

A thump rang out against the metal side of the trailer, followed by a scuffle, a smaller thump, and a cough. The wrangler flinched and banged a fist on the side of the trailer. "Settle down in there!" he ordered. Turning to Sam again, he touched the brim of his hat. "I got this paint gelding up front who thinks he runs the show. I better hit the road before he adds too many dents."

"I get it. I used to have a horse. A paint, it so happens." The fondest memories of her childhood were of exploring the countryside on Comanche.

"You have yourself a good day." He jogged down the side of the trailer, reaching up to slide open most of the high windows before he reached the pickup cab and hopped in.

She watched him pull out of the parking area, marveling that the pickup could tow that much weight. The dual rear tires spun briefly in the loose gravel of the dip between the highway and the dirt parking lot, but eventually caught on the lip of the pavement and hauled the trailer onto the asphalt.

Sam returned to her RAV4 and removed her pack, setting it on the ground against one of the signposts, then double-checked the interior of her SUV. In an attempt to dissuade any break-ins, she left a muddied pair of running shoes with dirty socks and a ragged T-shirt in the back seat, along with several dog-eared paperbacks. Few thieves seemed to be readers, and even fewer wore the small sizes that fit her petite frame.

Two crows perched on top of the trailhead sign. One hopped sideways to peck at the other, squawking. The bullied crow took off, but only flapped its wings a couple of times before landing on the sign again, effectively exchanging places with the aggressor.

Corvid dynamics of the unfathomable sort going on there. Sam often thought if her next life was an animal's, she might like to come back as a crow. The big black birds always seemed as though they were having a good time. When she closed her SUV door, both crows took to the air, complaining in loud caws about the sudden noise.

The thought about her next life inevitably brought her father to mind. He was a minister in a small town in Kansas and seemed certain that Heaven, not another life, was the destination after death. And that everything was part of God's grand plan, even after Sam's mother had wasted away and died a horrible death. And now his second wife, Zola, had been diagnosed with breast cancer. When he'd called last night to tell her, Sam had automatically asked if he'd like her to come back to Kansas, even though that was the last thing she wanted to do.

"No need," he'd said. "We're strong, and with God's help, we will beat this."

She'd noted her father's use of "we." Did Chase ever phrase his feelings that way? Did she? They were far from a traditional couple.

In less than a minute, the crows returned to the trailhead sign to bicker with each other again. One leaped off the sign and strutted across the ground purposefully toward her backpack, like a kid who had been dared to shoplift.

"Oh no, you don't." Sam strode quickly to her pack. The brave crow squawked and hopped sideways a couple of times before taking flight. It was joined by its fellow, both cawing loudly. Laughing? Calling each other names? Planning their next caper? If only Google could convert corvid language into English.

On the information board was a poster featuring the face of a young man with shoulder-length hair and a beard. Yet another Jesus look-alike. There were so many these days. She read the information below his photo, which started off with the headline: MISSING.

Alec Lysikov from Okanagan, twenty-seven, had set off for an extended backpacking trip on Ross Lake's East Bank Trail on April 22. His Ford Focus was found in the parking lot a week later, but no sign of Alec had ever turned up.

Sam clucked her tongue. Over the years, she'd seen so many "Missing" posters at Mount Rainier, Olympic National Park, and all over the national forests. She shared the trails with ghosts. According to the statistics, more than sixteen hundred people were currently listed as missing in US public lands. Official searches, when the missing were finally reported, typically lasted only a few days. If new clues were found or the family of a missing person was especially dedicated to plaguing the authorities and rallying the public to help, searches might be reactivated. Generally speaking, after a week or so, the missing were presumed to be dead.

People sometimes intentionally went missing to reinvent themselves elsewhere. Some had come to the wilderness to commit suicide. Others just fell victim to unfortunate accidents. An even smaller number were homicide victims.

How many had disappeared on purpose or accidentally fallen off a cliff or drowned in a river? The missing were men and women of different ages, most hiking alone. Like she was today. Most were never found. Or at least, not found alive. That was a grim reality, and one Sam knew all too well. In her worst nightmares, a parade of corpses visited her. The ones she'd known before death were the hardest to bear.

Yeesh, how morbid could she get? *Shake off all the depressing thoughts,* she told herself. She was here to enjoy nature and search for wolves.

To change the narrative in her head, she reminded herself she had found one missing person alive. A toddler, in Utah. A rare happy ending. She had no intention of searching for Alec Lysikov, but she would keep an eye out for signs of the man or his gear. Black windbreaker, red plaid shirt, gray hiking pants, green backpack, yellow tent. Taking out her phone, she snapped a photo of the poster.

Hefting her pack from the ground, Sam groaned at its weight. But her heart was celebrating to be heading out for her first backpacking trip since she'd been injured a little over a month ago. Her damaged ankle and shoulder were already protesting, but she willed them to shape up, and she knew from experience that with the aid of ibuprofen and movement, they would stop aching after a mile or two.

But even if they didn't, after all the recent trauma and drama in her world, it was worth a little pain to get outdoors again. She wanted her old life back. Nothing was the same after the avalanche of six weeks ago. Her housemate Blake was away, caretaking three gorillas in Evansburg and trying to get over his lover's betrayal and their subsequent breakup. He'd already been gone more than a week. Although Sam had imagined she would welcome the solitude in her house, instead she'd felt deprived, not only of Blake's companionship but also of his gourmet cooking.

Taking care of gorillas! *She* was the wildlife expert; *she* should be working with those apes. But Blake had spotted the opportunity and applied for the temporary job, while that had never even occurred to her. She'd been preoccupied with wolverines and Chase's injuries and the disaster on the ski slopes.

Blake definitely deserved the job, but she was still envious. Gorillas who knew sign language! He had sent her a few video clips of the apes, along with interpretive notes. Neema, the mother gorilla, asking in sign language for a cookie. The baby, Kanoni, signing *Chase* to her mother, and Neema scurrying after Kanoni inside the cage. The silverback, Gumu, had appeared fierce and intimidating as he pounded his leathery chest, but Blake explained Gumu's signs in that video meant, *"Fine gorilla."* Then the big male had joined in the chase, too, all three apes playing an ear-splitting game of tag as they rocketed around their fenced enclosure. When one gorilla grabbed onto the arm or leg of another, excited ape screams ensued.

If they were this loud when playing, Sam couldn't imagine what they'd sound like if they were fighting or frightened. But in the video, they were definitely having fun. She had to find the time to visit Blake while he was with those gorillas.

Maya, the former foster child who had brought so much trouble into her life, had gone with Blake, leaving behind a haunting residue of assorted lowlifes who still cruised past Sam's cabin at random times, hoping to spot Maya's tent in her backyard. Although she longed for Maya to clean up her act and finally become a responsible adult, she secretly missed the young woman, too. Maya had always added a certain spice to

Sam's life.

And then there was Chase. Her lover had deserted her as well, although it wasn't exactly his fault. He was finally out of rehab, but the FBI had restricted him to desk duty at the Bellingham office for now, a constraint that still chafed him He hadn't been willing to spend much time with her until he was "back to himself," as he described it. How long would that take? And what did it say about their relationship that Chase was unwilling to show any weakness in her presence? Had his near-death experience somehow changed his mind about being with her? What did that mean for the future?

Alone again, naturally. The chorus from Gilbert O'Sullivan's self-pitying song rang through her head. Had all those other lone hikers been regretfully reviewing their lives when they disappeared?

Yeesh, Westin, look where you are! She gave herself a mental slap. Mountains. Streams. Waterfalls. The lake. The forest. Wildlife. And with luck, wolves.

She'd picked an easy trip along the East Bank Trail, so named because it bordered the east side of Ross Lake. The mountain lake, created by damming the Skagit River coming down from Canada, was twenty-three miles long. With a few zigs and zags, the hiking trail was approximately thirty-one miles, but she didn't intend to hike all the way to the Canadian border, only up to Desolation campground and back. Her friend and fellow wildlife biologist, Gina, could spend only five days watching over Sam's house and her cat, Simon. Gina was still recovering from the serious injuries she'd sustained in the avalanche, but she could do her physical therapy and tend to her annoying parrot in Sam's house as easily as in her own.

Setting out on East Bank Trail now, she texted to both Gina and Chase, feeling slightly guilty she was currently more physically fit than any of her comrades.

Try not to kill yourself, querida, was the reply from Chase.

Didn't he know by now she was immortal? She'd survived all kinds of near-fatal disasters, even a few that had killed others. Or maybe, as her father had often suggested, she was addicted to taking risks, disaster prone, and simply damn lucky to still be alive.

Her phone displayed an earlier message from Blake's former lover, Claude. Found Blake's address yet?

No, she texted back. She regretted giving the Canadian her phone number. Blake no longer wanted anything to do with Claude, and she was determined to stay out of their drama. She was sick of dealing with other people's problems.

Enjoy! Gina texted. Fingers crossed for wolves.

That reminded her. She quickly texted Michael Fredd, her editor at *Out There*: Starting off to find the wolves now.

I need u for S2S. Else I'll assign another.

"S2S" was Fredd's shorthand for Ski to Sea, Bellingham's big seven-leg relay race that began near Mount Baker and finished in Bellingham Bay, with teams from all over the world transitioning from skis to bikes to finishing in kayaks, with running and canoes thrown in, too. It all happened on Memorial Day Weekend at the end of May. Six days from today.

I'll be there, she replied. She was tempted to add, *Don't get your jockstrap in a twist.* Gritting her teeth, she shut down her phone, glad to be off the electronic grid for a while.

Attitude of gratitude, she lectured herself. Her gig at *Out There* was part time, and she'd only been doing it for less than a year. But it was a steady income, and she was grateful for it. Yet she was already chafing at writing stories about other people enjoying the outdoor adventures she wanted to be doing herself. She was aching to get back to her usual treks in wild areas.

She'd sold Fredd on an article on backpacking this easy trail in the North Cascades. He had been frustrated she was leaving town just as major outdoor sporting events were finally ramping up around Bellingham, but he'd promised to also buy an article on wolves in the North Cascades if she delivered a good story with photos.

Pulling that off would require luck as well as her backcountry skills. Wolves were known to traverse many miles in a single day. The local wolves might be in the national park or in the adjoining Mount Baker National Forest or in the Pasayten Wilderness to the east.

But just last week she'd read an account of hikers who had heard wolves in the Ross Lake Recreation Area, east of Lightning Creek Campground toward Desolation Peak. So with luck, she might locate wolves in this trek along the lake. Not to mention—as it was only late May and the high peaks were still blanketed with snow—the East Bank Trail was one of the few clear paths available.

Her goal for the first night was Rainbow Point Campground, a little less than nine miles from the trailhead. The route there was mostly level trail, with the exception of ascending the nine hundred feet over Hidden Hand Pass. A good warm-up hike. Tomorrow she'd hike a little more than seven miles to Lightning Creek Campground, take a day to explore the trail to Desolation Peak and maybe stay below the lookout there for a day before retracing her steps to the parking lot.

At Ruby Creek, which fed into the southern end of Ross Lake, she stopped to take a photo of the emerald-green water and the impressive bridge that spanned the stream. The structure was a marvel of trail-building, with thick pole handrails and supporting logs beneath the planks that made it strong enough to carry the pack animals that were allowed on this trail. The bridge was starting to show the wear of many decades, though, with rotting spots visible in a few places along the flooring and rails.

She'd keep an eye out for the remains of cabins and other artifacts from the optimistic miners who had taken up stakes along the creek in the late 1800s, hoping to strike gold. Although together, over the years, they'd washed nearly $100,000 in gold dust out of the creek area, none of them had struck it rich. One prospector, John Rowley, had named Ruby Creek after finding a large "ruby" in his pan. The stone turned out to be a much less valuable garnet. Most miners in this area had been sorely disappointed, and they'd pulled out shortly after experiencing a winter or two in the high mountains, dreams dashed.

Sam used her phone to record a message to herself to look up the history of the bridge as well as more details about the mining history of the area. Although local history added interesting elements to her articles, she was here for nature and wildlife. She hoped she'd encounter a black bear or two, maybe a river otter, and at least find prints or scat from a lynx or cougar. Seeing a grizzly was a long shot, she knew, although a few had been sighted over the years. Grizzlies were considered endangered in Washington State, along with fishers and wolverines and the gray wolves she intended to write about.

10

She'd sworn to focus on the surroundings, but as she hiked, Sam found her thoughts wandering back to Alec Lysikov. The posters contained so little information. Was Lysikov a passionate outdoorsman? An experienced backpacker? A drug user or an alcoholic looking for escape? According to the poster, he'd hiked in over a month ago. Too much time had passed to find him alive, unless he'd escaped into British Columbia or hiked out of the park elsewhere to reinvent himself.

On the map, this section of the trail appeared to be close to Ruby Creek. But the path quickly rose into the forest high above the water, now so far away she could no longer see or hear the creek. She had the trail all to herself for several miles. The footing was gritty and occasionally muddy. Saplings of Douglas firs and young cedars crowded the edges. To her disappointment, she saw no derelict mining relics to photograph. A few semiflat areas might have held small cabins back in the local gold rush era but now were covered with thin saplings.

To her even greater disappointment, the only wildlife she saw along the route were the native Douglas squirrels, which flicked their tails and chattered at her, sounding more like birds than the rodents they were.

At the juncture of the Jack Mountain Trail, she paused and

considered climbing that path for half an hour. But the trail was steep and her ankle was aching, so she decided to continue on and have an early lunch at Hidden Hand Campground. When she was only a few steps beyond the trail junction, she heard distant rumbling in the high country. The noise stopped after only a few seconds. Likely a landslide somewhere up the mountain. When the snow was melting fast in spring weather, tunneling water tended to shift the landscape on steep slopes.

Several backpackers were leaving Hidden Hand Campground as she arrived, heading north in front of her. One woman had two boisterous boys in tow. They were practically bouncing with excitement. Sam took her time to hike out to the bluff and savor the view of the southern end of Ross Lake.

She spent the rest of her hike leapfrogging other backpackers along the trail until she reached Rainbow Point Campground in late afternoon. The area had only a handful of tent sites, and it was already getting crowded. She recognized a few hikers who had walked only a few miles from Hidden Hand.

Sam wasn't used to sharing her sleeping grounds with a crowd, but her permit specified Rainbow Point Campground for her first night, and so she pitched her tent in one of two remaining empty sites. She explored the area, locating the pit toilet and the heavy metal animal-proof container for storing food, commonly known as a bear box.

The other backpackers in camp were the usual motley crew. The mother and two boys tossed a frisbee back and forth in a grassy area near the lakeshore. Two adjoining sites were occupied by a cluster of young men chattering to each other in German as they scanned their cell phones. One phone blared music, and Sam groaned when she noticed the black rectangle of a compact charger on a nearby stump. Even wilderness campsites had become much noisier since battery chargers had become cheap and portable. Some backpackers she knew even watched movies on their phones.

She had one of those battery packs in her own gear for charging her phone to make notes and take photos. Not for entertainment. She hiked to escape from the electronic world as much as she could.

Two people were examining the bear box. A yellow nylon bag of food lay on top. A strawberry blonde stuffed into a long-sleeved T-shirt a size too small stared uncertainly at the black metal contraption. "How do you open it?"

The man with her was a generation older, with close-cropped, graying hair and a muscular body that might have appeared fit if his belly hadn't overlapped his fancy belt buckle by several inches. His attention was on his cell phone as he thumb-scrolled repeatedly, a frown on his face. His denim overshirt was open on top of a tee tucked into a belt with a huge brass buckle. The orange handle of a knife protruded from a sheath on the right side of his tooled belt. An unpleasant memory of finding the same type of knife recently on a dead poacher flashed through her brain.

"You saw a box just like that one last night," the man said. He didn't offer to help his younger companion, instead assuring her, "You got it, sweetheart."

The woman proved she clearly didn't "have it" by yanking on the steel handle. The heavy metal door did not budge even a fraction of an inch. "*You* opened the thing last night," she complained. "I didn't see you do it."

Sam said hello as she walked toward them. The man glanced up briefly and turned sideways, as if he suspected Sam might try to see what was on his phone.

"Let me show you," Sam said to the woman. She knelt beside the bear box. "You slide your fingers under this cover and press the handle inside." She demonstrated, opening the door, then stood up again. "Just be sure it's latched securely when you close it."

The woman's expression was skeptical, but she bent over and placed the food sack on the shelf inside, sliding it as far as possible from other packages on the shelf. An unopened package of Oreos peeked from the opening of the ripstop bag. The woman straightened, wafting the scent of coconut and pineapple toward Sam. Her eyebrows knit together in what passed for a frown. "*Everyone's* food goes in there?"

"Just like last night, sweetheart." The man jammed his cell phone into the back pocket of his blue jeans.

To both of them, Sam said, "We all share the food-storage space. It's an honor system, and you'll find most campers are pretty honorable. I'm Sam, by the way." It didn't seem the right situation to offer a hand.

"You a rodeo cowboy?" she asked the man. "That's some buckle."

His scowl shifted to a grin, and he hooked a thumb in his leather belt beside his buckle. "Champion team roper. Retired now."

"Wow," Sam remarked. "Nice to meet you." She faced the woman again. "Just FYI: you'll want to wash before you go to bed and store anything scented in the bear box here."

The blonde's eyebrows lifted. "*Anything* scented? Why?"

"Well," Sam refrained from adding *sweetheart*, "I can't help noticing you smell like a piña colada, and a bear might want to have a taste of that."

"That's just sunscreen." The young woman blanched. "I thought it smelled good." She tossed a look of alarm at her companion. "Why didn't you tell me that last night?"

"Like you said, hon, your sunscreen smells good. And

nothing happened last night, did it? You know I can always protect you." He crossed his arms and frowned fiercely at Sam for a second. After clearing his throat, he thrust his chin in Sam's direction and his expression softened. "But it's a good idea, what she said, sweetheart. Bears are pretty good smellers."

"This is your second night here?" Sam asked.

"No. Last night we camped at . . ." She turned to her companion. "What was the name of that place?"

Placing his hand around the back of the woman's neck, he squeezed as if grasping a snake, then looked back at Sam. "I don't remember, sweetheart. Our horses are picketed north of here tonight."

"Then we're headed in the same direction. I'm aiming for Lightning Creek tomorrow," Sam told them. "After that, Desolation, then back to the trailhead."

"We'll meet up with our horses tomorrow morning," the man told her. "I asked the wrangler to drop us here because I wanted to give Randi a taste of solo hiking and camping."

Sam stifled an incredulous snort. Sleeping in the crowded campground was hardly solo, but she supposed maybe it might seem that way to someone who was used to having guides set up their camp and cook.

"I'm Randi. With an *I*." The woman flattened her hand against her chest in case there was any doubt whom she was describing. "And this is my boyfriend, Mark. Are you saying bears could just walk into camp while we're in our tent tonight?"

"It's possible," Sam admitted. "Hence the bear box." She tilted her head toward it. "But a bear is unlikely to bother you if you don't keep anything in your tent it would be interested in."

Mark stepped forward and closed the door of the metal box with a clang. "We'll be fine, Randi."

He patted his hip with his right hand, shooting Sam a

meaningful look.

Muscles at the back of Sam's neck abruptly tightened as her gaze zeroed in on his gesture. That bulge under his shirttail had to be a pistol. The wrangler in the parking lot had a handgun and a rifle. Did everyone on this trail have a gun? Her consternation must have shown on her face, because when Mark glanced her way, he narrowed his eyes.

Sam averted her gaze and slowly inhaled and exhaled to tamp down a surge of anger. When traveling in the backcountry, she never worried much about bears or wolves or falling off a cliff. Her biggest fears involved ignorant, overanxious humans in the woods with loaded firearms. Years ago, her friends Kim and Kyla had lost their lives to bullets. More recently, a colleague in Arizona had been shot and killed. And there had been other hikers struck down by stray bullets in the years since. Most recently, in a national forest area, a man and his dog had been killed by a nervous camper shooting in the vague direction of "something growling."

Those were just the human casualties; she couldn't bear to think about all the innocent wildlife that succumbed to hunters, both legal and illegal.

Every glimpse of a gun reminded her of deaths in the past and deaths to come. She couldn't imagine what living in the American gun culture was like for the relatives of victims murdered in mass shootings that seemed to happen every day now. Chase was always careful to hide his duty pistol when she was around. She knew carrying a weapon was part of being an FBI agent, but she didn't want to see it, and he was respectful of her feelings. He understood how much all those deaths had hurt her over the years.

Mark stepped close, nearly treading on the toe of Sam's boot. When she glanced up at him, he slowly smiled, his eyes creasing at the corners as he peered down at her. She was reminded of a cobra rearing up over a mongoose.

What was this guy's problem? Turning her back to Mark, she told the other woman, "Honestly, Randi, you have more to fear from mice and mosquitos than from bears."

"Mice?" Randi chirped, apparently not reassured. Frowning, she accused Mark, "I *knew* I saw one in the tent last night. Oh, yuck." She wiped the palms of her hands on her shirt as if she had just picked up a diseased rodent.

"And crows," Sam said. "Watch out for them. They're thieves." Stifling a chuckle, she turned away toward her camp. "Well, have a nice evening."

"She's not a ranger," she heard Mark say before she was out of earshot.

Earlier in her life, Sam had wanted nothing more than to be a park service or forest service ranger. But she'd had a few tastes of those duties during contract assignments along the way, and now she was grateful she could enjoy the wilderness without having the responsibility of enforcing the myriad regulations of public lands. Rangers in all jurisdictions were few and far between.

The North Cascades National Park Complex was appropriately named. It was a complex conglomeration of the national park and two national recreation areas, with a state highway running through the middle and surrounded by national forest lands. She wasn't sure exactly which regulations applied in which section. The administration had to be challenging.

She assembled her backpacking stove and after scooping water out of the lake, heated it to boiling before pouring it into a bag of labeled beef stew. Freeze-dried meals rarely retained the flavors their labels promised, but they were lightweight and relieved her of the burden of packing a variety of ingredients. After the mixture had more or less rehydrated, she chewed her way through the salty meal, thinking her housemate would have found a way to make this more palatable.

What was Blake cooking in Evansburg? Something delicious, no doubt, for himself and maybe for Maya and the rest of the gorilla caretakers. Did he cook for the gorillas? Nah, probably gorillas only ate natural, raw foods. Or at least they should. For the tenth time, she wondered whether Blake would actually return when promised and cook for her again, or whether he'd fall head over heels with a professor at the small Evansburg college, or a cowboy like the wrangler she'd seen this morning.

After spooning up the last contents of pseudo stew—Two servings? Definitely false advertising—she rolled up the empty package, tucked it into an empty Ziplock baggie, and visited the bear box to lock up all her food items, grateful she didn't have to string a food bag from a limb and hope for the best.

11

Evansburg

After conferring over a few cups of desperately needed coffee at the police station with his usual detective partner, Perry Dawes, Finn drove to Grace's compound. When he arrived, Blake, the caretaker Grace had hired to gorilla-sit for six weeks, appeared shell-shocked. The tense expression on the poor man's face was no doubt due to the fact that Rebecca Ramey, Finn's media nemesis, had Blake backed up on the front steps of Grace's trailer. He had one hand clutched around the doorknob.

Driving up, Finn had grimly taken notice of the dark-red Volkswagen Golf parked beside the main trailer. A magnetic sign on the car's side proclaimed the arrival of *What's Up, Evansburg?*

Rebecca had clearly confronted Blake, either coming out or going in. The reporter was like a spider that way, lying in wait for an innocent bug to crawl across her web, then pouncing.

"Really," Blake was saying to the young woman, who held a cell phone in front of his face, "I know nothing of the history of the gorillas. I can't answer any of your questions."

Z was observing from behind a curtain in the window of the staff trailer. Grace's associate clearly knew better than to show himself right now.

When Blake saw Finn emerge from his car, relief washed over his features. "Detective Finn! Am I glad to see you!"

Ramey turned in Finn's direction, aiming her cell phone at him. Blake quickly escaped into Grace's trailer.

"And where have you been, Detective?" The reporter tilted her head. "Your colleagues at Evansburg PD tell me that you're in charge of this case."

Thanks a lot, guys. "I was on vacation when the original incident happened, Rebecca, but now I understand that the investigation has been assigned to me." Stifling a groan, he willed his expression to remain stern and professional.

When he'd first moved to Evansburg, Rebecca Ramey had been a journalism student at the small local college. Unfortunately, she was smart and dogged, monitoring the police radio nonstop for stories and hounding everyone involved for details. Now she was a "reporter at large" for the local Evansburg newspaper and starred in the weekly podcast the city produced: *What's Up, Evansburg?* She'd clearly moved up the local news ladder, short though it was, and Finn and all the city officials were forced to interact with her.

She thrust the phone in his face, nearly tapping his nose with it. "I understand the baby gorilla that lives here was shot."

Finn didn't like cell phone recording any better than he had liked Ramey's video cameras a few years ago. "I understand that, too."

"What can you tell us about this crime? Will the little gorilla live?" Ramey's eyes stayed focused on the screen rather than on his face.

Painfully aware he was on camera, Finn summoned his official voice. "The veterinarian tells me that Kanoni—that's her name—will live, but may have permanent damage. She was badly injured and will be needing veterinary care for several more days."

So don't show up here, he added in his thoughts to whomever might watch this. Over the years, many of Grace's problems had been due to the actions of the public who wanted to visit the gorillas.

"Who was the shooter?" Ramey asked.

"We're working on answering that question," Finn told her.

"Do you have a suspect?"

Before he could respond, she peppered him with multiple queries, designed to sound like a hard-hitting reporter who would not be put off. "Is it Frank Keyes, the man who poisoned one of Dr. McKenna's gorillas before? Or perhaps one of the people involved in Gumu's kidnapping a while ago? You remember, the illegal wildlife trafficking incident?"

Finn felt the blood rising to his face. Both were good questions that he needed to follow up on.

Ramey made Grace's gorilla compound sound like a hotbed of serious crime, and the *you remember* comment made him sound incompetent. Finn took a deep breath. "We're just beginning this investigation."

"Or does this have anything to do with your past cases here? Like the serial killer you discovered, or the kidnappers of those girls from the Gorge concert a couple of years ago? Or one of the county council reps who want these apes removed?"

For god's sake, Rebecca. She clearly wanted to record all these questions for future airing, in case she could develop any of them into a juicy feature story. It was annoying how the young reporter was developing a list of suspects before he'd had time to zero in on anything.

"We are still in the evidence-collecting stage," Finn said, trying to keep from frowning at the camera. "The media will be informed when we have any concrete information to share.

Nobody wants to spread disinformation." He telepathically begged her not to write *anything* yet. He didn't want Grace to discover the story on the internet. The report of a shooting along Grace's road had appeared this morning in the police blotter Facebook page, but without a specific address or other details.

With a loud exhale, Ramey shut down the phone and tucked it into her pocket. "You'd better keep me in the loop, Finn. You know that I will find out."

That sounded like a threat. "Now I need to do *my* job, Miz Ramey." He stepped sideways to walk around her.

"Have a nice day, Detective Finn." She left.

He stifled a growl as he strode toward the gorilla enclosure. Neema and Gumu tracked him with wary eyes. When he signed, *"Hello,"* both apes stayed sitting in place, sunken into their crouched positions. It was difficult to read gorilla expressions, but Finn would have described both Neema's and Gumu's demeanors as sullen. Or depressed. Or probably both. Understandable.

After a few seconds, Neema signed *"Grace here?"* and then watched closely for his answer.

Finn shook his head, then scanned the gorilla enclosure, noticing the bloodstain inside, only slightly darker than the surrounding dirt now that the blood had dried, and then he turned to look for the bloodstain outside the fence that Dawes had mentioned. Another dark patch was a few yards in front of him, near the rectangular portal Grace had installed so the caregivers could safely dispense food and toys to the apes. All was quiet inside the enclosure now, but he noted how the objects had been tossed around, no doubt by Gumu.

Turning and cupping his hands around his mouth, he yelled, "The press is gone. Come out, come out! Staff meeting!"

When Blake and Z and the girl—Maya, he now

remembered—emerged, he led them to the picnic table in the yard to quiz them. None of them remembered anything more than Finn had already gleaned from the police report. Two shots in the wee hours of the morning, then total pandemonium with screaming apes, then the realization that Kanoni had been shot.

"Oh man," Z moaned, stroking his beard. "You could hear those gorillas for miles."

Finn asked, "Could that have been the reason for the shooting? Maybe some sort of crazy TikTok challenge to cause a frenzy?"

"Shit, that would be insane," Z pushed a lock of his sandy hair away from his forehead.

Maya agreed. "Totally."

"I mean, who would hear?" Z added. "The neighbors are all miles away."

"But it could be a really sweet post," Maya's eyes sparkled with excitement. "It would get tons of hits."

Finn stared them both down. "Don't even think about it."

"Never, man." Z shook his head and held up both hands. "That would be, like, cruel."

Maya redirected her focus to the ground in front of her feet.

Like all law enforcement officers these days, Finn was aware of a variety of crimes committed by rabid TikTok followers. "I know it's a long shot, but would you two check that out for me? Find out if there's been any, er, chatter on social media that could lead to this?" Finn glanced from Maya to Z and back again. He was not about to admit that he didn't have a clue how to do that himself.

"Sure." Maya lifted and dropped a shoulder. "Could be fun."

Finn wasn't sure he liked the sound of that, but he could hardly warn her not to do anything stupid when he had just asked for a favor.

Blake reported that he had noticed the bloodstain on the outside of the pen only after the shooting, and that was largely because he'd stepped in wet blood while barefoot. The dark spot still held his footprint. He summarized, "So whoever the shooter was, looks like he got hurt somehow."

"Maybe a self-inflicted wound," Finn commented. "You said there were two shots."

None of them were aware of any recent threats against Grace or her gorillas.

"There's been nothing online or in the paper," Z assured him. "Only Grace would know if there were any phone calls."

Blake piped up. "I check her voicemail for messages every day. "There's been only one call while I've been here. Some man, complaining about the noise."

Finn thought about that. Grace's closest neighbors were a family named Ledford to the west of her property. When they'd first moved in, they'd been alarmed about the sounds coming from Grace's compound, but after she had invited them to meet the gorillas, they had not contacted her again.

"The caller didn't make any threats," Blake added. "I would have called him back to explain what the noises were, but he didn't leave a name, and his number showed up as private."

So maybe a house sitter or visiting relative of the Ledford family who didn't know what they were hearing. Or maybe someone hiking through the national forest close enough to hear the apes at play. A lot of nature lovers, especially birdwatchers, complained about any sort of intrusive sounds.

Finn faced Z. "How about you? Anyone who might want to hurt you by killing a gorilla?"

The ponytailed young man looked startled. "What?"

"A girlfriend you ditched, or a buddy you pissed off?"

"No way." Scowling, Z shook his head.

Finn turned to Blake. "Anyone back at home upset that you came here to babysit three gorillas?"

Blake's mouth tightened and his eyebrows knit together for a couple of seconds before he said, "There is one person who is definitely upset that I left Bellingham, but he doesn't even know where I am."

"Same here," Maya echoed. "Blake and I are sort of hiding out, I guess."

"Not from the law," Blake hastened to add, but then shot a · quick sideways look at Maya. "Just personal stuff."

Finn had already done background checks on both of them, so he knew that Maya had recently been involved in a shooting and had been summoned to appear at a trial in a couple of months. From what he'd read, her actions seemed to be self-defense during a kidnapping attempt. But there was also an older woman present at the time, and there was doubt about who had actually fired the bullet that killed the dirtbag. Still, he should check with the police department where that incident happened. He sighed. "Are you sure nobody knows where you are?"

They both nodded. Then Blake amended, "Well, almost nobody. Only my housemate, Summer Westin, and her boyfriend, Chase Perez, because I had him check out Grace McKenna before I took this gig. Perez is an FBI agent. Neither he nor Sam—that's Summer's nickname—would reveal our location to anyone sketchy, I'm sure of it."

The gorillas had been featured in various news articles online and even on the television news a few years ago, so their existence was not exactly a secret. Stifling a yawn, Finn said, "We may need to circle back to that. Call me if you think of any possibilities for people who might want to hurt the gorillas, no matter how remote."

He wasn't going to ask Grace about any complaints or threats. At least not directly. He'd have to think of a way to subtly get that information from her. Let her vegetate in the tropics a while longer.

No bullet casings, no sightings of the shooter, no known suspects. This was going to be as bad as his first encounter with Grace and her gorillas. Once again, apparently the only witness to the crime was a gorilla. Or, in this case, three gorillas.

Finn checked his watch. Two forty-two in the afternoon. The shooter had already had more than enough time to escape. He didn't know what more he could do here.

"Well." He stood up, yawning. "I'm headed back to the office to check the whereabouts of everyone Grace has ever tangled with."

12

At the police station, Finn spent several hours on the phone and computer, checking the whereabouts of everyone he could think of who knew about the gorillas and/or might have a grudge against Grace.

A computer voice informed him that the old cell number he had for Frank Keyes was no longer in service. Years ago, Keyes had poisoned Spencer, Grace's first silverback. Now he'd have to track Keyes down, find out if he had been in the area and had access to a gun. Finn remembered an old video clip of Keyes on the news years ago. He typed a query to Google to ask about that, and was amazed at how quickly a list of links appeared on his screen.

What's Up, Evansburg? was at the top of the list. Rebecca Ramey's weekly podcast. Shit. He clicked the link. "Baby Gorilla Shot" was the featured article. The text was mainly the recorded questions she had fired at him at Grace's compound. In the recording, his expression was strained, and the bags under his tired eyes were prominent.

Ramey had also incorporated the old video of the Frank Keyes case. Why did all news stories exist forever on the internet? Gritting his teeth, Finn clicked the arrow to play the old clip.

A reporter confronted Frank Keyes at the door of his

apartment, saying, "Mr. Keyes, years ago you were convicted of killing a gorilla named Spencer who belonged to Dr. Grace McKenna."

"A gorilla is not a who," Keyes snarled onscreen. "Animals are not people."

"Do you have any knowledge about Dr. McKenna's current missing gorilla, Gumu?"

Keyes' eyes darkened with anger in the video, and he spat out each word as he said, "You are harassing me."

"Did you kill Gumu, Mr. Keyes?"

Keyes took a step forward, jarring the camera, which swung wildly before refocusing on Keyes' face.

"*I* am not the criminal!" he bellowed. "People who believe in talking gorillas are the criminals. They are the sinners! Satan rules the earth and tries to persuade good people that we are descendants of monkeys." He turned toward the camera. "Armageddon is coming, people. Are you ready to face Judgment Day?"

The old video ended and Finn sat back in his chair. Was Keyes still such a rabid and violent opponent of anyone espousing animal intelligence? He'd never understood the vehemence, but then he didn't understand most conspiracies fanatics became obsessed with. The last time he'd tracked Keyes down, the guy was no longer on parole and seemed determined to stay off law enforcement's radar. Finn jotted down the man's particulars and decided to set one of the interns the task of finding the guy.

His sergeant stopped in front of Finn's desk, a folder tucked under his arm. Finn straightened in his chair. "Those gorillas," the sergeant complained. "For all the trouble those animals have caused, it's too bad they weren't all shot."

Finn met the man's eyes. "What if someone was shooting

cattle or horses?" He'd been assigned a rustling case just last year.

"That's different; livestock is livelihood." The sergeant pulled the folder from under his arm. "I've got another case for you."

"No." Finn held up both hands in front of his chest. "I came back only for this one, and as soon as I've nailed it, I'm back on vacation."

"Then you're only getting paid regular for the exact hours you work on this shooting, then. And you've only got seventy-two hours." He tucked the folder under his arm again. "It's just an animal, Finn." With that, the sergeant continued his search for another victim to assign to whatever case he had in that file folder.

Finn exhaled heavily. Although the public got up in arms over news reports of animal cruelty, in rural areas like this law enforcement rarely did. Animals were property. The laws on cruelty were often not strictly enforced, and penalties were light. When he caught Kanoni's shooter, the scumbag would probably get a sentence of only a few months in the county jail.

Naturally, most of the candidates on Finn's list claimed to have been sleeping at home when Kanoni had been shot. None of them lived close by. They provided the names of alibis. The drug kingpin, Jarvis Pinder, who'd caused him so much trouble in the past, was still in prison. That sleazebag had been obsessed with gorillas, and he certainly knew where Grace and the gorillas lived. Did he still have enough cohorts on the outside to get one of them to pull this off? Finn would put in a call to the prison to see if they'd hand over the recordings of any of Pinder's recent phone calls.

The complaint about the noise that Blake had mentioned was from a blocked number. Worth hassling the phone company to cough up the cell owner? They'd probably demand a search warrant, and the only judge likely to be sympathetic to that request had retired a couple of years ago. Finn set that task aside for now.

Blake had told him that Neema had repeatedly scanned the woods to the east of Grace's property. The report from the officers responding to the shooting had mentioned the USFS road back there. Although he'd never share the idea with his fellow officers, Finn had found over the years that the gorillas often provided useful clues to any mystery. Lacking the myriad distractions of human society, the apes noticed everything that took place in their world, from a beetle crawling up the wall to an errant gum wrapper in their cage.

He pulled up Google Earth to check an aerial map of Grace's area. He'd head out and drive that forest service road, see if anything unusual stood out, like an encampment in the woods. Homeless people were everywhere these days, and unfortunately, a lot of them had guns and sometimes problems with mental illness. It was entirely possible that one might get the idea to shoot a gorilla.

Finn followed the service road with his eyes, moving the map on the computer screen with his mouse. The gravel route snaked back through the trees for close to twenty miles before it reached an open area that was being clear-cut. He made a note to ask the Forest Service rangers about who was working on that project. He hoped that wouldn't glean too many names to check out. Along the road, there was also a Forest Service maintenance shed and storage area that should also be inspected, along with another structure, a small roof or tarped-over area. The image of that was too fuzzy to identify.

Double-checking the aerial map on his screen, he moved it back to the position closest to Grace's compound and zoomed in to see if he could spot a trail. Nope, the details were too blurry.

The USFS road and project crew working there seemed like a long shot, anyway. What interest would a forestry worker have in shooting a gorilla? Zooming out on the aerial view, he examined neighboring properties.

Outside the strip of forest to the north, there was an old farmhouse. He knew that property was dilapidated and had been abandoned for years. The county fire department considered those ancient wooden buildings a burn hazard, but according to the assessor, the owner of that property had died long ago. The heirs were overseas and didn't seem interested in managing or selling the old place. The property taxes hadn't been paid for three years, so the county would likely foreclose on it any day now.

By road, the farmhouse was miles from Grace's property. But if one hiked on foot, that house was only about a half mile away.

He stood up to stretch, his back stiff from the long hours of sitting on the plane and in the car yesterday, compounded now by hours at his desk.

Dr. Farin had told him that Kanoni was, in her words, "in serious condition, but strong," whatever that meant. She couldn't predict when Kanoni would be ready to return to the compound.

The sun had already set, and he could imagine Cargo howling inside his house for food and a pee break. He'd check out the road and that farmhouse tomorrow.

At midnight, Finn was sitting in his recliner and throwing the cats' sticky wall-walker toys at the sliding glass door and watching the cats studying the toys as they crawled down the glass. When one of the crazy-looking gummy octopuses dropped to the floor, Lok would bring it back to Finn to throw again. His cats fetched. While Cargo, slobbering at Finn's side, had never grasped the concept of retrieving or returning anything.

"Are you paying attention?" Finn said to the dog. "These cats are better dogs than you are."

The huge Newfie mix gazed at him with adoring brown eyes. Then with a dramatic sigh, Cargo laid his head on Finn's thigh and let his body sink to the floor. Finn put his hand on his dog's head and stroked his thumb across Cargo's broad skull. "Yeah, I missed you, too."

On his chairside table, Finn's cell phone buzzed. "What makes you think I'd still be up?" he asked on answering.

"I know you," Grace laughed. "Plus, you're still on Hawaii time. It's only nine here."

Finn could hear waves crashing on the shoreline and muted conversations nearby. "You're on the beach? At nine at night?"

"We have moonlight and tiki torches. Volleyball match coming up," she said. "We'll have to switch sides with every point because it's so windy, but it should still be fun."

"I'm envious." At his elbow, Cargo emitted a sharp bark, either excited to hear Grace's voice or annoyed that Finn was no longer paying attention to him. "My dog seconds that, although the doofus doesn't know what a beach is." He patted the big mutt, receiving in return a tongue swipe that slimed his palm and wrist with saliva.

"How's the case going? And how are Neema and Gumu and Kanoni?"

He wiped his hand on his pants leg and was at a loss for words for a second as he tried to remember what he'd told Grace. "Sorry, just distracted by Cargo slobber. The case is going. I'll try to wrap up everything tomorrow or the day after. And the gorillas are all okay. Neema asked about you."

"So you *did* go out there to check on them. Is Blake doing a good job?"

"As far as I can tell, Blake is handling things, and Z's helping when he's there." When she didn't respond, he told her, "I miss you, Grace." Cargo barked again, and Finn made a throat-cutting motion in the dog's direction. Cargo's tongue slid out and he appeared to smile.

"Not as much as I miss you," she replied. "I'm having to make do with the old beach bums here."

"Who you calling old?" a gruff voice interrupted.

Grace chuckled. "My team's up, Matt. I gotta go. Stay safe."

Both Lok and Kee simultaneously jumped into his lap from opposite sides of his chair, causing him to drop the cell phone on the floor. But it didn't matter. Grace was gone before he could say goodbye. He spent the night shoving Cargo off his bed and rearranging cats so he had enough space to turn over.

13

When the lights in both trailers went out, Rosaline walked back to the fence. She'd eaten the bread and the green thing last night, and this morning she'd found some mouse-chewed crackers underneath the kitchen sink, but now she was hungry again. Tonight, the go-rillas were high up in the net, not paying attention. Sticking her fingers through the mesh, Rosaline leaned back and tugged. The fence rattled, just a little bit.

Rosaline glanced nervously at the closest trailer. *Don't let anyone see you.* No lights. When she looked back, she noticed the small-big go-rilla was sitting up now, staring at her.

Rosaline touched her fingers to her mouth, like her mama had taught her when she was a baby. She whispered the word. *"Manje."*

The small-big go-rilla made a rocking motion with its arms. Rosaline didn't know what that meant. She touched her mouth again. She wished the littlest go-rilla was there. That small-small one was not so scary as the big ones.

Slowly, the small-big go-rilla walked down the net, like a giant furry black spider in a web. After plopping onto the ground, it walked, using its hands and its feet, to the food bin.

The black animal bent her head over the bin and then reached an arm inside. Was the bin empty? Maybe the go-rillas had eaten everything?

But finally, the go-rilla held up a big white thing, like a half melon, and then sat down and waited near the hole in the fence. Rosaline was afraid to go near the hole. When Johan had pointed his gun there, that made the go-rillas really mad. She didn't want them to scream again.

The small-big go-rilla walked back to the other side of the fence from Rosaline and sat down. The go-rilla bit into the white thing, then took the bite out of its mouth and pushed it through the fence.

Rosaline grabbed it quickly, stepped back, and sniffed. It didn't smell good, but it didn't smell bad, either. She nibbled it. It didn't taste good, but it was food. After swallowing it, she waited for the go-rilla to pass her another bite. The go-rilla still had a piece of the white thing in her hands, but it took the food away, moving back to the hole in the fence. Looking back at Rosaline, the small-big go-rilla curled her long black arm. *"Come."*

Rosaline could barely reach that hole, but when the go-rilla pushed the white thing through the hole, she stretched to take it. She backed up into the shadows and ate one more bite, then another, until the white thing was almost gone. At least her tummy stopped growling. She saved the last bite for her mother, pushing it into the pocket of her jeans. Maybe Mama could tell her what the white thing was. All the time Rosaline was eating, the go-rilla sat quietly, watching her with brown-red eyes. Rosaline decided the small-big go-rilla was a mama.

Then Rosaline curled her fingers over the bottom part of the opening, watching the go-rilla, hoping for more food. She was surprised when the go-rilla touched her hand with a giant black finger. The touch didn't hurt, but Rosaline didn't understand what the mama animal wanted. Then the mama go-rilla put her whole hand over both of Rosaline's. So big! Not soft, but so warm. Then the go-rilla turned away and climbed back into the net and left her all alone again.

Rosaline carried the piece of white thing back to the house. She had to run part of the way, because she heard a *hoo-hoo* sound high in the trees, and when she looked up, a giant bird was staring down at her, its yellow eyes huge and round. It might want to fly down and grab her.

The house was just as cold and dark as when she'd left a while ago. Johan had not come back. There was no food in the cupboard or in the cooler. Shivering, Rosaline climbed into bed beside her mother, pulling the blankets over her cold legs and feet.

"Mama, food." She held out the piece of white thing in front of her mama's face. "The go-rilla gave it to me. I eated some."

Her mother's eyes were closed. Mama was sleeping hard, with her mouth open just a little bit. Rosaline tried again. "Mama, food!"

She put her hand on mama's cheek. Cold. "Mama!" Using her fingers, she pried her mama's lips open, and then tried to push the white food inside, but it came back out. "Food!"

"I cover you up, Mama." Rosaline pulled the blankets over her mother and snuggled under them, too. "I cold, too."

Mama didn't put her arms around her to warm her up. Rosaline wished she could climb up into the net with that gentle mama go-rilla and share all those go-rilla blankets. The go-rilla was furry, like a cat. She would be warm.

14

North Cascades

Sam sat in the darkness on the shore, savoring the star-spangled sky that seemed to stretch forever over the lake. The water lapped gently in the breeze, revealing the tops of stumps that would protrude higher as the season wore on and water was released through Ross Dam. The scene would have been more enjoyable in solitude and silence, but she did her best to ignore the occasional shouts and the continuous background music from the campground behind her.

Too much time had elapsed since she'd glimpsed the Milky Way. She remembered when she and Chase had enjoyed the night sky together on a high Utah plateau. She missed her lover. His quiet humor. His touch.

Pulling her cell phone from her jacket pocket, she checked the time. Eleven twenty. Too late to call him. Only a couple of bars showed in the corner of the screen, and the power was running low. She'd plug her phone into the charger when she returned to her tent.

Lying back on the sand, she stretched out and let her thoughts wander through the galaxy. How many people had never seen this spectacle? How many had never seen the Milky Way? How many earthlings didn't even know all those stars existed in the heavens, their vision limited by the pollution of city lights? She listened for wolf howls but heard only the music from the campground and the melancholy, lyrical calls of loons from somewhere out on Ross Lake.

Ants were crawling up her neck and hypothermia was only minutes away from settling into her bones when she finally wandered back to her tent and zipped into her sleeping bag. All the other campers, with the exception of the Germans grouped around their cooking grate with drinking cups in hand and cell phone still playing music, were already in their tents.

Around midnight, the cell phone tunes finally ceased, and she drifted off.

Shortly after dawn the next morning, Sam knelt on the shore of Ross Lake and leaned toward the water, her cooking pot in hand to scoop up the liquid. Most of the backpackers were still in their tents. The site previously occupied by Mark and Randi was, surprisingly, vacant. They'd packed up at first light, maybe reluctant to face other campers this morning. Served the bozo right; he should be embarrassed.

The shallow lake water was liquid crystal, giving her a clear view of multicolored rocks on the lake bottom. She dipped her pot. Minnows darted away as her shadow moved over them. She heard only birdsong and the whispers of water brushing the shore. Further out, wind rippled the surface, gently splashing against a partially submerged cottonwood fallen from the bank so recently it still had leaves on the limbs she could see. The tree had floated in from its original location and become wedged between two of the underwater stumps.

An indistinct shape wavered beneath the wooden fingers of a limb. A fish, sheltering in the shade? Or something caught beneath the snag?

The blob moved again in the slight current. Back and forth. Fish usually hovered in place or flitted through the water. She removed her sunglasses and squinted to sharpen the image, cursing her aging eyesight. Broader than a fish, darker in the middle, pale edges vanishing into the murk. Maybe a lost item of clothing or a piece of gear the wind had blown from the camping area or from a boat. The water couldn't be more than three feet deep there; she should wade out and retrieve the flotsam.

She stared for a moment longer, trying to identify the object or creature. Abruptly, she gasped and averted her gaze. *No.* That had to be her imagination. She made herself focus again on the wavering shape beneath the water. A hand? A human hand?

Leaving her cooking pot on the bank, she returned to her campsite for her binoculars. Unfortunately, the lenses did little to confirm her horrific guess about what she was observing. The sun, fully risen now, glared off the rippling water. The waving digits vanished against the darkness of the lake. Through the leaves of the downed tree, she could make out a bundle of black clothing jammed up against the branches.

Maybe it was an optical illusion, a duffel bag or a jacket lost overboard. Sitting down on the bank, she removed her shoes and socks, and slid into the lake. The water was surprisingly cold, and became even colder as she waded out. And deeper, too. More like three and a half feet deep, nearly up to her armpits.

She tugged at the end of the half-submerged branch, and the mass beneath it moved, swinging around toward her. *Oh, God.* She'd guessed correctly. The bundle was a corpse.

The missing hiker, Alec Lysikov? No, this was a Black man with a balding head, floating face down, clad in a black jacket and blue jeans. Stenciled across the back of his jacket were the words NPS RANGER. A park service boat was probably floating, abandoned, somewhere on the lake.

There was no question the man was dead. The back of his ears were ragged. Fish had already nibbled on him. She had no intention of flipping him over to examine his face. She'd seen enough clouded eyes of the dead to last a lifetime.

When she released her hold on the branch, it snapped back, shifting the body again. Still pinned underwater by the sunken limb, the dead man's hand waved at her again, as if saying goodbye.

In a movie, a female character in this situation would scream or run away or at least stagger off a few feet and vomit. Sam's reaction, or more accurately, her lack of reaction, disturbed her. After digging out frozen bodies a few weeks ago, could nothing shock her now? Had she, like Chase in his FBI work, become inured to discovering corpses?

After wading back to shore, she perched on the bank, tugging on her socks and boots. A dead ranger. She didn't look forward to informing the central office of the North Cascades Park.

One of the Germans joined her on the lakeshore. Glancing at her, he asked how she had gotten so wet. She decided not to share her gruesome discovery. "I accidentally dropped my pot in the water and had to retrieve it."

He gazed briefly at the lake, but the glare kept him from noticing the body under the fallen tree. After filling his water bottle, he twisted the cap on.

"You should boil that water before drinking it," she advised.

He stared at her with a questioning expression.

"Boats move through this water. And all sorts of wildlife swim in this lake—deer, elk, raccoons, coyotes, bears." *And at least one human corpse.*

"Ah," he said. "Giardia. I have filter."

She nodded. "Even better."

Returning to her campsite, Sam retrieved her cell phone from her tent, realizing she had failed to plug it into the charger last night.

To her surprise, her cell phone had service, although the screen still showed only two bars. After eyeing the surrounding campsites to be sure nobody would overhear, she called the park headquarters.

"What!" the woman who answered the phone responded to her report. "We don't have a ranger missing." A brief hesitation. "At least, I don't think we do. Who did you say you are? Tell me you're pulling my leg."

Sam sighed. "I wish I could." She repeated her name and location.

"Just a minute. Don't hang up."

A few minutes later, Sam repeated the whole story to the district ranger. "Well, shit," he said. "Pardon my language." He sounded like a southern transplant. "Stay there, Miz Westin, and we'll get a boat out there ASAP. Has anyone else noticed the . . . uh . . . it?"

The body. He clearly was even more uncomfortable with the idea than she was. "I don't think so."

"Stay put, please. Don't call attention to the . . . uh . . . situation. I'll get someone there in half an hour or less."

She didn't want to waste half an hour cooling her heels here waiting for park personnel to come and see what she'd already seen, but Chase would tell her it was her duty. So she made herself a cup of coffee, boiling the lake water for a few minutes before pouring it through the filter, ate a bagel with peanut butter for breakfast, then stowed all her gear into her pack.

Around her, other campers were busy with their own meals.

She observed as a couple more hikers went down to the lake's edge, scooped up water or washed dishes, and never noticed anything out of place. They packed up their belongings and started down the trail. The Germans headed in the direction of Lightning Creek. She was the only hiker remaining at the campground when an NPS boat finally cruised up, scraping onto the small gravelly beach north of the downed tree and corpse. Sam carried her backpack to the shore to meet them.

Two rangers, a young man with a sparse blond mustache and a mature woman with graying hair held back in a ponytail, took down her contact information and questioned her about the find. No, she hadn't touched the body. No, she had no idea of who it could be. No, as far as she knew, none of the others in the campground had even noticed the body. No, she had no idea of the campers' names, except for Mark and Randi. She had no good response when the woman, whose nametag read CASTRO, asked her why she was the only person who had spotted it.

"Um . . ." She hesitated, then suggested, "I'm just more observant?"

When neither ranger responded, she added she was collecting information for an article on this area, so she was making notes on everything. "Plus," she said, "I'm solo on this trip. Everyone else is hiking with companions. They're focused on their friends."

Did that make her sound like a curmudgeon? Or maybe a recluse who hated people? Her brain flashed on all the news clips of neighbors of murderers who inevitably told a reporter, "I really never knew that guy. He kept to himself."

Sam was about to add an explanation about taking this trip to enjoy some rare solitude while working on her article, but the female ranger saved her by saying, "I know what you mean. It's amazing how many people don't even see their surroundings."

Ah. A kindred spirit. Sam felt comfortable enough to ask about where the wolves might be. When that caused Castro to raise an eyebrow, she added, "For my article."

"Last we heard, the wolves were east of Desolation Peak Trail." This came from Ranger Digby, according to his nametag. "But they move around, you know."

"I do," Sam assured him. "Still, I hope to get a glimpse of them."

"You might want to take the trail east, just south of Deerlick Creek Campground," Digby suggested.

Castro frowned at her younger colleague, then turned to Sam. "We didn't tell you that."

"Don't know where I heard it." Sam tugged her backpack upright. "Say, I saw the poster about the missing guy at the trailhead."

"Lysikov or Madura?" Digby asked.

"Oh god, there's more than one?" Sam was horrified. "Lysikov. Alec Lysikov."

"Of course, Lysikov." Castro frowned again at her colleague. "Madura was last year, up near Cutthroat. Lysikov went missing here." She puffed her cheeks with a big breath of air, blew it out in a signal Sam couldn't quite decipher—exasperation?

"Oh yeah, that's right," Digby agreed. He rubbed his mustache with an index finger as if the whiskers itched.

Sam switched her gaze from him to Castro. "Do you look for hikers who go missing?"

Castro folded her arms across her chest. "Of course. But it's a big place, and there are so few rangers." She held up a hand as if to stop Sam from commenting. "And yes, there are always volunteers who are willing to help, but there are only so many days and so many miles they can commit to."

"I get it. I've participated in wilderness searches myself."

Sam tilted her head toward the corpse in the lake. "Sorry about the . . ."

Castro shrugged. "Not my first floater."

"Really?" This was routine?

The female ranger grimaced. "Boats. Drunks without PFDs. Cold water. It happens."

The younger ranger melted into the woods and quickly jogged around the campground. "Just you here?" he asked on returning.

"Last night all the sites were full," she told him. Should she tell them about Mark and his pistol? Legal, she reminded herself, especially if he had a concealed weapon permit. They probably wouldn't care. Nobody had been shot.

After thanking her, the rangers shoved their boat off the beach and drifted out to the corpse as Sam observed from the shore, buckling on her pack. Voices carried across water, and she heard their conversation from her location.

"Oh, ugh," Castro remarked at first glance. "Take pictures, Lance."

Digby photographed the scene with his cell phone, and then the two of them awkwardly tugged the body over the gunwale, nearly tipping the edge of their craft into the water as they did so.

"Fancied himself a ranger, did he?" the woman remarked, by which Sam deduced the deceased wasn't actually attached to the National Park Service.

No wonder the lettering on the back of his coat had seemed amateurish. From her vantage point, Sam saw Castro tugging at the corpse. Digby seemed to gag, clapping his hand over his mouth. It was probably *his* first floater.

"Fish kisses. Suck it up, Lance." Castro reminded him, "Photos."

After he took a couple of pictures, he pocketed his cell and they both bent over, only their shoulders and heads visible from shore. Sam guessed they were going through the corpse's pockets. Before the boat drifted out of range, over the lapping waves, Sam heard Castro say, "No ID. Probably at the bottom of the lake."

A few seconds later, the outboard motor fired up and the NPS boat zipped away. Sam buckled the chest strap on her backpack and strode north on the trail.

Not Castro's first floater? Sam hoped she could wipe the memory of the body from her mind. This was supposed to be a nature expedition—backcountry beauty and amazing wildlife.

Should she add the corpse to her article? Would her editor think that was titillating, or a frightening and depressing way to taint a story in his outdoor adventure magazine? Should she ask?

She wanted to discuss it with someone, but this news seemed too grim to share with Blake. Maybe Chase. As if he'd read her thoughts, a moment later her cell phone buzzed from her pocket.

"Glad to hear from you, Chase! But I only have one bar, so this may not last for long. I should have plugged my cell into the charger last night."

"Good morning to you, too, *querida*. I haven't heard from you for more than thirty-six hours. And you can plug that phone in any time, you know."

Well, duh. Why hadn't she thought of that? "But then I'd have to fish the charger and cord out of my pack, and I'm hiking now." Sam couldn't decide whether to be annoyed or pleased he was keeping track of her. "I've been a little busy this morning. You do remember that I'm out in the North Cascades for a few days, right?"

"Got it; no cell reception sometimes. Are you on the trail of those wolves?"

After she told him about the body in the lake, he griped, "Damn, Summer. You're getting more excitement than I am these days."

"Not exactly the excitement I was hoping for."

His sigh rasped over the airwaves. "Of course not. I just guessed the fake NPS jacket probably meant he was up to some sort of criminal activity. I didn't mean to imply it was fun for you to stumble on a corpse."

"More like wade out to one. He was snagged under the branch of a tree that had fallen into the water. The rangers said boaters fall overboard and drown in this lake now and then." She focused on taking long strides, trying to make up for lost time.

". . . fading . . . and out."

"You are, too, Chase. I'm losing signal here. Later, *mi amor*."

She waited for his scratchy "Ciao" before shutting down her phone and zipping it back into in her pocket.

That swollen, waterlogged, waving hand. Ugh. How long would she keep seeing it in her mind?

15

Evansburg

In the morning, Finn fed Cargo and walked the dog around the block, then spent a half hour petting Lok and Kee and letting them chase the pinpoint of light from a laser pointer. After that, he brushed the pet hair from his pants and, yawning, drove to the USFS road behind Grace's compound. Even after two cups of coffee, his internal clock didn't know which time zone it was supposed to be in.

Before he reached the maintenance shed, he spied two large tents tucked between the trees. Three adults, two men and a woman, sprawled in lawn chairs around a primitive fire pit. He parked beside an old Subaru Outback off the side of the road. The car was piled high with clothes and boxes full of groceries.

When they noticed him approaching, the campers seemed surprised, but none of them ran for their tents, and as far as he could see, they were unarmed.

"Hello!" he called out before reaching them. "I hope you can help me with some information." He pulled out his identification wallet.

The woman stood up from her chair. Neither of the men moved.

"Isn't this national forest land?" The grizzled, bearded older man asked after checking Finn's shield. "And aren't you a city detective?"

Finn responded yes to both questions.

Graybeard leaned forward in his chair. "Then bugger off and leave us alone. We're camping here."

"Jonah, cool your jets," the woman said before turning to Finn. "The detective is only asking." She glanced toward the nearby stream. "Excuse my father-in-law, Detective. We thought it'd be fun to bring the kids out here for a few days." She tilted her head sideways. "School's out and all the campgrounds are reserved. This place is in our price range."

Through the trees, Finn glimpsed a small boy and girl throwing rocks into a small creek.

"I'm Amy Whitman, by the way." The woman offered her hand. "How can we help you?"

Maybe these people were homeless, maybe just scruffy campers. In any case, they didn't seem to be doing anything illegal. Finn shook Amy's hand, while keeping an eye on the men. "When did you set up camp?"

"Three nights ago," the younger man responded. He was wearing a plaid flannel shirt that Finn would have thought was too warm for a day in May. "Did you happen to hear gunshots?" he asked the trio.

"Nope," immediately responded the man in the plaid shirt.

"Wait a minute, Harley." The woman reached out to tap him on the arm before swiveling to face Finn. "My husband wouldn't wake up if a 747 landed right beside him. *My* answer is yes, I heard gunshots. Two nights ago, right?" She combed her fingers through her long dark hair. The gesture reminded him of Grace. "Two shots. They woke me up in the middle of the night. But they sounded quite a ways away."

Finn knew their camp was only about half a mile from

Grace's by foot. If they had heard the commotion, they probably knew that, too. "Do you have guns with you?" Finn shifted his gaze from one face to another.

While Amy and Harley shook their heads, Jonah scowled, clearly irritated. "Wouldn't be without one out here in the woods," he challenged in an angry growl.

Amy stared at Jonah. "What? With the kids? Where is it?"

"I get it." Finn ignored her, trying to be amiable to the old man. "Been hunting or shooting target practice with that gun lately, Mr. Whitman?"

"What's it to you?" Jonah fingered his beard, staring at Finn with cold blue-gray eyes. "Rifle's just for protection. What the hell's going on?"

"Someone shot an animal nearby a couple of nights ago," Finn told them.

"Oh no. That baby gorilla?" Amy guessed. "Was that what I heard?"

She obviously knew about the incident, so he nodded. "Yes, the baby gorilla."

"I saw that in the podcast," Amy confirmed. "Will Kanoni be okay?"

Finn stifled a groan. Not only did they know about the gorillas and the shooting, they even knew the baby's name. How long would it be before Grace heard about all this?

He asked if they knew anyone who might want to shoot a gorilla. The three all denied it. "Have any of you ever called anyone to complain about animal noises?"

Amy and Harley shook their heads, so Finn focused on Jonah, who finally said, "The neighbor's hound dog, once. But I didn't do nothing to it. People deserve peace and quiet in their own home."

"I agree, Mr. Whitman. Thanks for your time, folks. Have a

good time out here. It's a beautiful day." Finn turned back toward his car.

After sliding into the seat, he pulled out the little notebook he kept in his pocket and jotted down the Subaru's license plate number and their names. Amy, Harley, and Jonah Whitman. At least he'd assumed they were all named Whitman. Asking for ID tended to raise hackles out here, especially as he was technically out of his jurisdiction.

The maintenance shed that he'd seen on the map appeared to be just that. A rusting backhoe crouched under a pole structure with a corrugated aluminum roof. The building, if you could call it that, was flanked by a large, locked metal toolchest with USFS stenciled on top in peeling green paint. Finn made a note to ask the rangers about the contents. Alongside the shed was a medium-size pile of gravel.

The road was full of potholes that would have benefited from a lot of that gravel, and Finn was forced to drive slowly. It was hard to imagine a loaded logging truck navigating the rough surface. And maybe hauling logs was no longer happening, because when he reached the clear-cut site, there was zero activity. He'd need to ask the chief ranger about when the logging had ended and who had worked there. The ugly stumps reminded him of the stubble of a balding man who needed to start shaving his head.

On the way back, he spied another small hill of gravel covered by a tarp. That was the other anomaly he needed to check out, the object that appeared to be a small building on the Google Earth aerial image. But it was only gravel. Why the USFS felt it was important to throw a tarp over it was another question for the chief ranger.

After returning down the USFS road, Finn drove several miles to the derelict farmhouse on the north side of Grace's property. The long driveway was in slightly better shape than the forest service road had been, but with washboards that made his wheels chatter over the surface. He parked close to the old house, just outside a wooden fence that now lay partially on the ground. The place looked as if it had been deserted for years.

As he walked up the uneven stepping stones toward the house, he thought he heard a faint metallic click. He stopped for a minute, listening. Nothing. He shook his head and continued to the front door.

"Hello?" He knocked on the door. "Evansburg Police Department."

No response. The dirt-streaked windows were covered with shreds of curtains that had probably been white at one time, but now were gray. "Hello? Anyone home?"

He tried the knob. It didn't move. Locked, or rusted in place. Stepping over missing boards on the front porch, he gingerly navigated the creaking steps, then walked around the house to the back.

The vegetation there had grown knee-high, and the dry grasses whispered in the slight breeze, giving the place an ominous feeling. He knocked and called again at the back door. No answer.

When he tried the knob, it turned easily, surprising him. He pushed the door open and stepped in, and was immediately sorry. A foul odor engulfed him, one he knew all too well. The sweet-rotten smell was the scent of decomposition. The reek of death.

16

"Evansburg Police!" The place felt empty, but any cop who wanted to stay alive never assumed all rooms were clear. To assuage the creepy feeling that was crawling up his spine, Finn called the dispatcher to let her know where he was.

"Do you require backup?" she asked.

"I'll let you know what I find. Send help if I don't report back in ten." He ended the call, tucked his cell phone into his pocket and unholstered his pistol.

The room he stepped into probably had been called the mudroom when in use. Broken Linoleum covered the floor, and dust bunnies huddled beneath an old utility sink in the corner, flanked by water valves and outlets for a missing washer and dryer.

The mud/laundry room opened onto a spacious kitchen. Large empty spaces marked where once a stove and refrigerator had been installed. A Formica-topped table occupied center stage. A small one-burner camp stove, the type that backpackers used, sat on top of the table, along with a few well-used pans and a kerosene lantern. On the floor was a large cooler, its lid yawning open. An empty milk carton was the sole occupant, floating in a shallow lake of water from melted ice.

Holding his gun in front of him, Finn swung around the door frame and stepped into a living room. A decrepit couch sagged against one wall, keeping company with an old wooden rocking chair.

Finn discerned faint marks that might be partial footprints on the floor. The worn wooden planks appeared to be recently swept or mopped. After opening the closet door to reveal only a mildewing mop, he approached the staircase.

The stench grew stronger with each step he climbed. On the second floor were three bedrooms, but only one held a queen-size bed. Under blood-stained covers he could see the outline of a slight woman, unmoving. The closet door was open, revealing a few items of clothing hanging from the rack.

A pair of worn woman's tennis shoes lay beside the bed.

After a quick peek under the bed, he moved quickly to check out the other two rooms, his pistol still held out in front of him. One bedroom was completely empty. Its closet didn't have a door. In the third room, a small sleeping bag lay on top of a thin foam mattress, and the closet held a dirty pair of shoes, toddler size. In the lone bathroom, the small counter supported a hairbrush and a couple of toothbrushes in a glass, a large plastic water container with a spigot, and a generic black-on-white, pin-on badge that read WENDY.

Finn holstered his gun and walked back to the first bedroom, trying not to breathe too deeply. He didn't need to feel for a pulse; it had been clear on first glance that the woman was deceased. Rigor had come and gone, so she'd likely died at least twenty-four hours ago. After snapping a photo with his cell phone, he gently pulled back the blanket that hid her. She lay on her back, and the mattress beneath her had soaked up a great deal of blood.

A black hole under her rib cage was surrounded by the powder burns of gunshot stippling, indicating that she'd been shot at close range. She was thin but had obviously been attractive, with smooth, dark-brown skin, wavy black hair, and full lips that were now dried and stretched in a grimace across her teeth.

An unexpected element in this death scene was a small piece of cauliflower on the sheet next to the woman's ear. Peculiar.

Finn called the dispatcher again, reported the corpse, and asked for crime scene evidence collection, and the coroner. He didn't want to touch or move anything until at least one other witness arrived, so he studied the contents of the room. Suitcase open on the floor, a few clothes hanging in the closet. A woman's clothes, along with a dress and a T-shirt that looked as if they belonged to a small child. The size seemed a close match for the shoes he'd found in the other closet. The dress hinted at a tiny girl.

On the floor of the closet lay a pair of men's jockey shorts, as well as a pair of large, dirty socks. So a man had been here, and a child. But only the corpse remained.

Finn didn't see a gun, and it seemed unlikely that the woman had shot herself. So at least one other person had been here at the time of the shooting, unless the child had accidentally killed the woman. More probable, the man had shot the woman and then taken the child. Perhaps he was looking at a fatal resolution to a custody battle?

Crap. Now he had a gorilla shooter to find *and* a murder to look into. He hadn't yet located Keyes, but he was reasonably sure that Keyes had nothing to do with this, whatever this was. Was it possible that this shooter had also wounded Kanoni? He needed a lot more clues to these squatters' identities. And he needed the gun.

While he waited for his colleagues to arrive, he decided to explore the area surrounding the house. Several footprints led to and from the back door. Tiny bare feet indicated the child.

Larger imprints looked like tennis shoes, medium size. So probably the mom's prints.

The front side of the house held impressions of tire marks in the gravel and dirt. That surface was typically useless for discerning the brands of tires, but he could tell from the narrowness of trenches that it was a smallish vehicle, not a monster truck or van. In the soil to the side of the driveway, he found several imprints of a man's shoes, but none looked recent. The sole treads revealed no manufacturer's stamp.

The crime scene evidence tech arrived first. Multiple officers in the small Evansburg department had been trained in evidence collection, and today the job had been assigned to Guy Rodrigo, who grimaced at the news that this was a death scene.

"Sweet," he commented in a droll voice, extracting a pair of purple latex gloves from his kit. After snapping them on, he gestured toward the house. "Let's get this over with, Finn. Lead on."

Finn observed as Rodrigo dutifully collected fingerprints from the front doorknob, squinting at the results he'd lifted. "Smudged prints on top of other smudged prints."

Finn helped him label and pack the prints into his kit, then Rodrigo followed him to the back door, where the technician spent a good ten minutes collecting more prints that he deemed as useless as the first set.

"Hello?"

The coroner, a rotund man named Dave Severn, rounded the corner of the house. "Sorry to be late," he apologized. "I was, uh, in the midst of a delicate procedure when the call came in."

Severn had most likely been in the process of embalming a corpse. Finn shuddered, not wanting to think about it, yet unable to stop the image from forming in his imagination. It was already disturbing enough to him that the county coroner was not a medical professional but also a businessman who clearly had a financial interest in what happened to all the corpses he would inspect. But Washington State had no law that a coroner had to be a forensic pathologist, or even a physician. This was a rural county, and the voters repeatedly elected Severn, who had run unopposed in the two elections that Finn had witnessed since moving here from Chicago. Apparently, County Coroner was not a position that locals lusted after.

"Natural death?" Severn's expression was hopeful.

"Not unless you consider bullets natural," Finn told him.

Rodrigo, now sporting a bright-blue swimmer's nose clip, was already in the bedroom with the deceased when Finn brought Severn in. He'd completely uncovered the corpse. The jeans and sweatshirt she wore were soaked with blood. On her feet were socks.

"Alrighty." Severn stood back from the body. "Definitely homicide, then. Been a long time since I've had one of these."

"How many have you dealt with?" Finn asked, wondering if he should demand a forensic pathologist.

"This makes two. Or possibly three." He shot a sideways look at Finn. "You sent me the last one, Detective. That guy found rotting in the woods? With the neck wounds from wildlife?"

Finn had to stifle a gag reflex at the abrupt reminder of that horrific corpse. The way Severn described that scene made it sound as if he didn't believe the wildlife depredation story. Finn had personally suggested the cause of death. He stared Severn down.

"With his head chewed nearly off, there was no way to tell if he'd died from a broken neck. He could have been pushed from a cliff for all we know," the coroner added.

"I suppose." Finn shrugged. "Criminals usually don't live long happy lives. But like you say, there's no way to know for sure." He turned back to the corpse, eager to change the subject. "But this case . . ."

"No doubt about the cause of death here. Let's roll her."

Finn helped Severn roll the woman over. There was a large exit wound on her back. "No bullet hole in the bed," he observed. "So she wasn't shot here."

Damn. Finn had come back to solve Kanoni's shooting, and now he had not only an unexpected death scene to contend with but also an undiscovered crime scene somewhere. Would he ever get back to Hawaii?

"We'll need DNA," he told both men.

With Guy Rodrigo standing by, appropriate packaging in hand, Severn clipped fingernails and yanked out a few strands of hair, then used what looked like an implement from a manicure kit to scrape the insides of the deceased woman's cheeks and bag that, too. Then he turned to Finn. "I'll keep her for a few days in case you need bone marrow."

Ugh. Only a coroner could look pleased at the thought of breaking a corpse's bones to get DNA from the marrow, probably because that would be an extra charge to the county. "I'll have to let you know, Severn."

After the corpse was in the body bag and Finn had helped carry it to Severn's black station wagon, he returned to help Rodrigo finish with the scene. "No bullet holes in the walls?" he asked.

The technician shook his head. "Not that I found."

Damn again.

"Some decent prints, though, on the suitcase handles and in the bathroom. With luck, they'll match someone in AFIS."

"Let's hope," Finn agreed.

Rodrigo surveyed the room. Black smudges of fingerprint powder dotted nearly all the surfaces. "Do we take everything?"

He looked at Finn for confirmation.

"Yeah, I guess so. I'll help. Sing out about any identification you see, so I can stick that in a separate envelope."

By the time they'd bagged and packed the meager contents of the house, it was dark. In the small suitcase, they'd discovered a photo.

Finn studied it carefully. A handsome couple, in the twentyish to thirtyish range. The attractive woman was now the corpse in the body bag. The man was most likely the husband, or at least a temporary partner, who had shot the woman and taken the child.

The suitcase also contained a stash of money, hidden in the lining on the bottom. But after counting, it amounted to $185. So if the deceased was a drug dealer or a prostitute, either she'd been robbed or business had not been good.

Finn took possession of the photo and a large manila envelope enclosing two smaller plastic sleeves. One contained the ID badge from the bathroom and the other, a worn leather billfold containing $18.27 and a ragged identification card in the name of Gwendolyn Jones. California address. There was no state seal visible through the smudged laminated surface, which made the ID card seem suspicious.

It seemed likely that Gwendolyn and her child, and maybe the man, too, were homeless, in which case it could be hard to get more information about them. The second possibility was that they were on the run, in which case they might have left a trail he could find.

He and Rodrigo returned to the station and logged in the evidence from the abandoned house. With his phone, he snapped photos of the ID card, the badge, the billfold, and the picture of the man and woman.

After signing on to his desk computer, he discovered the California ID was fake, as he'd suspected. The address was a Burger King. He showed the plastic pin-on badge to the desk clerk on duty and the one officer in the station, who was writing up a report. "Restaurant or hotel" were their best guesses.

Great. He'd make the rounds tomorrow, and he'd try to call the owner of the farmhouse, but he didn't hold out much hope for more information there, as the heir hadn't even cared to do anything with the old house. He or she probably had no clue that squatters had taken up residence.

The thought that a child was out there somewhere in the dark, possibly in the hands of a murderer, was unsettling, but Finn didn't have a clue what he could do about that at this point.

17

Rosaline had hidden in the woods until after the scary men went away, then tried the back door of the house. Locked now. She couldn't get in. No blankets, no mama. It was dark and cold. She was hungry. She sat down on the step, sobbing.

Then she slowly walked back to the go-rillas. They had blankets. They had food.

They were sitting next to the barn. When she waved to them, the mama go-rilla that had held her hand came over. The mama watched Rosaline as she curled her fingers and toes in the fence and pulled herself up to the hole. The wire hurt her bare toes. When she reached the hole, she turned her head sideways, looking though the opening. Below, in the box, she saw a banana, a piece of bread, and more of the white and green things. Rosaline stretched one arm inside, trying to reach that food. She pushed her head all the way through the hole until she could wrap her fingers around the banana.

The big-big gorilla made a noise like Johan did when he was mad. Rosaline was upside down, but she knew the big-big gorilla was running toward her. She tried to yank her head out. But the scary gorilla wrapped his hand around Rosaline's arm and jerked Rosaline all the way in, dragging her over the food bin. He dropped her in the dirt, next to his big black feet that looked like hands, and then leaned over her and pressed his scary black face close to hers. Red-brown eyes. So big. Rosaline was so scared that she didn't even squeak. Would he bite her with those giant teeth? Would he put his giant hands around her neck?

She peed all over herself, she was so scared. A puddle spread across the ground.

Then the small-big mama go-rilla jerked Rosaline away from the big scary one. The mama go-rilla picked up the banana from the dirt and put it between her teeth. Then, with one arm wrapped around her, the mama go-rilla pressed Rosaline to her chest and stomach. Rosaline tried to wrap her arms and legs around the mama go-rilla, holding onto her fur as the go-rilla carried her, walking awkwardly on one hand and her feet, into the barn. Inside, the go-rilla sat down next to a tall pole. It was even darker here than outside, which might have been scary, but the go-rilla's arms and belly were so warm, like a hug from her mama.

The big scary go-rilla followed them in, and Rosaline clutched onto the mama go-rilla as tightly as she could. Rosaline's back scraped against the pole as the mama go-rilla climbed up to a flat place and snuggled them both into a pile of blankets there, like a nest in a tree. The big scary go-rilla climbed up the pole behind them. It stopped to sniff them, which made Rosaline shiver with fright.

But then the scary one moved on and Rosaline could hear it above them, higher up. Like maybe a giant daddy bird watching over the mama bird and baby bird.

The mama go-rilla took the banana from between her teeth and gave it to Rosaline. It was mashed and her own mama would have said it was dirty, but Rosaline peeled and ate it.

It was so very scary. She wanted her own Mama to wake up and come get her. Tears ran down her face, and the mama gorilla touched her wet cheek with a giant black finger and then pointed to her own eye, trying to talk to her with her hands. *Cry.* Rosaline was crying. But she had food and she was warm.

18

North Cascades

Lightning Creek Campground was nearly full when Sam arrived. There were two camping areas, one ringed by boats and another off in the trees, but within sight and sound of the boat-in area. The Germans had occupied three sites this time, and the music from their area competed with a harmonica across the small bay.

She'd known this would be a popular spot. Many visitors shared the goal of hiking to the Desolation Peak lookout, made famous by writer Jack Kerouac back in the '50s and '60s. She'd planned to go there herself, take photos, and at least mention him in her article, although personally, she had a hard time mustering the required respect for the Beat Generation poet and writer.

From everything she'd read, Kerouac had been a drunk and a druggie, always in search of the next high in any form: drugs, religion, sex, simply anything he hadn't yet experienced. His writing about his stay at the lookout included a lot of pages complaining about boredom and feeling sorry for himself and describing how he killed mice and then felt remorse for that. Kerouac was a unique literary soul for his era, though, and that was his main claim to fame. Like many authors who died young, he'd become more admired after his death.

As she had morosely surveyed the packed camping area, a drum began to thump from a site behind her. Someone had brought bongos to the campground?

No, no, and just no. No way in hell was she going to pitch her tent here. If, as the rangers had hinted, the wolves were anywhere near, the wild canines would surely keep their distance from this noisefest. So she decided that she would make tracks as well. Backtracking the short distance to the trail junction, she'd headed east on the main trail. South of Deerlick Creek Campground, Ranger Castro had said.

The sun was setting by the time she had reached the Boundary Trail junction south of Deerlick. She stepped off the trail and climbed over a rise, then followed a small creek until she found a space just big enough and flat enough for her one-person tent between a couple of tall Douglas firs, out of sight of the trail. It was close to the creek, handy for filling her water bottles. With luck, she wouldn't be discovered here, and if she was, maybe she could implore Rangers Castro and Digby for leniency. She had quickly set up her tent, rolled out her sleeping bag, and strung up her rope over a high branch to hang her food bag.

After assembling and firing up her camp stove, she boiled water under the beam of her headlamp. That night's dinner was freeze-dried macaroni with meat sauce. After pouring the water into the food bag and zipping it shut, she switched off her headlamp and sat on the ground with her back against a tree trunk, letting her eyes adjust to the darkness as she waited for the tomato encrusted cardboard to rehydrate into food. Then finally, magically, she had heard what she'd been hoping for.

The low harmonic notes seemed to come from the surrounding mountains, reverberating through her body as they repeated and blended, then separated, crossing over each other in the night air. She leaned back and closed her eyes, relishing the canine concert. A wolfish version of Pachelbel's Canon in D. The howls had started on a low note, as if a warm-up was required, then rose in volume and pitch to a high chorus that made the hairs on the back of her neck stand on end. Beautiful harmonies, deeper and richer than coyote yips. Haunting. Anyone not familiar with wild canines might believe there were demons in the forest. Packs of demons that sang together.

Sam had been thrilled to discover wolves still existed in the North Cascades. Studies in Yellowstone and other locations had proved wolves were beneficial to any wild ecosystem. Farley Mowat's *Never Cry Wolf,* originally published in 1963, detailed one of the first real studies of the feral canines. That book showed wolves were key to keeping caribou herds healthy in the Canadian arctic. Books and films about the coastal wolves on Vancouver Island always mesmerized her, and she had searched for signs of them every time she kayaked there.

Tomorrow, she'd search for these wolves. If Farley Mowat could find wolves, why couldn't she?

After eating her meal and sealing the packaging into her bear bag, she hefted her food stash as high as she could, tying off the rope around the tree trunk. By the light of her headlamp, she jotted down a few notes about the wolf howls for her article before crawling into her sleeping bag. This time she remembered to plug her phone into the portable charger.

Sleep had not been immediate. Her brain kept looping back to the "Missing" poster of Alec Lysikov, then the dead man in the lake, the delicate fish bites nibbled from his ears. How many people in the world were waiting for a father or husband or friend who wouldn't come home?

She'd once lost track of Chase. It was a horrible, hollow

feeling. She'd been in Ecuador; he'd been undercover in Arizona when he dropped off her radar. When she did finally locate him, she discovered he'd been shot. Friendly fire, they judged the incident, an accidental shooting by colleagues in a nighttime firefight. Those particular colleagues had turned out to be treacherous scumbags.

What had the dead guy in the lake been up to? Was he a scumbag? Was Alec Lysikov? Had he vanished on purpose? Was he living a new life in Canada?

Was her father's wife, Zola, lying awake right now in Kansas, worried that she might not survive breast cancer? She imagined their refrigerator stuffed with casseroles from the well-wishing church ladies. Sam herself had never been one of those, to her father's dismay, and she worried about him these days. After what he had gone through with her mother, watching another woman he loved die might undo him. Or maybe he'd just chalk it up to being part of God's plan, as he did most tragic events. It must be comforting to be so certain that a supreme being was in charge of life on this planet.

Shortly after dawn, Sam yawned as she poured hot water into the instant coffee in her cup. Last night, after she had finally exhausted her imaginings and drifted off, she'd dreamed she heard a horse neigh. Now, she wondered what her imagination had been playing with. Dreaming of the horse she'd had as a child? Visualizing the horseback camping trip with Chase this fall? She remembered small scurrying noises outside the tent, most likely rodents. Certainly not the clip-clop of hooves. She didn't remember anything else except the sound of a high-pitched whinny.

Packers. She remembered the giant horse trailer in the

trailhead parking lot. No responsible wrangler would be moving his string during darkness, but it was possible horses were picketed less than a mile away, near Deerlick Creek Campground. How far could a horse's whinny carry through a thick forest?

Or maybe she'd actually heard the scream of a rabbit caught in an owl's talons? A morbid idea to contemplate so early in the morning, but predators needed to eat, too. Maybe the wolves had taken down a meal.

She turned to her food bag to find the powdered creamer. And there, not more than six feet away, nearly cloaked by salmonberry shrubs, stood a wolf. The animal stared at her, unmoving. He—or she—was nearly all black with only a sprinkle of gray hairs on the chest and the top of the head. The wolf's eyes were an astounding luminous gold, and its gaze burned so intensely she questioned whether the animal had ever been this close to a human before.

How had he—or she—simply materialized in total silence? What was the appropriate reaction to a wolf abruptly appearing at your campsite?

Sam darted her gaze sideways to check for others. She saw no signs of more wolves. Just this loner. Could this be Wiley's "big black yellow-eyed monster"? The wolf was taller than most Huskies, but lean, hardly a monster; and its eyes were golden, not merely yellow. Was it a youngster searching for territory of its own, or a scout for the rest of the pack? Would they be here soon? She and the wolf contemplated each other for several moments, neither of them moving.

The wild canine's fixed amber gaze was unnerving, the moment so powerful it was almost painful. She could barely breathe.

How could anyone kill such a magnificent animal? For nearly

two centuries wolves everywhere had been poisoned with strychnine, maimed with neck snares and leg traps, and slaughtered with guns. Some Canadian provinces and states in the US still paid bounties to hunters for murdering them. Every year, some wolves were killed to protect free-ranging cattle that ranchers grazed for pennies on public land.

Sam didn't have much hope anything would change soon to protect wolves. Or any other wildlife, for that matter. She'd read more than sixteen hundred bison had been slaughtered recently when they migrated out of the protection of Yellowstone National Park onto national forest land.

Killing was too often considered heroic in the human world. Most people, like Mark What's-his-name, preferred the myth wolves were blood-thirsty monsters men needed to slaughter.

The black wolf in front of her looked more like a dog that might come closer if she held out a handful of food. She'd never do that. For their own protection, all wild animals needed to believe humans were dangerous. Their lives depended on it.

"Thanks for visiting," she whispered to the wolf. Wolves were mostly pack animals. Why was this one alone?

A cracking noise sounded behind her, and she hazarded a quick glance over her shoulder. A crow was pecking at her bag of coffee. The bird hopped away when his beady black eyes noticed her watching. When she turned back, the wolf was gone.

"Stay safe," she said aloud. "Live long and prosper." Would a world ever exist where humans truly respected the lives of other animals?

At least she'd finally seen a wolf. Why hadn't she had her camera at hand? Reaching for her phone, she recorded notes to herself about the wolf's appearance and the crow's interruption. She placed her phone on the log next to her and picked up her coffee cup again.

Her phone chimed, startling her. She'd assumed she wouldn't have service here in the forest.

"Chase! I just saw a wolf!"

"I was worried about you."

"I hardly think one wolf would attack me."

"Not that. I just found out your floater had been shot."

"Oh. So he didn't just fall out of a boat and drown."

"He might have, but after being shot."

Sam's thoughts immediately leaped to Mark. But whatever had happened to the dead guy had to be completely unrelated. She quipped, "I had nothing to do with that, Chase."

He groaned. "Of course not, Summer."

How could she be so flip about a dead man? She was mortified at her own callous attitude. "Sorry. I don't know what got into me. I'm just excited about the wolf."

Chase sighed. "I just thought you might need to know that your corpse was murdered."

"Not *my* corpse."

"Watch your back, Summer."

"Nobody's hunting *me*. I'm off in the woods by myself. Nobody even knows where I am."

"And that's supposed to reassure me? Hinky things, illegal things, are going in that area, Summer. Drug smuggling and God knows what else. Come back ASAP."

She was glad she hadn't told him about the missing hikers. "Were you listening, Chase? I saw a wolf! And I heard the whole pack last night. I'm going after them."

"You would." A phone rang in the background. "I have to go. Be careful."

"Always."

"Right." The line went dead, leaving Chase's sarcastic last word ringing in her ear.

Should she have been more concerned about the shooting? This morning, human problems seemed sordid and distant. She'd like to keep them far away. The wolf's visit, on the other hand, was enchanting. Breathtaking.

The spot she'd chosen for her tent was peaceful and private, mostly hidden beneath the spreading bows of a large Douglas fir, with the continuous soothing murmur of Lightning Creek only a few yards away. So far, her camping location had remained a secret from noisy humans and thieving predators that might steal her food stash. Sam resolved to leave her tent there another night and spend the day searching for the wolves. She'd still have two days before she needed to be back home.

Hiking would have been easier had Sam returned to the well-trodden trail, but that didn't seem likely to result in wolf sightings, so she decided to head cross-country in an eastern direction. She lightened her pack to include only her lunch and a couple of energy bars, a shrink-wrapped metallic emergency blanket, her cell phone, binoculars, camera, and her windbreaker. At the last minute, she added a down vest and her wool hat, which seemed like overkill now but might come in handy if the breeze picked up. Her water bottle, filter, small first-aid kit, roll of duct tape and short length of parachute cord lived in the pockets of her pack at all times.

After hours of tramping up hills and down gullies and threading her way through scratchy brush and ferns, she had seen no sign of wolves, except for one muddy paw print near a puddle.

Frustrated, Sam perched on a rock to eat her bagel and peanut butter for lunch. A gray jay, known locally as a camp robber, landed on a branch a short distance away and was soon joined by another. They watched her expectantly, and although she was well off the trail, she realized these birds were accustomed to seeing hikers. Breaking off a few bits of bagel, she held them up in the air, her palm flat. After turning its head to eye her for a second, one of the jays flitted down, clasped its tiny claws around her finger for a millisecond, snatched a crumb, and then took off. Its partner quickly repeated the performance.

"That's it, fellas." She wiped her hands on her pants leg. "The rest is mine. Tell me where the wolves are. Or a mountain lion. Or at least an elk."

One jay fluttered its wings near her head, its equivalent of begging. She was delighted to encounter them, but she wasn't buying the routine. After both jays flitted off, she caught a movement out of the corner of her eye. There, halfway up the slope to the south. She squinted.

A moving shadow in the shape of a canine. Coyote? Pulling her binoculars to her eyes, she studied the creature. It *was* a wolf. A black wolf, perhaps the same one that had visited her only hours ago, trotted across the flank of the hill. And then another, this one dark gray, appeared out of the trees, walked over and touched noses with the black, and then bowed down on its front legs in a canine "play" position. The black wolf pounced, bowling over the gray, but they were both quickly up and running. The black wolf nipped the gray one's flank, and she—Sam was convinced the gray was a female—leaped up, reversing directions in midair. Then the black wolf dashed off with the gray in hot pursuit.

Grabbing her camera, Sam zoomed in on the wolves, and hit "Record" in the video mode. She caught a few seconds of the two playing tag, racing in circles around a tree, knocking each other over. Three more dark shapes emerged from the trees to join the pair, and then all five wolves all took off, vanishing into the forest, racing effortlessly up the slope toward the summit of Spratt Mountain.

Yes! She'd not only found a pack of wolves but also captured video footage of them. Maybe she could pull a few worthwhile still images from the video as well. She still had an hour before she needed to start back toward her camp. Keeping her camera slung around her neck., she started up the slope in the direction the wolves had taken, trying to keep her steps as quiet as possible in the hope of encountering them again.

As she pulled herself up the slope with the help of a small sapling, she caught another flash of movement in the rocks up ahead. Moving into the shadow of a tree, she stopped and waited.

A sway of tall grasses in front of the rocks, and then the nose of a small furry creature emerged. At first Sam thought it might be a marmot, but another furball jumped on its back, and together they rolled a foot down the slope. She couldn't believe her luck. Wolf pups!

She slowly raised her camera and zoomed in. Thank heavens she'd brought a real camera on this trip; there was no way her cell phone was up to long-distance photography. Now she could see not only the pups, which turned out to be four in all, but also an adult wolf lying near the entrance of the rocky den. She quickly snapped as many photos as she could, but even with the sound turned off on the camera, after a moment the adult wolf heard her, or maybe scented her. At some signal she didn't see, all the wild canines vanished from sight.

19

Evansburg

The corpse in the farmhouse was not a quick match for any missing women in the Washington State database. Finn would have to make a more thorough search through NamUs, the repository for missing individuals and unidentified corpses, but that could take hours. There was the chance that he could offload that task onto one of the clerks. Across the room, he observed the department's newest criminal justice graduate intern, whose ID badge proclaimed her as Jax. She stared morosely at a stack of folders on her desk, then swiveled her chair to peer out the window. A silver nose ring glinted in the shaft of sunlight that illuminated her, and when she turned back to her desk, he noticed a tiny matching ring in her eyebrow.

That conjured up the uncomfortable image of rings piercing the noses of Brahma bulls and camels overseas. Those rings were all about control of the animals, a sign of bondage, not for decoration. He wondered if young women ever thought about that. Seemed unlikely.

Jax looked bored, like she was about to do a runner. She reminded him of Maya's demeanor at Grace's compound. When Finn approached Jax about doing online research, she was thrilled to be assigned a "real investigation" job instead of her usual photocopying, scanning, and filing assignments. Finn suspected Jax's boss, the sergeant, might not be as thrilled, but with luck he'd be out of the station when the sarge discovered the switch.

He scanned local rap sheets for Black men who had committed recent crimes but wasn't surprised when none of the photos looked anything like the man in the photo with the dead woman. For one thing, this area of Washington State was mighty white, so it would have been surprising to see many African faces among the local convicted. For another, if, as all appearances indicated, the family was homeless, they could be vagabonds from anywhere. He needed a name for at least one of the adults.

A message from Rodrigo popped up on his screen. No matches in AFIS. Crap, the fingerprint analysis came up with nothing. But that only meant that the individuals had never been fingerprinted. Like the majority of Americans. The DNA analysis would no doubt come back with the same results: no match to any known individual. Typically, only convicted criminals, military personnel, and high-security jobs were legally required to submit samples.

Finn's tour of restaurants and hotels took several hours. Most establishments used black nametags, tan nametags, or no nametags for their staff. Nobody on duty recognized the photocopy of the California ID, the picture of the dark-skinned couple, or the name Wendy or Gwendolyn Jones.

On the seventh establishment, a run-down motel on the outskirts of Evansburg, he finally got lucky. As he parked before the office, a maid exited from a room wearing the same white nametag. Hers said ESTELA.

"Jes, I know Wendy," she responded to his question, her words heavily tinged with a Hispanic accent. "But she don' work today. Maybe she don' work here now."

Curious answer. When he continued to stare at her, she shrugged. "Dey come; dey go."

"Does Wendy speak Spanish?" Finn asked.

Estela shook her head. "I don' know what dat girl speak. No espanish, no inglés."

"Did she have a child? A little girl?"

Estela's eyes darkened. "I don' know, sir."

Finn had the feeling that might be a lie. "Do you know how she came to work? Did she drive?"

"Sometime she take a bus, but a man drop her off mos' time."

Finn pulled up the photo of the dark-skinned couple on his phone and pointed to the man. "This man?"

Estela shrugged. "He never get out of da car."

"Do you remember what kind of car it was? Did you by any chance see the license plate?"

"Small blue car. Wit' hatchback."

He wrote that down.

"I don't see license plate, sorry, sir." She shifted her gaze meaningfully to her cart and busied herself refolding a hand towel there. "I got to work now, okay?"

In the office, the manager's expression stiffened when Finn flashed his badge. "What can I do for you, Detective? I hope none of our clients has gotten in trouble." He nervously ran a hand over his bald head.

After Finn explained that he was seeking information on Wendy Jones, the manager's shoulders lowered a bit. "Yes, Wendy worked for us. But her husband called a couple of days ago to say she'd taken another job."

Finn showed him the wedding photo. "These the people you're talking about?"

The manager squinted at the photo. "That's Wendy, alright.

I can't be sure about the guy. I only saw her husband a couple of times."

"Do you know where Wendy was from?"

"California. That's what her job application said." He turned toward a file cabinet behind him. "We do a background check on all our employees."

The manager was too eager to please. "I'm sure you do," Finn assured him. "But the maid I talked with earlier said Wendy didn't speak English well. So I wondered if you knew where she came from originally."

The manager shook his head and then smiled. "Sorry. Not a clue. She did her job well and she had a California ID, so I figure it's none of my business, is it? Good help is hard to find these days, as I'm sure you know."

Finn didn't respond to that. "Where did you send her checks?"

The manager pulled open a file drawer, fished out a sheet of paper, and handed it over. The address was a P. O. box in the main Evansburg post office.

At the post office, the clerk, a stern woman taller than Finn's own six feet, was at first reluctant to tell him who rented the box, insisting that information was federal data so she didn't need to share it with local law enforcement.

"We could go to the station and have a conversation about that with my captain," Finn suggested.

The clerk peered down her nose and engaged Finn in a stare-down for a long moment, then her gaze broke away. "I suppose it does no harm to give the name to you." She clicked and typed on the desktop computer for a moment, then wrote down the name of the person who had rented the P.O. box: Johan Vincent.

"Not Wendy Jones?"

The clerk tucked her chin. "No. Only this Vincent guy."

"Was there ever any mail addressed to Wendy Jones?"

The bell over the doorway dinged as a new client, a chunky silver-haired woman, entered. She wore so much perfume that it made Finn's nose twitch.

"I'll be with you in a minute, ma'am," the clerk said to her before turning back to Finn. "I wouldn't know about everything that went into that mailbox. If something has the right box number on it, I stick it in there. That's my job, alright?"

"What does Johan Vincent look like? Did Wendy Jones ever pick up the mail?" He held out his phone with the photo of the couple. "Recognize either of these people?"

The clerk narrowed her eyes at him. "Not that I remember. But how would I know? At least half the box holders come in after the desk is closed. The front door is unlocked from six in the morning to midnight, and I'm here only from nine to five. Anyone with a key can access their box."

Finn blew out an exasperated breath. So much of police work was evasive answers and lies. "Thanks."

He drove back to confront the motel manager. "Did you make out Wendy Jones' paychecks to a man named Johan Vincent?"

The manager licked his lips, glanced toward the back of the office as if he might bolt, but then finally nodded. "That's what they wanted me to do. Wendy was right there with her husband when we did the paperwork."

"Did she have a valid social security number?" Finn leaned on the counter between them.

"Well, they gave me one, and I used that on the quarterly payroll forms. That's all I know."

"Write it down for me, please."

When the manager had done that, Finn asked to see the manager's ID.

"I've done nothing wrong." The manager, who turned out to

be Eric Strickland, handed over his driver's license.

"Then you have no reason to be concerned." Finn compared the photo to the man in front of him. They matched. He took a photo of the license with his phone, then handed it back. "Thank you, Mr. Strickland."

Back at the police station, Jax had left for the day but had emailed him a message saying there were no matches with the names of Wendy or Gwendolyn Jones in NamUs, but a sad, lengthy list of African American women who had gone missing in the last few months that he might want to compare photos to. He grimaced, realizing he should have expected that. He'd give Jax the deceased woman's photo and approximate measurements tomorrow so she could do that herself.

Finn assigned a part-time data analyst, a student from the local community college, to research Gwendolyn Jones, Johan Vincent, and the social security number.

"I'm on it, Detective," the kid said eagerly, bending over his keyboard. "I'm Joseph, by the way."

In less than an hour, Joseph presented Finn with the information that not only was Johan Vincent an actual person but also his social security number was used to hire Wendy Jones. It made sense, then, that the man had been able to easily cash the checks. Johan Vincent was most likely pocketing the paychecks earned by Gwendolyn Jones.

"Gwendolyn or Wendy Jones was a harder search." The young analyst handed Finn a sheaf of papers. "There are so many women with that name."

Finn sifted through the listings. None of the Wendy Joneses were from California, and none were described as African American. Johan Vincent and Wendy Jones were clearly up to something illegal, and it seemed likely that Wendy was not an American citizen.

Most migrants, even if they were using borrowed names, kept their original IDs somewhere. It especially bothered him that there was no paperwork for the missing child.

With no clues rising to the top of his imagination about the corpse in the farmhouse, Finn decided to start with motives for shooting one of Grace's gorillas. Back to the list Rebecca Ramey had thrown at him, the individuals who had harmed the gorillas in the past. He wearily punched in the numbers for the prison that kept Jarvis Pinder, his first suspect on the list.

"Yeah, all phone calls are recorded. How far back do you need us to go with Pinder?" The prison's chief deputy warden, a man by the problematic name of Marlin Raper, asked Detective Finn.

Finn toyed with a pen while he considered. "A month, just to be safe."

"Damn, Detective. That's a lot of work. Jarvis is a popular guy. Looking for anything in particular?"

"Any hints about shooting animals or threatening Dr. Grace McKenna or me. Maybe a mention of Gumu, Neema, or Kanoni."

"Spell those for me." When Finn did, Raper remarked, "Weird names."

Finn was tempted to make a smart remark about weird names for deputy wardens at prisons, but the guy had probably heard that a million times. "They're African names. And no last names. Those three are gorillas."

"Are you shittin' me?"

When Finn didn't respond, Raper hesitated, then said, "Oh, yeah, I see in Pinder's record that his last conviction had something to do with gorillas. The guy's obsessed. I heard he has a private zoo on the outside."

"So I've been told."

"He showed me a photo of a freaky-looking bird. A crested crane, he called it. And the guards say his cell is full of photos of animals."

Finn was not inclined to spend an hour talking exotic creatures with Raper. "Thanks for your help, Raper. The sooner I can get those recordings, the better."

Fervently wishing he were still in Hawaii with Grace, he sighed heavily and set about locating Frank Keyes. He hated phone work, but that was often the fastest way to find a suspect or witness. After talking to Keyes' former employer, he discovered his last paycheck had been sent to Boise, Idaho. Given that his previous employment had been at a warehouse, Finn started down the list of the warehouses in Boise, and on his third try, hit gold with an Amazon warehouse on the outskirts of town.

When he identified himself, Keyes immediately hung up on him. His boss swore he'd been at work the last ten days. "He's raking in the dough," she commented. "We have a lot of overtime right now, and he volunteers for most of the hours. I wish I had more employees like him."

So he was back to square one with Kanoni's shooting, and he didn't have much to work with in the murder case, either. Frustrated, Finn called Guy Rodrigo, the crime-scene investigator who had worked with him at the death scene. "Did we collect *everything* at that house?"

"There were a few things that I didn't collect, like the bags of garbage. I went through that, though, and took photos. Yuck. And I left a few cosmetic items in the bathroom. I don't see how those could help, and if we brought all that junk in from every crime scene, we'd need a warehouse to store it."

"Cosmetic items?"

"You know, lady things. Lipstick, tampons, toothpaste, hand lotion . . ."

Finn sat up straight in his chair. "Tampons? In a box?"

"Yeah."

"Did you empty that box?"

"Well, no."

"Next time, look through everything, Rodrigo. I do mean *everything*, got it?"

"Okay, got it. Want me to go back and check again?"

"No. I'm on my way over there right now."

When he ended the call, Perry Dawes, his fellow detective sitting at the next desk, commented, "Tampons in a box. Are we having fun yet?"

Finn snorted. "I'm driving all over the county. What are you on?"

Dawes looked up from his paperwork. "Motorcycle theft, and suspected drug sales to teens at the hamburger stand. Want to help?"

"I'm on vacation." His imagination immediately filled in a scene of volleyball on a white sand beach, with Grace handing him an ice-cold drink.

Dawes pulled a wry face. "I can see that."

"Well, I will be again as soon as I wrap this up."

Dawes leaned back in his chair. "I'll trade you the motorcycle theft for the gorilla shooting, but I'm not touching the murder."

"No deal, Perry." Finn shut down his computer and stood up.

In twenty minutes, he parked in front of the derelict farmhouse, cursing when he found a familiar red car parked in the gravel driveway. The front of the house appeared undisturbed, so he quickly strode around to the back.

Rebecca Ramey was snapping photos of the back door crisscrossed with the yellow crime-scene tape. She grinned as soon as she spotted him. "Well, well, well. If it isn't our star detective."

She quickly switched her cell from camera mode to video and held it out in his direction. "What can you tell me about this murder investigation?"

Shit. Finn would have bet $1000 that the coroner, Severn, had let the exciting news of a murder slip to the reporter. He broke the yellow tape over the back door. "There's nothing to report. And you'd better not have touched anything, Miz Ramey."

She coyly placed one hand on an outthrust hip, but kept the cell camera aimed in his direction. "I know the drill, Detective. But people need to know about a murder in our community."

"Not yet, they don't. And do *not* follow me inside." He glared at her.

Shutting down the camera, she held up both hands in a protest of innocence. "Wouldn't dream of it."

Inside the house, he scanned the lower level. Few items had been left behind. Snapping on a pair of latex gloves, he pulled out the garbage can under the sink. It had been emptied, but now he made sure there was no false bottom. After climbing the stairs, he checked the bedrooms, then the bathroom. He pulled out the small box of tampons inside the cabinet and upended it, emptying it onto the bathroom counter. The usual paper-wrapped tubes fell out. He shook the box, and dislodged a rectangle of thin cardboard that had been pressed into the bottom. It fell onto the countertop. A dark-blue passport and a folded document landed on top.

"Bingo," he murmured to himself. This would never have been overlooked at his old precinct in Chicago, where it was well known that women sometimes hid possessions and money in feminine hygiene packages because men were so often squeamish about touching those items.

The passport was Haitian, with a photo of the deceased. Widelene Pierre, twenty-six years old.

The folded document was a birth certificate for Rosaline Margarite Baptiste, born in Spokane to Widelene Pierre, no father listed, now just a few days shy of her third birthday.

When he stepped out of the house, Finn was relieved to see that the reporter had already left. He had gained a few more clues, but he felt as if he was still spinning his wheels, given that Widelene Pierre was dead, her daughter Rosaline was missing, and he didn't have a clue where Johan Vincent might be, or whether he was the father of the missing Rosaline.

A message chimed on his cell. Blake, the caretaker at Grace's compound, informing him that Kanoni, the baby gorilla, was doing well, according to Dr. Farin, and would be returned to her home in a few days.

Excellent news, Finn responded. Keep me posted.

God, he was tired. He stopped at the local drive-up coffee kiosk to stock up on caffeine. While he idled in line, he made mental notes about what to do with this new information. He needed to visit Grace's compound and learn whether Blake or Z knew anything about Haitians in the area, then try to figure out who to call at Homeland Security or maybe Immigrations and Customs Enforcement to ask about migrants passing through the Evansburg area.

But he still had no clues about who had shot Kanoni. Abruptly, he remembered that he'd never run background checks on that Whitman family camping out in the woods.

20

Sam could have watched the wolf family forever, so pleased with her day's exploration. Michael Fredd would be satisfied with the article and photos she was now capable of delivering. It was already late afternoon, and she needed to find her way back to her camp before darkness fell.

After trudging up and down over the uneven terrain and noisily plowing through thickets of vegetation like a buffalo, she chanced on a narrow, overgrown trail winding through the trees. It was not well traveled, certainly not the main hiking trail. It was probably a game trail, but it proved to be slightly easier than the bushwacking she'd done this morning.

A chipmunk flashed across the trail in front of her, chittering as it went. A raven flew overhead, talking to itself or maybe to an unseen companion, issuing gurgling croaks, deeper and more melodic than its crow relatives. Sam always marveled at the variety of sounds a raven could make. Scientists had classified more than thirty different raven vocalizations.

She paused to take a photo of some tall purple lupines and check for a cell signal. Nothing here. The trail snaked southward to hug the side of a cliff, with a steep drop-off into a brush-filled ravine below. A rockslide from the precipice above had deposited a cluster of large, jagged pieces of granite across the path, narrowing the route. More sharp-edged rocks spilled down into the ravine, transitioning to smaller scree and finally vanishing into the vegetation. On the cliffside above her, a small tree hung precariously, barely clinging to the earth with its roots.

Had this been mining country, Sam might have thought the rockfall was the product of a dynamite explosion. But based on the position and the sharp vee etched into the cliff above, this geological shift was more likely the result of an avalanche during the spring melt. Beneath the rocks she could hear the trickle of moving water that probably flowed into a creek below, hidden from her viewpoint under dense foliage.

Her campsite was west and slightly north of her current position, she knew, next to Lightning Creek. Unfortunately, she hadn't downloaded the local topo maps onto her phone, so the map provided by the GPS app was far too general to be of much use. This game trail seemed to be headed south now, but she wondered if it might zag again to the west on the other side of the ravine, or if she should abandon it to bushwack cross-country again. Pulling out her binoculars, she surveyed the terrain.

The trail seemed to continue on southward, into the forest beyond the ravine. Not helpful. She twisted to focus the lenses on the ravine itself. Maybe following its edge would offer a shortcut through the woods to the west.

About thirty feet down the vertical incline, a fragment of red stood out among the tumble of gray rocks. Not far from that, what appeared to be the green strap bisected a flat stone. Human detritus.

A memory flashed through her brain. Alec Lysikov had been wearing a red and black shirt when he vanished, hadn't he? And carrying a green backpack, if she remembered the poster correctly.

Flaming crap! Why did *she* have to be the one to find him? Surely searchers had explored this route after Lysikov's disappearance, even if this path was only a game trail. She followed game trails all the time; that wasn't such an unusual thing to do, was it? Especially for wildlife photographers and hunters and such.

Alec had vanished over a month ago, in April, and it was possible, even probable, that the terrain would have looked different then. At least part of this rockslide might have been covered in snow at that time.

A tiny flare of hope sparked in her brain. Maybe he had lost his pack in the snow. Maybe she had spotted only his clothes. Maybe these items didn't belong to him at all.

And maybe a dinosaur is roaming the North Cascades. Stop with the wishful thinking, Westin, and get on with finding real evidence.

Her mouth and throat were suddenly dry. Pulling out her water bottle, she took a gulp, swishing it in her mouth as she reviewed her options. She was here; she'd seen the clues. She could just put a pin in the location on her phone and send rangers here, couldn't she? But they'd ask her what she was doing so far off a main trail when all the signs—and the rangers—urged hikers to stick to the marked course. And what if it wasn't Alec after all?

Shit. She needed to be sure. Leaving her pack beside the trail, she pocketed only her cell phone and carefully scrambled down the jumble of rocks, steadying herself with her hands at times, keeping her gaze on the shred of crimson. Loose stones slid under her feet, making her gasp at a sudden vision of careening down the slope on her own personal rockslide.

Balancing on the relatively flat, stable stone across which the green strap lay, she scanned the site. The red she'd spotted was a flap of plaid fabric snagged under a rock. And there, between the piled rocks, was a fold of black nylon. He'd been wearing a black windbreaker.

Just clothes, she told herself. There were no macabre skeletal fingers jutting from the rocks, no flashes of a white skull. It was possible for even a careful hiker to lose clothes; over the years she'd lost a sock to a curious weasel and a glove and spoon to thieving crows.

An unlikely curve of black caught her eye. *Shit.* The heel of a Vibram-soled hiking boot was barely visible, sunken a few inches between sharp pieces of granite. Hikers might lose clothing, but they didn't go far without boots. It had to be Alec Lysikov under the slide.

Sam blew out a long slow breath and swallowed against the lump forming in her throat. Such a sad ending. If only Alec had stuck to the popular main trail, this wouldn't have happened. Then she snorted at the irony of that thought. She of all people knew the popular trails weren't likely to reveal the surprises of awesome wildlife encounters and fascinating details of rare landscapes few hikers saw.

The young man buried under these rocks was likely a kindred spirit. She wished she'd met him. "Rest in peace, Alec," she murmured. "I hope it was quick."

What did it say that she had felt nothing but curiosity about the dead guy in the lake, but such a deep sorrow for this fellow backpacker? In life, both men might have been scumbags society was better off without, or both might have been generous, compassionate men who would be missed every day by family and friends. She should be ashamed of herself; Summer Westin should know better than to make snap judgements. A few years back, she'd nearly been murdered in a vendetta against the US government because of such a snap judgement when she'd worn a National Park Service uniform shirt on a temporary assignment.

She extracted her phone from her pants pocket, pulled up the GPS map, and marked her position on the green blob that the GPS app said was her general location. A rustling sound from behind and below startled her, and she turned quickly. The rock beneath her boots tilted, and she flailed her arms and danced a step sideways to stay on her feet. At another sound of breaking twigs, she focused on the ravine. Something was moving around below.

Something big.

21

Sam identified the snapping and cracking of small twigs, the rustle of leafy vegetation, and . . . huffing and snorting sounds? She scanned the bushes in the gulley below, watching for movement. A bear, feeding on carrion? She'd seen at least a hundred black bears over the years and knew they were rarely a threat. Grizzlies were being reintroduced back into the North Cascades, and while she'd be thrilled to see one, she had no wish for her first encounter to be this close.

If it was a grizzly, she hoped it would stay at the bottom of the ravine. No way could she run up this perilous incline faster than a bear.

Could it be a wolverine? She'd love to see a wild wolverine. She'd come close a few weeks ago but ended up only viewing a mother and kits on a wildlife camera. With muscles tensed, ready to bolt, she anxiously perused the bottom of the ravine. The terrain was a thick jumble of stones, tall grasses, and shrubby vegetation. Between leafy branches, she spied the gleam of water, a thin trickle of stream running from beneath the rock spill down the center of the gulley. That line of water quickly disappeared from sight under all the green growth. She expected to see dark fur, a carnivore rummaging in the bushes.

There! The brush moved, and she squinted, wishing she had carried her binoculars down the rockslide. Was that . . . a *horse*?

She blinked several times to be sure. Its dappled coat was barely distinguishable from the shadows of the scrubby trees surrounding it, and the animal was nearly hidden by shrubs that enclosed its legs.

"Easy, now, I'm coming," Sam crooned as she descended the steep flank of the ravine toward the horse, the scree sliding under her boots toward the bottom. Pushing her way through thick bushes that clawed at her clothing, scratched her face, and nearly poked out one of her eyes before she reached the poor animal. Indeed, the trapped creature proved to be a horse.

And the horse proved to be a mare, with a reddish roan coat from nose to belly, and Appaloosa spots on her rump. She wore a pack saddle, a contraption of wooden frame and leather straps, with one canvas pannier sagging off the left side. The right pannier rested on the ground a short distance away. The bedraggled animal stood with her head low, held there by the reins of her bridle, which had snagged in a bush, twisted and entwined between small branches there. The ends of the reins were trapped beneath a boulder. The mare gazed at Sam mournfully with huge brown eyes but stood immobile, as if resigned to her fate. Dried blood from several nasty looking gouges on her forehead streaked down to her muzzle.

"What happened, girl? How long have you been stuck here?"

Given the horse's condition and the way the reins were trapped under a large stone, it seemed likely the mare had tumbled off the trail and slid down the rock slope, dislodging stones as she rolled.

"I'm just going to check you out, sweetie. I'll try not to hurt you."

To get close enough to see the poor animal's rear limbs, Sam had to break branches off several shrubs to prevent stabbing herself in the face again. With each crack of a breaking branch, the skin on the mare's sides flinched and her ears swiveled back. She tried to pull up her head, but the reins held her tight.

The mare's right flank and rear leg were covered with dried blood from a gash on her haunch near her tail, and she was standing with that leg cocked. Sam's heart skipped a beat. *Oh God. Please don't let this horse have a broken leg.*

Squatting beside the horse, Sam ran her hand gently down the rear leg. The mare made the huffing sound Sam had heard from above, but then straightened the injured leg.

"So you can put weight on it. It's not broken, then, is it?" Sam asked the horse. "That's good. Let me get you loose." She struggled, tugging on each rein separately, but neither of the leather straps would budge. The rock that rested on them had to weigh around two hundred pounds, and she suspected the reins were knotted together beneath the chunk of granite. She finally ended up pulling the knife from her belt sheath and cutting off the ends of the reins to free the unfortunate beast from the heavy stone.

The mare raised her head and shook it and backed a few steps, until her rear legs smacked into a cedar sapling. Snorting, she rolled her eyes.

"Take it easy." Sam held tightly onto the reins. "We don't have much space to work with here."

Sam stood for a minute, stroking the mare's velvety muzzle as she examined the walls of the ravine. From this angle, she saw that the slope she'd scrambled down bore broken vegetation and rock gouges from sliding stones. "So you fell off that trail, girl? That must have been terrifying. But I think we can both get back up."

Grabbing up the loose pannier by a strap, Sam slung the bag over her shoulder and then slowly backed the mare in tiny increments, turning her head and backing a step or two again and again, as if the horse were a car hemmed in by other vehicles. In the process, both horse and woman were thoroughly jabbed and scraped by unforgiving vegetation. The remaining pannier on the pack saddle snagged a couple of times and Sam had to yank it free, but the mare remained docile enough, until the stream was in sight. Then she thrust her nose eagerly toward the water, nearly jerking Sam off her feet.

"Of course you're thirsty." Sam let go of the reins and the mare crashed her way to the water, lowered her head, and slurped up water from the shallow creek. Sam thought longingly of her own water bottle in her pack up the hill.

When the mare had drunk enough, Sam started up the steep slope, tugging the horse behind her. Loose rocks skated from beneath the mare's hooves, but she gamely leaped upward and gained purchase on the uneven ground again, quickly bypassing her rescuer and pulling Sam up the incline, dislodging a slide of stones along the way.

"Whoa there!" Sam gasped, trying to stay on her feet as she clung one-handed to the frame of the pack saddle, reins in her other hand and heavy pannier dangling from her shoulder.

They finally gained the trail. Both woman and animal stood facing each other, their sides heaving. When breathing seemed normal again, Sam pulled the mare forward a few steps, watching her legs. The Appaloosa was limping, but only slightly. She held the reins in the crook of her arm as she adjusted the pack saddle so it rested again in the middle of the horse's spine, and lifted the other pannier into place to balance out the load. Neither bag seemed excessively heavy, so the mare could probably carry them easily enough if Sam led her.

She checked her cell. No service here. *Damn it.*

She couldn't believe any horse owner could watch a horse tumble off a trail and go off and leave it to die. "You're a beauty," she told the mare as she adjusted the straps of the pack saddle. "Where's your human? How can someone not be missing you?"

A low moan answered her question. Sam pulled back to look at the horse's eyes. "Was that you?"

22

The mare stood on the trail, gazing at her with sad brown eyes. Sam heard the moan again, a feeble sound coming from below, followed by an even feebler cry. "Hep!"

"Shit!" Sam yelped, startled by the sound of a human voice. She peered down into the ravine again but saw only rocks and shrubs.

No, it was impossible for Alec to still be alive under all those rocks. Wasn't it? A horrific thought, to be pinned under all that weight but still alive. She stared for a long moment at the place he was buried. No movement.

"Hep me!" The man's voice seemed to be coming from farther down the gulley, somewhere under the shrubbery, not too far away from where the horse had been imprisoned.

Jesus. And this day had started out so well, with the lone wolf and then a whole pack, including pups. And now, what the hell had she stumbled into? It would be dark soon, she had no cell service, she wasn't certain of the exact location of her camp, she was already burdened with an injured horse, and now a human was calling for help?

"Guess we'll be here a little longer, Freckles. I'll be back." She scratched the mare between her ears. The horse leaned in and exhaled a long sigh.

After leading the mare down the game trail away from the

rockfall, Sam tied her to a small tree and then trotted back to the head of the ravine. Strapping on her pack this time, she wearily scrambled down the tumble of rocks again, dislodging more gravel with every step.

"Keep calling out so I can find you," she yelled.

Only a moan answered. "Keep moaning, then," she grumbled under her breath.

"Hep!" Did the shouter have a mouth injury, or was the word "help" a foreign word to him?

"Come!"

That word was clear enough. She parted bushes with her hands, trying to see into the thicket. "Where are you?" A twig speared into her side and then slid between her pack strap and her ribs. She twisted and backed a few steps to disentangle herself, then finally spotted a shoe ahead in the brush. The sole of a sneaker. Black. Thrashing her way through the shrub branches, she found the shoe was connected to a blue-jeaned leg.

A man lay beside a pile of rocks, halfway under a bush, his head and shoulder resting near the trickle of the creek. Spying her, he waved weakly. His right leg was bloody, and it was clear from the gash in the fabric and the lump stretching the denim at midcalf that at least one bone was broken. Kneeling beside him, she took his closest hand in hers. "I'm here."

Blood from a cut on his scalp mingled with muddy sludge on his chin and lips, but Sam thought he might be handsome once cleaned up. His skin was a smooth dark mocha, the irises of his eyes were the shade of black coffee, and he had a strong jawline and tightly curled hair, close-cropped like a sheep recently shorn. Judging by the gouges and muck on his hands, he'd dragged himself to the water. Sam knew that's what she would have done.

But the stream was only maybe a half inch deep, and she had no clue how long he had been lying here. She extracted her water bottle from her pack. "Water?"

When he nodded weakly, she carefully lifted his head and held the bottle to his mouth. He coughed a couple of times after the first gulp, but his eyes seemed to imply he was grateful.

"Do you have injuries other than your head and your leg?" she asked.

His first response was to groan. The words that tumbled next out of his mouth were unintelligible. Thanks to Chase, Sam might have been able to handle some Spanish, but this was some other language. He confirmed that by mumbling, "No much inglish."

Double shit. This guy was not going be of much assistance in his own rescue.

"I'm just going to check you out, okay?" she told him, although she doubted he could understand. She unzipped the jacket he wore. No obvious wounds on his torso. That was good. Well, maybe. After the avalanche, Chase hadn't had obvious injuries on his body, either, other than bruises, and he'd nearly died from internal damage.

She ran her hands gently over the man's ribs and abdomen. He grabbed her sleeve to stop her and then pointed to his leg, jabbing his finger in the air and saying something that started off sounding vaguely like *jam* but then segued into a string of incomprehensible syllables.

"Yes, I can see your leg is broken." She didn't want to inspect that leg closely. With just a quick sideways glance, she had noticed the shin bone poking out of the mangled skin.

"Does your head ache?" She pointed to his forehead as she focused on his eyes. His pupils were equal, a good sign.

He gingerly touched his temple close to the gash at his

hairline and mumbled something else.

"Can you sit up?"

He stared, not comprehending. She grasped his wrist and pulled up. He understood and used both hands to push himself to a sitting position, where he sat moaning and breathing hard, gesturing toward his broken leg.

What was she supposed to do? She wasn't an EMT. She'd had rudimentary first aid, and this was far more serious. It could be miles and hours before she could find cell service.

"Stay." She gestured with both hands. "I'm going to get something to stabilize your leg."

When she stood up, he gurgled, grabbed her ankle, and quickly spat out a string of mystery sentences, his eyes round with panic.

"I will be back." She pointed to herself and made a circular motion ending with him.

His face relaxed a bit. She thought he understood her intention.

Walking only a short distance away, she chose the bush with the straightest branches and using her knife, cut two about a foot long. Returning to the man, she took off her pack, pulled out a bandana and the ace bandage she always carried in her emergency kit. Kneeling, she positioned the twigs, one on either side of his injured leg. He understood what she was doing and held them in place while she lifted his leg, trying to be as gentle as possible. He whined like a wounded animal as she gritted her teeth and wrapped the bandana around his calf and tied the makeshift splint in place, trying not to look at the splintered bone.

It seemed a positive sign that the bleeding had stopped, but it certainly couldn't be good that the bone had broken through the skin. How long had the poor fellow been lying here? She finished by wrapping the ace bandage around his calf and securing it in place with a safety pin. She should probably feel his foot to see if he still had circulation, but she didn't have any idea what she would do if his foot was ice cold, and she'd rather not know.

She was afraid to give him aspirin for fear he might start bleeding again. Should she leave him here and go for help? But how long would that take? She'd have to find the main trail again, hope for a cell signal, get rangers to respond, wait for them, and lead them back. She didn't have extra food or clothing to leave with him. He could succumb to hypothermia and blood loss in her absence.

The injured man was panting in pain. Tears streaked down his cheeks, but when he could open his eyes, he met her gaze and made an upward motion with his hand.

She stood and grasped both his wrists, and with his efforts in addition to hers, he got to his feet, or rather, his one good foot. He leaned heavily on her shoulder for a moment, blinking away tears, his chest heaving.

After hobbling one step, Sam realized she needed to be on the side with his broken leg, so she stabilized him with a hand on his chest while she ducked under his arm to his other side and tucked her shoulder into his armpit. He was at least eight inches taller than she and probably outweighed her by fifty or sixty pounds. The best she could do was serve as a crutch for him to lean on.

And he did lean, heavily. After the first time he slipped and nearly fell, she grabbed onto the hand he had wrapped around her neck and held it securely to keep him upright. The whole process was agonizingly slow, and more than once, she thought maybe he'd be better off if she left him and went in search of a cell signal. But he needed food and water and shelter as well as medical care, and she'd left most of her supplies back at camp.

They made their way to the slope hobbling and cursing. At least Sam was cursing, and she assumed the foreign words coming from his mouth were swear words, too. But for all she knew, he could be praying.

The steep rockfall slope seemed as insurmountable as Everest, and Sam had the brief inspiration to tie a rope onto the Appaloosa's pack saddle and haul the man up with horsepower. But then, she remembered the length of parachute cord she carried was far too short and far too stretchy. Her longer rope was back at her camp, holding her food stash high.

The wounded man had to more or less crawl, trying to hold his splinted leg above the uneven ground but forced to drag that foot on the ground part of the time, while he used both hands to clutch rocks along the way and pull himself up. Sweat poured down his face and dampened his shirt. Twice the rock he grabbed onto slipped and Sam had to seize his arm to keep him from sliding back down the slope.

At intervals, he stopped and closed his eyes to simply breathe, lowering his forehead to his hands as his chest heaved. She felt useless. The most she could do was to encourage him in a language he probably couldn't even understand.

But finally, they reached the trail, and he sprawled across the dusty horizontal surface. Lying there, his face pale and sweaty, he looked as if he might pass out at any second. Or die.

But they had to go on. The sun was sinking fast.

23

Sam again motioned she would be back, and returned to the Appaloosa mare and untied the reins from the tree. The horse was chewing a mouthful of grass it had ripped from the hillside, and still stood with its hind leg cocked to keep the weight off her injury.

"I'm so sorry, girl, but I need your help." Thank God the mare was amenable to being led to where the man sprawled across the trail.

The man gasped at the sight of the horse. When she lowered her head to him, he patted her nose, saying something that began like *"chwal."*

"You know this horse?" Sam asked.

"Chwal mwen an." He stroked the mare's nose again.

His was not any language Sam had ever heard, but the first word sounded a bit like *cheval*, which she thought might be French. *"Caballo?"* she tried in Spanish.

He frowned.

She gave up trying to find a mutual language. "You're going to need to ride this *caballo*. In a pack saddle, no less." That would be damn uncomfortable. Maybe she should pull her jacket and hat out of her pack and use them to pad the frame between the saddle bags. Maybe he could hang his legs in front of the panniers, but that would still be painful and might injure him even more.

What was in those panniers, anyway? She hadn't even looked. Now she unstrapped the leather fasteners on the nearest one and peeked in. Rolled on top was a large oiled canvas slicker, the type cowboys used when riding the range in wet weather. That would help as padding. She pulled it out. Beneath that were . . . packages of flour? Pancake mix? The packages were sheathed in clear plastic and securely wrapped in shipping tape. Whoever this horse belonged to had gone to great trouble to be sure the packages didn't get wet. But who needed that much flour? It looked like enough for a group to camp out for a month. And there might be more in the other pannier.

Then, it came to her, and Sam wanted to slap herself for being so naive. These bricklike packages didn't contain food. More likely cocaine or heroin or whatever else was craved by addicts these days. She glanced at the man again. Had she just rescued a major drug dealer? He lay with his eyes closed, not watching her. She quickly buckled the pannier shut, padded the saddle with the slicker as best she could, and knelt by the man.

Criminal or not, she couldn't keep calling him "the man," could she? She crouched beside him. "Hey."

When he opened his eyes, she gestured to herself. "I'm Sam."

"Sam," he repeated. He slapped his hand on his chest. "Diego."

She repeated it. She'd met a few Diegos over the years.

Next, he said, "I am from Miami."

That sentence sounded oddly rehearsed, but then, English was clearly not his first language. "You're from Miami, Florida?"

He nodded. "Diego Cruz. I am from Miami."

Somehow, she doubted that, given that he hadn't known the word 'caballo,' but now was not the time to grill the poor guy. She tugged him to a sitting position. "Okay, Diego, we need to get you on this horse." She pointed to the mare.

His expression darkened as he anticipated how painful that might be, but he nodded, his jaw clenched, and grasped her arms tighter.

If only she were a tall, hefty man instead of a petite muscular woman, this would be a lot easier. Leaning backward to counterbalance his weight, her back and arms and abdominal muscles straining, she pulled him to his feet, where he swayed, standing on the right side of the horse, grasping the wooden frame of the pack saddle with clenched fists. His face was several shades paler than it had been a few minutes ago.

"Sorry," Sam said. She wasn't sure what she was apologizing for.

He tried to pull himself upward, gasping in pain, but gave up after a few seconds.

"No," she said. He was on Freckles' right side, and his right leg was broken. This wasn't going to work. "Wait, Diego." She peeled his fingers off the pack frame, and pulled his arm around her neck. She backed the mare a few steps and leaned Diego against the hillside. "Stay," she said, gesturing with an upraised palm toward him, feeling like she was commanding a dog.

Leaving him reclining against the vertical slope, she backed the mare farther and carefully turned her around in a wider spot down the trail. Then, stepping in front of the mare, Sam placed one hand on the animal's head and kept one on the reins, tugging down and urging the horse to slowly back toward the injured man. "Good girl, Freckles. I'm sorry to make you do this."

She left the reins trailing the ground, hoping the horse had been trained to "ground tie" and stay in place that way. Walking around the mare's rump to Diego, she took his arm again and once more wrapped it around her neck. Together they hobbled back to the left side of the mare, sidestepping to keep from falling off the edge of the trail. The motion was exceedingly awkward, and Sam again wished she was taller so she could provide a better crutch.

At the mare's side, Diego grasped the wooden pack frame again.

"Don't pull yet, Diego. Here's how we're going to do it." Sam bent over and wrapped her hands around the calf of his left leg, then looked up to meet his gaze. "Okay?"

His expression indicated that he probably understood. Maybe he'd had help mounting a horse like this before.

"Now!" When he pulled upward, she jerked his left leg up from the ground, lifting him to throw his weight across the saddle frame.

With a cry of agony, he managed to swing his broken leg across the frame and rest it awkwardly on the pannier. The knuckles of his hands were white. His face paled as he hunched over, his jaw tight. Tears streamed down his cheeks and dripped from his chin.

Sam paused for a minute, breathing heavily. How the hell had she gotten into this predicament? How was she *always* getting into messes like this?

Wolves, she reminded herself. She'd taken the trail less traveled—less peopled, anyway—to find wolves. And it had made all the difference, just like the poet Robert Frost had written. Although he'd written about roads diverging, not trails. How many people had his poem influenced to make bad decisions? How many found it had made all the difference, in a good way?

She had found wolves on her "road less traveled." One checkmark in the positive column.

She'd also, sadly, found the remains of Alec Lysikov. And

more sadly, she'd discovered a seriously injured foreigner and a slightly less injured horse. Three checkmarks in the negative column. Or maybe one check for the dead hiker and two question marks for the wounded man and horse.

She checked her phone. Still no service. Gritting her teeth, she started slowly back down the trail. Freckles seemed resigned to follow her over the rolling terrain, limping slightly and balking only briefly when Sam tugged her off the game trail and headed westward, skirting the ravine, following the featureless map on her phone until she was sure she was walking in the right direction. When the GPS app reported "No connection," she knew the forest was too thick for the satellite signals. Then the screen flashed a "Low Battery" warning. *Shit.* From taking photos and the GPS app constantly seeking a satellite signal, her old phone was nearly out of juice. She turned the phone off and stuck it into her pocket.

On the mare's back, Diego groaned intermittently, his whimpers punctuating the continuous squeak of the pack saddle frame and rustle of the panniers. Sam tried to make encouraging sounds but her noises came out more like moaning and groaning, too. Footsore and exhausted, she wanted food and water and a warm sleeping bag in a peaceful campsite. Instead, she had an injured man she couldn't communicate with, a limping horse, and saddlebags full of illegal drugs.

After another twenty minutes of walking, Sam pulled her cell phone from her pocket to check for service again. The face of the damn thing refused to even light up.

Her watch indicated it was after midnight and the woods were so dark when they finally reached her camp that Sam recognized the area only after she'd sunk one boot into the creek. Her tent

and food bag were as she'd left them, thank heavens. She let
Freckles drink her fill from the creek, and a few minutes later,
while Sam was debating how to get Diego down, he leaned in
her direction and fell off into her arms, knocking her to the
rocky ground on her back. She grunted in surprise; he shrieked
and went limp.

"Diego?" His head lolled against her chest.

Only fainted, she hoped. She rolled, letting his heavy body
slide off hers, then did her best to straighten his body out on the
uneven ground. She checked the pulse in his neck. Faint, but
there. Under the makeshift splint, his pants leg was soaked with
fresh blood.

Shit. Diving into her tent, she found her battery charger and
plugged in her cell phone. A lightning bolt appeared on the
screen, indicating it was charging. Sam stuck her flashlight into
her pocket and pulled her sleeping bag from the tent and spread
it over the unconscious man. Freckles seemed content to graze
on the sparse grass nearby, so Sam wound the reins loosely
around a shrub to keep her from running off.

"Sorry," she apologized to the mare. "I'll get you something
better to eat as soon as I can."

Diego would need food, too. Assuming he regained
consciousness. Assuming he lived. She filled a cooking pan with
water from the creek and lit her camp stove to boil it. Her food
bag contained coffee, creamer, two bagels, a half-filled tube of
peanut butter, two freeze-dried meals, and two apples. Stark
reminders she was scheduled to be home the day after
tomorrow. But it was 1:00 a.m., already tomorrow, so that
meant she needed to be home even sooner.

She checked on Diego. When she shook his arm, he moaned.
His eyes fluttered open. "Food?" she asked, using the universal
symbol of putting fingers to her mouth. His dark eyes bore into

hers, but he remained immobile.

"It'll be cooked in a couple of minutes." She held up her water bottle. "Water?"

He dipped his head a fraction. A nod? She chose to interpret it that way. Sliding her hand under his head, she raised his head and held the water bottle to his lips. He took a couple of gulps, coughed, and she lay his head back down on the ground, thought better of that, and then retrieved her down vest from her tent and slid it under his head.

The water in the pan was boiling, and she poured it into a pouch of dried beef stroganoff and sealed the pouch shut again to reconstitute the meal. Freckles snorted and crunched a short distance away. Sam wanted to remove the poor mare's pack saddle and bridle, but she was afraid she wouldn't be able to get all the gear back on by herself. "Sorry," she apologized again.

When the stroganoff was sufficiently gloppy, she opened the bag and waited for it to cool off. Checking her phone, she saw only the charging symbol. How long would the old device take to regain enough umph to wake up? She really needed to get a newer cell. And maybe a newer charger, too. She hoped this one had enough power left to do the job. If not, she'd have to leave Diego here, find the main trail, and hope to run into rangers. Or at least backpackers or boaters with working cell phones.

She managed to dribble a couple of spoonfuls of stroganoff into Diego's mouth, but when he started coughing again, she gave up. His eyelids were closed and he didn't respond at all when she asked if he was okay. If she insisted on feeding him, she'd probably end up choking him to death, and she had a sudden unwelcome and ridiculous vision of being convicted of murder. A Good Samaritan law protected someone trying to help, she thought, but she wasn't sure it would cover death by stroganoff.

Settling her back against the tree, she wrapped her metallic emergency blanket around her shoulders and slowly ate the rest of the lukewarm stroganoff. The dark sky seemed to be humming somewhere high overhead. Peering out from under the branches, she saw the far-away lights on a jet passing in the distance. Exhaustion was making her hallucinate. She barely managed to set down the empty stroganoff package before she fell asleep.

Nearly two hours later, she opened her eyes. The moon had risen, casting enough light between the branches to wake her. Shivering, she stood up, her muscles stiff. After stumbling to Diego and holding her hand above his mouth to be sure he was breathing, she checked her cell phone. Two bars.

Finally! She called the ranger station. Got a recording telling her the station was closed, leave a message. She did, not that she held out much hope for action at 3:15 a.m. Dialing 911 resulted in connecting with a sleepy-sounding woman who kept asking her where she was.

"You're in the US?" the operator asked.

"Yes. In North Cascades near Ross Lake, off the trail."

"Miss, this is Hope, British Columbia. I'll relay the message, but odds are nobody could get to your location for more than a day. You should call the North Cascades Ranger Station."

Sam hung up. Multiple missed calls and texts from Chase were listed on the screen. An FBI agent would know how to rally the troops. At least she hoped he would.

"Summer!" His voice was hoarse with sleep. He paused to clear his throat. "Where have you been, *querida*? I've been trying to call you all day. I was afraid you'd fallen off a cliff."

"Not me. But I found a body and a horse and a man that did."

"What!"

"I found a whole wolf family, with cubs. So I was following

the wolves, and then I found this game trail—"

A loud bang cut short her explanation.

Her cell phone exploded in her hand. Bits of plastic shrapnel speared into her cheek and forehead.

24

Evansburg

The sleeping platform was too high. The mama go-rilla carried Rosaline up there in the barn and then left her there for a whole day, going out into the daylight. Her own mama would never let her sleep there. Crawling to the edge, she looked down. It was so far; she could fall to the ground. She was hungry and thirsty, so she put her thumb into her mouth and sucked on it, curling up in the blankets and trying not to make crying noises. Not until after dark did the mama go-rilla come back, but she brought Rosaline a banana and a big piece of bread. Rosaline ate the banana while the small-big go-rilla hugged her close and rubbed her big black hands over Rosaline like she'd rubbed the cat outside. That felt nice, until the mama go-rilla tried to bite her eyelashes.

"*Non!*" she told that mama go-rilla, pushing her big black rubbery mouth away. Too big teeth, too close. Scary. Next, the mama go-rilla tugged on Rosaline's braids with her lips, trying to pull off the beads on the ends. That hurt. She pulled one off and rolled it around in her big black mouth.

"*Non!*" Rosaline said again. Did the mama go-rilla want to eat her? The go-rilla pulled the bead out of her mouth and looked at it, so tiny in her big black fingers.

Rosaline took the bead back and hid it in the red blanket. The mama go-rilla pushed Rosaline back on her bottom and then smelled her pants where she'd wet them. Would she be punished? *"Padon,"* Rosaline said. She couldn't help it. But her pants were almost dry now.

"Desan!" she pointed to the floor far below. *"Desan!"*

The big-big go-rilla was climbing the pole. He stopped to study her, a mean look in his eyes.

"Desan?" she asked, more softly.

The big-big go-rilla ignored her and grunted and then climbed up to the top platform like he had last night.

Instead of carrying her to the ground, the mama go-rilla pushed Rosaline into the blankets, lay down beside her, and covered them both with all the blankets. Rosaline put the piece of bread into her mouth and sucked on it.

25

North Cascades

The pain and shock of the blast was eclipsed a second later by a piercing burn in Sam's hand. Blood gushed down her palm from a ragged tear between her second and third fingers.

What the—?

She didn't have time to finish the thought before a projectile buzzed past her ear and struck a tree in the woods beyond. Freckles whinnied in terror. A branch cracked.

Sam dropped to the ground, shouting, "Camper! Stop shooting! I'm not a bear. I'm camping here! Stop shooting!"

A third shot rang out. The mare screamed. Popping and cracking sounds issued from the darkness as the mare thrashed. Sam prayed she hadn't been hit. Freckles was yanking wildly on her reins and would probably free herself within seconds.

The shots had seemed to come from northeast of her position. Sam's thoughts raced to the drugs in the panniers still on the mare's pack saddle, and then to Diego himself. Maybe he was a drug runner, or at least a mule. Maybe he hadn't been alone. Maybe a cartel sniper had caught up with him.

She crawled to him like a lizard, staying close to the ground, and urgently whispered, "Diego, what's happening?"

A fourth bullet whizzed into camp, kicking up dirt near the

flashlight she'd left on a rock near the tent. She scrabbled her way there with elbows and feet and switched off the light, jamming it into her back pocket. She slithered back to Diego. "You okay?"

His eyes showed more white than dark pupil, and he gasped out a string of words unintelligible to Sam. When she didn't respond, he said, "Go!"

He was right. They had to go. The shooter was far enough away his aim was none too accurate, thank heavens, but that could change quickly. Her cell phone with its lighted display had been the first target, and then her flashlight. Now that the camp was dark, there were no more shots. But the shooter was still out there, and had obviously zeroed in on her position. She pushed herself to her feet, wincing at the jolt of pain in her injured hand. Hunched over, she jogged to Freckles, who was leaning back onto her haunches, pulling on her bridle with all her might, her eyes wild, nostrils distended in fear. Sam tried to make her voice soothing as she untied the reins. Her right hand, slippery with blood, was next to useless. "It's okay, girl. Let's get out of here."

The panicked mare dragged her a few steps before Sam gained control, clutching the reins tight. Freckles nervously trotted alongside her toward Diego. He had already pushed himself into a sitting position, and as she struggled to keep the dancing mare in place, he grabbed hold of Sam's leg and then her belt and pulled himself to his feet, balancing awkwardly on his one good leg. He grabbed for the pack saddle frame as Sam grasped his left calf and lifted with all her might.

As well as the burning agony in her hand, a sharp pain in her lower spine zinged through her body when she tossed him onto the saddle. She gasped. Diego made a hissing sound as he settled on top of the panniers. His face became only a silhouette in the darkness as he screwed his eyes shut.

Something cracked in the trees to the east. Sam quickly led the horse out of camp and up a small rise to the southwest, then down the other side. If luck was with them, they might connect with the main trail headed south before the shooter caught up with them. With more luck, a law enforcement ranger would be standing there, waiting for her. *Yeah, right.*

A crescent moon dimly illuminated the open spaces, but the valleys and shadows were black pools of vegetation and filled with invisible rocks. Sam, afraid using her flashlight would pinpoint her position, tripped several times over obstacles before she ran headlong into a bush, adding scratches her already smarting face and neck. The horse, yanking at the reins, pulled her out. Afterward, Sam slowed to a more careful jog. Diego whimpered and swayed, bending over the mare's neck to hold on to her mane. His fractured leg had to be agonizing; her own injured hand and cuts and scratches on her face were nothing in comparison.

The off-trail travel was rough, threading through crowded tree trunks and skirting rocks jutting from the soil. By a quarter till five, the sky was brightening with the coming dawn. Bathed in sweat, Sam had stopped long enough to tie her bandana around her bleeding hand, but in the growing light, she saw her clothes, the bridle reins, and no doubt her face were spattered with her own blood. Diego was similarly covered in a mix of his blood and hers. Thankfully, the cuts on Freckles' flanks and back legs seemed to have stopped bleeding, although the poor mare still limped. Sam was torturing both man and horse.

When she heard voices, she knew she was nearing the main trail bordering the lake. Backpackers? She was in the trees only twenty yards from them, but above the trail, and cloaked from their view by a cluster of trees.

"You asshole!" she heard one say. "You were supposed to

bring the booze."

"I did. I drank it last night when you were asleep."

Young men, then, joking with each other. She could hear only snatches of their conversation as she wound her way through the trees. Then she abruptly heard the unmistakable rhythmic pounding of a horse galloping past.

"Watch it, you jerk!" yelled one disembodied voice as the hoofbeats retreated. The other voice complained, "Asshole almost knocked me off the trail."

The hoofbeats stopped, and Sam heard the snort of a horse and a few clopping steps returning. "Sorry, man," a third male voice said. "Seen a woman and a dark-skinned man this morning? Might have had a horse with them."

The backpackers apparently shook their heads, because the hoofbeats moved on southward down the trail. The hikers resumed their march north.

"Did you see that rifle he was carrying? I thought hunting wasn't allowed."

"He had a pistol on his belt, too. Maybe he was a ranger."

"Maybe. I didn't really notice."

Sam halted. A man with a rifle and a pistol on a horse? A sudden chill shot down her spine. That had to be her shooter. Was it Mark, the overweight gun-toting camper she'd run into two nights ago? He and Randi had seemed like such anomalies on the trail, and he'd mentioned meeting up with horses. With his rodeo buckle, he had to be an experienced rider.

She waited a minute in silence, listening. The throbbing of her hand seemed strident enough to hear. Freckles nudged her shoulder and dropped her head to the closest bush to rip off a mouthful of green leaves. Diego slumped lower over the mare's neck. Sam prayed he would not fall off the pack saddle, because there was no way she could get him back on without help.

When she heard no returning hoofbeats, she led the Appaloosa down the slope to the trail. Two backpackers were striding north, already a hundred feet beyond her position. She couldn't summon the energy to run after them. "Hey!"

One of the young backpackers glanced over his shoulder, grabbed his buddy's shoulder, and when his friend turned, pointed down the trail at Sam. They quickly jogged in her direction, their packs bouncing on their backs.

"A guy on a horse was just looking for you. What happened?" the shorter one asked. "Man, you look like—"

She cut him off. "Was the guy a big man? Muscular, but with a gut?"

The shorter one shook his head. "Didn't really get a close look at him. He was up on a tall horse and he had on a hat."

"I was sorta focused on the guns," said the tall one.

So maybe Mark; maybe someone else. "Do you have a cell phone I can use to call the rangers?"

They exchanged glances, their expressions uncertain.

"Mine got shot up. This man"—she gestured to Diego—"and I are in a bad way. I know we look terrible. We need help. I'll stand here so you can hear me, and I'll give the phone right back."

While the taller one continued to stare at her suspiciously, the shorter one stroked his beard once before pulling his cell phone from a pocket on his waist strap. "I don't know if there's any service right here . . ."

One bar. She punched in the number of the North Cascades Park headquarters. A female voice answered. "North Cascades, this is Ashlee."

"Ashlee, listen. Can you grab a piece of paper and take notes? I have a bad connection and I have some important things to tell you."

"Who is this?"

"You have paper and pen? Can you write this down?"

"Um, okay." There was a brief hesitation. "Okay, go."

"My name is Summer Westin. I'm hiking the East Bank Trail of Ross Lake, and I called a couple of days ago about"—she glanced at the backpackers—"a . . . um . . . floater . . . in the lake. Ask Rangers Castro and Digby. Yesterday I found an injured man and a horse in a gulley off the trail. And drugs. And the missing guy, too."

"What? Wait!"

"I'm going to try to get back to the trailhead along Highway 20, but someone has been shooting at me."

"Wait, wait. I can't write that fast. Are you pulling my leg?"

Just then, Sam heard the faint clip-clop of a horse returning on the trail. "I gotta go. Send help." She pressed "End," wiped the blood from the phone on her shirt, and shoved the phone at the backpacker. "Thanks. You never saw me."

Sam pulled the mare back into the trees, jogging now to get up and over the rise before the shooter returned on the trail. Would the backpackers tell the guy where she went? She didn't wait to find out, but turned south, paralleling the main trail several hundred feet away.

"Sorry, sorry, sorry," she whispered to Freckles. To Diego. To herself. How many times had she said that word today? Was it still today? She certainly *was* sorry about the way this trip was turning out.

The panniers repeatedly snagged on shrubs and small trees, causing Freckles to stumble, and the terrain was thick with an appalling number of thorny plants they had to push through. At intervals, Sam stopped to listen for anyone following her. She heard only rustling leaves, the mare's snuffling, and Diego's heavy breathing and occasional whimpers.

When a flutter of wings above her head startled her, she glanced up to see a pair of crows settle on a limb. "Fly, bozos. Go get help," she whispered.

In the distance, a horse whinnied. Freckles answered with a loud neigh, making Sam flinch. "Quiet!" She laid her hand on the horse's nose. Was there a way to clamp a horse's nostrils and mouth shut? Her hand wasn't big enough.

26

Praying that either the shooter hadn't heard Freckles, or that the whinny she heard didn't belong to the shooter's horse at all, Sam hurriedly led her sad party further east, where she stumbled upon a game trail, perhaps a continuation of the one she had followed to the ravine yesterday. Yeesh, was that only yesterday? In a nightmare, time quickly became a blur.

Most of the path was overgrown and narrow. In places, it widened as though an elk or bear had blazed a route through the brush, and in others dissipated down to a trail sized for a chipmunk. Still, it seemed easier to follow even a faint trail rather than fight her way through unmarked forest and underbrush.

Her feet didn't feel like they belonged to her body, they were so numb. Her injured hand, however, hurt like hell, throbbing against the tight kerchief. It had swollen to twice its normal size. The mare seemed resigned to her enslavement, hobbling slowly along with her head down.

"I'm depressed, too," Sam assured her. *Who wouldn't be?*

Diego sagged over the front of the pack saddle like a half-full sack of grain. His straddle position on the mostly unpadded frame had to be excruciating, but she wasn't sure he was alert enough to register the pain. The blood on his jeans leg was wet. Sam feared at any moment both horse and rider would drop to the ground and refuse to move. Why hadn't she paused to grab her food bag, or at least a bottle of water?

As she crested and then descended a small rise, the noise of crackling vegetation ahead of her made her gasp. A doe and two fawns raised their heads from the trickle of a creek beneath their hooves. Spying her, they wheeled and vanished into the forest.

Sam fell to her knees at the water's edge. "Thank God!" Leaning over, she put her whole face into the cool water, drinking deeply. She'd rather risk giardiasis than die of dehydration. Beside her, Freckles too was slurping and snuffling in the creek.

After a few gulps, Sam sat up and studied Diego. He was still slumped over the front of the pack saddle, held there by the crossed uprights of the wooden frame. Sleeping? No, more likely unconscious. Or dead.

She stood up, tottered over on wooden legs, and tugged at his arm. "Diego?"

A groan answered her.

Not dead, then. At least semiconscious. Having lost a lot of blood, he'd need water even more than she did. She had no cup or glass. If only she'd been at the seashore, she could probably have found a shell to serve as a vessel. But here? Could she form a cup of leaves? Maybe, but there was no way she could hand that to Diego, and if he leaned far enough to drink from her hands, he'd surely fall off the horse.

Maybe soak some of her clothes in the water and squeeze that into his mouth? Everything she wore was filthy with sweat and blood. Her bandana? But disgusting water was better than no water.

She peeled the kerchief from her hand and tried to wash out the blood, thinking of everything she'd used it for on this trip. A washrag in the morning and evening. A napkin at breakfast, lunch, and dinner. Her brain lingered on the memory of food.

No, she couldn't think about food now, about the freeze-dried meal she'd left behind. Last night, the contents of the foil envelopes had tasted like spiced cardboard; today they beckoned like gourmet cuisine. Bagels and peanut butter. Or had she eaten the last of those for lunch yesterday?

Lunch yesterday. She'd carried a bagel in a plastic bag, eaten it while she watched the wolves, and stuffed the baggie into her pocket. She patted that back pocket now. Yes! Pulling out the crumpled plastic envelope, she rinsed the trace of peanut butter from the inside, and eased the bag sideways in the creek until it filled.

The baggie leaked a bit from one corner, but it was the best she could do. "Diego."

When he opened his eyes, she held the bag in front of his face. "Water."

He struggled to sit more erect, and carefully took it from her and slurped the contents. "Tanks."

She filled it for him three more times until he shook his head. He was clearly in agony, his face pale and his brow sweaty, but he briefly touched his chin and held his hand out to her in the universal gesture of thanks. That sign made her think about Blake and the gorillas. How she wished she were in Evansburg with him, peacefully observing those clever apes. She wrapped the bandana around her wounded hand again and plodded on, both her body and her mind growing more and more numb with each step.

Did she dare go back to the main trail, stop at one of the campgrounds and try to call for help? No, she decided. The shooter would expect her to do that. Even if she was able to contact them, how long would it take rangers to come to her aid? What were the odds that the shooter would show up before the rangers did? She didn't even know what he or his horse looked like.

The map had indicated only about sixteen miles on the main trail from the Lightning Creek campground to the trailhead parking lot. She'd added more by going off trail on a meandering path and now overland, but the total journey would probably not be more than eighteen, and she'd already covered part of that. She could do that, couldn't she? Couldn't Freckles?

Her sketchy route led up and down over the rugged landscape, and at times vanished altogether, but she was proceeding in the same general direction, which she was reasonably sure was more or less south. At times, she found a narrow path made by wildlife; at others, she made her own. Normally she enjoyed exploring cross country, finding new flora and fauna to investigate in a journey of discovery. This particular expedition seemed more like a journey of torture. Self-inflicted torture. But she wasn't ready to die, and the shooter could still be out there on the main trail.

The hours blurred together in a symphony of pain and exhaustion as she staggered and wove to avoid a jab from a branch in the eye, urged the limping horse around boulders and between trees. When darkness began to descend, anxiety crawled up Sam's throat from her stomach. How could it be sunset already? She checked her watch. A few minutes after 8:00 p.m. This journey was taking way too long. But Freckles didn't seem able to move any faster, and truth be told, she probably couldn't, either.

27

Soon a sliver of moon shed a minimal amount of light on the trail. Sam wanted nothing more than to lie down and sleep, but Diego and Freckles both seemed like they could expire at any moment, so there could be no stopping. And after the last rays of sun disappeared, the air cooled rapidly. Sam's clothes were soaked with sweat and the dampness of the vegetation she wandered through. Hypothermia was a definite possibility for the sweat- and dew-soaked two of them, and it was probable that Diego, severely injured, was already in that zone. They'd gained substantial elevation during their escape; they were definitely traversing the flank of a mountain. With luck, it was Jack Mountain, the peak close to the main trail. The going was rock-strewn and steeply sloping. Mountain goat country.

Sam's whole body ached from walking on a slanted surface, but she was too anxious to go downslope and get onto the flatter trail. At intervals, small creatures skittered across the path in front of her. Mice, probably, or ground squirrels or chipmunks. Twice, something medium-size— possibly a fox or a weasel of some sort. She wished she could clearly view the wildlife. When had the flashlight fallen out of her pocket?

After sunset, it was impossible to verify whether she was still headed south. If they were moving in the right direction, they would eventually encounter a trail or Ruby Creek or even the

North Cascades Highway, and then she'd be able to find the trailhead. But what—or who—would be waiting for her there?

Please let me be close to the trailhead. Please let me be close to the trailhead. During the long hours of darkness, the words had become a mantra Sam repeated over and over in her head. She felt like she had been walking—or more accurately, staggering—for days. Maybe a month. Surely, she would stumble onto something recognizable soon.

She tried to picture everything she'd left in her RAV4 at the trailhead. A blanket. Some books. She was reasonably sure there were still a couple of power bars in the compartment with the spare tire, triple-wrapped and sealed in a dry bag to thwart the sensitive noses of black bears. A big bottle of stale water in that same compartment.

As well as the high-pitched yips of coyotes in the distance, she discerned the distinctive hoots of a barred owl close by. One even more distant call might be a great horned. If she'd had a flashlight or even her headlamp, she might have looked for them.

Headlamp. Good thing she hadn't been wearing her headlamp in camp last night. A bullet aimed for that might have pierced her skull.

The moonlight was short-lived as clouds moved in. Then it began to rain, lessening the visibility and increasing the misery.

She stumbled and practically fell down a steep rocky section. Freckles slid and then leaped the last few feet, nearly jerking Sam over the edge of the trail they'd landed on. Diego whimpered. The mare snorted a few times in sympathy, her head low. Sam was amazed Diego managed to stay on, but now his chest seemed to be firmly wedged between the uprights of the pack saddle. His arms dangled along the sides of the horse's neck, and his head lolled against the mare's mane. Sam prayed he was only sleeping.

The path they'd landed on was a well-used hiking trail, wider and smoother than any game trail. Maybe East Bank Trail. No, she couldn't see the lake, and although the trail slanted downhill, it didn't slope down into Ruby Creek. Maybe Jack Mountain Trail, then. Which would lead down to the East Bank Trail and eventually back to the trailhead. Much easier than cross-country scrambling, especially in the dark and rain, and all three of them needed easier now. But if the shooter was waiting for her, that was where he would expect her to travel.

She fixed her gaze ahead on the trail, searching the shadows for the form of a man, or a horse, or a man with a rifle on a horse. Still too dark to see much of anything. Nothing seemed to be moving.

The howls began, just a solitary wolf. Another answered. Then the whole pack joined in. Freckles' ears swiveled, alarmed by the canine chorus. The mare snorted nervously and butted Sam's back with her bony head before hauling back on the reins in an attempt to turn around.

"Easy, girl," Sam crooned, pulling down on the reins with as firm a grip as she could master with her left hand. Rain dripped off her nose and the horse's forelock. She paused to rub the mare with her injured right hand, the fingers now frozen into an unusable claw. "They're not after you; they're far, far away."

"Let's do it," she said to herself, and tugged on the reins. "We're going down." Was using the maintained hiking trail more dangerous? Probably. But using the popular trail was a risk she was willing to take in the middle of the night. Surely her shooter had given up finding her by now. Anything to end this torture. She wiped the wetness from her forehead with her shirt sleeve, which wasn't much drier.

Sam welcomed the wolf symphony to keep her company during her trek. *Sing me back to the trailhead,* she silently commanded the wolves.

"Woof," Diego muttered, followed by something she couldn't understand in whatever his native language was. Then, "Many woof."

She was startled to hear his voice after hours of silence interrupted only by intermittent moans. "These woofs are far away," she assured him. Did the man have an innate fear of wolves? Maybe they had terrifying fairy tales about murderous wolves in whatever country he was from. God knows there were enough of those stories in European and American lore.

The howls soon died away, and she was left with only heavy breathing and the rhythmic clop of hooves behind her. The rain seemed to be lessening, thank goodness. She tried to picture the wolf pack meeting up, shaking the wetness from their fur, and setting off for a successful hunt in these mountains.

Chase had shared with her some of the Lakota legends about wolves. Native Americans generally regarded wolves as cunning experts in stealthy travel and cooperative hunts, but above all, the wild canines were celebrated for being loyal, generous, and sharing with their families. Many tribes included wolf clans and considered wolves their brothers.

Sam appreciated that image of wolves much better than the typical European horror stories, and based on what she knew of wolves, it was more accurate. She tried to remember what Chase had said about the lone wolf who had visited her campsite.

Chase! He had to be frantic. What would he make of the abrupt stop to their conversation? She'd mentioned an injured man, a horse, the corpse of the missing man. Then, *blam!* End of conversation.

She'd never hear the end of this. Assuming she lived to hear from him or anyone else again.

Her feet had transitioned from numb blocks of wood to spasming with rippling cramps. Her hand throbbed with every step. Every muscle in her body ached. Her stomach growled. While her clothes and hair were soaked, her mouth was a desert. And pitiable Freckles, limping bravely behind her. And Diego, whoever he was, with his shattered leg and God knew what other injuries. She hadn't been part of such a pathetic set of survivors for quite some time. Well, for more than five weeks, anyway, remembering her recent near-death avalanche disaster. She was forced to admit that she did have a penchant for this sort of misfortune.

An unnatural shape appeared ahead, just to the side of the trail, one arm outstretched. Sam's breath caught in her throat. Her heart hammered a few staccato beats before slowing as she neared. Just the leftover stump of a broken tree, one branch threatening to intrude into the path.

Her footsteps continued, along with her dark thoughts of everything that had gone wrong on this adventure. Alec Lysikov, under all those rocks. And oh yeah, the dead guy in the lake. How could she have forgotten about the floater? Were her future backpacking trips all doomed to be this creepy?

The air had grown cold during the night. Steam wafted from the mare's nostrils, and Sam blew out a breath to see her own exhalation materialize briefly in front of her face. If she hadn't been walking for what seemed like days, she'd be curled up into a hypothermic ball by now.

Something cracked loudly in the dark forest to her left, and she startled again. A vision of an armed man reared up in her imagination. But she couldn't see anything in that direction, and she didn't hear anything beyond a deep sigh from Freckles and another low moan from Diego. Probably just a dead branch falling, or maybe a deer stepping on a twig. Time to focus on something other than dead people.

Concentrate on the positive. The wolf puppies she'd seen. *Oh jeez, her camera!* She'd left it in the tent. What had happened to her camera and all the wonderful photos and video she'd taken of the wild canines? Would the shooter have ransacked her camp? Would the rangers be willing to recover her gear? Or maybe she shouldn't tell them about her off-trail activities. She could kayak to Lightning Creek and hike in from there, hoping to find her camp untouched. But when? Would her hand heal in time to paddle?

Ski to Sea duties. She'd promised Fredd she would cover that contest this weekend. And she needed the money. There were no groceries in the house, and Blake wasn't there to help. How in the hell was this going to work? She was a walking disaster. Correction: a stumbling, bleeding, aching disaster.

They finally gained the intersection of the trail, and with the faint sound of Ruby Creek in the distance and the slope down to the water, she knew they were now on the trail she'd originally hiked in on, headed back toward the parking lot. She was grateful to be close, but as the last few miles passed and the trail descended toward the footbridge, her anxiety ratcheted up. Dawn wasn't far away. The shooter could well be waiting for her at the trailhead.

Her worst nightmare materialized. Out of the shadows, strolling her way, a bulky monster blocked the trail. Sam stopped. The black bear—at least she prayed it was a black and not a grizzly—also halted a few yards away on the narrow trail, standing stiffly with its head raised, sniffing the air. When the creature opened its jaws, a wisp of steam emerged as it exhaled. Was that a challenge?

A cliff rose to Sam's left. To her right, the hill fell away steeply from the edge of the trail. There was nowhere to pass.

In the dim light, Sam and the bruin engaged in a staring contest for a long moment. Behind her, Freckles snorted and yanked at the reins, jerking Sam back a step. She was abruptly, painfully reminded that every member of her party smelled like blood. How long would this standoff last?

"For crap's sake," Sam grumbled to the bear. "We don't have the energy for this now. *You* move." She raised her wounded hand to point at the bear.

The beast raised its head and sniffed at her again, apparently considering the bloody offering.

No. Sam bellowed, "Move!"

The startled bear bolted sideways off the trail down the steep slope toward the creek, crashing through the vegetation as it vanished.

"Thanks." Light-headed with relief, Sam listened until the sounds of the bear's retreat faded. *Please, Supreme Being, if there is one, don't let anyone have heard that shout.* Animals, she could handle. Men with guns were another matter.

Finally, the footbridge. Freckles' hooves echoed across the structure, clip-clopping so loudly on the wood it seemed anyone within a mile would hear.

To her horror, another apparition approached the far end of the bridge. Had the damn bear circled back?

As the creature trotted swiftly in her direction, she could more clearly make out its outline. This silhouette was definitely human.

The shooter had found her.

28

The man shone a flashlight on the trail ahead of his feet, and then raised it to blind Sam with its light. There was nowhere to hide. If she had an ounce of energy left, she might be able to squeeze between the railings and drop into the creek below. But her body was no longer obeying her frantic thoughts. With her heartbeat thudding in her ears, Sam twisted sideways to make herself as small a target as possible. She braced for a gunshot.

"Summer! *Querida!*"

Even after his arms enclosed her, she remained dazed. "Chase?" Could he really be here, or was he a hallucination?

"I heard you shout," he told her. "'*Move?*'"

Sam snorted. "There was a bear." She gratefully relinquished the bloody reins to him. "Meet Freckles and Diego."

Moving to the horse's side, Chase Perez pressed two fingers against Diego's neck. The injured man didn't react at all.

"Alive?" Sam asked.

"I think so." Chase turned toward Sam again, and urged her with a forward thrust of his hand to continue down the trail. "You're almost at the parking lot."

"How are you here?" she asked him over her shoulder.

"How could I *not* be here after your phone calls? Especially the last one."

She relived the phone exploding as she held it. Her hand

throbbed anew with that memory.

He said, "The rangers told me about your call to the headquarters. Someone shot at you?"

"Yeah. Did they catch the guy?"

"No. Nobody seems to know anything about that. So did this guy—Diego—get shot?"

"No." She wearily remembered the snatches of conversation between the two backpackers, a man on a horse with a rifle. Those two had at least seen the shooter. "But I talked to two backpackers on the trail. And they saw the shooter. Didn't they give his description to the rangers?"

"Apparently not."

Well, *that* was just great. She hadn't seen the shooter. How the heck was she, or the rangers, supposed to find two young male backpackers when there were probably a hundred on the trail every day? For all she knew, those two had hiked in from the Canadian side and were already back in British Columbia. She tried to remember their appearance. Not much beyond *young, male, backpackers* came to mind.

Sam wearily shuffled up the final switchbacks, barely able to move her feet, her wet hiking pants clinging to her shaky legs, flapping around her ankles. She might never hike again.

Chase's voice came from behind her. "We need to get those pants off you."

"Really, Chase? Romance *now*?"

"Funny," he groaned. "I have sweatpants in my trunk."

"You carry them around in hopes of collecting women's wet pants?"

"They're *my* old sweatpants," he told her.

"Even kinkier."

He chuckled. "I can't believe you have the energy for this conversation."

I don't, she thought. But being silly seemed easier right now than relating everything she'd been through in the last couple of days.

After a few seconds of silence, Chase asked, "What's Diego's story?"

"I have no idea. He says he's from Miami. But his accent doesn't sound Hispanic, and everything else that came out of his mouth was in some language I've never heard. I found him and the horse down in a steep gulley. Looked like both of them fell off the trail. And the dead guy was there, too."

"Dead guy? The floater from the lake?" When she didn't immediately respond, he added, "*Another* dead guy?"

She realized she'd already moved the missing hiker into the "dead guy" category, along with the floater in the lake. Was it just her fatigued imagination, or did she know more dead people than live ones? "The guy on the "Missing" poster in the parking lot," she clarified. "Alec Lysikov."

Finally, a clearing appeared between the trees ahead, and in a few minutes more, they staggered off the hiking trail into the gravel parking area.

It wasn't quite dawn, but the blackness of night had lifted to a dull gray. A Park Service SUV in the lot had its interior lights on. Her RAV4 was still where she'd left it. Chase's car was parked alongside, as if to keep hers company. She couldn't wait to get at the energy bars in her glove box, drink the water in the spare tire compartment.

A door abruptly slammed shut on her eager anticipation. Her car key was zipped into her pack. Her pack was zipped into her tent.

Sucking in a deep breath to keep from bursting into tears, she leaned dejectedly against the dust-covered back bumper. Now that she wasn't moving, the frigid morning air quickly seeped through to her skin. A thin vapor of steam rose from her wet clothes, transforming her into a filthy, bloody wraith.

A pickup hitched to a two-slot horse trailer huddled near two other vehicles at the far side of the lot. The ebony tail of one horse streamed over the back door, and a light vapor of steam wafted from its haunches in the cold morning air. Another pickup and horse trailer, a nearly identical but empty combination, was parked next to the smaller one. She'd never imagined so many horse packers used the East Bank Trail.

The headlights in the park service vehicle flashed on, spotlighting Sam and company. She and the mare turned their heads away from the painful glare. Chase shielded his eyes with his hand. Diego remained slumped over the *V*-shaped frame of the pack saddle like a sack of dirty laundry, and in the glaring light, Sam noticed fresh blood dripping from his horrific wound. Chase was again pressing his fingers to Diego's neck, murmuring, "Hey, buddy, *amigo*, you still here?"

She held up her right hand in the light. Her fingers were coated in red, and the same crimson paint decorated her shirt sleeve all the way to her elbow, as well as the right leg of her pants. She peeled the bandana away. Blood slowly trickled down her palm from a ragged hole between her second and third fingers. That hand refused to respond to her command to move; the fingers remained painfully curved in a clawlike position.

She was a writer. She was right-handed. How the hell was she going to type?

Ranger Amelia Castro emerged from the NPS vehicle. She jogged over, saying to Chase, "You found them!"

"More like *they* found *me*," Chase informed her. "We need an ambulance. This man is in a bad way, and Summer is also injured."

Castro did a quick inspection of the situation. "It will be

fastest to transport them ourselves. The ambulance can meet us down the road, or we might be able get a Life Flight chopper to land in Newhalem or Rockport. I'll make some calls now." She pulled a satellite phone from her duty belt and tapped in a number.

"Let me take the horse." A man appeared out of the dark to grasp the reins from Chase. His voice sounded familiar.

"Life Flight, forty minutes, Newhalem," Castro reported after hanging up, then confirmed the new man's identity by saying, "Thanks, Wiley."

"No problemo." The wrangler studied Diego, then remarked, "Damn, what happened to this guy?"

"Wiley Thompson is one of the local volunteers," Castro informed Chase. "He often helps with search and rescue." She turned to face Sam. "As soon as we knew we had trouble and a horse was involved, I asked if Wiley could come. He works at a local ranch that does packing trips here."

"We've met." Sam tried to remember how many days ago that was.

A brief smile crossed Wiley's lips as he regarded Sam. "Looks like I don't need to saddle up and search for you, after all."

Wiley's sandy hair was tousled and his face was weary and whiskered, as if he hadn't looked in the mirror for a couple of days. He was dressed in the typical wrangler clothes she'd seen earlier: denim jacket, plaid shirt, blue jeans, and boots, although he wasn't wearing a nametag or a pistol this time.

The sound of clopping hooves announced the arrival of another rider. Ranger Digby emerged from the forest on a tall bay gelding, announcing to the park service vehicle, "No sight of—" On seeing the gathering in the parking lot, he stopped, staring at Sam. "You're here!"

Digby wore his ranger uniform with a jacket open over his

duty belt, on which was holstered a revolver and a can of bear spray. When he dismounted, Sam noted a rifle scabbard hanging from the saddle, which had been tucked under his left knee.

Sweat striped the bay's belly and chest. Digby took a moment to pull the reins over his horse's head, patting the animal on the nose. "Guess I didn't need to hustle, after all."

"Westin just arrived a few minutes ago," Castro told him. "She found this injured man on the trail."

Digby studied Diego, still clinging to the mare. "Damn," he said. "How'd he end up like that?"

Facing Sam and Chase, Castro explained, "Digby was on horse patrol up at the north end of the trail today. We sent out the SOS after your call."

Just how many horsemen with guns routinely rode around the North Cascades? They could be up to anything. They could be criminals. Or maybe they were just horsemen with guns. Or gunmen with horses. Her brain was too fatigued to sort anything out at the moment.

Digby dismounted. "I've been riding all night," he grumbled, shoving his green Park Service cap back on his head.

Sam felt she was expected to comment on that, although she found it difficult to muster much sympathy at the moment. "Thanks?"

The younger mustachioed ranger nodded in acknowledgment, then led the bay to the trailhead sign, where he tied his mount to a post and began to loosen the cinch. When the gelding whickered, Digby trotted to the rear of the park service SUV, opened the back door, removed a bucket and a large plastic container of water and gave his horse a drink. "I'll call HQ and get someone up here with the horse trailer," he told Castro.

"Larkson's on today," the senior ranger told him. "She can do it."

The bay drank noisily from the bucket. "How about Freckles here?"

When his horse was finished drinking, Digby transferred the bucket to the Appaloosa. Sam wondered if she could join the horses in the slurpfest.

Castro briefly examined Diego's leg, then tried to rouse him, tapping his arm gently. "Hey buddy, how're you doing? Can you look at me? Can you sit up?"

"His name is Diego." Sam's voice was hoarse with dryness. "He says he's from Miami, but I don't think he speaks much English.

"*Amigo*?" Castro shook Diego's arm again. He did not respond and remained slumped forward. She turned to Sam. "Why is he riding on a pack saddle?"

"Don't ask me," Sam replied. "I found them in a ravine. I think they both fell off the trail." She'd get to the dead missing hiker later. This was all too complicated for so early in the morning.

"Digby! Open the back door, then get over here and help me get this poor man off this horse," the senior ranger commanded. "Lead the horse over here."

While the rangers and Chase discussed how best to move Diego, Sam's thoughts tumbled in her exhausted brain like sodden clothes in a dryer. Dead guys, shooter, wolves, horses, drugs, hiking up and down, up and down, through thorns and saplings and rocks. She couldn't focus.

Was the shooter still out there? She studied Wiley. "Do you know who that other trailer belongs to?"

"No, ma'am. It was empty when I got here"—he checked a watch on his wrist—"less than an hour ago, just a few minutes before the rangers showed up."

"I should be able to check that with vehicle registration," Castro volunteered. "All hikers, boaters, and horse packers need to register to stay in the campgrounds, and they should have left us their license plate number."

Uh-huh, Sam thought. Like a rider aiming to kill someone would just fork over that information.

"Is that your horse?" Sam asked the wrangler, jutting her chin at the horse in the other trailer.

"Yep. The rangers said they might need to look for you, and a horse seemed like the fastest way, so I brought Diamond, just in case." He tilted his head toward the trailered horse. "He's my search and rescue horse."

Sam nodded, trying to marshal her thoughts. Although the parking lot was growing lighter by the minute, a dark fog seemed to be settling in her mind. She shivered. Hypothermia was quickly closing in.

"I got some water in the truck," Wiley volunteered. "And some jerky. You gotta be powerful hungry and thirsty. I'll go get it."

Finally. Was it her imagination, or did his aw-shucks accent seem to be getting thicker? He was back in a flash with a bottle in one hand and a stick of jerky in the other.

"Thanks." She unscrewed the lid from the commercial water bottle. It was only half-full, and she swallowed a few gulps. She bit into the jerky—beef, teriyaki flavor—before glugging the rest of the water. The wrangler wasn't so bad; she'd have to excuse his anti-wolf comments a couple of days ago. "By the way, Wiley, I found the wolves."

"Yeah?" He combed his fingers through his hair. "You said you wanted to." When she continued to watch him, he shrugged. "Live and let live, I guess."

"There are pups. I have a video."

"Oh, man. I'd like to see that." He flashed her a grin.

Shit. The camera. The tent. *Did* she have a video?

Castro cradled Diego's broken leg while Chase and Digby hefted the inert man from the pack saddle. After shrieking a sharp cry of pain, Diego went completely limp. The team nearly dropped him on the ground.

"He's passed out," Digby observed. "Probably a blessing."

The three rescuers managed to wrestle the unconscious man onto the back seat of the Park Service vehicle.

Wiley turned Freckles in the direction of his double horse trailer.

Sam stood up. "Stop, Wiley. Chase, Ranger Castro, you need to check those panniers on the horse."

Inside the Park Service SUV, Castro raised her head over the seat. "That can wait. Wiley will take care of unloading them."

"I'm on it." The wrangler led the horse out of the headlights toward the trailer.

"No!" Sam blurted, too loudly, causing everyone to stare at her. "You need to check them *now*." She shot what she hoped was a meaningful glance at Chase.

He nodded once, his dark eyes flashing. "Hold up there, Wiley." Chase quickly strode toward the horse and unbuckled the flap on the heavy canvas pannier. Illuminating the contents with flashlight, he whistled a low note, moved to the other side and checked the pannier there, shaking his head. "Thousands of dollars' worth in there. Probably hundreds of thousands. No wonder someone was shooting at you, *querida*."

Wiley peered over Chase's shoulder. After a minute of awed hesitation, the wrangler said, "Hoo-wee! Whoever lost *this* is going to be in *big* trouble."

"Ranger Castro, get over here," Chase commanded.

With a frown of annoyance, Castro backed away from the door of the Park Service vehicle and, pulling aside the canvas flap on the pannier closest to her, inspected the cargo inside. "Oh, crap!"

Digby looked over his boss's shoulder. "Whoa."

Chase frowned. "This happen a lot in this park?"

Ranger Castro faced him, grimacing. "Some. Too often. Drugs coming down from Canada. But usually on a boat. And never in this quantity, as far as I know." She turned to the wrangler. "Wiley, can you unload these panniers now and stash them in the back?" The ranger strode to her SUV and opened the rear door. "And we need to find out who this horse belongs to."

"Yes, ma'am." Wiley began to undo the straps holding the panniers to the pack saddle frame. "I'll check around. Maybe somebody stole this mare." He patted her forehead. "Poor girl." Freckles raised her nose toward him.

"We need to take photos of this horse," Sam announced loudly, glancing again at Chase.

Everyone stared at her, questions written on their faces. "The owner will need to describe her," Sam said. "You don't want to hand this mare over to just anyone."

"Good point." Castro sounded annoyed.

"And I want photos of Wiley, too, because he was helping to look for me."

"Nah." The wrangler waved a hand in the air. "I didn't even get started. That's not necessary, ma'am."

"Yes, it is." The words made her dry throat tickle, and after Sam started coughing, she couldn't stop.

Chase jogged to his car and came back with a full bottle of water, twisting off the lid before reaching her. After a few swallows and a few more coughs, Sam added, "I'm a journalist."

Her conscience added, *Really?* But she ignored that, and continued, speaking to Wiley, "I want to include you in my story."

Everyone continued to gaze at her, as if waiting to see what she'd do next. "I don't have a phone," she explained. *Or a camera,* her brain added. *Or a tent, a sleeping bag, a first aid kit.* She'd left it all back at her illegal camp.

Chase pulled out his cell phone and, walking around Freckles and the wrangler, took photos from several angles. The sun had now peeked over the mountains to the east, but Sam noticed he had the flash turned on.

"And I need your address, Wiley," Sam added. "I'll want you to verify the story before I publish."

After a brief hesitation, he said, "I'll write it down for you. Let me find a pen and paper."

He turned toward the trailer, leaving Freckles standing with her head down, the straps dangling on the ground, the heavy panniers still resting on her back.

Chase quickly strode toward the wrangler. "I can see you have your wallet in your back pocket. I'll just snap a quick photo your driver's license. That'll be perfect."

Wiley patted himself down for a minute. His jaw was clenched as he extracted his wallet and withdrew his license. After Chase snapped a photo, the wrangler returned to Freckles, pulled off the panniers and transferred them to the rangers' vehicle.

When he started to lead the mare away, Sam stood up, tottering a bit on her aching feet. "Wait! Give me a minute."

Taking the horse's cheeks in both hands, she bent and touched her forehead to Freckles'. "Thank you, girl. You are the bravest, toughest horse I've ever had the pleasure to meet." She gently kissed the mare's salty forehead. Straightening, Sam said to Wiley, "Take good care of her. She's a hero."

Sam couldn't stay standing a moment more. Her shivering was getting worse. Any second now, her teeth would start chattering.

Stumbling toward Chase's car, weaving like she'd consumed a whole pitcher of margaritas, she yanked on the backseat door handle with her still-functional hand. When the door opened, she collapsed full length onto the seat.

29

Evansburg

Finn had been back in Evansburg for almost a week, and he was starting to feel like he was never going to solve either of his cases and he was never going to return to Hawaii. Jarvis Pinder's phone calls turned out to be mostly sweet-talking to women, maybe one of those inexplicable romances between pen pals and inmates. Of course, Pinder being the sleazebag he was, was romancing several females at a time. The warden confirmed that Pinder did receive letters from people with female names, but that all the correspondence seemed innocuous enough.

Z and Maya had texted that they'd turned up only short videos of gorillas on TikTok, and no references to harming apes of any kind. He needed to go to Grace's compound and ask to view those gorilla videos, and chat with everyone there about Haitians they might have noticed in the area.

Jonah Whitman, the armed man camping with his son and daughter-in-law, did have a criminal record for hunting out of season, but he'd only shot a deer. Finn winced when he read that, but he figured it was likely that a good percentage the male population had done the same things. There was also a record of the old grouch firing a gun at his neighbor's dog for howling, but the dog hadn't been hit, and it turned out the dog was howling because the neighbor had chained the hound up, so that incident resulted in only a warning to both men. Finn debated whether it was a good strategy to interview all the members of the family again, or whether that might earn him lifelong animosity from the locals. Due to the rampant gossip vine and everybody knowing most everybody else, detective work in midsize Evansburg was much pricklier than it had been in Chicago.

The USFS district ranger had left Finn a voicemail about the timber-harvesting project. It had been subcontracted out and was finished six weeks ago. He'd left the name and number of the harvesting company, but that seemed like another dead end.

If only Finn could just file both cases in the Unsolved category and be done with them. But a child was still missing, and whoever had shot Kanoni might come back. There were too many loose threads to leave uninvestigated. And he knew Grace was getting impatient and suspicious and likely to hop on a plane home any day now. And then she'd be in the line of fire, too.

He decided that he'd spend the next couple of hours driving back to the Whitman's campsite and then walking from there to Grace's boundary, and maybe to the old farmhouse to see if any clues were lurking in the woods there. He didn't have a lot of hope for a breakthrough, but you never knew when you might stumble across something that would point to a conclusion.

The only good news was that Rebecca Ramey hadn't shown up to plague him for several days now, and although all the questions were still on the site, the *What's Up, Evansburg?* blog was currently focused on the local rodeo.

His phone chimed, and he picked it up from his desk. Blake had texted. Dr. Farin is bringing Kanoni home tomorrow.

That was good news. Asking the caregiver and Z about

Haitians could wait until then. He replied: I'd like to be there. Call when you know the delivery time. I have more questions for you, Z, Maya.

Maya's gone, Blake responded. I'll call tomorrow.

Why had Maya left? Did she know something about Kanoni's shooting? He decided those questions could wait until tomorrow, too, and headed to his house to grab his hiking boots and Cargo. The Newfie would be ecstatic about an outing. Finn knew that taking the dog to the forest service road might result in a wrestling match, but at least he could get some exercise and see some greenery instead of staring at a computer screen.

30

Bellingham, Washington

An ear-shattering wail woke Sam Westin, and as Chase pulled into a parking space, she pushed herself to a sitting position in the backseat. Ahead, an ambulance was pulling into the emergency entrance to St. Joseph hospital.

Chase twisted in the driver's seat. "Good day, sleeping beauty."

Her mouth was full of cotton. She had to work her tongue around her teeth to find some saliva before she asked, "Did they bring Diego here?"

Chase slipped from the driver's seat and pulled open the backseat side door, leaning in. "Life Flight picked him up in a field outside of Rockport. He arrived here over an hour ago. They didn't have space for you on the chopper."

"Thank God. I don't need that." Not to mention she was pretty sure her low-cost, high-deductible insurance wouldn't cover even a tenth of that cost.

Her feet were clothed only in socks. She fingered the sweatpants bagging around her legs. Chase had pulled her pants off, after all. At least she hoped it had been Chase.

He gestured toward the hospital entrance. "You're here now."

"No, no, no." She loathed hospitals. With all her mother's emergencies and years of wasting away from ALS, Sam had spent too many days in these places as a little girl. Those were days she'd never get back.

"Summer." Chase reached in, grabbed her right wrist. She yowled as a sharp pain shot through her entire body. Mercilessly, he pulled her arm up in front of her face. Her hand was a swollen, bloody mess, her fingers curled in a position that reminded her of a garden rake. "I expect you may want to use this hand in the future."

She examined her injury. "Maybe it can star in a horror movie. *Zombie Hand Rising.*"

He continued to hold her wrist. "Summer . . ."

Shit. "Just . . . let . . . go," she hissed.

He finally did. She scooted to the edge of the seat and reluctantly swung her legs out. "Not to mention all gunshot wounds have to be reported," he added, grabbing her good hand and pulling her from the car.

"That only applies to hospital personnel," she argued.

"And to law enforcement," Chase continued. "Of which I am a member."

She caught a reflection of her face in the side-view mirror and gasped. Streaks painted her forehead and cheeks, rusty trails of blood from black starbursts spattered across her face. "Yikes! Why didn't you tell me I looked like Frankenstein's monster?"

"You were out. And we are building a case here, remember?"

Oh, yeah. But a case against who? Or should that be "whom"?

"Summer!" He grabbed her good hand again.

"I'm coming, aren't I?" she said. He insisted on towing her by her left hand. "I can't believe I have my cell phone all over my face."

"You're lucky it's not in your eyes."

Good point. After she was checked in and ensconced in a cubicle, Sam asked about Diego.

"I'll check on his status." But Chase didn't move from the side of the bed.

"So go." She flicked her left hand at him.

"I don't trust you to stay here until the doctor comes."

An unwelcome recollection of the last time she'd been here, after the avalanche, floated to the surface of her memory. Her housemate had guarded her at that time. "Yeesh, you are as bad as Blake."

Blake, that lucky devil. Cavorting happily with gorillas. Well, maybe not cavorting, and maybe not happily. But taking care of apes, learning about them, maybe even conversing with them, had to be more rewarding than stumbling across dead people and getting shot. The wolves were her consolation prize.

After a tetanus shot, an antibiotic shot, a pain shot, and a still-painful cleaning of her face and right hand, Sam was shuffled off to X-ray and finally to a consultation with a yawning white-haired man in scrubs who identified himself as an orthopedic physician.

"You're lucky," he told her. "The bullet mainly took out the fleshy web between your fingers. There's a small chip on the knuckle bone of your third finger and some tearing of the muscle between your fingers, but that will likely heal on its own. If it isn't better in a few days, you'll need to consult a hand specialist and investigate surgery."

Her hand was swathed in gauze and topped with an elastic bandage. Wincing, she tried to flatten her fingers on the desktop between her and the doctor. The resulting pain brought tears to her eyes, and as soon as she released the pressure, her fingers curled again.

The doctor grimaced. "Even with the local anesthetic, you

probably shouldn't do that. You'll find your hand will remain swollen for several days."

She frowned at the bandages. Her hand now looked more like a boxer's glove than a functional hand. "I'm a writer. I need to be able to type."

"Good luck with that." He yawned again. "I suggest you try a voice app and dictate."

"Okay." *Easy for you to say. Piece of cake.* She'd never used one.

"Keep that hand dry." The doctor pushed himself to his feet. "Get some rest, Ms. Westin. A shower wouldn't hurt, either."

A rush of blood heated her face. "Sorry. I've been hiking for"—she tried to count back—"oh, most of forty-eight hours."

He nodded. "I heard you brought the open fracture from Ross Lake."

Not quite an accurate statement, but she guessed he meant Diego. "How is he?"

"Lucky to be alive." The doctor headed for the door.

Three hours had passed since she'd come through the door at St. Joe's. More hours lost to a hospital. When she escaped from the emergency room, Chase was waiting for her in the lobby, texting away on his cell phone.

It suddenly felt weird to be unable to check her own phone messages. "Chase, I need to stop by the store and get a cell phone to replace mine."

A self-satisfied smile spread across his face. He stood up and extracted a cell phone from his jacket pocket. "Here you go."

The phone was a Google Pixel, several versions newer than her cell that had been obliterated. When she turned it on, the face lit up, displaying her old phone number. She positioned it on a table and poked at the icons with her good hand. It was all there, her contacts, her photos, her texts, her emails. "How—?"

He shrugged. "I had the time. Gina helped me find your passwords."

She grimaced. "It was that easy? I hope you two are a lot smarter than the average burglar."

"The transfer was all Google. Good thing you had most of your info stored on your Google Drive."

She had two missed calls from Michael Fredd. A picture from Gina showed Sam's cat Simon sitting on the table with a paw raised in the direction of Gina's parrot's cage. The parrot, Zeke, was leaning toward the paw, no doubt determined to come away with a beakful of cat fur if Simon's paw appeared between the wires of his cage.

She called the editor first.

"Thank God you're back early." He sounded harried. "I need you yesterday."

Early? It seemed as if she'd been on the trail for a week, but looking at the date on the phone, she realized she had actually returned half a day earlier than she had promised. She had told him Saturday evening, and it was a little after one on Friday afternoon. She laughed.

"It's not funny," he protested. "I need you to cover the prep for Ski to Sea on the cross-country leg up at Baker."

Fredd consistently operated in panic mode. "I told you I'd do the race." Frowning, she raised her right hand and studied the bulky bandage. Could she learn to use a dictation app overnight?

"But—"

"You said nothing about the day before. The race is a day away. I'm not home yet, Michael." That wasn't precisely a lie. Back in Bellingham did not equal back at her home address. She wanted food, a shower, and her bed. "I'll call you tomorrow and we'll work out the logistics for race day." She ended the call before he could argue.

Chase parked his car in her driveway next to an unfamiliar red Honda. Oh yeah, Gina's. For a disconcerting moment she imagined her RAV4 had been stolen, but then she remembered her car was still in the trailhead lot. Her key was in her tent near Lightning Creek, unless a bear or raccoon or crow had stolen it by now.

"I need to call Ranger Castro," she said. "And pray she will forgive me."

Pulling open the glove compartment, Chase slid out a business card and handed it to Sam. "What does she need to forgive you for?"

The card showed a private number for Senior Ranger Amelia Castro. "Uh," Sam said. "I was sort of camping outside the regular campgrounds. And I had to leave everything there. Including my car key. I need all that gear: tent, sleeping bag, camera, food bag, backpack."

"I'm sure the investigators will be thorough. They need to recover the bullets, in any case."

He had a lot more faith in the budgetary allowance and forensics expertise of NPS rangers than she did.

"The Whatcom County Sheriff will want to interview you, too."

Sam frowned. "I've already talked to the park service."

"Whatcom County deputies handle most of the park crimes and missing persons, and I believe you said you found one of those."

He slid out of the driver's seat and walked around the front of the car. Sam awkwardly unlatched her seat belt with her left hand and twisted to reach the door handle.

It would be interesting if she was interviewed by her old buddy, Whatcom County Deputy Ben Ortiz. He'd been her liaison for the avalanche disaster and helped her dig two wolverine-trapping teenagers out of the snow. What would he make of all this? She seemed destined to get a reputation for wandering into places she shouldn't be and ending up surrounded by corpses.

All because she liked to take the trail less traveled. Like Alec Lysikov, apparently. And maybe Diego, too. She still didn't know his story. Robert Frost had said it so eloquently. Something like, "I took the road less traveled, and it has made all the difference."

Tripped over a few corpses along the way, her brain added. She chuckled at the absurdity.

Chase pulled open her door. "What's funny?"

"Life." *And death.* She chuckled again as she slid out of the car, winced as her feet hit the ground. She had a hard time straightening her spine to her full height, and then she had an even harder time making her legs propel her to the door.

Yeesh. "Shower," she mumbled, shuffling like a ninety-year-old through the living room toward her bedroom. Odors emanating from the oven made her mouth water.

Her friend Gina appeared in her peripheral vision. "You're alive!"

"Not sure about that," Sam said. "I'll let you know in a few minutes."

"Hello! Hello!" Gina's macaw, Zeke, squawked. *"Trade you for a dog!"*

Sam snorted. She knew the parrot was repeating the threat Gina had told the bird multiple times, but it sounded as if Zeke were threatening her now. "Might be a good idea, Zeke."

"Hello! Alexa, play NPR," the bird commanded. Fortunately, Sam did not own a smart device to respond.

"Mac and cheese in the oven," Gina said. "Cold beer in the

fridge. Now I'm making myself scarce. And I'm taking Zeke with me."

"Thanks for the mac and cheese. And the house- and cat-sitting," Sam said. "Speaking of which . . ." She scanned the living area and kitchen.

Her friend smiled. "Simon's laying low outside, I think."

"*Meow!*" Zeke screeched.

Sam couldn't help smiling, although it hurt to flex the skin on her face. What had the docs cleaned her cuts with, anyway?

"Bag that hand," Chase reminded, handing her a plastic produce bag from the recycle bin.

"Talk to you tomorrow," Gina said. "I need to hear all about this."

"Tomorrow," Sam promised, continuing her slow shuffle toward hot water.

31

Sam woke up a few minutes shy of 5:00 a.m., surprised to find Chase Perez curled around her. He hadn't stayed overnight since nearly being killed in the building collapse over a month ago. He'd excused himself by saying he wanted to fully recover from his injuries, "get back to himself" before "inflicting himself" on her.

She tried to slide out of his embrace without waking him, but he rolled over onto his back and lay staring at her from his pillow, his square jaw darkened with whiskers.

She smiled and sat up. "This is a welcome surprise."

"I'm not letting you out of my sight this morning until I can deliver you someplace safe." Grabbing her left hand, he pulled her back down to him, and she lay her head against his bare torso. "I almost lost you. Again." His voice reverberated in his chest.

Raising her head, she kissed his lips. "Now you're just being dramatic."

"How's the hand?" His gaze shifted to her bandaged right hand that rested on his abdomen.

"Feels like I caught it in a threshing machine." She yawned. "When did we go to bed?"

"You, about two yesterday afternoon." He grinned. "Me, more like ten."

"Did I take a shower? Did we eat the mac and cheese?" She remembered *thinking* about eating the casserole, but she didn't remember actually chewing and swallowing."

"You don't remember the shower? I'm offended."

"Sorry?"

"As for the mac and cheese, *you* ate two plates of it. You also drank two IPAs. *I* consumed a *reasonable* portion of food and drank *one* beer." He ran his fingers through her fine, tangled hair, combing it away from her face. "But I'll give you a pass this time."

She sighed and lay her head on his chest again. "Did all that really happen?" Chase was adept at interpreting her non sequiturs; he'd know she was talking about the last few days.

His voice rumbled through his chest as he said, "I'm afraid so. I'm also afraid you'll get to relive every moment of it today. The park rangers and the Whatcom County Sheriff want to talk to you."

"Yay." Lifting her head, she made a face at him. "*And* I've got to work this afternoon for *Out There*. And somehow figure out how to type with this"—balancing on one elbow, she held up her bandaged right hand—"or use a recording program."

Chase abruptly rolled over, tugging at the sheet and flipping Sam onto her back. His dark eyes gleamed as his face neared hers. "How sore *are* you this morning?"

Sam raised an eyebrow. "Stiff, but not so sore."

"I'm stiff, too." Smiling, he traced his index finger lightly around her bare nipple.

"Maybe we can loosen each other up." She curled her left arm around his neck to pull him closer. "And then I'm eating the rest of the mac and cheese."

* * * * *

Sam was still smiling when Chase dropped her off at the Whatcom County Sheriff's Office in downtown Bellingham a few minutes before 10:00 a.m. Her lover, her best friend, was back. Or nearly back. Chase told her his assessment was in an hour. He was confident he'd pass the physical tests and get back to regular assignments, and then his attitude toward life might get back to normal, too.

What had been the turning point in their relationship? That phone call cut off by a gunshot? If that were true, how many times would she have to come close to dying to keep him in her bed and in her life?

The North Cascades National Park had sent Senior Ranger Amelia Castro to town to ask follow-up questions, and after some grumbling, the Whatcom County Sheriff's Office had agreed to do a joint interview with NPS personnel. The Sheriff's Office had also towed Sam's RAV4 to the station and called to ask her to bring an extra key, which she'd eventually managed to find in her underwear drawer. When she glanced inside her SUV, she saw her extra clothes and books on the floor as she'd left them. A few smudges of a powdery substance had been added to the dashboard and steering wheel and the inside of the doors, and when she stepped to the back of the vehicle, she noticed more of the powder around the back door latch.

Why had they searched and fingerprinted her SUV? She couldn't imagine why they were suspicious of *her*.

Inside the building, the man at the front desk directed her to a door off the main lobby. When she entered the interview room, four uniforms were already seated at the table with steaming cups of coffee in front of them.

She recognized Ranger Castro, of course. And Whatcom County Deputy Ortiz, who took one look at Sam, suppressed a grin, and groused, "Of course it's you, Summer Westin."

The others in the room glanced curiously at Ortiz, probably wondering if she had a criminal history. Should she explain she and Ortiz had recently been involved in an incident concerning wolverines and dead teens?

Ortiz did not volunteer that information, and before Sam could, the two strangers stood up and introduced themselves. Deputy Owen Yates was a short, blocky man, with thickly muscular arms and chest. A few gray strands threaded through his black hair. A tall, trim middle-aged woman in a navy blazer, white blouse, and black trousers was dressed to appear the epitome of professionalism with her chestnut hair tightly coiffed in a French braid. She identified herself as "Carole Erickson, HSI," and promptly took her seat.

"I'm starting the recording now." Reaching out, Ortiz pressed a button on a gizmo in the middle of the table, which looked to Sam more like a tortoise than a recording device. He then recited the date and time and the names and departments of everyone present.

"I thought your name was Sam," Ranger Castro remarked, looking at her.

Sam explained that was her nickname, but her birth certificate and driver's license showed Summer Alicia Westin.

Ortiz leaned forward. "I understand you were shot?"

Sam raised her bandaged right hand. "He mainly murdered my cell phone. But I was holding it at the time."

"He?" Yates and Erickson asked simultaneously.

What? Did they think she was being sexist or did they think she knew her shooter? Sam told them about overhearing the hoofbeats on the trail and her conversation with the two backpackers about the armed man on horseback. Of course, then everyone present wanted to know who the two backpackers were, and Sam had to explain she had few clues to their identities. Then she told them about Mark, the pistol-carrying camper she'd encountered at Rainbow Point a few days ago.

"Last name?" Ortiz asked.

Sam shook her head. "No idea. He was with a woman by the first name of Randi, with an *I*. They said they were on a horse-packing trip. He said he was a champion roper, and had a big brass buckle to prove it."

"Great," Erickson snidely remarked. "Mark and Randi."

Castro told the group she'd see if she could get a list of everyone who'd registered for the campsites in that time frame, but that she'd need help to contact them.

Sam noticed nobody in the room volunteered for that duty. She directed her gaze to Erickson. "Pardon my ignorance, but what is HSI and why are you here?"

The woman's lips curved in a condescending smile. "Homeland Security Investigations. We're a division of ICE."

ICE, Sam knew. Immigrations and Customs Enforcement. "I'm still not sure what your part is in this."

Erickson leaned forward, putting her hands on the table. She exhaled loudly, like she was already tired of explaining the obvious to a clueless civilian. "I'm an investigator. I'm not yet sure what role ICE or CBP will need to play in this situation; I'm here to make an initial determination of that."

CBP, Sam repeated in her head. *Customs and Border Patrol.* Yeesh. How many government operatives were crawling around the national park?

Erickson continued, "There are obviously illegal drugs involved. Also, I was told the first word that Emmanuel Baptiste uttered when he regained consciousness in the hospital was 'asylum.'"

Sam asked, "Who is Emmanuel Baptiste?"

Erickson practically rolled her eyes. "The injured man you

found." Why did the investigator's voice hold a note of skepticism?

Sam leaned forward in her chair. "You mean Diego? Diego Cruz? The guy from Miami that I brought in?"

The woman's blue eyes were cold. "His name is Emmanuel Baptiste. He's a noncitizen; a migrant from Haiti. Why do you say he was from Miami?"

"He told me so." She adopted a Hispanic accent as she imitated, "'Diego. I am from Miami.'" She then sat back in her chair, feeling like she'd just been jolted awake from a confusing dream. "But now that I think about it, the other things he said didn't sound much like Spanish—or French, for that matter—to me. Then again, he was barely conscious most of the time, so there wasn't a lot of conversation."

"Wait, wait, wait." Deputy Ortiz waved his hands as if erasing the words zinging back and forth across the table. "Let's start at the beginning. What were you doing in the Ross Lake area? When and where did you arrive?"

Oh crap, she *was* going to have to relive it all. "Can I at least have a cup of coffee?"

After a long-held look from Ortiz, Deputy Yates pushed back his chair.

"With cream, please," Sam told him. "Thank you."

Yates nodded as he left the room. Within minutes, he was back with a cup of surprisingly good coffee. After a sip, Sam took the people at the table through the whole four days and nights of her disastrous trip. Yeesh, had it only been four?

Only Ranger Castro scribbled in a notebook as Sam talked. The others apparently intended to rely on the recording.

When Sam finally paused, Erickson leaned forward. "So you don't know the deceased in the lake? You'd never seen him before?"

Sam shook her head. Ortiz frowned and gestured toward the recorder. "No and no," she said aloud. "Who is he?"

Yates looked as though he were about to answer when Erickson stated, "We're still working on that," ending any further conversation along that line.

"And you never before met Emmanuel Baptiste?" Ortiz, this time.

"Obviously not. I thought his name was Diego Cruz." Sam took another sip of her coffee. It was growing cold. Did she dare ask Yates to get her a warm-up?

Erickson clasped her hands on top of the table. Her nails were perfectly shaped and painted a tasteful shell pink. Sam was reminded of Nicole Boudreaux, Chase's immaculate former FBI partner, who often made her feel like a used dishrag. "How did you happen to be in these convenient places to discover both of these individuals, Miss Westin?"

Sam, caught scrutinizing her own ragged nails, lifted her chin in surprise, disturbed by the tone of the woman's question. *Shit.* Could they think she was involved in any of this? "As for the floater in the lake, I just saw something strange from the shore in the campground when I was washing my breakfast dishes, and so I waded out to be sure of what it was." She paused, remembering the hand shifting beneath the waves. "What *he* was. Whether it was actually a corpse."

"And Baptiste?" This came from Deputy Yates.

Sam moved her gaze to Ranger Castro. "Like I told the rangers, I went off-trail to look for the wolves. I accidentally stumbled across Diego, I mean Emmanuel, and a horse down in a ravine they'd fallen into."

"And the drugs?" from Ortiz.

She faced the deputy. "They were in the horse's saddlebags. Or to use the right term, panniers, because the mare was not actually saddled but outfitted as a pack horse. At first, I thought the bags might be pancake mix or flour, except there was way too much."

Skeptical looks ricocheted from person to person around the room.

What the heck? Shouldn't it be to her credit she didn't recognize illegal drugs? And she hadn't even mentioned finding the missing hiker. Her head was spinning; it was all too much. She took another sip of lukewarm coffee before asking, "What did Emmanuel Baptiste say about the drugs?"

Carole Erickson caught her eye. "He said he didn't know anything about any drugs."

Sam blinked and again lifted her coffee cup to her lips, but found it was empty. She set the cup back on the table. "He's probably scared for his life. Especially after the shooting. Clearly, someone out there is not happy I found the drugs . . . or Diego, I mean Emmanuel . . . or the horse." She shrugged. "Well, probably all of that."

And the dead guy in the lake, and the dead guy in the rockfall, her conscience added. No wonder this group had so many questions.

Ortiz summed up the situation by ticking off statements on his fingers. "So we have drug smuggling, an illegal alien, a corpse in Ross Lake, and a mysterious sniper on the loose." He groaned and flattened his hands on the table top. "And we don't have a single description of a suspect or a single bullet for evidence."

Sam frowned. She'd told them about Mark, but they didn't seem to think that was important information. Then she perked up. "I know where you can find bullets."

"We're listening," Erickson said, somehow making those two words sound ominous.

Shifting her focus again to Ranger Castro, Sam explained about her camp and all the equipment she'd left in it. "I have the approximate location marked on this contour map." Standing up from her chair, she pulled the folded map from her back pocket and indicated the *X* on it. "Maybe you can bring back all my gear? Especially my camera." She slid the map across the table to the ranger.

Castro studied the map. "It's looks like it's only a couple of hours walk from the trail junction at Lightning Creek, but it will involve some bushwhacking." She looked at Sam for confirmation.

Sam hoped the ranger's next question would not be whether Summer Westin had a special permit to travel off-trail.

Deputy Ortiz checked his wristwatch. "We've been at this for two hours, and we don't seem to be making a lot of progress." He leveled his gaze at Sam. "So better than us wasting time searching for this camp, Westin," he stated, "You'll take us there."

Déjà vu. Ortiz had insisted on the same thing a few months ago when she'd reported the wolverine and dead teens. Sam pursed her lips, thinking about all the hours it would take to return to that camp, even if they boated into the Lightning Creek campground.

"We'll also need to examine the location in which you found Baptiste and the drugs," Erickson added.

Sam swallowed against a constriction in her throat. "That would be almost a day's hike from the camp area. I'm not even sure I can find it again. I registered the coordinates on my phone, but like I said, my phone was destroyed." Unfortunately, the data from several of her apps hadn't survived the transfer to her new device.

"Maybe tomorrow?" Ortiz suggested. He turned to Ranger

Castro. "Can those sites be accessed from a helicopter?"

"I don't know." Castro's tone was doubtful. Her head was down as she studied the map, and Sam felt a kinship to her when she noticed the part in the ranger's graying dark hair was far from straight. "Maybe we could land somewhere on Spratt Mountain, but that's rugged country." Castro paged through the notebook she'd laid on the table. "When you called in, Westin, I see you said something about finding our missing hiker, Alec Lysikov?"

"Missing hiker?" Carole Erickson raised her eyebrows. So did Deputies Ortiz and Yates.

Oh god. Now she had to add this? Sam mentally counted to ten before starting. "Yes, that's what called my attention to the ravine in the first place. I was returning to my camp after finding the wolves and I saw a flash of red in this rockslide, then I spotted what looked like a scrap of black fabric. I remembered he had a red plaid shirt and a black jacket."

She did a quick survey of the faces around the table. Yates was shaking his head. Erickson's eyebrows were knit together, her expression skeptical. Castro merely looked interested. Was Ortiz really rolling his eyes?

"I memorized the description from the 'Missing' poster at the trailhead," Sam explained.

Describing all the events that had transpired in the last few days made her story sound suspicious, even to her own ears. She briefly considered adding something about the road less traveled. Her conscience quickly vetoed that. She already sounded like some sort of corpse-seeking nutcase. How was a woman supposed to demonstrate her innocence?

"We could at least do a flyover," Ortiz suggested. "I'll see if I can get a helicopter for tomorrow."

"Maybe we can recover the GPS data from Westin's old

phone, so I suggest we start there. I'll arrange a floatplane this afternoon," Erickson offered. "Two o'clock?" Giving nobody time to respond, she added, "Gear up for a hike. Meet in the airport near security." She turned to Deputy Ortiz. "But we can only take four passengers, and even that will be cozy."

"Done. Yates will stay here." Ortiz stood up from his chair. Ranger Castro followed his lead, and the others filed out the door to the lobby area. Sam heard Castro ask Ortiz in a low murmur, "You and Westin have a history?"

Sam, now alone at the table, pulled out her cell phone. Her boss at *Out There* was going to love this.

32

Was flying in a floatplane a benefit of working with law enforcement, or a detriment? Sam decided that, although taking off and landing on water would be new and interesting to her, this unscheduled expedition was grossly unfair. All the law enforcement types and the pilot were being paid for their time by their various employers, while she was going broke in a hurry. They were doing their jobs while preventing her from doing hers. Michael Fredd had already replaced her for the Ski to Sea coverage, and to make matters worse, she was going to miss the big relay race day and all the accompanying celebrations tomorrow as well.

"Half-time pay for twenty hours of work per week," he reminded her of their agreement.

"Believe me, Michael, I don't want to go, either. But Homeland Security, the Whatcom County Sheriff's Department, and North Cascades National Park have commandeered me."

"Humph. I'll have to think up something else useful for you to do when you get back."

She'd barely had time to eat lunch and change into her hiking clothes before she had to meet the team at the airport. She'd tried to call Chase, got his voicemail, and left him a long message whining about what a pain the interview session had been and telling him she was being forced to return to the scene

of the crime this afternoon. After ten minutes, he texted back
he'd passed his fitness assessment with ease. I have a new
investigation on the Quinault rez, but I'm not going out there
until I know you're safe. You shouldn't be home alone,
especially while you're injured.

Don't be ridiculous, she texted back. Go! I am fine.

If you're sure . . .

She knew how eager he was to get back to real work. He'd
been frustrated for weeks at being confined to a desk. Go! I can
get a friend to help if I need to.

He sent back a thumb up emoji, along with the short note
You could come with me.

Not now, she responded. The investigation team needs me.

She knew Chase would respect that. She was glad for him to
be back in action, but . . . so much for sympathy from him about
everything *she* was ensnared in. So much for his company at
home tonight. So much for his help changing the bandage on
her hand. Maybe she could pull off the bulky wrap with her good
hand and her teeth, and at least liberate her fingers. In the end,
she didn't have time to even attempt that. A quick stroke over
Simon's fur and an apology and extra food in his dish, then she
was out the door, her most minimal pack slung over her
shoulder.

The flight over the mountains took less than an hour, and
Sam, squeezed into a middle seat between Ranger Castro and
Deputy Ortiz, didn't even have a chance to enjoy the bird's-eye
view of the snow-covered peaks and lakes below. Their landing
on the lake caused a flurry of interest from the nearby campers.
The pilot, a middle-aged woman, broke out a fishing rod and sat
down cross-legged on the dock. Sam's comrades ignored
questions from the campers as they passed through the sites,
which were only half-filled at this hour. Feeling sorry for herself,

Sam grudgingly led the group over the miles from the boat landing at Lightning Creek to her camp. Every muscle in her body complained about being forced to hike cross-country again so soon.

The upside was her camp was intact, except for the food bag, which had clearly been ravaged by wild creatures. Canine prints, too small to belong to the visiting wolf, as well as tiny handprints, surrounded the scattered remains. At least one coyote and one raccoon had enjoyed her food. And there were large bird prints, too, so she added crows to the gang of raiders.

Just as she recalled, her cell phone had been reduced to sharp splinters of glass and plastic. Erickson delicately fished out the memory card, but even that was bent and chipped. "Probably useless," the HSI investigator complained as she tucked it into her pocket.

A few dark splashes indicated where blood had seeped into the earth. Hers, by the tree, and Emmanuel's, closer to the creek. Ortiz stowed samples of the bloody dirt in evidence bags.

Sam's tent still held her sleeping bag and clothes. Her pack was still leaning against the tree trunk, although the zippers were all undone as if someone had searched it. The tent had been unzipped as well, and she bit her lip when she didn't see her camera, which was the possession she most needed to recover. As the deputy and the feds searched for bullets and speculated about trajectories and photographed the man-size footprints near the creek, Sam awkwardly attempted to wad her sleeping bag into its stuff sack, a task that proved nearly impossible one-handed. Thankfully, Ranger Castro came to her aid and finished the job, and as the sleeping bag vanished into the sack, her camera was revealed beneath it.

"Wahoo!" Sam chortled, hugging the device to her chest. "I have all my photos of the wolves!"

"The idiot who shot you probably assumed all your photos were on your cell phone," Castro observed. "Nobody uses dedicated cameras anymore."

"Photojournalists do," Sam told her. "Most cell phones don't have the same zoom capabilities and polarizing filters."

"I suppose that's true." Castro crawled out of the tent first. After Sam followed, the ranger began to pull apart the poles holding up the structure. Castro was clearly an expert at this. She pushed the sleeping bag and other gear into Sam's pack and zipped it up, then lashed the tent to the top.

When Sam tried to hand her the small pack she'd brought today to stuff in as well, Castro said, "You keep that. I'll carry yours back to the plane." The ranger stuffed her own minimal pack into Sam's backpack.

"Thank you so much. I'm truly grateful."

The ranger smiled. "I know you're truly tired."

"Got that right." With her good hand, Sam helped the ranger pick up the detritus of scraps of cell pieces and food packaging littering the site, adding them to the garbage bag Castro had brought. Then Sam circled the campsite, pushing her way through the brush, inspecting the ground as she went.

"What do you think you're doing?" Erickson materialized beside her. "Did you bury something nearby?"

Why was this woman so mistrustful of her? *She* was the victim here. "There were footprints around my tent, but the shooter came on horseback, I'm fairly certain. I'm looking for hoofprints."

"Stay within sight."

As Erickson turned away, Sam stuck her tongue out at the investigator's back, and waded farther into the undergrowth toward the main trail. She soon found a small cleared space, brush trampled by hoofprints, and a pile of horse manure. Boot prints led away from a low branch to which the horse had likely been tied.

She could visualize the scene all too well, a man with a rifle slipping off his horse and slinking through the woods in hopes of surprising her at her tent. Thank God Diego, Emmanuel, whatever, and the poor mare had cooperated as quickly as they had to flee the campsite.

After taking a photo of the clearing, Sam marked the coordinates on her new phone. Ranger Castro showed up to watch and inform her, "We're done processing the campsite."

Sam tried not to moan at the cramps in her calves as she trudged back to the dock and floatplane. At least all the law enforcement types now understood her tale of the shooting at her campsite was true, although Erickson had asked multiple times where Sam had kept the drugs while in camp.

Erickson waited until they had crawled back inside the floatplane to grill her some more. Peering at Sam over her shoulder from the front passenger seat, she asked, "You tried to hide your camp, correct?" The investigator seemed hell-bent on making everything Sam had done sound like a crime.

If camping off-trail was a crime, it was a minor one. Sam glanced at Ranger Castro, who fortunately was focused on some hikers outside her window, before answering Erickson. "I wanted solitude, yes."

The investigator thought about that for a few seconds. "Then how did the shooter know where you were?"

Ortiz had already settled in and was staring at Sam, stroking a finger over his moustache as he awaited her response.

Crap. Double crap. That unsettling detail hadn't even occurred to her. Sam focused on fastening her seat belt in the nonexistent space between her and Ortiz without groping the deputy's leg or backside. She ran through the possibilities in her head. No way could Diego have alerted anyone, even if he was part of a drug-running gang. Only whoever had been with him would know that Diego and the horse were missing. Had a search dog been brought in to locate them? The only canines she'd seen were the wolves. A search horse? Her lips curved at that silly thought.

"Why are you smiling?" Erickson demanded.

Why did her brain throw out these ridiculous ideas at the most awkward times? She couldn't mention the errant search horse thought. She willed her expression to be somber. Then a memory with the most probable explanation dropped into a slot in her brain. The sky humming. "There may have been a drone. I thought I heard one a short time before the shooting."

The engine noise of the plane taxiing across the water and lifting off stopped that line of interrogation. Before turning around in her seat, Erickson lifted a questioning eyebrow as she mouthed the words, "You *thought* . . .?"

The group was back at the Bellingham airport by eight that evening and agreed to meet there again in twelve hours to board a helicopter, arranged once more by Erickson. Sam didn't seem to have a choice, since she was the only one who had been to the ravine where she found Alec Lysikov, Diego Cruz/Emmanuel Baptiste, and Freckles. In her head, she heard Erickson's voice add, "And the drugs."

As she drove back to her cabin, Sam's legs rippled with cramps, her wounded hand was throbbing with its own heartbeat, and her stomach growled. What in the freezer might be edible? Please let Blake have stowed some of his gourmet leftovers there. The alternative might be sharing a can of cat food with Simon.

When she opened the front door, her cat was lying sprawled across the side table formerly occupied by Gina's parrot, Zeke, in his cage. Simon opened his eyes and flicked his tail a few times, acknowledging Sam's presence, but did not lift his head. "Admit it," she told him. "You miss that bird, don't you?"

He switched his tail hard enough to thwack the table, lifted his head and stared regally through the living room window to the trees beyond, either insulted or simply avoiding the question.

"Or maybe you're just reclaiming your space?" she amended. Simon looked at her and slitted his green eyes.

The house was quiet. Too quiet. She could almost hear the ticking of a grandfather clock. Which was disturbing, because she didn't have a grandfather clock. While she had often disagreed with Blake's choice of dinner preparation music, she missed his tunes. He'd taken his portable stereo system with him.

At the back of the freezer compartment, she found a container labeled BOEUF BOURGUIGNON. She lay her bandaged hand against the frozen package for a few minutes, feeling the pulsing pain subside a bit with the cold. Of course, Blake wouldn't call this beef stew, but after nuking the contents for a few minutes, that's what it turned out to be, except much more delicious than most average Americans would prepare, with hints of red wine, and . . . yes, bacon. Gourmet beef stew. Accompanied by two ibuprofen and a glass of merlot, it was perfect. Her meal would have been improved by a nice crisp salad, but that would require a trip to the grocery store. Maybe in a couple of days.

A thump let her know Simon had jumped from the table, and a meow told her it was time to feed him. After she did, she paced around her house, cradling her right hand against her stomach, at a loss for what to do next. No Blake. No Chase. How had she lived completely alone for years before meeting both those men?

She needed a shower and then bed, but first, she would call her housemate to see how he was getting along with those gorillas. And to tell him thank you for the boeuf bourguignon. Besides, after all she'd been through, she needed an audience who would appreciate the drama and suspense of the last few days, and maybe even sound a wee bit sympathetic.

"Sammie," he answered. "How was the hiking trip?"

"Long story," she said. "Very long story." She ran down the list in her head. "So first, tell me about the gorillas. I need to hear something happy is going on somewhere."

"The baby gorilla got shot."

She chuckled. "You win! Not exactly a happy suggestion, but you made me laugh, anyway."

When Blake did not respond, Sam realized he wasn't kidding. She was rendered speechless for several seconds. "Did you say he got *shot*?" she finally gasped.

"Yep. *She*. Kanoni is her name. Some nutcase came in the middle of the night and shot *her*."

"Oh my God, Blake, did they catch her, I mean him—I mean the shooter?"

"Not yet. But there's this detective who is handling the case. I met him when I interviewed for this gig. The gorillas' owner, or keeper, or handler—I don't know what to call her—Dr. Grace McKenna, is in a relationship with this detective. His name is Matthew Finn. And the vet, Dr. Stephanie Farin, is bringing Kanoni back soon.

"Thank heavens for that. I was going to tell you I got shot, too, while I was out on the trail."

"Really? Are you okay? Did they catch the person who shot you? Was it some hunter who can't aim?"

"No. This was intentional; he was aiming at my cell phone, I think, and he blew that to smithereens. But he also nailed my hand, because I was holding the phone at the time. Unfortunately, I need both hands to earn a living."

"Why was he aiming at any part of you?"

"Probably because I picked up his drugs. Like I said, it's a long story."

Blake sighed. "Why are there crazy people with guns everywhere?"

"Uh . . . this is America?"

"I don't have a response for that." An audible intake of breath indicated Blake was yawning. "Sam, I want to hear the whole story, but—"

She interrupted. "It's complicated, and it's not over yet."

"Same here. Can we save it for later? I'm so tired I can barely stand up."

"Ditto, Blake. I've got to head back to the North Cascades tomorrow morning to show the rangers what's what, but I'll try you again after I get back. Be careful out there. Thanks for the boeuf bourguignon."

"You ate it?"

"Bye, Blake."

33

Evansburg

The adult gorillas were in the barn when Dr. Stephanie Farin brought Kanoni home at twilight, tranquilized and wrapped in a blanket like an extra-large burrito. At the gate to the gorilla enclosure, Farin handed Kanoni to Z, then pulled out a syringe.

"This will reverse the tranquilizer quickly, so please open the gate ASAP and lay her just inside, and then close it in case Gumu and Neema come roaring out."

To Detective Finn, she handed a plastic pill bottle with a metal fragment inside. "The bullet," she said needlessly. "I only touched it with a pair of forceps."

"Good thinking," he told her.

Blake stationed himself next to the latch, his fingers already on it. Farin pulled the blanket down from Kanoni's shoulder, injected her, and then motioned to Blake, who opened the gate. Z quickly positioned the little unconscious ape on the ground on her side just inside the fence, and then slid back out as Blake anxiously watched the barn door. As he double-checked the lock, Kanoni began to stir, whimpering softly.

Only a few seconds had elapsed before Neema and Gumu both appeared in the doorway to the barn, their black fur making them nearly invisible in the shadows. Neema rushed to

Kanoni and gently peeled back the blanket to reveal a large white bandage on the baby's shoulder. The mother gorilla crouched over Kanoni and lowered her head to her baby, sniffing her face and shoulders and even pressing her lips to the bandage as if trying to determine what it was.

Gumu uttered a warning growl and neared the fence. The knot of humans stepped back in unison as if they'd rehearsed the move.

When Kanoni whimpered again, Neema pulled her by one arm out of the blankets, clutching her awkwardly to her chest. After dragging her sleepy daughter back toward the barn, Neema sat on the ground, pulled Kanoni into her arms and pressed her daughter's head against her breasts, inspecting her carefully from her feet to the top of her head. The baby gorilla roused, put her arms around her mother, and pulled one of Neema's elongated nipples into her mouth.

"Is Neema still nursing Kanoni?" Blake asked the veterinarian.

"It's possible," Farin said. "But more likely, that's the gorilla version of a pacifier."

Gumu neared his mate and offspring. Balancing on his feet and one arm, he stretched out the other arm to touch the baby, grunting all the while.

Baby happy me, Neema signed. Blake was pleased he could interpret the gorilla's gestures.

"Kanoni will most likely be okay now," Farin murmured. "Although I suspect that bandage probably won't stay on for long. Call me if she seems lethargic or doesn't eat in the next few days. I've pumped her full of antibiotics, but you never know."

"We won't be able to watch them inside the barn. The camera's not working anymore," Z grimly informed all of them. "Gumu strikes again."

"Well, do the best you can to look out for Kanoni," Farin said. "Pay attention to whether she can use her left arm as well as her right. I'm a bit worried about muscle and nerve damage in that shoulder." She asked Finn, "Any news on the shooter?"

The detective shook his head. "Not yet. I'm working on it."

Blake apparently was not relieved of guard duty. Still, it was a relief to see all three gorillas back in the enclosure and sitting calmly. Night was falling fast, but he could still see the eyes of the trio focused in his direction.

34

Outside the barn door, the go-rillas were very noisy. They were excited. Maybe something good to eat? Rosaline could hear people out there, too, but she couldn't see anything except the brighter light of the door, and she couldn't go there. But she shouldn't, anyway. *Don't let anyone see you.*

She was a little bit cold on top of the nest of blankets, and that made her think of her mama. Was her mama still sleeping? Was she still cold?

The small-big go-rilla would bring her something to eat soon, Rosaline was sure. But she was tired of eating bread and green and white things. Apples were better. Would there be apples?

The mama go-rilla had left her way up high on the platform again. It was a long way to the floor. She couldn't climb down by herself. She needed big feet like hands, like the go-rillas used to wrap around the pole and go up and down. Her hands wouldn't reach around, and her feet didn't work like that. It wasn't fair. It was so dark inside. She wanted to go outside, too.

She crawled to the edge of the platform, sat down there, and wrapped her arms and legs around the pole. She twisted her bottom off the platform and slid down to the next platform, hitting it with her leg. That hurt. She slid again down, down to sit in the dirt. Her arms and legs hurt where she'd wrapped them around the pole, but she was down.

She tottered to the doorway, but stayed in the darkest spots, watching outside. The small small gorilla was back. People stood outside the pen, talking. Loud.

Did they put food in the bin? *Don't let them see you.* She had to wait until the people went away.

35

Pulling out his cell phone, Blake took a quick video of the gorilla family. The video was very dark; maybe he could brighten it somehow before he sent it. If not, he'd try again in the morning, assuming the apes came out of the barn.

"Your baby's back, Neema." He signed the words as he spoke, proud that he'd learned that much. "Everything will be okay now."

Baby love, the mother gorilla signed back. *Baby, baby here.* Even Gumu signed *Baby*, then *Mine, mine, fine gorilla.* Then all three apes rose to their feet and ambled into the dark barn.

Satisfied, Blake stopped the video. He'd be able to sleep peacefully tonight, knowing he wouldn't have to report a disaster to Grace McKenna. He decided to send the video of the gorillas signing to Sam; she'd enjoy it even if it was a little dark.

As soon as he pressed "Send," another text came in. Claude again.

I miss hearing about your day. What have you been up to, love? I'll be in your area in few days. Can I stop by?

Blake was sorely tempted to tell his former lover about the gorillas and the shooting; that would sound exotic and had to be much more exciting than Claude's sales routine or his family life in Canada. Instead, he just deleted the man's text.

Another text arrived, and for a second, he feared that Claude had somehow realized Blake had just deleted his message. But no, the new message was from Ross Irwin, a colleague Blake barely knew from the greenhouse he worked at near Bellingham. Ross had only been with the company a few weeks, and they'd only shared a few shifts, but Blake had liked him on sight. He looked to be a bit older than Blake, with a few gray hairs salting his hairline. When he had told Ross about the cooking classes he was taking in the evening, Ross had told him his own specialty was Ethiopian cuisine; he'd served in the Peace Corps there.

The text was a surprise.

When are you coming back, Blake? The place isn't the same without you. I think we have a lot in common. I'd like to get to know you better.

Interesting. Did Ross know he was gay? Blake wasn't closeted, but he kept his private life, well, private. Was Ross gay? Blake had suspected he might be, and while a twentysomething might just ask nowadays, most men in their age bracket didn't run around broadcasting their history. After all, Blake had been married to a woman and was the father of a teenage daughter. Maybe Ross had a similar history. While Bellingham was a very progressive town, not all its citizens progressed at the same rate.

36

The noise outside went on for a long while, and then finally the people voices went away. The go-rillas came into the barn. Now there were three of them. The littlest go-rilla climbed up the pole first. It had a white bandage on it, and it smelled like medicine. The mama go-rilla picked up Rosaline and carried her up the pole and sat her down next to the nest of blankets. She had two bananas in her mouth, and she gave one to Rosaline and one to the new small go-rilla. When that littlest go-rilla saw Rosaline, it poked her with a finger and then smelled her.

Then it screeched and raised up its arms, and then it smacked her on the head, hitting her hard. Rosaline screamed and started to cry. The littlest go-rilla leaned close, like it was going to bite her, and Rosaline scooted as far away as she could. The mama go-rilla pulled the littlest away from Rosaline, wrapping one long black arm around the littlest and hugging her on one side, against the mama go-rilla's stomach.

Rosaline's head hurt. She sobbed as she opened her banana. Her arms and legs hurt where they'd rubbed against the pole. She didn't want to slide down again. But she wanted her own mama. When would she get to see her own mama? She wanted to go home.

Then the mama gorilla wrapped her other arm around Rosaline and hugged her tight. The littlest go-rilla looked at her with mean eyes from under the mama's other arm, and Rosaline pressed her face against the furry side of the mama go-rilla so she didn't have to see. The mama go-rilla pulled the blanket over Rosaline's head, and they all lay down to sleep.

In the morning, Rosaline would climb on that mama go-rilla's back and make her take her down to the ground. Then she'd find a way out.

37

North Cascades

The next day was both exhilarating and terrifying as the helicopter flew low over the spectacular terrain of the North Cascades. The group had allowed her a window seat this time. Sam struggled to quash her acrophobia as she surveyed the dizzying landscape below.

The pilot, Alberto Solis, a grizzled, square-headed fellow with the air of ex-military, had asked her to direct him, and she insisted they begin at the site where she'd camped, then fly a little south and west of Spratt Mountain. The view of that peak brought back warm memories of seeing the wolves gamboling on the wooded hillside there. Then she instructed Solis to fly in an expanding spiral. As a scuba diver, she'd learned this search technique to find a lost diver, and it seemed the pilot and ranger knew it, too.

After she finally spotted what she thought was the location of the rockslide, they were blocked by steep hillsides and forest. Solis tried to land the chopper in a small clearing on the top of a hill about a mile and a half away. As they dropped in elevation, even that purchase proved too rocky and unstable, with no flat surface bigger than six feet across. The pilot expertly hovered a couple of feet above the ground as the four of their party sat down one by one in the open doorway and leaped to the ground.

"I'll land near Lightning Creek Campground," Solis told them. "And I'll meet you back here. Call when you're ready to be picked up." He tossed a handheld radio to Ranger Castro.

Carole Erickson narrowed her eyes at that, conflicting expressions crossing her face. Sam guessed the investigator assumed she should be in charge of all communications. But the ranger was the person most likely to know the park and its topography.

The investigator and Deputy Ortiz traded complaints as they hiked down the rocky slope, viewing the multiple steep hills and deep gulleys creasing the landscape ahead. Sam sulked silently. She was the person who should be complaining. She was wounded, she was worn out, and she'd been shanghaied into this forced march by the authorities surrounding her.

"Why the hell would you come here?" Erickson demanded to know, panting and glaring at her as the party emerged from the second ravine onto the ridge above. "Why would you choose this godforsaken area?"

Sam had to unlock her jaw before answering, "I didn't exactly plan it. I was on my way back from filming the wolves near Spratt Mountain, and I came across a game trail." She pointed to the narrow path they'd just stumbled onto minutes ago. It had better be the trail she remembered; all the tracks looked pretty much the same through the brush. "I thought it might be a quicker route back to my camp if the trail turned west."

It was the correct game trail, as soon proven by hoofprints and prints from her hiking boots in the few spots dampened by the nightly dew. As the group approached the brushy ravine, Sam pointed out the rockslide: "And then I saw . . ." her voice trailed off as she thrust her index finger toward the scrap of red in the rocks, and the backpack strap.

"Our missing hiker," Castro finished, beginning the steep climb down to the remains.

Sam stayed in place on the trail with Erickson, pointing to the clumps of brush halfway down the ravine, where she'd found the injured man and horse. Broken branches indicated the route they'd forged through the vegetation.

"How'd they get down there?" Erickson asked.

Sam waited a beat to see if the investigator would answer her own question, but she didn't. "I'd guess Diego, I mean Emmanuel, was riding the mare when she got spooked and fell off the trail, taking her rider with her."

Erickson frowned. "I thought you said the horse was outfitted as a packhorse, not for riding."

"She was," Sam assured her. "If you don't believe me, you can ask the wrangler, Wiley, who took her at the trailhead. Ranger Castro was there, too. If Emmanuel had been riding another horse, he wouldn't have ended up at the bottom of the ravine. Did you ask *him*?"

The investigator ignored the question. "How does a horse *fall* off a trail?"

Sam thought about the few intelligible words the man had uttered. "He said something about wolves, I think. So maybe there were wolves on the trail, or maybe they heard howls and the horse just spooked. It happens. As you can see, the trail right here has mostly fallen away, so it might be hard for a heavy four-legged animal to navigate, especially with panniers on both sides and a man on top. It's a miracle both man and horse survived."

"Uh-huh," Erickson's voice radiated suspicion. "And that you found them. What a coincidence."

What was it with this woman? After a last questioning glare at Sam, Erickson clambered down the slope, trailing Deputy

Ortiz, dislodging a few loose stones along the way.

From her vantage point above on the trail, Sam watched Amelia Castro below as the ranger examined the rockslide area. Exclamations drifted up from Ortiz and Erickson as they plowed through the thorny brush in the ravine. Sam was grateful they hadn't insisted she accompany them. Finding an uncomfortable rock of convenient height, Sam sat. When Chase had driven her home after her disastrous hiking trip, she'd thought she was done with this section of the park and this story. Instead, she seemed to be caught in an endless loop of repeating the same tale and even visiting the same remote areas again.

She studied the landscape beyond the rockfall that had obliterated a section of the trail, remembering she'd wondered if the game trail would skirt the gulley and continue south back toward the parking lot or bend west, as she'd hoped a few days ago. She stood and pulling herself up on a root, she stepped cautiously over the river of rocks. Several stones slid a few inches, but then stopped.

"Where are you going?" Ortiz shouted from below.

"Not far," she shouted back.

The narrow path meandered a bit but continued mostly south through the forest. Most interesting, she discovered a section of damp dirt containing more hoofprints, many overlaying each other, proving multiple horses had traveled this way.

"Westin! Where are you?" Erickson's voice.

"Coming!" She snapped a photo of the prints before turning back.

She'd returned to her sitting rock on the trail by the time the three others had climbed back up.

"How'd you get the horse and Baptiste back up here?" Castro wanted to know.

"It wasn't easy," Sam told her. "But they both wanted out. Freckles was such a willing horse, even though she was injured. And Emmanuel was motivated."

"I'll bet. So you know that horse by name?" Erickson pressed.

Sam shook her head. "She's a leopard appy, and I had to call her something."

Ortiz raised an eyebrow. "Leopard appy?"

"Appaloosa, with spots all over. Like freckles," she explained. "And look, she wasn't the only horse on the trail." She held out her camera with the photo of the multiple hoofprints on the screen.

"Drug smugglers for sure," Ortiz muttered.

Everyone nodded, and Ranger Castro promised to arrange for a more thorough examination of the trail later. She added, "I'm surprised the smuggling crew left a man behind."

"I can envision exactly how it happened," Sam told them. "Freckles was no doubt the last horse in a pack train, and slid off the trail after the preceding horses had loosened the rubble left from the past landslide. Their fall probably made a hell of a racket. It's likely both the mare and the rider screamed, and the rest of the drug runners took off to be sure they could escape."

"They probably thought they were both dead. No honor among thieves." Erickson tapped Sam's wrist. "Send me that photo."

"Okay." Sam continued, "Whoever was in charge of transporting the drugs came back later, looking for their lost shipment. And found my tracks instead. And then my camp."

"I'll have to arrange to get a body recovery team out here for Alec Lysikov," Castro interjected.

Ortiz and Erickson looked startled at the ranger's statement. Castro rolled her eyes. "The missing hiker?"

Sam guessed they'd totally forgotten about the missing man

in their excitement over assembling the probable pieces of a drug smuggling operation. After they'd mulled it over for few seconds, Castro added, "Unrelated to the horse or drug thing. The rockslide that buried him was weeks ago. Probably was a snowslide on top when it happened."

As they hiked back to the rendezvous spot with the helicopter, Sam thought about Freckles, about the self-sacrificing way the injured mare just kept on going. She was definitely going to call Wiley, the wrangler with the alluring eyes, and ask if he had discovered who owned her. Maybe she could visit the mare.

She wanted to visit Emmanuel, too. She couldn't believe he had been involved in smuggling drugs. An experienced smuggler would have arranged to ride in a comfortable saddle, not astride a horse outfitted with a wooden frame and panniers.

Maybe she could visit him in the hospital? Would he be under guard as a suspected smuggler? Would the authorities protect him from the smugglers who might want to silence him?

Wait a minute! An alarm began to buzz in her head. Should *she* be under guard? "*I'm* the one who got shot," she abruptly said aloud. "Am *I* in danger?"

38

They all stopped, Erickson and Ortiz panting from exertion. No one seemed surprised by Sam's question. "Did the shooter ever see you?" Ortiz asked.

Sam shook her head. "I don't think so. It was dark. He aimed at the light on my phone, and next, my flashlight." She was still peeved about losing that pocket flashlight during her escape.

"Then watch your back," Ortiz advised. "But it seems like you're safe."

"As long as you weren't involved," Erickson added. "And you don't go blabbing."

Sam couldn't wait to be rid of the HSI officer. Her own foul humor was made worse by the fact she had only an antique energy bar in her pack for sustenance. When the ranger handed her a brown paper bag containing a sandwich and an apple, that helped her mood immensely. Amelia Castro was proving to be a kindred spirit indeed.

After regaining the mountaintop where they'd been dropped, Castro summoned the helicopter, which arrived twenty minutes later. Again, Solis didn't want to touch down, so he hovered a couple of feet above the ground. Ortiz clambered in first, and hauled the other three of them in by their arms. Although he tried to tug on her forearm instead of her bandaged right hand and wrist, Sam ended up landing inside on both hands and knees, which hurt like hell. Erickson commandeered the passenger seat up front next to the pilot. Sam had been bumped to the rear middle again, so she crawled there, and held her breath as the chopper rose from the ground before Castro managed to fully close the door.

After they landed at the Bellingham airport, Erickson demanded Sam and Castro immediately collaborate to produce a marked topo map showing Sam's wandering routes on the day she'd found Emmanuel and the horse.

"Tomorrow morning," Sam responded wearily, sharing a look with Ranger Castro.

Erickson opened her mouth to protest.

"Tomorrow," Castro quickly agreed. "I'll find a decent topo of the area and meet you at the sheriff's office. But not before nine."

"Let's meet at nine thirty," Sam answered.

Castro and Sam walked off in different directions, leaving Deputy Ortiz grumbling about needing to reserve the conference room again and Erickson standing with her hands on her hips and a scowl on her face.

After checking her watch, Sam realized the Ski to Sea relay race had already concluded. The winners would have hit the beach hours ago. She bit her lip, sorry to have missed Bellingham's biggest event of the year. But she knew the celebrations would be ongoing in the Fairhaven district, the site of Marine Park, where the kayakers in the last leg ran up and rang the bell, signifying their team's finish.

Instead of returning to her lonely house and empty refrigerator, she headed for the music and food booths in Fairhaven. After a day of reliving her experiences with corpses and faceless would-be murderers, she needed to share a couple of hours with carefree people.

Sam ran into her friend Gina at one of the Fairhaven beer gardens. "How's the hand?" Gina immediately asked.

In answer, Sam held up her bandaged limb. The elastic wrap that encased her palm and fingers was stained with blood and dirt.

Gina pulled a face. "Nasty. Is Chase helping you with that?"

"He's back at work, out at Quinault right now. I've been in the Ross Lake Recreation Area all day, showing the ranger, the cop, and a super snotty investigator all the exciting places I've been in the last few days. We hiked for miles all over the place."

"That explains it," Gina said.

"Explains what?"

Her friend held her nose by way of demonstration.

"Sorry," Sam apologized. "I know I need a shower, but I totally missed Ski to Sea, and I had nothing in the fridge, so—" Her words trailed off as she waved a hand to encompass the noisy party around them.

Gina grinned. "Fortunately, I'm used to stinky beasts." The two women had met and bonded years ago on a wolverine research project. Wolverines, nicknamed "skunk bears," were famously odiferous creatures.

"Hey!" Sam protested.

Gina offered to help Sam change the dressing on her hand, and after sharing beers and hot dogs and Sam's wolf stories, they met back at Sam's house. On unwrapping her friend's bandage, Gina remarked, "That's a really ugly sculpture, but it sort of resembles a hand, don't you think?"

From the tips of three fingers down to her wrist, Sam's hand was swollen and blackish purple, with a ragged wound between her second and third fingers. "You're not going to be able to type for a long while," Gina concluded.

Sam groaned. "Maybe I'll surprise you. I *have* to surprise my editor. Since I missed my Ski to Sea assignment, my bank account will soon be near zero. I've got to write."

"Good luck with that." After completing the rebandaging job by fastening the outer elastic wrap with a clasp, Gina stood up. "Need help fixing this for a shower?"

"I can pull a plastic bag over it. Thanks, girlfriend."

"Anytime, Skunk Girl."

"Out!" Sam pointed to the door.

She noticed that she had a text from Blake, sent yesterday evening. The baby gorilla is back! Attached was a video clip and an additional note: This is a little dark, but I wanted you to see it. She hit "Play" and watched a big gorilla drag a small one from the fence to the outer wall of the barn. Neema and her daughter Kanoni. Neema examined Kanoni all over, smelling and nuzzling her. The small gorilla wore a white bandage on one shoulder.

A huge silverback appeared next to them. He gently poked at the youngster with a long black finger. Gumu, Kanoni's father.

She heard Blake's familiar voice reassuring the gorillas. Neema turned and made a couple of signs to the camera. A brief rocking gesture, followed by the universal sign, crossed arms for *love*. Baby love, maybe? Clearly the gorillas were content again. Sam was glad for Blake.

She sent him a message with a thumb-up emoji and then moved the slider back a bit to watch the signing again. This time she noticed a shadow move in the background. What was that? She restarted the video and watched carefully. Either she was losing her mind or the dark video was deceptive or a small child was standing half-hidden in the shadows, hugging the dark doorway of the barn.

Is it safe to have a small child in there with the apes? she texted Blake.

Her housemate did not immediately respond, and she guessed he was busy with gorilla care, whatever that consisted of. Or he'd misplaced his cell phone again, as he often did. He usually found it within a few hours.

She sent another message: Can I come visit soon?

After showering, Sam was so tired she headed to bed at 9:00 p.m. But only minutes after she'd shut her eyes, her phone buzzed.

Probably Erickson, checking the whereabouts of her number one suspect. For exactly which crime, Sam wasn't sure.

"What?" she demanded on answering. Simon laid his ears back and leaped off the bed.

"I love you, that's what."

She sat up in bed, shocked to hear Chase say those words. In English, no less. He generally murmured all his affections in Spanish, in a low, sexy voice. "I'm sorry, Chase. I was asleep and I thought you were this annoying investigator."

"I have been called that more than once," he said. "What are you doing in bed at this hour? It's only"—there was a brief hesitation while he checked—"nine twelve p.m. What's going on? How's your hand? What annoying investigator?"

"Oh yeesh, Chase. They've had me flying back and forth to Ross Lake for the last two days to show them where everything happened. This HSI gal, Carole Erickson, acts like I was involved somehow."

After another hesitation, he said, "I can see how it would look suspicious to her."

So much for sympathy. "I'm sick of explaining every little detail over and over. And I talked to Blake. He's not having a great time, either. What's up at Quinault?"

"I wish you were here with me." Electronic dings and chimes of slot machines filled the background.

"In a casino? No, thanks." She could almost smell the cigarette smoke. Or did people still smoke in casinos these days? The casino Chase was speaking from was on the reservation; she supposed smoking regulations were up to the tribe.

He interrupted her mental meanderings on gambling and smoking. "I was thinking more about romantic walks along the seashore. Sunshine, warm sand, waves gently rolling in off the magnificent blue Pacific . . ."

That image made her moan with longing. "But you're working, right?"

"Finally!" He failed to disguise the enthusiasm in his voice. "A real case in my jurisdiction. I'm checking out questionable financial processes at the casino."

She leaned back against her pillow. "Are there ever financial processes at a casino that *aren't* questionable?"

"A couple of employees who might be involved are in the wind, so I need to track them down."

"Sounds like fun." *Not,* she added in her head. "Unfortunately, I need to work, too."

"But you can write from anywhere, correct?"

Sam scoffed, "That's a common misconception among nonwriters. Simon needs me. And I need to be able to unexpectedly drop in on law enforcement types who won't answer my calls."

"Seems more likely they might unexpectedly drop in on you," Chase observed.

Sam thought about Erickson's suspicions. "Probably true. Damn it."

He made a huffing sound, which might have been an aborted laugh or an expression of frustration. "Okay, so you're not coming right now. What's up with Blake and those gorillas?"

"Someone shot the baby gorilla a few days ago."

"What?"

"She spent a few days at the vet's. She's back home now. But they don't have a clue who shot her, or why. Why are there yahoos with guns everywhere these days?"

"Tell me more about the shooting. As for your second question, what can I say? Those yahoos keep all of us law enforcement types employed."

They talked for a few more minutes, during which time Simon returned and crawled into her lap. The cat grew drowsy as she stroked his fur, slowly closing his eyes, his purr fading. Sam was fading fast, too.

She concluded the conversation. "Stay safe, *mi amor*."

"Seems like you're the one who needs that advice," he said. "*Te amo*, Summer."

"I love you, too, Chase."

39

"Matt?" Grace asked as soon as Finn answered his phone the next day. "What's going on there in Evansburg? When are you coming back?"

He hesitated, turning his back on the gorilla enclosure. What could he tell her that wouldn't send her rushing for the first plane home? He swallowed and said, "A body was found in an abandoned house."

She gasped. "In Evansburg?"

"In the county, but you know how the sheriff's department depends on mutual assistance. It looks like a domestic dispute. And as I am the only experienced detective in cases like this, it might take a while to solve. I'm moving it along as fast as I can. I'm sorry."

"You don't need to be sorry. I just miss you." He heard a horn honk in the background.

"Me too," he said. "I'll be back as soon as I can. Where are you?"

"Farmers market. You wouldn't believe all the luscious fruit here. The ripe pineapples and mangos are to die for."

"While the rock-hard fruit in the market here might actually kill you," he joked. The noise behind him increased. Kanoni was apparently feeling like the three-year-old she was this morning, rushing around, twirling in circles and picking up toys, begging Neema to chase her and tickle her, cackling maniacally.

"I hear gorillas. Don't tell me I don't hear gorillas."

"Yes, I'm at your place, Grace," he admitted. "The gorillas are fine. Here, I'll show you." He turned on the camera and held the phone out toward the gorilla enclosure.

Neema chased Kanoni a few times, but then retreated to the food bin, where she inspected the contents. Seeming disappointed by the cauliflower and broccoli and whole-grain bread, she signed *cookie* to the humans standing outside the fence, her eyes hopeful.

The baby gorilla, seeing her mother's signs, repeated *cookie cookie cookie* in Finn's direction. Or maybe the signs were aimed for Blake, who stood beside him, watching the antics.

Grace's voice emanated from his phone. "Is that a bandage on Kanoni's shoulder?"

He'd forgotten about that. "Uh, yeah. She got a little hurt, but Dr. Farin and Blake took care of it, and now she'll be fine in a few days."

"What happened? How did she get hurt?"

"Don't worry about it, Grace, honey. That's why I came out, to check for you and see if everything is being handled. And it is. Blake and Z are on it." He pointed the phone at Blake, who accommodated by smiling and making an okay signal with his right hand. Finn turned the camera off and pressed the phone back to his ear. "Don't worry about it," he repeated. "I'll be back as soon as I can. I need to go now. I love you." He ended the call, hoping she was reassured.

"Looks like everything's back to normal," Finn commented to Blake. He eyed the contents of the gorillas' food bin. "Have you been feeding them a lot of cauliflower?"

Blake arched an eyebrow in surprise. "As directed by Dr. McKenna, I feed them vegetables and fruits and whole-grain bread. Why do you ask?"

Finn shrugged, thinking of the curious piece of cauliflower by the dead woman's head.

"I suspect some creature is stealing from the food bin," Blake told him. "I found a piece of cauliflower out there by the woods a couple of days ago." He pointed in that direction. "Z told me that crows have been known to steal the gorilla food."

"Interesting," Finn remarked, his eyes briefly focusing in the direction of the forest and then swiveling back to study the opening in the fence above the food bin. Anyone could reach an arm in there to grab food. Small animals and birds could also get in. In his exploration, he'd found a crust of bread, and he'd assumed a hiker had lost a piece of his sandwich.

"Say, Blake, while you've been here, have you heard anything about Haitians in the area?"

The guy was taken aback. "Haitians? Are there normally a lot of people from Haiti in Evansburg?"

"No, but ask Z when he gets up, okay? And what happened to Maya?"

"Maya took off for New Mexico yesterday afternoon. She got a call from her half sister's mother and just left."

Finn briefly wondered if Maya Velasquez had permission to leave the state, given she was involved in a pending court case. But he had enough on his plate; he wasn't going to add anything more. "Half sister's mother?"

"It's complicated." Blake said. "Maya had a drug-addict mother and a missing father who got found a few years ago. Dead. And then a half sister. And she was bored out of her mind here, which, with Maya, means she was an inch away from getting into trouble." He waved a hand in the air as if to dismiss the whole snarl of history. "What's this about Haitians?"

Finn decided to come clean, in case Blake or Zyrnek might notice clues he had missed. "Keep this to yourself, but a dead woman found in the area turns out to be a migrant from Haiti."

Blake's expression was concerned. "Is this drug related?"

Good question. "I don't know yet."

"Was she shot?"

Finn supposed the guy had jumped to that conclusion because of Kanoni's shooting. He didn't want to divulge any details yet. "It's still an active investigation."

"Any news on *our* shooter?" Blake asked. "It's alarming to think he's still out there somewhere."

"Still following up leads," Finn answered. "Do you know anything about the house through the woods back there?" He pointed north, beyond the barn.

Blake shook his head. "I didn't even know there *was* a house back there." He shifted from one foot to the other and ran his fingers through his short dark hair, betraying his discomfort with that idea. "How far away is it? Is *that* where you found the dead woman? Do the owners of that house have guns? Do you think our shooter came from there?"

Finn was saved from answering all those questions when Z emerged from the staff trailer, letting the screen door bounce shut behind him with a clap.

"Maybe Z knows something," Blake suggested.

The crunch of gravel in the driveway drew the attention of all three men. Rebecca Ramey stepped out of her car, clad from the waist up in a professional-looking red blazer, and from the waist down in blue jeans and sneakers. The cell phone in her hand was already aimed in their direction.

"Shit," Finn said under his breath.

Blake groaned. "I second that."

The screen door on the staff trailer slapped again as Z vanished inside. Blake seemed poised to do the same at any second.

"Detective Finn!" Ramey beamed her ultrawhite smile as she strode toward them, her cell phone camera fixed on Finn.

He waved a hand toward the gorilla enclosure. "As you can see, Miz Ramey, everything's back to normal now."

"Call me Rebecca," she crooned. "We're old friends, after all."

Finn grimaced, but said nothing, hoping Ramey's cell phone hadn't recorded that. The last thing he needed was that "old friends" comment circulating in town.

"Normal? I wouldn't say *anything* was normal," Ramey commented. "You haven't tracked down the shooter, have you?" She waited, her large blue eyes expectant. The eager expression on her face reminded Finn of Cargo when he was preparing the dog's dinner.

"We're following several leads," he told her.

Her lips curved up in a slight smile. "And now you have a murder on your hands as well."

Beside him, Blake startled and turned in Finn's direction. "What? That Haitian woman was murdered?"

Finn's gaze stayed focused on the reporter, and he clenched his jaw for a few seconds. "No comment," he tried.

"No comment?" She raised her voice to a shout. "*No comment?* We have a murderer running around, and the police have no comment?"

This situation was quickly becoming a train wreck. Finn abruptly pulled his cell phone from his jacket pocket and frowned at the screen. "Excuse me," he said to the reporter and Blake. "I've got to take this. In private." He race-walked to his car, holding his phone to his chest so nobody could see that the screen was blank.

40

Blake watched the detective slide into his car. He suspected that Finn's phone call was a ruse to escape the reporter.

A cell phone buzzed, and Blake finally spied his on the picnic table, where he'd probably left it last evening. He walked over and picked it up, expecting a message from Detective Finn to tell him what was going on. But no, it was a cryptic text from Sam Westin: Well? Blake thumbed through messages she'd left last night, then gasped and quickly pulled up the video he'd sent her, stretching the dark window to a larger size on the screen.

"Oh my God!" He slapped a hand over his mouth.

"What's up?" Rebecca Ramey hovered at his elbow, her attention darting back and forth from Detective Finn's car to Blake's face.

Alarm bells were clanging in his head, but Blake wasn't about to show the reporter Sam's text or the video he'd sent her.

"Detective Finn better be coming back." Ramey tossed her head and glared at Finn's car, where he was still pretending to talk on the phone. At least he was holding it to his ear and nodding now and then, although his lips weren't moving. With a disgusted snort, Ramey focused on Blake and repeated, "What's up with *you*? Interesting news on your phone? Anything to do with this case?"

Blake's thoughts were reeling. Surely it couldn't be real,

could it? A little girl in the gorilla barn? Maybe a trick of the evening shadows? And a murderer on the loose? Ramey edged closer. Blake quickly shoved his phone back into his pocket. "Personal drama."

Marching intently toward the staff trailer, Blake pulled the phone back out and texted Detective Finn. Urgent. Need to talk to you. As he opened the door, he watched with dismay as the detective turned his car around and drove down the long driveway to the street.

"Shit!" Rebecca Ramey yelled, thrusting both arms in the air. Then she started after Blake, who quickly closed and locked the door of the staff trailer behind him.

Z waited inside, drinking a cup of some herbal tea that smelled like stewed hay. "She's still here, isn't she? Save yourself, man."

A few seconds later, Ramey pounded on the door. They both ignored the loud thumps as Z reviewed the video on Blake's phone. He started to hand it back, commenting, "Happy gorillas. Neema signing. What's the big deal?" He glanced at the door, which bounced with each blow of Ramey's fist. "Damn it," he cursed under his breath. "Just go, girl!"

As Ramey's footsteps finally thudded down the steps and then faded away, Blake pushed the phone back at Z. "Back up the video. Focus on the doorway of the barn."

Z's frown intensified as he followed Blake's instructions. "No way! Is that . . . ? It can't be!" His eyes met Blake's. "How the hell did a kid get in there?"

They both stared at each other for a long moment, each clearly hoping the other would come up with a good answer.

When a knock sounded on the door, they both jumped. "Finn here," the detective announced. "Come out, come out. The wicked witch is gone."

"Gone where the goblins go, oh ho," Z murmured, following Blake out to the courtyard between the trailers and the gorilla barn.

Finn stopped at the picnic table and put one foot up on the bench, turning to Blake. "You wanted to talk to me? Urgently?"

"I thought you'd left," Blake said.

"I have my hiding spots," the detective told them.

"We have a big problem," Blake said. "I think there's a small child in the gorilla barn."

Finn laughed. "What would make you think that?"

Blake shared the video. "Look closely at the barn doorway."

The detective's expression jetted from amused to anxious. "Christ." He handed the phone back to Blake, and then focused on Z. "Can you get in and look?"

Shaking his head, Z backed a step, holding his hands in the air. "I'm not going in there, man. Gumu's been in attack mode since the shooting."

"Maybe we can get Neema to tell us?" the detective suggested.

"Grace might be able to convince her," Z hinted.

Finn licked his lips and said, "I don't want to involve Grace if we don't have to. She needs this gorilla-free time."

"May I suggest bribery?" Blake headed for his trailer. "I'm going for cookies."

"Get the gate key, too," Finn yelled after him.

Supplied with sufficient material for bribery, the three of them stood at the fence. "Neema," Z called, signing as he did so, "Is there a baby inside?"

Neema glanced at Kanoni. *"Here baby,"* she signed, then, *"Kanoni here."*

"Kanoni's outside," Z said. "Is there *another* baby inside?" He repeated the sign for "inside," sliding the fingers of one hand behind the other upraised hand. "More baby inside?"

The mother gorilla folded her arms in a show of stubbornness.

"Bring the other baby outside," Detective Finn said, his tone stern.

Z signed the detective's words. Neema sat in her hunched position, staring at their faces. Finally, she signed, *"Cookie."*

"Bring the other baby out," Finn repeated.

Z repeated the message, and then added, "Trade. Trade for cookie."

Blake held up a cookie. All three gorillas were interested now.

Neema looked doubtful, glancing first at the cookie and then at the barn door, and then back at the cookie. Kanoni made excited ape sounds, signed *cookie cookie cookie*, twirled in place once, and then vanished into the barn.

"Cookie," Neema signed. Gumu repeated the gesture.

"Trade," Finn insisted.

A child's screams erupted from inside the barn.

"Jesus!" Blake yelped. "Is Kanoni killing her?"

"I sincerely hope not." Finn crossed his arms impatiently.

On all fours, Neema scrambled inside the barn. Gumu walked closer to the fence, sitting only a few inches away from the feeding portal. *"Cookie now,"* he signed, glaring at Blake.

The shrieks continued, along with a small child's sobs. *"Nooooo!"*

Then Kanoni dragged a screeching dark-skinned toddler out of the shadows into the sunshine, clutching the little girl fiercely by one arm and yanking her through the dirt. Blake winced, knowing the strength of an ape, even a young one.

Neema intervened, putting her arms around the child and pushing Kanoni away. The little toddler burrowed her face into Neema's chest, sobbing and moaning, *"Nooooooo, nooooo."*

"Cookie," Gumu signed again. So did Kanoni. Even Neema repeated that.

"Bring that baby to the gate," Finn instructed, seeming amazingly calm, even pointing to the gate in the fence. "Then trade." He nodded at Z, who translated.

Blake thought he might have a heart attack. This was the weirdest hostage negotiation that he'd ever heard of. Placing the cookies on the picnic table, he pulled out his cell phone, wishing he'd thought to film the earlier interaction. Sam was not going to believe this.

"Oh my God! Who is *that*?" Rebecca Ramey dashed up to the fence, holding her cell phone in front of her. "How could you put a toddler in a pen with three gorillas?"

"Nobody put her in there," Finn told her, his eyes still on Neema and the baby girl. "Stay out of this, Rebecca." He repeated, "Bring the baby to the gate, Neema. Then cookie."

Gumu growled and stood up, beating his fists against his leathery chest in a loud tattoo.

Cookie, cookie, cookie, Kanoni signed, then yanked the little girl out of Neema's embrace, pulling her by one arm in the direction of the gate. The baby girl screamed in fright or pain or both, and Neema reached out, taking hold of the girl's ankle, stretching the child between her and Kanoni. The shrieks increased in volume.

"Oh my God. Oh my God!" Ramey gasped, her camera focused on the scene. "They're going to kill her. How can you let this go on?"

Shooting the reporter an angry glare, Finn walked around Rebecca Ramey and stopped in front of the gate. "Bring that baby here now!" he shouted. Then, "Blake, cookies!"

Blake awkwardly held his cell phone, hoping he was aiming correctly, while he trotted in Finn's direction with the cookies, holding the treats up so the gorillas could see them.

Neema finally gave up the battle of wits, and she and Kanoni transported the sobbing child to the gate, the mother gorilla dragging her by one leg and Kanoni hauling her by the arm.

When Neema, Kanoni, and the shrieking toddler were at the gate, Blake nervously unlocked the heavy padlock, panicking as Gumu started in their direction.

Fortunately, Z noticed, too. "Gumu," he shouted, dashing to the food portal. "Cookie! Gumu, cookie!" He shoved a cookie through the opening, leaving it balancing on the edge of the metal bin inside.

The silverback glanced at the cookie and then at the scene by the gate, and made his decision, returning to the far corner of the enclosure for the cookie. As he neared, he bared his teeth to Z, but then, with a snort, sat and pressed the cookie to his lips.

Opening the gate, Detective Finn pulled out the little girl, then took the cookies from Blake and tossed them inside before closing and locking the gate.

"Who the hell is that?" Ramey pressed, speaking loudly so her voice would be captured on the cell phone video. "What's happening?"

Finn told her to put the phone down.

Blake crouched beside the hysterical child. "Sweetheart." He tried to make his voice soothing. "Are you okay?" Her dirty face was smudged with tears. Snot trailed from her nostrils. A strand of hair hung loose on the right side of her head. He gently touched her on the arm.

"Nooooooo," she sobbed, looking up at him. "No, no, no!"

Underneath all the tears and dirt, the girl was beautiful. Her eyes were dark brown and glistening, her skin was the color of strong coffee, her black hair twisted into dozens of tiny braids along her scalp. Someone loved this child.

She began to crawl away on her hands and knees, and Blake grabbed the back of her shirt. The tiny girl screeched like a bird when he picked her up, but then fell against his chest, sobbing and hiccupping. Carrying her to the picnic table, he sat down on a bench, cradling her in his arms and stroking her head and back. "It's okay, sweetie. You're going to be okay."

Z sat down heavily on the other bench, shaking his head. "I can't believe all this. Grace is going to have a cow. Or more like a water buffalo."

At the gate, Rebecca Ramey and Finn were engaged in a loud argument about privacy and freedom of the press and the public's right to know.

The girl felt so small and light in Blake's lap. A baby bird that had fallen out of a nest. He remembered what his daughter Hannah was like as a toddler. This child had to be so frightened to be alone among strange people and strange animals. She'd be hungry and thirsty, too.

"I'm taking her into my trailer," he announced to Z as he stood up with the child in his arms. "She needs food and water and a bath and clean clothes."

He had no idea how he was going to provide clothing for a toddler. She probably needed medical attention, too, but that would have to wait until she was calmer.

Rebecca Ramey pounded a fist against the chain link fence of the enclosure. "Answers, Detective Finn. I'll be back for them. You know I can find you."

She turned on her heel and strode back to her car. Inside the fence, the three gorillas sat in a row, their backs against the barn, signing, *"Cookie, cookie, cookie,"* over and over again. But at least they were quiet. To the west, storm clouds were gathering, and the forecast was for a thunderstorm this evening. He'd get Z to feed the apes the fruit, vegetables, and bread that he'd cut up this morning. And then, with luck, all three apes would retreat into their barn for a quiet night.

That might end the gorilla drama for now, but clearly, the human drama was just beginning.

41

Finn sat in his recliner, staring at the sun setting behind the mountains to the west beyond his sliding door. Both cats lay across in his lap, and he held a glass of Scotch in his right hand that Cargo was eyeing from the side of his chair.

Stunned, Finn decided, was the best adjective to describe how he was feeling at this moment. The dark-skinned child was most likely the toddler missing from the abandoned house, and the dead woman her mother. But what had happened to the man who had been living with them? Had he murdered Widelene Pierre? Had he shot Kanoni? What could his motive be? Tomorrow morning, he'd hike the area from the gorilla enclosure to the abandoned house and hope to find footprints or other signs of travel between the two properties.

How the heck had the kid gotten into the gorilla cage? He hadn't reported the girl's discovery to his colleagues before he'd headed home. There were no Child Protective Services immediately available in Evansburg, and he doubted there were foster parents available, either.

Blake had seemed to know how to take care of a toddler, so he'd left the girl in that man's capable hands. The authorities would either be annoyed or relieved at that. The fly in the ointment was Rebecca Ramey, who remained clueless about how all the pieces fit together but had still witnessed and filmed most of the commotion.

When Cargo leaned too close to his drink, Finn shifted it to his other hand. The dog whined and trotted around the chair. When Finn shifted it again, Cargo repeated the performance.

"Doofus, you're making me dizzy." Upending the glass, Finn emptied the small amount of remaining liquor into his mouth and set the glass on the table.

Cargo eagerly stuck his tongue into it, sliming the glass and slurping up an ice cube, which he promptly dropped on the carpet. The dog tried again and managed to keep the ice in his mouth long enough for an obviously satisfying crunch before two pieces escaped his slobbery lips. One flipped into the chair with Finn and the cats, and Lok, disgusted, leaped off and slinked down the hallway toward the bedroom, switching his tail from side to side.

The phone chimed and Finn retrieved it from the table to his right. Grace, of course. He pressed the speakerphone button, and told her, "I think I have an alcoholic dog."

"Matthew Finn!" Grace sounded as if she were berating him from across the room instead of from Kauai. "I just read *What's Up, Evansburg.*"

"Okay." Man oh man, that Ramey gal was fast. Finn thumbed the phone screen to find the blog.

Oh, sweet Jesus! In the latest post, Ramey had added to her list of inflammatory questions designed to make his life miserable.

WHAT'S UP, EVANSBURG?

How did a baby girl end up in a gorilla pen?

Who shot Kanoni, the youngest gorilla?

Who is the dead woman found in the derelict farmhouse near the gorilla compound?

Does Detective Matthew Finn have the smallest clue about what's going on?
Stay tuned to this blog for exciting developments.

Ramey had included a brief video clip of him and Blake and Z at the gate as they dragged out the crying girl and tossed in the cookies, and a still shot of the abandoned farmhouse bordered by yellow CRIME SCENE tape.

Could he possibly avoid going into the station tomorrow? He rubbed his stubbly chin and tried to remember if he'd shaved this morning. Maybe he should dump this whole mess in Rebecca Ramey's lap and fly back to Hawaii right now.

"Matt? Matt! Are you there?"

Grace was still on the line. He closed the blog site so he could focus on their conversation. "Uh, yeah."

"I asked you—twice—how could a little girl end up in the gorilla barn? Where did she come from? I told Blake no visitors!"

"Hon, that's a long story, and I'm still missing most of the chapters. But no, Blake hasn't been letting anyone visit. He seems trustworthy."

"How trustworthy can he be? Kanoni was *shot*? Who shot her? Why? And that dead woman was in that old house behind my property?" Grace's tone rose in pitch, bordering on hysterical.

Cargo nosed the whiskey glass off onto the carpet with a clunk. The remaining cat, Kee, dug his claws into Finn's thigh, vaulted to the floor, and followed his brother down the hall.

"Ow." Finn rubbed his thigh through his pants.

"What?" Grace's exasperated sigh filled the room. "I'm getting on the first plane back."

"No, Grace, don't do that. Yes, this case is a little messy at the moment, but the gorillas are okay. That little girl is being taken care of. Turns out that Blake is as amazing with small humans as he is with gorillas. I'll have everything wrapped up before you could make it back to Evansburg."

Fat chance of that, his conscience commented. *A little messy at the moment? Really?*

"You really think so?" she asked.

"Yeah. And you have no idea how much I'm looking forward to being back on the beach with you. I've never been to Kauai."

There was a hesitation before she said, "The condo here is beautiful, even more special than the one on the Big Island. It's like sleeping in a treehouse."

"I can't wait to see it." He eyed the clock. "But it's nearly one thirty in the morning here, and I can barely keep my eyes open. As you can tell, it's been an eventful day. I'll call you tomorrow with an update, okay?"

"You'd better."

"Good night, sweetheart. Sweet dreams." He clicked off the phone, picked up his empty drink glass, and headed for his bedroom. "Sweet dreams to you, too, Matt," he murmured in a high-pitched voice.

Padding down the hall right behind him, Cargo nudged Finn's butt cheek with a wet nose.

Things couldn't possibly get any weirder tomorrow.

42

Blake had made up a bed for the tiny girl on the floor with an air mattress and a comforter and soft pillow, but after lying there for only a minute, she had climbed into bed with him and snuggled close. It had been a long time since a small child had sought his affection like that. His daughter Hannah was now a teenager and delivered very few hugs. After getting over her initial terror, the toddler seemed desperate for a kind touch, or at least bodily warmth. Had she curled up with Neema while she was in the gorilla barn? Probably. He'd witnessed how affectionate the mother gorilla could be with Kanoni, and even with the cats that lived on the property. What a bizarre temp job this was turning out to be.

Rosa, the girl in the gorilla pen. At least he believed that some version of Rosie, or Rose, or Rosa was the child's name. She didn't seem to know many English words, and he couldn't comprehend any of her chattering. Some sort of Haitian dialect, most likely.

She was a beautiful child, with dark skin, slightly slanted brown eyes, and ebony hair. He'd gone through the usual gestures, touching his own chest and saying "Blake," then pointing to her and finally holding out his hands in a questioning gesture. It took several repetitions of this pantomime before the girl finally offered something that sounded like "Rose Allen." Or maybe Rosalind? He would call her Rosa.

She'd eagerly eaten everything he'd cooked for her, wolfing it down while watching him warily as if he might snatch it away. When he served her a small dish of steamed cauliflower, she giggled and said, "Go-rilla," and then scarfed that down as well. Most likely, Neema had shared her food with Rosa, or the child had stolen some from the food box. That would explain the bits of cauliflower and bread in the woods.

When he'd first run a bath for Rosa, she was afraid to take off her clothes and step into the tub. Finn had told him her family had most likely been homeless and had been camping out in an abandoned farmhouse with no running water. It was possible the child had never had a bath before. Relieved that there were no witnesses to accuse him of child molestation or something equally awful, Blake ended up shucking off his clothes down to his shorts and then stepping in and sitting down to prove to her it was okay. Seeing that, she eagerly climbed in, clothes and all, but then allowed him to pull her clothes off and drop them in a sodden mess on the floor. She delighted in the soap, the washcloth, the shampoo, and the towel, chuckling and babbling as if the bath process were all new and wonderful to her, and maybe it was. Poor kid.

After the bath, her smooth brown skin glowed. He'd shampooed her scalp and braids as much as he could, while wondering if he should unbraid her hair and comb it out, or if that might hurt, or would frighten her more. He had no experience with Black hair; he'd read it was notoriously tricky to deal with. The clothes Rosa wore were practically rags, her shirt and jeans filthy and ripped in front, probably from when she'd crawled through the feeding portal in the gorillas' fence.

He tossed all her clothes in the washing machine, anyway,

including her tiny sneakers, because he didn't have immediate access to any little-kid clothes. Then he dressed her in his smallest T-shirt and socks so big they practically reached her thighs. If she stayed with him, he'd buy her some new clothes. But he didn't know if staying with him was even possible. Detective Finn had said he'd let him know tomorrow.

As he lay there in the dark, Rosa's small warm body curled up against his, he speculated about her history. Finn had mentioned a homeless family and Haitians, although he hadn't specifically tied all those things in with the dead woman found in the abandoned house. Haitian heritage fit with Rosa's skin color and lack of English. Had her mother been in the US illegally? Had she been involved in shooting Kanoni? Was it her blood outside of the gorilla enclosure?

He studied the little girl's face, relaxed and angelic in sleep. Did she understand her mother was dead? He had no idea what would happen next to the poor waif.

His cell phone was on the table next to the bed. Blake picked it up and snapped a photo of the sleeping child and texted it to Sam, adding, The excitement continues. Look what we found in the gorilla barn.

43

Bellingham

The next morning, while she was waiting in the parking lot of the sheriff's office, Sam decided to call Wiley Thompson.

The number turned out to be not his personal cell phone, but the main number for Grafton Stables. A woman answered. Sam explained she was looking for Wiley Thompson.

"He's not here right now. Can I take a message?"

Sam gave the woman her name and number and said she wanted to know how Freckles was doing.

"I assume Mr. Thompson will know what that means," the woman replied. "I'll give him the message." She hung up without saying goodbye.

Sam squirmed in her seat, frustrated. Of course, the woman wouldn't know Freckles. That probably wasn't even the mare's real name. She should have said something like "the Appaloosa mare he picked up at the trailhead."

Freckles had been such a brave partner that whole night, just kept going and carrying such a load, even though she was injured. Some might think it was silly, but Sam wanted to see for herself that Freckles was okay and thank her.

She couldn't stop yawning. At 3:06 a.m., she and Simon had been awakened by headlights shining through her bedroom window. The cat had leaped to the windowsill to stare out at the driveway. She'd wondered if Chase or Blake had decided to come back early. She'd anticipated the front door opening. But after listening to a truck engine idle for a long minute, a trickle of fear had snaked down her spine. The last time this had happened, drug dealers had been searching for Maya, her reckless former ward. Next, they'd invaded her house.

Sliding out from beneath the blankets, Sam had crept to the window and peeked around the curtain, but the vehicle had already backed out of the driveway and was turning on the dark street beyond.

Reassured, she went back to bed. Simon, now perched on her bookcase headboard, had chirped a question at her. "Maya's not here; they know that. So maybe just a lost driver searching for the house number," she'd told the cat. "Or maybe Investigator Erickson, making sure I haven't left town."

It was irritating to think any authority suspected her of any crime, and even more irritating that nobody would tell her what they had discovered about the dead guy in the lake or whom they suspected had abandoned Diego and Freckles in that remote ravine. She'd call Chase later to see if an FBI agent could discover what the heck the investigators were thinking. Or maybe she'd drive over to the coast to surprise him with a visit. Or when the drama of the investigation was over, she'd drive south and east instead, to see Blake and those amazing signing gorillas.

In the morning, she'd noticed that she had a text waiting, and when she'd displayed her list, she was surprised she hadn't noticed the message from Blake yesterday. Even after opening it, she couldn't quite believe it what she'd read. A child really had been in the gorilla barn? She called him. The call went to voicemail. "What? How did that little kid end up in the gorilla barn? Without you knowing?"

She ended the call, but remained staring at the image of the sleeping child, moved back to the earlier video Blake had sent her. That had to be the same child who had been standing in the shadows there.

A knock on her driver-side window startled her back to the here and now. Amelia Castro, wearing her ranger uniform, stood beside Sam's RAV4. She held up a topo map, and gestured toward the building. Nodding, Sam slid out of her seat and followed the ranger inside.

They were nearly finished marking up the map with Sam's meanderings to and from her campsite when Investigator Erickson walked in. Her hair was again arranged in its immaculate roll at the back of her head.

Grabbing up the map, Erickson first squinted at the markings before turning her focus to Sam. "This is where you found the floater?" She stabbed an index finger at the map.

"Yeah, there at Rainbow Point. I was washing my breakfast dishes when I spotted him in the lake."

"And you're sure you never saw him before?" Erickson's blue eyes were glued to Sam's face as she awaited her response.

"He was floating upside down. I never even saw his face. And no, I don't think I ever saw the back of his head before, either."

The investigator hissed with impatience, pulled out her cell phone, and then thumbed through it for a bit before thrusting it out to Sam. She stared at the image for a long moment, trying to visualize the face less bloated. Black man. Black curly hair fringing a bald spot. Maybe middle-aged. Hard to tell in his current waterlogged and deceased condition. She hit Share and sent the photo to her own cell phone.

"Hey!" The investigator yanked her phone out of Sam's hand. "I did not give you permission for that. Have you seen this man before or not?"

Sam shook her head. "I don't think so."

"You don't *think* so?" When Sam didn't respond, Erickson's brow creased, and the investigator turned to Ranger Castro. "Doesn't the wind typically blow from south to north at Ross Lake?"

Castro's shoulders lifted and fell in a shrug. "Depends on the weather. Sometimes it blows more east, and sometimes it doesn't blow much at all."

"So I'm guessing not much floats from north to south on the lake." Erickson continued to scan the map.

Castro said, "You're mostly right. Like I said, sometimes there's not much wind at all, and there are eddies here and there along the shores. And if there's no wind, there can be a slight current moving south when we're releasing water from the dam at the south end, as happened earlier this week. Do you have a theory on how he got there?"

Erickson did not respond, but focused again on Sam. "So you walked all over the area, found a corpse and an injured man and horse, then made it back to your campsite, where you got shot."

"You left out the wolves, but that pretty much sums it up," Sam responded.

The investigator slapped the map back onto the table. "Hardly. How did you get from that campsite back to the trailhead with Baptiste and the horse?"

Sam explained fleeing toward the main trail, then overhearing the horse and the hikers, and next, heading back across country on game trails to avoid the armed man on horseback.

"Draw your route," Erickson commanded.

As Sam did her best to mark her journey on the topo map with her left hand, the investigator peppered her with questions about how she knew the floater in the lake, the dead hiker, and Emmanuel Baptiste.

"I don't *know* any of them," Sam protested. And obviously, she would never meet the dead guys.

She handed the finished product to the investigator. "Am I done?"

"For now." Map in hand, Erickson turned to leave the room, then turned around. "But please don't leave town. I may need to speak to you again."

As soon as Erickson left the room, Castro rolled her eyes, making Sam smile. *I will bloody well leave town if I feel like it,* she thought as she stomped to her car.

She was finally forced to go to the grocery store. Simon was out of food and the cat could hardly shop for himself. In the past few weeks, she'd realized how much she'd depended on Blake over the years to take care not only of the cooking but also the grocery shopping. With six cans of whitefish mixture and a prebaked chicken, a dozen eggs, grapefruit juice, a packaged salad, and a bottle of wine in a bag slung over her shoulder, she headed home to try to repair her reputation with the editor at *Out There.*

After a bit of one-handed online research, she found she could record and transcribe through Google, so she paced around her house as she practiced with her cell phone, feeling as if she had developed schizophrenia. Simon curiously studied her every move. She wasn't used to dictating sentences and punctuation. Her writing process turned out to need an intermediary keyboard and fingers to work efficiently. Eventually she gave up and spent the time recording notes about how her wolf article should go. She printed those out and then used them as prompts to complete the entire text, awkwardly typing with her left hand.

After nearly four hours of fits and starts, the result was a messy rough draft that would require a lot of correction, which she would have to do herself, because Michael Fredd had been hesitant about paying for this article at all, so she couldn't expect him to edit it as well. To prove she was still useful, she wanted to submit the wolf article to him at the same time she asked for her next assignment.

Her cell phone dinged, and she picked it up, expecting a text from Blake. Instead, there was a photo of foam-crested waves crashing on the beach at Quinault. Seagulls spotted the sunny blue sky beyond. View from my room, Chase had texted.

Stop distracting me, she texted back. She attached a photo of her bandaged hand on the keyboard in front of her computer. Her hand was throbbing. Black bruising showed at the edges of the elastic wrap.

He responded with a heart emoji.

"Argh!" Shutting down the phone, she walked to the window overlooking the backyard. A ladybug was strolling up the outside of the glass toward another of its kind. Were the insects intent on mating, or fighting, or maybe just greeting an old friend? She needed to do research on ladybug lifestyles. Toward the back of the yard, a pileated woodpecker was noisily enlarging a hole in the dead cedar. Sam hoped he—or she— would build a nest inside. She'd never seen pileated chicks. It would be fascinating to watch the young birds learning to fly. Like seeing baby pterodactyls stretch their wings for the first time. Did the males help raise the chicks? Clearly she also needed to do research on pileated woodpeckers.

Simon leaped to the windowsill. Instantly spotting the movement of the huge bird in the distance, he switched his tail and uttered excited little hunting chirps.

"In your dreams, bud," she told him. "That bird could drill a hole in your skull."

Work, she reminded herself. She had to finish something ASAP and make some income. Although she and Fredd had a deal for half-time work, she wasn't an employee, and unemployment pay and sick leave did not exist for freelancers. She redirected her thoughts to reflect on everything she'd been through in the last several days. Michael Fredd might be more excited about a writeup describing the floater in the lake and the dead hiker and her shooter and fleeing through the wild terrain than he was about her wolves.

As far as she knew, the floater had not yet been identified, so she suspected any mention of the dead guy in the lake might piss off the Whatcom County Sheriff's Office, law enforcement types in North Cascades National Park, and, most definitely, the HSI investigator, Carole Erickson. So Sam dictated a few notes about her experiences and left it at that for now.

It occurred to her this was exactly the sort of salacious story her old boyfriend and now television reporter Adam Steele would be interested in. He paid big bucks. However, she was not eager to be featured in any documentary ever again, and she didn't have the whole story, anyway. Still, she had to give Adam credit for the stellar avalanche coverage he'd pulled together last month, and there was a chance that his decision to feature the wolverines had influenced the feds to finally put them on the endangered species list. His documentary had also helped shine the spotlight on a missing Latina photographer down by the border wall in Arizona. Adam Steele could be useful, but he could also be a self-serving pain. She shelved the thought of bringing him in for now.

But the missing hiker . . . She could write a story about all the people who'd gone missing in Washington State's public lands. Some were still unaccounted for; others had been rescued or their remains found. She could call Alec Lysikov's family and ask more about him. He was from Okanagan, Washington, she recalled. How many Lysikovs could there be in the small town of Okanagan?

The last time she'd sat down with a grieving family, only a month ago, had become the basis of a magazine article and part of Adam's most recent documentary. Tragedies of people dying in the wild were always enthusiastically welcomed by publishers of e-zines and streaming channels on television, and that paid her bills. But finding his remains was only the tragic end of Alec's story; she needed to discover who he was to make his history memorable. Most relatives wanted to contribute to stories that memorialized their loved ones.

"'Death in the Wild,' by Summer Westin, whose specialty is stumbling over corpses," she announced to the empty room in a pathetic imitation of a television reviewer. Why did her assignments always get sucked into that black hole, when she set out to write about the pleasures of exploring wild places? She resolved to finish her wolf article before revisiting the topic of death in the backcountry.

After spending a few more hours painfully editing the text and sorting through her photos from the trip, the wolf article was finally coming into focus. And the pictures brought back happy memories of watching the wolves romping in their home environment. Maybe she'd even put a video on YouTube after she sold the article.

A text from her editor came through. Your assignment to do ASAP: interview the winning team of Ski to Sea, ask about training, conditions this year, secrets for winning three years in a row. Need this completed in two days.

Oh, that was just great. She sighed. Eight people to interview and submit the final result in forty-eight hours. With a nonfunctional hand.

Don't muck up this job, she told herself. The pay might be only half-time, but was the only regular income she could depend on.

Sighing, she replied, Got it, and set about looking up the winners. Turned out it was an extreme team, with only five members, not eight, thank heavens, and they all worked for one local company. She fired off the same email message to all five about doing an interview that afternoon. At least she could interview the two canoeists at the same time.

Surprisingly, the answer was swift, and it came from the company's CEO, who said the team would be thrilled to be interviewed this afternoon.

She'd get this Google recording thing down fast . . . or get fired.

44

The interview of the winning Ski to Sea team turned out to be reasonably painless and actually enjoyable, as Sam was able to talk to the whole team at one time. She explained about her injury, raising her right arm as if asking a question. Admitting that she'd been shot in the hand was both gratifying and embarrassing, because then naturally they wanted to know how that had happened. And then they asked about her face. She'd completely forgotten about the myriad cuts and scrapes; she really needed to start checking her appearance in the mirror before she left the house.

The HVAC company they all worked for were so proud of their athletes that they lent her their conference room to do the interviews. Best of all, when all the recordings were done, the company CEO escorted her out, and on his way past the receptionist, said, "If you'd like to give your recordings to Emily here, I'm sure she'll be glad to transcribe them for you, wouldn't you, Emily?"

The receptionist raised her gaze from her computer screen, a surprised expression on her face. But then she smiled and nodded. "Sure. I can have them delivered to you by noon tomorrow."

Sam felt a twinge of guilt that the boss had ambushed the receptionist that way, but she was not going to turn down that offer. And the odds were good that Michael Fredd would never hear about it. She gratefully handed over the tiny recorder she'd used and waved her bandaged hand. "You're my savior, Emily."

Back home, Sam couldn't stop thinking about that child in the gorilla barn. She called Blake again, but again got no answer. Left another voicemail. But Blake was nearly as bad as she was about not carrying around his cell phone. He sometimes didn't respond for days. Sam told herself there was a perfectly logical explanation for the kid in the barn, and if Blake was now caring for her as well as the gorillas, he'd be pretty busy.

Her brain also refused to let go of Freckles and Diego. She googled Grafton Stables and discovered it was on the way to Okanagan and the Lysikov family. It was much too late to head there today. She'd visit there tomorrow.

As far as she knew, Diego was still in St. Joseph Medical Center, so she drove there, trying to recall what Erickson had told her was the man's real name. Emmanuel. Nothing like Diego. And the last name? Nothing close to Cruz, like he'd told her. Something that also sounded vaguely religious, though. Santos? No. Baptiste, that was it.

"I'm looking for Emmanuel Baptiste's room," she told the man guarding the front entrance to the hospital. He consulted a chart on his computer, then turned to her. "Visitors are restricted. He's under government protection."

"I know that." She affected annoyance, glancing over her shoulder at the two women and a sullen teenage boy who waited behind her.

"It's the very least you can do to visit your grandpa for half an hour," the younger woman told the boy.

A man carrying a bouquet of flowers walked up and stood

behind the family.

The door guard, whose nametag identified him only as "Volunteer," continued, "There's an investigator from Immigration with Baptiste right now. She went in just a while ago."

"I know that, too. I'm supposed to take her an urgent message. She's wanted back at HQ and she's not answering her phone." Sam waved her notebook in the air, praying Volunteer wouldn't ask to see her credentials, where HQ was, or what was in the notebook, which were only a few left-handed scribbles about how she'd met Diego. She wasn't even sure she could read them herself.

"Room 271." Volunteer handed her a Guest press-on tag and waved her out of the way to face the family standing behind her. "Can I help you?"

One hurdle leaped over. Sam headed for the elevator. When she reached Room 271, the door was partially closed. She peeked through the slit, hoping the investigator was not Carole Erickson.

She lucked out again. A young Black woman sat by Emmanuel's left bedside, notebook in hand. When Sam entered, both Emmanuel and the woman glanced up. Emmanuel's curious expression morphed into a smile.

"*Zanmi*. Friend!" He raised his left hand until the clank of a handcuff attached to the bedrail stopped the motion.

Emmanuel was a thousand times cleaner and healthier-looking than when she'd left him a few days ago. A clean white bandage stretched across his forehead, an IV snaked into his left arm, and his right leg was enclosed in a temporary cast from thigh to toes. He probably couldn't wear plaster until his wound was healed.

The woman said something to him in a language totally

unfamiliar to Sam, then stood up, facing her across the hospital bed. "I am Madeline Chery, a translator for immigration services. Who are you?"

Stepping forward, Sam gently grasped Emmanuel's shoulder. "Like he said, I am Emmanuel's, friend. I met him a few days ago."

Emmanuel fired off a few rapid sentences to Madeline, and she responded, nodding, and then wrote down something in her notebook.

Sam told the other woman, "We couldn't share much because he doesn't seem to have much English, and I have absolutely no knowledge of whatever language you two are speaking."

Madeline dipped her chin. "Few people do. It's Haitian Creole."

Emmanuel rattled off another long stream of words, and then faced Sam, a grin lighting up his face.

Madeline interpreted. "He says thank you for saving his life, and how is your hand?"

"I'm glad I was there." She held up her bandaged hand. "It's healing. Although the docs say I may need surgery to make it right."

After hearing the translation, Emmanuel uttered another incomprehensible phrase, which according to Madeline meant, "God bless you." Sam found it frustrating not to be able to actually converse with the man.

"Tell him I'm glad to see he's doing well, and if I can help him, to let me know." After giving his shoulder a gentle squeeze, she walked around the bed to face Madeline. "He's here illegally, right?" she asked in a low murmur. "What's going to happen to him now?"

Madeline sat down again. "Yes, he's undocumented. He's claimed asylum, and his status has not yet been determined."

The interpreter then lowered her voice until she was nearly whispering. "The authorities seem to think he may be mixed up in drug smuggling from Canada."

Apparently, Emmanuel understood some of that, because he stirred and began to protest loudly. Sam guessed he was declaring his innocence. Madeline grasped his handcuffed hand and said something that calmed him down. He responded and thrust his chin in the direction of the bedside table.

"He wants you to see a picture of his wife. He says she's here in Washington State waiting for him." Madeline slid open the drawer in the table, extracted a worn billfold, and then slid out a dog-eared photo and showed it to Emmanuel. When he nodded, Madeline handed it to Sam.

The photo had been worn to a softness resembling newsprint. It depicted Emmanuel in a tuxedo, his arm around a stunning Black woman with luxurious curly hair tucked into a bridal veil.

"Your wife is beautiful." Sam raised her gaze from the image to the man's face. "Can I take a picture of this photo with my phone?" She placed the photo on the bed and pulled out her phone. He nodded. "How long has she been in the US?"

"Three years," was the answer that came back through Madeline. "And now they have a little girl, too. He can't wait to see them."

"How can I keep in touch with Emmanuel?" Sam asked the interpreter.

The woman shrugged. "Why don't you leave your contact information, and maybe he can try." Her brown eyes were sad as she whispered, "I have no idea where he will end up."

After jotting down her information and wishing Emmanuel the best of luck, Sam thanked Madeline and left. As she approached the exit, she spotted Carole Erickson entering through the hospital's sliding doors. Sam took a quick right into the gift shop to avoid the investigator.

So Diego Cruz was actually Emmanuel Baptiste, and he was from Haiti. As she drove home, Sam reflected on the latest news of chaos and violence from Haiti. The Middle East. Africa. Starvation. Kidnapping. Killings. Life could be so brutal for those unlucky enough to be born in a poor, strife-ridden country. Emmanuel's story would be so different if only he had really been from Miami.

Refugees. They reminded her of the wolves, born in the wrong time and in the wrong places, always in danger and always searching for a safe place they could call home.

45

North Cascades Highway to Okanagan

Finding the Lysikov family was easier than Sam had expected. The internet simply coughed up the current information. After she'd expressed her condolences to Alec's parents, they said they'd welcome a chance to tell her more about their son.

"We were beginning to think nobody cared," his mother told Sam in a shaky voice. "It would be nice to see an article about him."

She gulped. She hadn't promised an article would be published, but she didn't want to discourage them from talking, so she simply arranged for an interview in the afternoon and set off. She planned to drive up State Route 20, known locally as the North Cascades Highway. According to their website, Grafton Stables was not far from Rockport, on the way to North Cascades National Park. Since Wiley never answered the phone, she'd try to surprise him by showing up in person to ask about Freckles.

Many would find her attachment to the horse irrational, but she and the mare had been to hell and back together. Emmanuel, even more so. This had to be how soldiers felt about their comrades in battle.

After a little more than an hour of driving, she pulled under a Grafton Stables arch on a gravel road only a few miles from the Skagit River. It was a pretty place, with a sprawling ranch house, large stables, and what looked like a separate accommodation for relatives, or more likely, for employees of the ranch. Maybe a bunkhouse. Since Wiley was a wrangler, he'd likely be there, not in the big house that had to belong to the owner. She headed in that direction, noticing as she drove closer that the buildings needed paint and the gutters were rusting and dented.

Horses grazed in the pasture that bordered the parking area. A handsome paint that reminded her of her old horse, Comanche, a buckskin and a sleek bay. Two Appaloosas stood nose to tail in the dappled shade of distant cottonwoods. Freckles? She recognized the pattern of spots. Her owner hadn't arrived to pick the mare up yet?

After sliding through the split-rail fence, Sam strode across the pasture toward the trees, the tall grass swishing against her pant legs. When she was about thirty feet from the horses, she called, "Freckles? Is that you?"

Sure enough, one of the Appaloosas raised a head and whickered in recognition. The mare craned her neck, intently watching Sam's approach. The other horse slowly shuffled away through the tall grass.

"Freckles," Sam crooned affectionately as the horse pressed her head into Sam's chest. She scratched the mare between the ears. Freckles blew a happy sigh through her nostrils. Sam hoped her shirt wouldn't be spotted with snotty grass stains for her interview this afternoon.

"How are you doing, girl?" The injuries to the mare's flank and forehead were painted with some kind of purplish medication. The gashes had scabbed over nicely. Wiley was taking good care of the mare while waiting for the owner to pick her up, and she had plenty of grass and water and equine company. Sam was relieved to see her battle buddy was doing so well.

"You were such a trouper." She stroked the mare's neck. "Emmanuel and I couldn't have made it without you. That's Diego's real name, Emmanuel."

"Hey!"

Sam turned to see a woman frantically waving from the other side of the fence. She waved in return, and then walked back.

"What the hell do you think you're doing?" The woman demanded, an angry glare on her face. "You can't just trespass whenever you feel like it. What do you want?"

The woman was several inches taller than Sam, and broad across the shoulders and chest. Her boots were worn and dusty. Another wrangler, Sam guessed. She stuck out her unbandaged left hand. "Sam Westin. I was with Freckles a few days ago up along Ross Lake."

The woman ignored the outstretched hand. "Freckles?"

Sam dropped her hand and twisted her head to thrust her chin in the mare's direction. "That appy mare."

"You mean Gypsy."

"Okay." Freckles seemed like a much better name for a spotted mare. "Is Wiley here?"

"Nope." The woman fisted her hands on her hips, clearly eager to get rid of Sam. "Wiley is out on business today. Did you want something?" She radiated hostility.

"I just wanted to see that Freckles, I mean Gypsy, was okay. I'm glad you found out her name."

The expression on the woman's face said she thought that was a statement from a fool. "Unless you're here on business, I've got tons of chores to do." She thrust an arm in the direction of the road.

Sam took the hint and returned to her SUV, murmuring an apology. She drove back to the highway. The jagged peaks and waterfalls of North Cascades National Park were stunning as always, but the highway was busy with huge campers and motorcycles and even a few clumps of bicycle riders, forcing Sam to stay focused on the road as she mulled over her stop at the stables. That strange hostile woman. Gypsy. For a wrangler, Wiley rarely seemed to be at the ranch, but maybe he was out guiding tourists again.

At least she'd seen the mare was doing well. "Mission accomplished," she murmured. But she still would like to talk to Wiley and find out what he knew, if anything, about shady goings-on in the park.

Descending from the highest passes, she drove east through the Old West facades of the tourist town of Winthrop and beyond, headed for the town of Okanagan.

The entire region of rolling hills and lakes and canyons in northeast Washington State was known by Washingtonians as "the Okanagan." Adding to the confusion, the southeast section of the province of British Columbia, just north across the Canadian border, famed for its vineyards and fruit orchards, was called the Okanagan Valley, and the biggest lake there was Okanagan Lake. Everything seemed to be named after the Okanagan indigenous band that traditionally claimed that territory. Sam wondered how many of the original people were left, and whether they also called themselves Okanagan or went by another name these days.

The city of Okanagan was small, only a few thousand people, and Sam found the address of the Lysikov house without difficulty. Parking in the driveway of a well-kept one-story home, she took three deep breaths, gathered up her notebook and cell phone, and mentally prepared herself to meet a grieving family. As she slid out of the car, two bearded men and an older woman emerged from the front door to greet her.

Inside the house, it appeared that the entire extended family had come to meet her. She explained that she'd injured her hand in an accident, and they were kind enough not to inquire about her face. Each of them insisted on shaking her good hand, and several gave her those weird double European air kisses. The whole situation felt awkwardly ceremonial. Two of the most elderly relatives had heavy accents, so it seemed natural to ask where the family had originated.

"Belarus," offered a nearly toothless wrinkled woman. A woman about Sam's age added, "A long time ago."

"I see," Sam said, for lack of anything better. All she knew about Belarus was that the country bordered Russia and Ukraine, and she had no intention of stepping into that political minefield. "I'm so sorry about Alec."

"Please." Alec's father gestured to a long dining table covered in a gold tablecloth. Everyone positioned themselves behind the chairs as if they had familiar seating assignments, and Sam feared that she'd been given Alec's vacant seat. After they'd all settled themselves, the silver-haired man asked, "You were the one who found him?"

Sam described finding Alec's body under the rockslide rubble, omitting the discovery of Emmanuel and Freckles. No need to throw in all the extraneous drama.

When she'd finished describing the situation, silence stretched out for a few uncomfortable beats before Alec's mother remarked, "So you are a lonely hiker like Alec."

Sam straightened in her chair, surprised by the description. "I guess I am, sometimes. He loved to explore, didn't he? I am an animal lover and I saw wolves out there, so I followed them. Maybe he did, too."

One of the cousins, a black-haired woman whose name Sam had already forgotten, smiled. "Alec would like that, to see wolves in the wild."

"Crazy boy." This comment came from his mother. "Who chases wolves?"

Nobody had a response to that. They all probably thought Sam was crazy, too. "So Alec was a fellow nature lover. I'd like to know more about him. Tell me what he was like," she urged, leaning forward.

"Of course," said Alec's father. "But first, refreshments." Several of the relatives stood up, the women going to the kitchen and the men to a bar at the side of the room. Soon the table was littered with plates of cake and small glasses of vodka and cups of steaming tea.

Sam accepted a cup of tea and a slice of poppyseed cake. From the conversations that ensued, she learned that Alec Lysikov had been a troubled soul who couldn't keep a job, according to his parents.

"He had a girl who loved him." His mother shook her head, her expression sad. "He could have had a family."

"But Alec was an adventure seeker," his younger sister Daria countered. "He spent a lot of time by himself in the wild." She sounded wistful, as if she could identify with that way of life.

"He was never the same after he came back from Afghanistan," his sister Nadia added.

"So Alec was a soldier." Sam took a sip of tea.

Nadia slowly stirred her spoon in her own cup. "For a few years." She drew in a breath. "And the things he experienced over there—"

The father bristled, glaring at Nadia. "Alec was a hero."

Unspoken emotions swirled in the room, and an awkward silence reigned for a long moment before Alec's uncle Sergei mercifully ended it by saying, "Alec was always such a happy little boy when we went out fishing."

Others added remembrances of Alec's childhood and accomplishments as a young adult. The conversation left Sam feeling melancholy. Several family members promised to text her photos of Alec, and after nearly two hours of sitting with them, she gathered her notes and her cell phone and stood up. "I've got to head back now. Thank you so much for meeting me. I'll send you the article as soon as I have it done." In her head, she vowed to make good on writing and marketing Alec's story.

The family insisted on hugging her and giving her more air kisses and a piece of poppy seed cake before she left. Their gratitude was disturbing. She thought about their stories during the four-hour drive back to Bellingham. Crazy. Couldn't keep a job. Troubled. Could have had a family but was always wandering off into the wilderness.

Was this how people talked about her? She'd sometimes overheard her father remark he wished his daughter Summer had a normal existence. Did Reverend Mark Westin think she'd wasted her life? She felt a pang, remembering her father's suffering with her mother's illness and now with Zola's. She hoped that her choices hadn't always disappointed him. So many people assumed that an unmarried, childless woman was a tragic figure. She loved her life, at least most of the time. She'd rather die in a rockslide in the wild than waste away from a long illness in a soulless hospital.

As she drove back, a brilliant sunset lit up the highest mountain peaks surrounding the highway, painting their glaciers with a rose and gold alpenglow.

Alex Lysikov had appreciated this view, too.

"I get you, Alec," she said aloud to the surrounding mountains.

As she passed the turnoff to Grafton Stables, she briefly considered stopping there again to see if Wiley was back yet. No, that female wrangler had been so hostile; she'd better not stop without calling first. She pulled over and tried the number again, but was told by a familiar resentful woman's voice that Wiley was still not available.

As she reached the dark outskirts of Bellingham, her cell phone chimed. "Westin," Investigator Erickson hissed in a voicemail message. "Where have you been? I told you not to leave town."

She gritted her teeth. Apparently, she was still considered a suspect. But of what? Drug smuggling? People smuggling? Were the authorities tracking her? She decided to inspect the undercarriage of her SUV tomorrow for tracking devices.

That message was followed by one from Michael Fredd, asking about the interviews. After finding a package with the transcribed and printed interviews of the Ski to Sea team propped against her front door, she texted him back that she'd get that article to him first thing tomorrow.

Sam found a text message from Chase on her phone. I'm wrapping up this case. I'll return tomorrow. Can't wait to hold you!

She responded, I'll be waiting, and added a happy face emoji.

46

The next day, Sam busied herself editing the Ski to Sea transcript to add descriptions and histories of the team members and make the conversation sound less formal. Typing with one hand made for slow progress, and it was midafternoon before she sent the results to her editor and could turn to her notes from yesterday about Alec Lysikov. She added a few other thoughts about more missing hikers in the Pacific Northwest. The rangers had mentioned a Madura who'd vanished the previous year near Cutthroat. There was a Cutthroat Lake and a Cutthroat Pass in the area. She googled the story of the missing backpacker.

Yes, there it was. Suzanne Madura had last been seen headed through Cutthroat Pass in August of the previous year on a solo backpacking trip to Hart's Pass. Nobody had reported whether she had camped near the pass or hiked north over the pass to some point beyond. That section of the Pacific Crest Trail unspooled through stunning scenery, Sam knew, where often the path hugged vertical mountainsides, passing between craggy spires, overlooking boulder fields and alpine lakes at the bottoms of the steep valleys between Cutthroat and Hart's passes. Potential rockslide areas, Sam thought, remembering the grim scene where she'd found Alec Lysikov.

Did she really want to get into another missing hiker story? While there was always the possibility that the person might turn up alive, most of the time they didn't. Readers were fascinated by missing persons cases, but the ones that had no documented conclusion left them feeling dissatisfied. It was human nature to want mysteries wrapped up in neat packages.

With so many hikers missing across the US, she could probably put together article after article of their stories, but would any editor want to publish them? Certainly, no business that catered to outdoor adventures would want to advertise in any publication that featured their customers vanishing into the wild, especially if they perished in terrible ways. If Michael Fredd agreed to publish Alex Lysikov's story in his magazine, it would only be because she had a personal angle on it, having found his remains.

Fredd was currently considering her proposal to write about everything that happened to her on her short expedition. "It's a cliff-hanger," he agreed. "But our mission is to encourage people to celebrate and explore the great outdoors. Corpses in lakes and dead hikers and drug smuggling and shootings of innocent hikers could hardly be considered a celebration, could they?"

She saw his point. But if he turned it down, maybe she could sell it elsewhere. She'd tackle it later. After she could really type again.

Her hand was aching. She looked up from her computer screen to her office window and watched a flock of Pacific bushtits crowding into the branches of her aronia bush. They were some of her favorite birds, but she rarely saw them. She'd never seen a lone bushtit, she'd never seen an individual sit still for more than a second, and they often even hung upside down as they searched for insects. They were lively, teeny-tiny birds that traveled in flocks, impossible to count because there were always so many and they were so active. It was always a special moment when they visited her suet feeder, and as they took off, she hoped that was where they were headed. She got up to check, but if they'd landed there, they were already gone by the time she arrived at her back window.

The glass near the sill was smeared with Simon's paw swipe marks, and now she noticed the window sill also held dirty paw prints. When Blake was in residence, he'd probably cleaned those areas on a regular basis. Feeling ashamed of her sloppy housekeeping and knowing Chase would be arriving tonight, she located the cleaning supplies in the laundry room and set about wiping down windows and sills in all the rooms in her house.

At 5:46 p.m., a message came in from Chase. Unexpected complication, he wrote. Might not arrive in Bellingham until the wee hours of the morning. Want me to come in or drive on to my cabin?

Come in! she responded.

She was actually relieved. While this meant she was on her own again for dinner, it gave her time to wash and dry the sheets on her bed and shampoo her hair and spend some quality time with Simon.

Headlights again woke Sam in the middle of the night. Simon stood up from his sleeping position near the foot of her bed, his furry outline highlighted in the beam shining through her bedroom window. But this time, the car engine turned off and the lights went out.

Chase. Her lover had returned from his assignment at the reservation on the coast, as predicted. After a few minutes of rattling around at the front door, she heard him come in. Smiling, she snuggled back under the covers and eagerly awaited his arrival in her bedroom. Her cat remained tense in his alert position, gazing toward the living room.

"It's just Chase, Simon," she murmured, closing her eyes and drifting off. A few seconds later, Simon's growl shocked her awake, and then the cat leaped from the bed onto the hardwood floor. His claws scrabbled against the oak planks as he vanished under the bed.

She rolled over. A dark figure stood by her bed. "Chase?"

When the man didn't respond, her heart leaped into overdrive. She abruptly sat up.

The man wasn't Chase.

47

"Get out of my house!" she screamed, reaching for her cell phone on the bedside table.

The man slapped her phone to the floor, but his motion turned on the touch-control lamp on the table. Her heart was pounding so hard she didn't recognize him for a few seconds. Dark-blond hair, moustache. Incredible hazel eyes. Now he wore a baseball cap instead of a Stetson.

"Why?" He pointed a pistol at her.

She couldn't make sense of the situation. Adrenaline flooded her system and her body started to shake. "What? Wiley? Wiley Thompson?"

"Why couldn't you just leave it alone? Leave *them* alone." The wrangler's voice cracked; he sounded as if he might cry.

She found it impossible to lift her focus from the black hole of the gun barrel to his face. She would hyperventilate and pass out any second.

Leave them alone? Who was he talking about? Was she going to die?

Her throat was a desert. She swallowed painfully, focused on enunciating. "Wiley, please put the gun away."

The logic came to her in snatches. The way Freckles had raised her head to him. The way the woman wrangler answered the phone for him. He probably owned Grafton Stables; he owned Freckles. Why the "aw shucks" demeanor at the trailhead? Why the lies?

The packets of powder in the saddlebags. Drug trafficking. Diego Cruz/Emmanuel Baptiste, a migrant from Haiti. The thumps and scuffling she'd heard from the front of his eight-horse, slant-load trailer. More undocumented migrants? Human trafficking? Had she stood only feet away from a load of migrants without realizing?

"Did you hope Diego and Freckles would die in that gully?" she asked.

Wiley scowled. Simon dashed from under the bed, his claws scratching on the hardwood planks as he fled through the doorway. She didn't blame the cat; he had been shot in a home invasion not too long ago. She wished she could follow him.

Wiley's gaze danced to the doorway and back. He licked his lips before saying, "I don't know who you're talking about. Let's go outside."

She didn't understand why he wanted to do that, but it couldn't be good. She swung her legs over the side of the bed. "Can you just put that gun away? We can work this out, Wiley."

"Hurry up." He waved his pistol in the direction of the doorway as if to urge her in that direction. "Backyard."

Before he could point it at her again, she leaped to her feet. Thrusting out her fingers, she jabbed him hard in the neck. He stumbled back, clutching at his throat, but before she could slap at his arm, the pistol was pointed at her again. She sprang and grabbed him in a bear hug, forcing the pistol down between them.

The gun fired. Sam yelped as a hot flare shot down her leg. Wiley howled. "Fuck!" he yelled. "Shit, shit, shit!"

She heard a loud ringing sound as they both crumpled to the floor. He hit first, the back of his head whacking the floor, and she felt his grip on the pistol slacken. Pushing herself away, she grabbed his crotch with her left hand and squeezed with all her might, and slapped the gun out of his hand with her right. The weapon spun across the floor to disappear under the bed.

Pain shrieked through her injured hand. Black spots danced in front of her vision as she frantically considered what she could grab to defend herself. Why didn't she keep a baseball bat by the bed? Why didn't she *have* a baseball bat?

But it was Wiley who writhed in agony beside her, both hands on his genitals, his feet thrashing on the floor. One of his cowboy boots was gushing blood.

"Unh! God! Jesus Christ!" he groaned. "How could you *do* that?"

Sam pushed herself to a sitting position, gasping. One of her breasts was hanging nearly out of the loose shirt she slept in. She tucked it back in, feeling as if she was starring in a bad movie.

Pushing himself with his feet and one hand, Wiley scooted backward like a crab to the wall, still clutching his balls with the other hand and muttering, "I didn't really mean it, I didn't."

A really bad movie.

"Shit. Fuck!" He pressed his back against the vertical surface and used his hands to push himself up the wall, his boots skidding in blood. Then he limped, hunched over, to the front door. His truck engine roared to life. Gravel crunched. He was gone.

Sam slithered halfway under her bed to grab the pistol, spied her cell phone, grabbed that, too. She sat with her legs extended on the floor, her back propped up by the bed, her breath ragged.

Go lock the door, she told herself. But Wiley had already come through a locked door. And the adrenaline had her shaking so hard she wasn't sure she could stand and walk to the front door. Or even crawl there.

She fingered the pistol in her lap. Was it loaded? She assumed it was. Did she know how to use it? Looked as if all she needed to do was put her finger on the trigger.

Call 911. But she couldn't slow down her panicked gasping enough to talk. Wiley was gone. Her heart continued to pound like it was determined to break through the ringing in her ears.

Did she have wine in the refrigerator? She pressed her good hand against her chest, willing her lungs and heart to slow down. Should she have a glass of wine to calm down before she called? Then she was ashamed of herself for even thinking that.

This was a really, really bad movie. She closed her eyes. *Breathe in; breathe out. Slow down.* Maybe it was a nightmare. She hoped to wake up soon.

A footstep sounded outside her bedroom door, and her brain shifted back into warp speed. Oh God, he was back, he was back!

48

Sam grabbed at her cell phone, but her bandaged right hand was useless and her left hand was shaking so badly she couldn't focus on the numbers. The pistol slid from her lap to the floor and she fumbled for it. Before she could grasp the weapon properly, the man was there beside her. She wanted to scream, but only a pathetic squeak emerged from her petrified lips.

Crouching in front of her, he clamped a restraining hand on each of her arms.

"*Mierda*, Summer! What happened here? Are you okay?"

Chase.

He gently pulled the pistol out of her hands, took the cell phone from her lap, and placed them both on the bed, then sat on the floor beside her and pulled her into his arms, settling her on his lap. Where she dissolved into a blathering blob of snot and tears, unable to form a single intelligible word for several minutes. He gently ran his hands all over her body as she leaned against his chest. Chase Perez, her lover, her best friend, was really there. Solid, warm, calm.

Finally, when her sobs lessened a bit, Chase said, "The front door was open. Who came in?"

"Wiley."

He frowned. "Wiley? That horse guy we met in the trailhead parking lot? Is that his blood on the floor?"

Sam raised her injured right hand, realizing only now how excruciating the pain was. A crimson stain seeped through the bandages, but no blood dripped from the mess. Letting it drop to her lap, she wiped her face with the fingers of her left hand, sat erect, and met his eyes. "Yeah, that's his blood. Sorry to be so dramatic."

His eyes crinkled at the corners. "Looks like you earned that right."

Sam swallowed hard to clear her throat and then surveyed the room. Chase's service weapon lay on the floor an arm's length away. He'd obviously drawn it when he came in, after noticing her front door standing open. A large smear of crimson stained the floorboards only a foot from her position, and continued in an uneven ribbon to the wall. "That's all his blood, Chase. The gun's his, too."

Then she grinned, remembering. "He shot himself in the foot."

"I noticed the bullet hole." Chase pressed himself to his feet, offered her a hand and pulled her up beside him.

Now she noticed the dark circle in the floor, too. "Well, crap. I'll have to fix that." She turned to Chase. "Wine? I want wine."

"*Por el amor de Dios*, Summer, it's four in the morning."

"So?" She strode toward the kitchen. The front door still stood open, the cool night air wafting in. She detoured to close it, noting that a circle had been neatly cut from the small glass pane close to the door. "Shit. I'll have to fix that, too."

Awkwardly holding the bottle under her right arm, she used her left to pull the stopper from a bottle of Shiraz. After pouring two glasses, she held one out to Chase. "How's your investigation at the rez going?"

Grimacing, he ran his fingers through his ebony hair. "I should never have left you alone when I knew all this was going on. I thought the cops and rangers would be looking out for you."

She scoffed at that. "They think I'm a suspect." She took a sip of the wine. "And it's me, or actually I, who should have gone with you." Holding out her bandaged hand, she intended to point at him, but of course the dang fingers were still packaged in gauze and elastic wrap, and she ended up just waving her bloody claw at him. "I knew you were eager to get back to work, and you invited me to share your room with a view on the beach, and I just selfishly—"

"Stop, Summer." Chase grabbed her wrist and towed her to the couch. "Sit. You've just survived a traumatic event; I think you're in shock. Tell me why this Wiley would attack you, and what happened here tonight."

It took more than an hour and two glasses of wine—hers, and then Chase's as well—to get through the story of everything she'd been through in the last several days.

"It has to be Wiley, Chase," she summarized. "He's the one smuggling drugs and migrants down from Canada. He assumed I'd figured it out before I did."

Chase pulled his cell phone from his back pocket. "Tell me who you've been dealing with on this case. Anyone from the FBI?"

"No. Sheriff's department, Ranger Castro—you met her—and this annoying investigator from Homeland Security, Carole Erickson."

"Okay." Chase took the wine glass from her hand and placed it on the coffee table next to the other one. "I'm going to make a few phone calls. And you," he pulled her by her good hand, "are going back to bed."

Grabbing a blanket from the linen closet, he led her to the living room couch. When she sat down, they both noticed a long red line streaking down her left leg. And now that she'd seen it, she felt it, too. A slight burning sensation, like her leg had been partially sunburned.

"Gas burn from the bullet," he informed her. "Do you have some salve?"

"Yes, but I don't need it. That mark will probably be gone in a couple hours. It really doesn't hurt."

"Well, that may change. I'm going to take a photo of it now." Pulling his cell from his pocket, he snapped the picture. "Don't go in the bedroom, Summer. It's a crime scene. We need to preserve evidence, okay? And uh, I'll need your clothes."

He vanished into Blake's bedroom and came back with one of her housemate's T-shirts, then helped her change.

As he pushed her back, she held onto his neck. "Get down here with me, *querido*. It's already dawn and I'm not sleepy."

He gently loosened her hand. "Phone calls, remember?"

"Don't invite anyone back here. And your DNA is already all over this house, remember?"

He tried to suppress it, but his stern professional expression morphed into a smile. "I'll be back."

49

As Sam had guessed, she and Ranger Castro were summoned to talk to the authorities again that afternoon. Her rebandaged hand still hurt like hell, and the salve she'd smeared on her leg kept sticking to her pants. She was sick of the sheriff's office and the meeting room there. Even the coffee seemed to be more bitter. By the time she finished her tale of Wiley's attack, she was lightheaded. She clasped her bandaged right wrist with her left hand to keep her hands from shaking, and went on to explain her assumptions about the wrangler's participation in events along the East Bank Trail. Ranger Castro listened to Sam's speculations, rubbing her lower lip with a knuckle, a horrified expression deepening on her face. When Sam had finished, the ranger frowned, lowered her hand, and focused on the tabletop, saying, "Well, shit. That all fits."

"Except." Investigator Erickson raised a finger in the air. "We still need to prove it." Then she pointed that finger at Sam, as if proving the case was all up to her. "How does the floater in the lake fit in?"

They all pondered that for a few minutes. Finally, Deputy Ortiz broke the awkward silence. "I suspect Wiley Thompson will be able to fill in that missing piece. But first, we have to apprehend him. Bellingham Police and Whatcom County Sheriff are on the lookout. But his ranch is in Skagit County. I gotta get them on board ASAP."

With that, he stood up, adjusted his service belt, and stomped out of the room.

The meeting broke up without anyone divulging their plans for what came next, if indeed any of them had definite plans in place.

"Hey!" Erickson yelled after the deputy. "Keep me posted!"

"Gotta go inform the superintendent," Castro muttered. "Wiley might have disappeared into the park."

"You too," Erickson tossed at the ranger's back, clearly frustrated.

Sam guessed Erickson's non sequitur was intended as a follow-up command to the ranger. Sam slipped out the door before the investigator barked an order at her.

Sam thought it likely that Emmanuel Baptiste might have some useful information about the dead man, but she didn't volunteer his name. As an undocumented migrant, the guy was already in trouble. She'd visit him again in the hospital, and talk to him about this. The clank of his handcuff against the bed rail rang in her memory.

Why did her imagination conjure up an ugly image of a wolf caught in a trap?

Chase was waiting for her in the parking lot, pacing near his car. "Did they offer you protection?"

She hadn't even thought of that, and clearly, neither had any of the other participants. "I guess this is nothing like the movies," she told him.

"Good thing you know an FBI agent, then," he said.

"Damn good thing," she echoed. "And for what it's worth, Wiley Thompson seems like the most inept criminal I've ever run into."

"He shot you, Summer. And he broke into your house and

threatened you with a gun."

She considered that for a moment. What would have happened in the backyard if Wiley had gotten her out there? "He just didn't seem like a killer."

"I believe most of Ted Bundy's dates would have said that when they met him."

After Chase had thoroughly checked her house and yard and measured the destroyed window, they parted company for a couple of hours while Chase made a quick trip to his house and office and she worked on her article about hiking the trail and the one about Lysikov.

Then Chase returned, overnight bag in hand and a bag of groceries in the other, and a sheet of plywood in the car. He had volunteered to make dinner. She was always amazed and grateful that some people actually liked to cook; to her, the whole process was too time-consuming and stressful. After nailing the plywood over the window, Chase crafted handmade green chili and cheese enchiladas and a crunchy salad with sliced jicamas and strawberries, accompanied by margaritas he'd whipped up in the blender.

She oohed and aahed over the food.

Chase asked, "As good as Blake's cooking?"

"Different, but yes, definitely as good. I don't think Blake has ever cooked Mexican food for me." Like Blake, Chase loved to experiment with recipes, although his schedule as a roving FBI agent rarely left him much time to cook. He always felt he was in competition for her taste buds. Sam couldn't think of a better position for her to be in.

Chase grinned, satisfied.

Beneath the table, Simon rubbed against her ankles, and she reached down to stroke his fur. "Speaking of Blake," she began.

"Yes? How's the gorilla-sitting project?"

Sam had to think for a few seconds to come up with an appropriate adjective. "'Dramatic' is probably the best way to describe it. I told you that some scumbag shot the baby gorilla, Kanoni."

He scooped a last bit of enchilada from his plate with a scrap of tortilla. "Did they catch the shooter?" Placing the bundle in his mouth, he chewed as he waited for her answer.

"Not yet." Sam took another sip of margarita. Tart with extra lime juice, just the way she liked it. Simon levitated into her lap, and she scratched the cat gently under the chin. "But Kanoni survived and is back with the adult gorillas."

"That's good, isn't it?"

"But there's another development. A three-year-old child was found in the gorilla barn."

Chase sat back in his chair. "How could that happen?"

"They think that she got in through this feeding portal, a hole in the fence for the caretakers to drop in food. Apparently, the silverback can be violently protective, so they needed a safe way to feed the troop. But the gorillas didn't attack the little girl. It looks like Neema, the mother gorilla, protected the child and even fed her. Now, Blake is taking care of her."

Clapping a hand to his forehead, Chase stared into his half-empty margarita glass. "Shades of Tarzan! My head is spinning with all this. You find a dead guy in the lake and rescue a man and a horse and then get shot on the trail and later attacked in your house. Blake's gorillas were attacked, there was a murder nearby, and Haitians are in the mix? And I thought my work was complicated."

Simon leaped down to the floor to check his food dish. Sam was gratified that Chase had noted the confusion of details and understood her situation. "You forgot the wolves and the other dead hiker, but never mind. Can you take a few days off? Blake is down to only a couple more weeks, and I really want to go see these signing gorillas."

"Did they say you could leave town?"

She scowled at that. "I don't know who *they* would be, and I didn't ask." Then she softened her tone and suggested, "I could get Gina to drop by and check on Simon. We could drive to Evansburg in less than a day, and spend two nights in a classy hotel, then drive back."

He quirked an ebony eyebrow. "Do they have classy hotels in Evansburg?"

"Okay, maybe in a B and B. But I'd love for you to come with me. We haven't spent much time together since the avalanche."

He hesitated. "I still have a lot to wrap up on this Quinault investigation. Don't you have articles to write?"

She raised her injured hand and twisted it in the air as if modeling her bandage. "It's a long way. I'm not sure how well I can handle the drive with this. And there are still two shooters on the loose, one here and one there. And I have nobody to watch my back . . ."

Chase rolled his eyes. "Your helpless female act really needs work." Whatever he was going to say next was interrupted by the chime of his phone. After scanning the screen, he pressed the phone to his ear, murmuring, "Need to take this."

After listening to the caller for a minute, he said, "Okay, I'm in. Keep me posted."

Sam ran a finger around the rim of her empty margarita glass, annoyed at Chase's business dealings during dinner. "What are you 'in' now?" He'd probably announce next that he needed to return to the coast.

He pushed his phone back into his shirt pocket. "Since I obviously have a connection to this case, Erickson and Ortiz are formally requesting my assistance. It'll probably take the Seattle office at least a day to cave and approve. Bureaucracy, you know."

Sam had him now. "So?"

"So you'll pack tonight and go home with me first thing tomorrow morning so I can pack, and then we can take off, okay? We should be in Evansburg by noon."

50

Evansburg

Outside of Evansburg, Sam sat cross-legged in front of the gorilla enclosure, entranced by the interaction of the little girl and the mother gorilla. Rosa, the dark-skinned toddler, stood beside Sam, both hands thrust through the fence. She chanted "Nee-ma, Nee-ma, Nee-ma," followed by other words Sam didn't understand.

The mother gorilla lumbered over to the fence, sat on her rump, and placed both of her giant hands on top of the little girl's. Ape and tiny human gazed into each other's eyes. The girl laughed and chortled a few more words.

Kanoni emerged from the barn dragging a large branch. Observing the tender scene between her mother and Rosa, the young gorilla screeched, dropped her toy and rushed over to yank on Neema's arm. The mother gorilla swatted Kanoni away, and Kanoni squealed and dramatically rolled head over heels.

"She's healing quickly. Good thing, because that bandage won't stay in place much longer," Blake observed, tapping his own shoulder in the same location where Kanoni had been shot.

The little girl, seeing Blake's motion, pointed to Kanoni's bandaged shoulder. "Johan."

Blake and Sam exchanged a confused glance. Then Blake

shrugged. "I don't know who confuses me more, Rosa or Neema."

They watched as the youngest gorilla bounced up again, signing to Neema.

"Chase me," Blake interpreted. "Tickle me."

"Wow," Sam whispered. "They even sign to each other. And you can understand them."

"Yeah." Blake laughed. "I'm not sure how much future use I'll have for ape sign language, though." Standing on the other side of Rosa, he commented, "This whole experience has been pretty wow, for sure. But zookeeping is definitely not my next career. Especially when it comes with gunshots and dead neighbors."

Neema chased her gorilla daughter around the pen, both cackling maniacally. Outside the fence, Rosa giggled and clapped her hands.

Sam looked at her housemate. "It will be great to have you back in Bellingham. I've really missed you, Blake."

He twisted his lips in a wry expression. "You've missed my cooking."

"That, too." Sam stood up and dusted off the backside of her jeans. "I should probably tell you that Claude stopped by the house about two weeks ago, but I shooed him off."

"Good."

"Are you over him?" Truth be told, she kind of missed Claude. The three of them, often with Chase, too, had had some great times together. But the charming Canadian had lied to Blake for nearly two years about living a completely different life north of the border. Blake deserved so much better.

"I'm definitely over him." Blake paused, a blank look on his face as he considered. "Well, mostly. I don't want to see Claude again. And I'm ready to get back to my own kitchen and my spice rack, and to the greenhouse and the gang there. I think the manager must have missed me, too, because he promised me a raise if I came back."

Sam studied the little girl, who was now poking a dandelion flower through the fence, burbling in her language at the gorillas. Neema came over to accept the flower. Then she ate it, making Sam blink in surprise. Rosa giggled and began to search for more dandelions at the edges of the lawn. "What's going to happen to Rosa?"

Blake shook his head. "No idea. A child protection service type visited me this morning. She said she's working on a placement, but it might be in another town. That poor kid has been through so much, I hate to think of yet more strangers taking her to another strange place."

"As opposed to bunking with three gorillas, which is not strange at all." Sam looked for Chase, who was conferring with Detective Finn at the picnic table. She couldn't hear what they were saying. Law enforcement talk, no doubt.

"Rosa's mother is the dead woman they found?" Sam asked Blake. Yet another dead person in the same time short period. The stars must be out of alignment or something. Then again, humans did tend to kill each other all too often.

"It looks like that's the case." Blake patted himself down until he located his cell in a hip pocket and pulled it out. "I have a photo that Detective Finn sent me. He says this is Rosa's mother, Widelene Pierre, and most likely, Rosa's father, too." Blake showed her a photo of a woman and her husband in their wedding finery.

Sam gasped and reached for her cell phone in her back pocket.

Blake didn't notice her reaction. He continued, "Finn found her passport from Haiti. And a birth certificate for Rosaline Baptiste. This little girl is a US citizen, but her mother probably wasn't. And who knows about her father? Finn doesn't even have a name for him."

"A passport from Haiti? That's so weird. The man I found on the trail turned out to be Haitian." She'd flicked to the photo in her own phone. Balancing Blake's phone awkwardly in her bandaged hand, she compared both photos. "And *this* is even more weird."

"What's weird?" Blake asked. "That Haitians are escaping to the US? Have you been paying attention to the news out of Haiti? I'd sure be on the first boat out."

"I know." She held up both phones. "*Here's* the weird thing. This is the very same man I rescued in North Cascades."

He squinted at her. "Are you sure?" He took his phone back.

"Absolutely." She showed him her cell. "See, I have the exact same picture. I took this from a photo he had with him. His name is Emmanuel Baptiste. He's in the hospital in Bellingham."

Blake stood up. "Finn's got to hear this. This means that Rosa most likely has a parent in the US." He took both phones from her.

"Well, Emmanuel's in the US for now. But who knows how long he can stay? He's waiting for his asylum hearing." Sam strode with Blake over to the two law enforcement professionals.

Chase had already filled Finn in on a few of Sam's recent adventures, and Sam now provided details to the detective on the rest. When she'd concluded her summary and shown them both phones, the detective rubbed his forehead as if he had a headache. "So the man in the photo is Emmanuel Baptiste. It looks as if *he's* Widelene's husband, and he's in custody in Bellingham. Have I got that right?"

"Let me try something." Gesturing to Rosa to come, Blake

knelt down and showed the toddler the wedding photo. "Who's this, Rosa?"

Her little face darkened and she put a saliva-sticky finger on the woman's image. "Mama." Then she rattled off something that sounded sad. When she looked up, her eyes were shiny with tears.

"And this?" Blake put his finger on the groom in the photo. "Who is this man?"

Her little forehead creased and she glanced at him for reassurance. "Papi?"

Blake patted her on the back and then stood up. "Inconclusive, but I'm guessing someone, probably her mother, showed her that photo and told her that was her 'Papi.'"

"Emmanuel Baptiste told me he had a wife in Washington State, but he hadn't seen her for three years, and 'now a baby girl, too.'" Sam made one-handed air quotes around the last few words. "He's never seen his daughter."

"Sounds somewhat plausible." Finn frowned. "But then who the hell is Johan Vincent?"

That question elicited only curious stares from the rest of them. Finn explained Johan Vincent was the name of the man who'd been collecting Widelene's checks, and with whom she had most likely lived.

Sam said, "I think Rosa said that name just a few minutes ago. She was pointing to Kanoni's bandage, and she said 'Johan.'"

Finn perked up. "Like this Johan had something to do with the shooting?"

"Was he a Black man?" Sam asked.

The detective nodded. "According to the manager and a maid at the hotel where she worked. Vincent was likely Haitian by birth, but he has a US social security number and ID."

"There is—was—another Black man near Ross Lake in the North Cascades. Actually, *in* the lake. I don't know if he was Haitian." She held her phone out to Detective Finn to show him the photo of the floater. "He's dead."

"I can see that." Finn examined the photo for a long time, then pulled out his own phone and brought up a photo of a driver's license. "His face is bloated, so it's difficult to say whether or not he's the guy in this driver's license photo, but there's a definite possibility that he could be Johan Vincent."

"Emmanuel, the man in the hospital, might know," Sam told both men. "Seems very coincidental, doesn't it? Two unrelated Haitians in North Cascades National Park?"

Detective Finn tapped icons on her phone. "I'm sending this photo to myself now. I'll share it with the others in the station."

She smiled, thinking how that would probably irritate HSI Erickson. She took her phone back and then strode toward the little girl.

"Oh Sammie, don't show her a picture of a dead man!" Blake whined.

"She won't know." Squatting down beside Rosa, she showed the tiny girl the photo of the floater. "Rosa, who is this?"

The toddler stared at the phone for a long moment. Then she barked, "Johan!" and angrily slapped her pudgy hand down on the screen, nearly bouncing the phone out of Sam's hand. Next, Rosa abruptly sat down on the ground and started to sob.

"Enough." Blake scooped up the child and cuddled her against his chest.

Chase pulled his cell phone from his pocket. "I've got to talk to Investigator Erickson." He moved a few steps away to make the call.

Finn's phone buzzed. He extracted it from his pants pocket. "Grace!" he answered. "We're close to cracking this case. I'll be back with you in no time."

Inside the gorilla enclosure, the apes were becoming more and more rambunctious, their games increasingly boisterous. Finn plugged his other ear with a finger as he spoke with his girlfriend Grace McKenna in Hawaii. Chase was relaying information to Erickson in Bellingham. Sam and Blake watched the antics of the animals, who were playing a rough game of tag, interspersed by excitedly tossing objects around the cage. The branch that Kanoni had been dragging went flying, and then a half-deflated beach ball bounced against the fence.

Sam tried to imagine how these games played out in the wild. Tossing rocks and branches? Was there a goal, or were these displays of strength just plain gorilla fun? Were apes this loud in the jungle? That would seem to signal they had no worries about predators. She wished she could talk to Dr. McKenna about all this.

"Back in town late tomorrow," Chase told whomever he was talking to, his gaze connecting with hers as he walked toward her.

Annoyed, she frowned, realizing he had just cut short this visit. She turned back to the fence to watch the apes play. Chase's cell pinged, and he turned away to read a text.

Sam was surprised that in addition to Kanoni and her mother Neema, the silverback Gumu was also playing like a kid. A massive, superstrong kid. He threw the branch across the enclosure and beat his chest, and then picked up a giant tractor tire that lay next to the barn and hurled it toward the fence.

Blake grabbed Rosa's hand and pulled her away from the chain link as the tire clanged into it. The child's expression was perplexed, unsure whether to clap and laugh or contort her face in fear.

Rushing to the spot vacated by the tractor tire, Kanoni picked up an object from the dirt. Black. Heavy-looking. Shaped like a pistol.

"Uh, guys?" Sam raised her voice, trying to get everyone's attention. "Do the gorillas have a toy gun?"

51

All three men turned to regard the gorilla cage.

"Shit!" blurted Finn. "That is *not* a toy. Everybody take cover!"

Blake ran for his trailer carrying Rosa. Detective Finn dashed to the side of the barn, out of the gorillas' sight. Sam and Chase raced in opposite directions for the trees closest to them, and ducked behind the trunks, peeking out every few seconds to check the gorilla enclosure. From his position off to the side, Finn could see Sam, or Summer, as the FBI agent called her, but not much of Chase.

On Finn's cell phone, Grace was shouting now, her voice tinny on the device. "What's going on? Matt? Matt! Did someone mention a *gun?*"

Finn took a breath and then raised the phone to his ear. He thought his voice sounded remarkably calm as he said, "Grace, honey, somehow a pistol ended up in the gorilla cage. And now Kanoni has it."

He watched Sam Westin shoot a concerned glance to Chase Perez as Grace shouted questions over the phone line. "A pistol? How did that get there? How did Kanoni get hold of it?"

"Uh," said Finn. "We'll talk about all that later. For now, any ideas on how to get Kanoni to give it up?"

"Let me talk to her. Put me on the screen, and turn the

speakerphone up as loud as you can."

When Grace's image came into view, Finn held out the phone beyond the safety of the barn, where the gorillas could see it. "You're on, Grace."

In the trailer window across the courtyard, Blake's face appeared behind a screen.

"I can see the gorillas." Grace's voice rose in volume. "Kanoni, come! Kanoni! Come now!"

Finn peeked around the corner. Not only was Kanoni approaching with gun in hand, but Gumu trailed behind her, curious about what was happening. Neema calmly observed from the other side of the pen, idly chewing on a stalk of broccoli.

The baby gorilla held the pistol upside down, with one finger looped through the trigger guard. When Gumu noticed the new toy the youngster held, he wanted it. Grunting, the silverback jerked Kanoni's arm. The baby gorilla shrieked her outrage and tried to hide the gun by bending over and holding it against her belly. Finn feared that any second now Kanoni would shoot herself.

"Kanoni! Gumu! Put that down! Put the gun down now!" Grace's voice was nearly drowned out by the shrieks and growls of the gorillas as they contested ownership of the pistol. With an impressive snarl and baring of his long incisors, Gumu finally wrested the gun away from his daughter. Kanoni rained ineffective fisted blows down on her father's massive shoulder, until Gumu turned and roared at her, again flashing his fangs. Kanoni raced for the comfort of Neema's arms, whimpering.

Finn groaned.

The silverback now had his massive hand around the grip of the gun. The tip of one finger was looped through the trigger guard, just below the trigger.

"Gumu! Gumu! Put the gun down! Put the gun down *now!*"
Grace shouted. "Matt, for god's sake, where's Z?"

"He's running errands in t—"

The pistol went off with a loud bang. A bullet thudded into
the front of Sam's tree. She flinched at the impact and clutched
her wounded hand to her chest.

Shrieking at maximum volume, Gumu dropped the weapon
in the dirt, and he, too, fled to the other side of the cage, where
he sat, looking embarrassed and grunting nervously.

"Anyone hurt?" Grace wanted to know.

"Not so far," Finn told her. "But here they come again."

Indeed, all three gorillas were slowly, warily, approaching
the pistol on the ground, sniffing the air as they approached.

"Any ideas, Grace?"

"Neema's your best bet. You know how she likes to trade."

Apparently Blake heard that, because after a count of ten the
trailer door opened, and he slid two cookies out onto the steps,
then closed the door again.

"Cookie!" Grace announced over the phone. "Neema, trade
gun for cookie."

Nobody in the compound moved. "Grace, it's not safe for any
of us to come out in the open and make that trade," Finn told
her.

Neema touched the pistol with a tentative finger, and then
leaped back as if the gun were a snake. Grace had told him that
Neema had some knowledge of guns, gleaned from films the
gorilla had seen, and possibly from watching poachers kill her
mother when she was a baby. Neema had even learned a sign
language gesture for gun, which she used to give Finn a name,
Gun Man. Sometimes this was preceded by Dog Cat, as in Dog
Cat Gun Man. His service pistol had been the focus of the
gorilla's attention, but apparently Neema could also smell his

pets on his clothing.

The tree Sam sheltered behind was the closest to the trailer steps and the cookies. The gorilla enclosure was only steps away in the other direction. Sam apparently glanced at Chase Perez, because Finn heard the FBI agent say "No."

Ignoring him, Sam broke from her cover, trotted to the trailer steps, scooped up the cookies, and walked to the feeding portal. "Neema!" she called. "Trade gun for cookie!" She didn't know the signs for "trade" or "gun," but she made a motion like a gunfighter drawing from a holster, and then signed, *"Cookie."*

"Get out of there!" Finn urged her.

Signing *"Cookie,"* Neema stepped over the pistol on the ground and held her hand out through the feeding portal.

Behind the mother gorilla, Kanoni once again bent over the pistol, eyeing it carefully.

"Summer . . ." Chase hissed the warning.

Sam took a step back from the feeding portal. "Neema! *'Gun'"*—she signed it again—*"for cookie!"* She held a cookie in each hand up in the air. "Trade gun for two cookies!"

From Finn's phone, Grace's voice echoed the command. "Neema, trade gun for cookie. Gun for cookie, now!"

The mother gorilla's nostrils flared as she considered the offering. Finn was terrified that Kanoni would grab the gun again to make the deal.

Finally, Neema turned. Seeing Kanoni hovering over the pistol, she shoved her daughter out of the way and grabbed the gun, hooting nervously, her massive hand wrapped around the whole pistol as she carried it against her belly to the opening. She thrust the gun through the feeding portal and dropped it in the dirt outside.

Heaving a sigh of relief, Sam handed Neema the cookies, and then signed, *"Thank you."* Neema moved back against the barn, her treats held tightly to her chest. Kanoni swooped in and managed to snatch one away, cackling, but Gumu reached for Kanoni's cookie, breaking it in half. Then all three gorillas reclined against the side of the barn, munching.

The drama concluded, everyone stepped out of their respective hiding places. Blake held Rosa's hand as they walked down the steps, then the little girl pulled her hand from his and signed, *"Cookie."* Rolling his eyes, Blake went back into the trailer and emerged with a cookie for her.

Detective Finn crooked a finger in Sam's direction and then held out his phone, and Sam met Dr. Grace McKenna for the first time. The woman wore a red flower in her long dark hair. Behind her chair was a bush with more of the same blossoms. "Thank you, Summer," Grace said. "That was an incredibly brave thing to do."

"More like crazy," Chase grumbled, sliding an arm around Sam's shoulders. "But Summer's prone to doing things like that." He waved at the phone and introduced himself. "FBI Agent Chase Perez."

"Hello?" Grace said, confusion in her voice.

Finn pulled the phone back, tapped off the speakerphone and held it to his ear. "Yes, I can explain everything. Well, nearly everything. It's a little complicated."

Chase pulled Sam close and kissed her. *"Por el amor de Dios,* Summer, don't ever do that to me again."

"No promises," she told him.

"I thought you'd say that," Chase grumbled.

"Chase, Sam, Finn, how about a round of margaritas and nachos?" Blake gestured toward his trailer.

Finn held up a finger to signal he'd be there in a minute.

"Amen!" Sam slapped her hand against her leg. Turning to Finn, she shrugged and excused herself with, "Preacher's daughter."

Inside the gorilla pen, Neema signed *cookie* again, then gestured a couple of more signs.

"Tree candy," Blake interpreted, glancing at Sam. "That's Neema's absolute favorite treat. She wants a lollipop."

"Tree candy. Clever." Sam nodded. "And some people believe that animals don't think. Neema understands the shape of a tree and the concept of candy. Her description makes perfect sense."

Finn turned his back to murmur into his phone. "I'll be in Kauai in forty-eight hours, Grace. We'll still have ten days of vacation left."

52

As Finn drove to his office, he struggled to think through all the unraveled threads of this case that needed to be woven into place. He still had to solve the murder of the Haitian woman, Widelene Pierre. The man she had been living with was apparently not her husband, but could still be the father of Rosa. There were simply too many coincidences involving Haitians here to be totally unrelated. Summer Westin, a.k.a. Sam, caretaker Blake's housemate, had rescued a Haitian man in the North Cascades Park complex who had a wedding photo of himself and Widelene Pierre. Another Black man found shot and floating in Ross Lake was also most likely Haitian, and Rosa had seemed to identify his photo as Johan and associate his name with Kanoni's shooting. But why would he have shot Kanoni, and was he Widelene's murderer?

As the news about the Haitian connection swept the station, Jax, the intern, told Finn she had worked a summer for a relief organization in Haiti, and she had a passing knowledge of the Creole language.

"Really?" Finn was astonished. "I didn't think anyone went to Haiti."

"You'd be surprised," she said. "Haiti used to be a major tourist destination, so lots of Americans have visited it in the past. These days, some relief organizations, including the First

Christian Church here in town, have ongoing projects there, especially since the 2021 earthquake. So much of the infrastructure was destroyed, and hundreds of thousands of people were left homeless." She sighed heavily. "And then the gangs filled the gap when the government didn't come through. And our own government keeps wavering back and forth about whether Haitians deserve protection, when people are dying there every day, being murdered or just starving to death or dying from lack of medical care."

Finn felt like an ignoramus. "I don't think I've ever met a Haitian."

She shrugged. "Most of them end up in Florida, for obvious reasons."

"The closest point," he said.

"Right. Anyhow, about this little girl. My Creole is pretty rusty now, but I could try to interpret," she promised, her eyes gleaming. "But only in exchange for seeing these gorillas Rebecca Ramey keeps going on about."

When he asked whether Jax had any experience talking to a three-year-old, she'd laughed. "You know, Detective Finn, you might try getting to know the personnel here. I have a son. He'll be four in September."

He'd squinted. "How old are you? I assumed around nineteen or twenty."

She chuckled again. "Then it would still be possible that I had a four-year-old, you know."

He blushed, thinking of teen mom Brittany Morgan's missing-baby case, which had been his first big challenge in Evansburg. "I guess that's true. Sorry."

"I'm twenty-four, by the way." She turned back to her computer, smiling at his discomfort. "I'll see you and—what's the little girl's name?"

"Rosaline."

"And Rosaline, tomorrow at eleven out at Grace McKenna's."

Finn had just been dismissed. By his own intern, no less.

The next day, while he waited at Grace's compound for Jax to arrive, he mulled over the evidence needed to prove most everything having to do with this case. Rosa's testimony could be vital, if a three-year-old could be trusted to provide information. He'd learned from Neema that even limited memories and experiences such as a gorilla's could offer useful clues, although he would never admit that to anyone except for Grace, Z, and maybe now Blake.

Widelene had been shot, as well as Kanoni, most likely at more or less the same time. The two shots Blake had heard in the middle of the night. The bullet had been recovered from Kanoni's shoulder and was being compared today by a ballistics expert with the pistol found in the gorilla pen. He had no idea how that gun had ended up so far inside the enclosure. With luck, forensics would find some useful fingerprints on the pistol. He feared those might include gorilla fingerprints, because while the pistol could not have originated with the gorillas, based on its hidden position, it had likely been tossed or concealed there by one of the gorillas. He hoped the gun would include at least one human fingerprint.

If only he had bullets from Widelene's body. Her injury had been a through-and-through, unfortunately clipping part of her liver and an intestine. She'd probably lived for hours in excruciating pain, slowly bleeding out as her young daughter waited by her side.

He watched Blake playing with Rosa at the picnic table now, stacking ABC blocks and then knocking them down. The dense plastic blocks had teeth marks on them, so he suspected Grace had used them in gorilla training at one time or another.

The sound of gravel crunching alerted him to Jax's arrival. "Ah," she said, sliding out of a Prius. "The gorillas!" She immediately walked to the cage.

"Neema," Finn called, signing, *"Come say hi."*

The mother gorilla ambled over, followed closely by Kanoni. After an introductory sniff at Jax, Neema raised a hand in greeting, then thumped her hand on her chest.

"Hello. Neema fine gorilla," Finn translated.

Jax chuckled. "Detective! You speak gorilla sign language!"

"Tell anyone and you'll be filing carbon copies of useless information for a decade," he threatened.

"Got it," she said.

"Neema, Neema!" The little girl joined them at the fence.

"You must be Rosaline." Jax knelt down beside the dark-skinned toddler.

When Rosa regarded her curiously, Jax rattled off a melodic sequence of sentences. The little girl grinned and pointed at Neema, chattering. Finn understood only one word, which Rosa pronounced "go-rilla."

Jax chuckled. "Rosa says Neema is her gorilla mother, and Neema likes green things and white things and cookies. And she's warm to sleep with."

Finn nodded. "It seems like Neema may have taken care of Rosa when she ended up in the pen."

When Kanoni sidled up to Neema, Rosa scowled and told Jax something else.

"She says Kanoni is mean to her." Shifting her glance up to Finn's face, Jax added, "Probably jealous, just like a human sibling."

"Makes sense. Can we shift this interview to the picnic table?" Finn pointed.

Jax and Blake introduced themselves, and then Blake tried

to excuse himself. But Finn asked him to film the interview, handing him a tiny video recorder. Blake eyed the device suspiciously.

"Sorry," Finn explained, showing Blake the controls. "It's department-issue. Courts and judges tend not to trust stuff on personal cell phones, and you never know where things will lead."

After they were settled at the table, Finn instructed Jax to ask about what had happened to Kanoni. The little girl glanced in the direction of the gorilla enclosure and then became very animated, making her hand into a gun and chattering loudly. Even Gumu noticed, growling at the gesture and thumping his chest.

"I think she said Johan wanted to kill the gorillas because they were so noisy, and he had a gun."

Rosa slid off the bench and scampered over to the feeding portal, patting the metal lip there. Gumu growled again, and Rosa ran back.

"Johan pointed the gun inside that hole," Jax interpreted.

"Bang!" Rosa shouted, startling everyone at the table.

"It went off," Jax narrated. "Obviously."

Then the little girl grabbed Jax's arm and pulled it back and forth, chattering animatedly.

"Then the biggest gorilla grabbed the gun, too," Jax told them.

Rosa shouted "Bang!" again, and then mumbled a few more words. Her face crumpled and she began to sob.

"They shot her mother," Jax finished sadly.

The small child climbed into Jax's lap and lay her head against the woman's chest.

"That's enough for today," Blake turned off the recorder and handed it back to Finn. "Time for lunch and a nap, I think." He held his hands out to Rosa. Jax transferred her over.

Finn thanked Jax and offered to buy her lunch at the diner in town, which she gratefully accepted. "I'll be there in about forty-five minutes." He waved to her as she backed out of the driveway.

He returned to the blood-stained area outside of the pen and paced back and forth, scuffing his shoes over the dirt around the perimeter. His actions turned up two small rocks before hitting pay dirt, a bullet that had plowed into the soil, burying itself by a couple of inches. He pinched it up, his hand inside an inside-out evidence bag from his pocket, then sealed and labeled it. The forensic tech hadn't looked very hard for this, because at the time, the department had assumed the crime involved only injury to an animal, and not even a valuable cow or horse at that. If he was right and Rosa understood what she had seen, this bullet would also match the bullet extracted from Kanoni, and the pistol found in the gorilla pen. It looked as if Gumu had won that wrestling match for the weapon, but if the blood in the courtyard matched Widelene's, Rosa's mother had been collateral damage.

53

Bellingham

By the time Chase and Sam arrived back in Bellingham the next day, the puzzle pieces were starting to fit into place.

Carole Erickson, at Chase's urging, reluctantly gave permission for Sam, Deputy Ortiz, and Ranger Amelia Castro to observe their interview of Wiley Thompson on a computer displaying the video feed from the camera in the corner of the interview room.

A joint SWAT team from Whatcom and Skagit counties had located the man on his own ranch, hiding out in a storage shed at the back of the property. Now, a Whatcom County jail employee manhandled him into the room in a wheelchair and transferred him to a chair, locking his handcuffs into a chain attached to the table. He wore one jail slipper. His other foot was swathed in bandages. Sam couldn't stifle a smile, remembering how he'd shot himself in the foot. Were his testicles black and blue? She sincerely hoped so.

Ortiz was watching her, a curious expression on his face.

"I was there when he shot his own foot. And I squashed his balls, too."

The deputy squirmed and shoved his hands into his front uniform pockets. Ranger Castro winked at Sam from Ortiz's other side.

In the interview room, Erickson and Chase detailed the events and evidence from his assault on Summer Westin. Wiley seemed resigned and acknowledged the details.

"I didn't want to do it, but I had to. If only Westin hadn't found the Haitian guy and Gypsy in that ravine. I mean, really, nobody but me even knows about that trail. Why the hell was *she* there?" His tone grew angrier as he explained. "And then, she just wouldn't leave it alone! Why did she have to look in those panniers, and why did she have to take the guy and the horse with her instead of just calling for help like a normal person?" He shook his head. "She made me go after her."

"Interesting defense," Ortiz commented dryly, rubbing his moustache.

Erickson asked about the people Wiley had been smuggling in.

"Look," Wiley told her. "To them, I'm a hero. They come from God knows what hellholes and just need someone to help them."

He refused to tell how many he'd "helped," saying, "I don't know any names; I don't know any countries. None of that is my business."

"Where did you meet them? Who handed them over? Where did you deliver them? How did you get paid?" Erickson fired off questions in rapid succession, waiting only a beat of time for an answer before rattling off the next. "Did you always transport drugs along with migrants?"

"I'm not a drug dealer. That was just a one-time deal; I needed the money for my ranch."

"Who delivered the drugs?"

Wiley's response was to ask for an attorney.

Chase tried another question. "Was it the man who ended up in the lake? Was his name Johan Vincent?"

Wiley pounded on the table with his free hand. "Attorney, I said! You're supposed to stop asking questions until I get an attorney."

Then the interview was concluded and Wiley Thompson was removed from the room. Deputy Ortiz went in to participate in a debate about whose responsibility it was to secure an attorney for the accused smuggler, and exactly which court this mess would end up in. Carole Erickson finally held up her hands in exasperation and told the others she'd sort it all out and get back to them in a day or so.

"That was sort of unsatisfactory," Sam told Chase when he came out.

"Welcome to my world. The wheels of justice sometimes grind themselves into squares instead of circles, but eventually things get sorted out and moving again. At least we have the main guy in custody."

"Is Wiley the 'main guy'?" she asked.

"For now." Putting a hand on her shoulder, Chase said, "Let's go to lunch. Blake and Finn should be there any time with the little girl."

Blake, Detective Finn, and Rosaline were already seated at the local restaurant when she and Chase arrived. The three-year-old was wearing an adorable lavender dress that she was clearly proud of, running her hands repeatedly down the front of it, giggling every time she did so.

"Nice choice, Blake," Sam told him. "Did you braid her hair?"

"No need, apparently," Detective Finn surprised them by saying. "One of the Evansburg police interns, Jax, fixed that one braid, and told me to shampoo her head with the braids still in."

"Clearly, that worked." Rosaline's braids were shining in the overhead lights.

"Baids!" The toddler patted her head with both hands.

"She's learning English quickly," Blake observed.

Their food arrived, burgers for the adults, macaroni and cheese for Rosaline.

"Chow down." Chase checked his watch. "We have an appointment at the hospital in fifty-five minutes."

"Will Investigator Erickson be there?" Sam asked.

Chase appeared surprised by the question. "Of course."

"Wonderful." Sam said sarcastically, spreading her napkin across her lap. "I can hardly wait to spend time with her again."

Erickson was already in Emmanuel's hospital room, along with Madeline Chery, the interpreter, when Sam, Chase, and Finn entered, making the small space suddenly seem crowded. Blake and Rosaline waited nearby in a small waiting room filled with children's toys.

Emmanuel's expression grew more concerned with the introduction of the FBI agent and the police detective. Sam's stomach knotted with dread. Whatever Emmanuel was expecting from this gathering, she knew the reality was going to be far worse.

She hovered near his shoulder, touching him lightly, as Detective Finn delivered the news of his wife's death. Tears ran down Madeline's cheeks as she interpreted.

"Your wife was living with a man called Johan Vincent. He'd promised to help her, I'm guessing, but he ended up somehow killing her."

Emmanuel's face contorted as he struggled not to cry. Sam grasped his shoulder more firmly, and he reached up with his free hand to grab hers.

"Do you know Johan Vincent?" Finn asked.

After swallowing hard several times, Emmanuel nodded.

Tears were flowing freely now, dripping off his chin.

Erickson showed him the photo of the floater. "Is this him?"

Another nod.

"What happened to him?"

The breath that Emmanuel sucked in was long and slow, and he gazed at the wall, his voice cracking now as he began to talk.

"Johan guided us from Canada to the lake. At first we walked, but the last part was in a boat. We arrived just as two other men were leaving in a different boat." Madeline translated, then gestured for Emmanuel to continue.

"We met a cowboy there. He had horses for us, but the men who just left had delivered big bags of drugs, and the cowboy was loading the horses with those. When Johan saw that, he refused to pay the cowboy and he refused to let us go with him. Johan said he didn't want any part of drugs. They fought."

"This Johan was okay with smuggling people, but not drugs?" Sam asked, surprised.

The interpreter looked at Erickson for direction about whether to translate the question.

Erickson shook her head at Chery and then turned to Sam, shrugging. "You'd be surprised about the moral codes of some of these smugglers. To him, bringing people in was probably not a crime, but drugs were a different story." She turned back to Emmanuel and signaled for Madeline to continue. "Then what happened?"

"The cowboy shot Johan. He fell in the lake. The cowboy pulled the boat up onshore and hid it, and we all got on the horses and rode until the trail got bad with sliding rocks. Wolves howled, and my horse fell off the trail. The others left me there."

Emmanuel looked up at Sam and concluded with, "You know the rest. My friend saved me." Letting go of her hand, he wiped his cheeks.

"Did you know Johan before you came here?"

He shook his head.

"He never told you he knew your wife?"

Emmanuel continued to shake his head, and he reached up with his free hand to stifle a sob coming from his lips. In a shaky voice, he asked how his wife had died.

"She was shot," Erickson said.

Apparently, that needed no translation, because Emmanuel immediately sobbed aloud, tears now streaming from his eyes.

Erickson surprised Sam by thanking Emmanuel for telling his story. He looked down at the bed and crinkled the sheet in his free hand.

Sam wanted to be the one to break the good news. "Emmanuel, we have your daughter."

The investigator made a hissing noise of disapproval. The DNA tests had not yet been completed to prove they were father and daughter. Sam ignored Erickson.

Emmanuel's head jerked up and he searched Sam's face with his eyes.

"Are you ready to meet her?"

Emmanuel gulped wiped his tears with the back of his hand. "Please," he croaked in English.

Sam left and returned with Blake, Rosaline clutched in his arms. The child was solemn on seeing so many people in the hospital room. She stuck a thumb into her mouth to suck on it.

The wedding photo was already displayed on Sam's cell phone, and Blake drew Rosaline's attention to it, pointing and saying "Rosa, who is this?"

"Mama and Papi." She gazed up at Blake for confirmation.

To Erickson, Blake explained, "Her mother probably showed her this photo a hundred times." To Rosaline, he said, "And who is this?" He then pointed to Emmanuel.

Rosaline looked again at the photo, and then at the man in the bed. "Papi?"

"Papi," Emmanuel echoed, holding out his free hand in her direction.

"That's right," Blake said, "He's your papi."

After checking the child's expression to see if she were afraid, Blake set her down on the bed next to Emmanuel, and father and daughter simply gazed at each other for several minutes.

"I think it's amazing that a three-year-old can make that connection," Detective Finn remarked. "But I've learned recently that I'm pretty ignorant when it comes to three-year-olds."

Finally, Rosaline reached out and softly patted Emmanuel's cheek, and then said something to him.

"Papi, you're sad," Madeline interpreted for the rest. Then, "You are so beautiful, my daughter," when Emmanuel responded, touching the little girl's cheek.

Emmanuel focused on Madeline. "Where will she stay?"

Madeline turned to Erickson, her brow wrinkling.

"We have someone coming for her tomorrow," Erickson said. "Foster family tonight."

Blake crossed his arms. "She'll stay with me at Sam's house tonight." His tone dared anyone to disagree. Nobody did.

Detective Finn looked at his watch. "I have a flight to catch in Seattle in three hours. You all know where to reach me." After Erickson and Chase had nodded, he left.

Erickson stood up, too. "We'll settle the details tomorrow."

When she looked at Madeline, the interpreter nodded.

"Say adieu to Papi," Blake told Rosaline.

The little girl leaned forward and kissed her father's cheek. Emmanuel, overcome, simply grasped her little hand, shaking it up and down.

As they all filed out of the room, they heard agonized sobs from Emmanuel Baptiste. Sam nearly turned to go back, but Chase stopped her.

"I don't think anyone can comfort him right now, Summer. Let him come to grips with all of it. We'll see him tomorrow."

Blake's expression wavered between anger and sorrow. He hugged Rosa closer to his chest and kissed the top of her head.

"I thought you needed to get back to Evansburg," Sam said.

"Z can hold down the fort for a night." When Rosaline looked up from his arms, he added, "Or more, if need be." Then he forced a smile. "We'll see Papi tomorrow, Rosa."

"Okay," she chirped. And then lay her head against Blake's chest again.

54

Investigator Erickson summoned Sam and Blake for a two-o'clock meeting in Emmanuel's hospital room, which naturally meant that Rosaline was coming as well. Any command from Carole Erickson caused butterflies to hatch out in Sam's stomach, and at this meeting, it was likely that Emmanuel's and Rosaline's immediate futures were going to be announced.

"I'm coming, too," Chase announced from her office. He'd commandeered her computer and had been busy with phone calls and research since they'd returned from Evansburg. "And I've invited an important guest."

Sam frowned. "And you're not going to tell me who that is."

"Correct."

When they walked into the room, Emmanuel's expression was sober, and Sam was sure that the presence of Carole Erickson and Madeline Chery was not helping. They'd probably been grilling the distraught widower for more details about his illegal entry to the country. But as soon as Emmanuel spotted Rosaline, he brightened, breaking into a smile.

"Papi!" the little girl chirped, and they began happily chattering in Creole. Blake set Rosaline on the bed next to her father. It was gratifying to see how quickly they'd bonded. But the ugly fact remained that the three-year-old was an American citizen, and her father an undocumented migrant.

Emmanuel and Rosaline burbled back and forth. Erickson scowled at Madeline, no doubt awaiting translation.

"Just kid chatter," Madeline explained. "She's telling him about the cat she met yesterday."

"My cat," Sam clarified.

Rosaline told her father something that made his eyebrows shoot up in surprise.

"She just told him that you don't have any gorillas," the interpreter told Sam. Then she faced Erickson. "I'll let you know if they say anything significant."

The investigator was only slightly mollified by that. Erickson rubbed her hands over her thighs, smoothing her pants, then gazed at those present and stated, "As you know, Emmanuel Baptiste entered the country illegally."

Madeline interpreted for Emmanuel.

Erickson continued. "He will likely be released from the hospital tomorrow, and he will be allowed to remain in the country until his asylum hearing, which is set for six weeks from now."

On hearing Madeline's translation, Emmanuel's expression darkened, but when he saw Rosaline's face mirror his, he swallowed hard and then gave his daughter an uncertain smile.

Chase's phone buzzed, and everyone turned to watch as he pulled it out of his pocket. That was less painful than everyone in the room frowning at each other in dismay over what the future would bring.

"Back in a few minutes," he said. "There's someone you all need to meet."

"I didn't—" Carole Erickson began, but Chase was out the door, so she let that sentence trail off.

Sam guessed she was about to say something along the lines of *I didn't authorize that.*

The woman Chase brought back with him had the same smooth dark skin as Emmanuel and Rosaline. Her curly black hair was twisted up into a bun, and she wore makeup and a smart red blouse over black slacks.

Chase made the introductions. Addressing Emmanuel, he said, "This is Mirlande Delva, your wife's cousin. She lives in Seattle."

The woman moved forward, greeting Emmanuel in Creole. Leaning in, she kissed him on the cheek, then hugged and kissed Rosaline, too. A tear escaped from Mirlande's right eye to roll down toward her chin, and Rosaline reached up and wiped it away with her pudgy little hand, then made a gesture down her own cheek.

"*Sad, cry,*" Blake interpreted. "Sign language."

"Gorilla sign language?" Sam asked, a note of incredulity in her voice.

Blake shrugged. "Rosaline learned from Neema." When Mirlande faced him with curiosity in her eyes, he said, "Neema is a gorilla."

Rosaline chuckled. "Go-rilla!"

Mirlande rattled off several sentences to Emmanuel, and then they both laughed.

"Talking about the gorilla," the interpreter said to the room.

Caroline Erickson cleared her throat. "Well, I've got to hear about that sometime soon. But for now, we are discussing Emmanuel Baptiste's future, and that of Rosaline Baptiste here. First of all, we will need to determine a genetic link between father and daughter."

"Okay." That would likely be just cheek swabs from both. "So then, will Emmanuel be allowed to stay in the country since Rosaline is an American citizen?"

"Not necessarily." The investigator's tone was grim.

"Will he be allowed to work?" Blake pressed. "Will Rosaline be allowed to stay with him?"

"There's an immigrant detention center in Tacoma, and that's where he'll likely be sent. Maybe a foster family could be found close by for Rosaline."

"No!" Mirlande shook her head. "I will sponsor Emmanuel. He and Rosaline will stay with me." She relayed this to Emmanuel, and they conversed back and forth, with Madeline translating.

"You and Rosaline are family." [Mirlande]

"I want to pay my way and earn money for my daughter." [Emmanuel]

"I have a job for you." [Mirlande]

Erickson protested. "No, no, no. Asylum seekers are not allowed to work until they receive permission. There's a form he'll need to fill out, but he can't do that until he's been in the US for several more weeks."

Mirlande answered the investigator. "Until he has work permission, Emmanuel will *volunteer* for the Haitian Refugee Support Center in Seattle. They will pay his room and board and a small stipend for his *volunteer* work."

"Fine," Erickson conceded. "But he may still be deported if he isn't granted refugee status."

"What about Rosaline?" Blake asked.

"She would have to live with a foster parent or go with him. She could come back when she's eighteen."

Sam was beginning to feel like crying herself. She stifled the urge to sign *sad, cry* as Rosaline had.

"That's it." Erickson stood up and pointed to Mirlande. "Come with me. I'll take down your contact information and someone will let you know when your . . ." Her brow furrowed, no doubt trying to sort out the family relationship between a cousin and the husband of the deceased. ". . . when Emmanuel can leave the hospital." They left the room.

Brief exchanges followed between the interpreter and Emmanuel, and then Madeline Chery departed, too, leaving Emmanuel, Rosaline, Chase, Blake, and Sam in awkward silence.

"Well," Blake finally said. "If they'll let me, I can take Rosaline back to Evansburg with me tomorrow." He touched Rosaline gently on the shoulder. "Say goodbye to Papi for now, Rosa."

The little girl dutifully leaned forward and grasped Emmanuel's face with both hands. "Bye-bye, Papi!"

Blake swept her up, and the toddler clung to him, uncertainty clouding her features.

"Poor tyke." Blake rubbed his hand across the back of her braids. "She's been through so much in just a few days."

55

The next morning, Investigator Erickson waited with Mirlande for Sam, Blake, and Rosaline outside Emmanuel's hospital room. Chase returned to the FBI office to do paperwork.

"Look," Erickson said. "I'm not heartless. Immigration is in charge of Emmanuel's future, and the current government keeps swinging back and forth. In the last two weeks, more than a hundred Haitians have been deported back to Haiti, and it seems like more are being repatriated every day.

"That sounds grim," Sam observed needlessly.

Erickson shrugged. "That said, Baptiste has a decent case for refugee status, and he's a vital witness in two smuggling cases. I'll lobby for getting both Emmanuel and Rosaline released to Miss Delva here, but that could take a few days. Make sure, all of you, that I know where to find you."

After a visit with Emmanuel, Blake and Sam took Mirlande back to Sam's cabin.

"I need to head back to Evansburg," Blake told the women. "I'll take Rosaline." He inclined his head toward the coffee table, where the little girl was scribbling on a piece of scratch paper with a red felt pen.

"No," Mirlande protested. "*I* am her aunt. I will take her to Seattle. There are other Haitians at the center who speak her language. Other children her age, too. And her father will be there soon as well."

"Thank you," Sam said.

Blake's expression was sorrowful. "I'll miss her."

They packed the few items that Blake had purchased for the tiny girl and said their goodbyes.

Closing the door behind them, Sam remarked, "I can't believe any authorities in their right minds would send Rosaline and Emmanuel back to Haiti."

Blake snorted. "Then you haven't been paying attention to the national news, have you?" He hugged her to soften the cynicism. "See you in a couple of weeks, Sammie. Don't give my room away."

"Never."

"Or my spices, or my cookware."

She gave him a three-fingered salute. "Don't let those gorillas boss you around."

He snorted again.

She tried to focus on editing her article about Alex Lysikov and writing a rough draft about her experiences on the East Bank Trail, but her efforts were frustrated by still having only one functional hand. Her brain kept wandering back to Emmanuel and Rosaline and the dead wife/mother and how everything in life seemed to be dependent on the place you were born and the family you were born into.

Feeling grateful to be American and be born into a kind family, she called her father in Kansas instead of waiting for him to call her as she usually did.

Zola answered. "This is a pleasant surprise. How are you, Summer?"

"I'm fine. Well, I got shot in the hand, but I'm healing."

"What? Did you say you were shot?"

"Yes, but I'm going to be fine. I called to hear how *you're* doing, Zola." She braced herself for bad news as she watched through the back window as the pileated woodpecker returned to enlarge the hole in the dead tree in the yard.

"I couldn't be better."

"Really?" Sam asked.

She heard a click in the background, and then her father's voice joined on the landline. "Really, Summer. The oncologist says she's all clear."

"Thank God. That's wonderful."

"Amen!" Mark Westin chuckled.

Sam was pleased that for once, she'd voiced a response that her father appreciated. They chatted for a few more minutes before hanging up, Zola full of news about her grown twin daughters, and her father telling her about the upcoming church picnic and all the games they had scheduled.

After ending the call, she couldn't stop thinking about families and how unfair life had been for Emmanuel and his daughter. More Americans needed to hear this story. She decided to call Adam. He lived in California, but could be anywhere his television work took him.

As she punched in his number, Simon jumped onto her desk and tramped across her keyboard, then leaped to her lap.

To her surprise, Adam answered on the third ring. "Well, well, well, if it's not Sizzling Hot Summer in the City. What disaster have you been involved in recently?"

"Um . . . I got shot."

He laughed. "Aren't you always getting shot?"

She was annoyed. "Hell, no, Adam."

"Buried in an avalanche?"

What a jerk. "Not recently. And don't make fun of all the

people that died only a few weeks ago. You got a lot of attention and made a lot of money from that story."

"I stand reprimanded."

He didn't sound at all chastened. His documentaries had brought well-deserved attention to several situations in the past that she had wanted the public to know about. She was confident he could do the same for Emmanuel and Rosaline. "I called to tell you about a couple of opportunities for stories that would be perfect for your skills."

"Fire away." She heard him take a sip of something.

"First, did you know that there are over a thousand people that have gone missing in our public lands over the years? I found the remains of one just a few days ago."

"Old news. Like you said, over a thousand. Over time. Too much research required, although I'll file the idea away for a potential series in case I get desperate in the future. There will probably be even more in the future. Maybe a series could fit in with the police shows that are proliferating like maggots on a dead rat."

"Nice image." She groaned. "That's going to take me a while to unsee."

"You're welcome. What are you wearing right now?"

"Focus!" How could she have dated this guy for so long? "Here's another idea, Adam. Illegal migrants from Haiti. The wife comes in along the southern border, and the husband sneaks across the border from Canada."

"The immigration issue is on the news every night, my princess of the mundane."

Yeesh, whatever he was sipping had to be alcoholic, and probably not his first drink, either. She continued, "The wife gets murdered by her smuggler, and the husband ends up in a ravine in the North Cascades with a broken leg, abandoned by a drug smuggler after his horse fell off a trail. And they have a three-year-old daughter who ends up in a barn with a signing gorilla who takes care of her."

Simon butted his head against her arm to remind her she was supposed to be petting him.

"Did you say a signing gorilla?"

She was surprised he was still paying attention. "I was there for all of this. I'm going to write the story. I'm sure I can sell it quickly, so if you're not interested . . ."

"Whoa, whoa, whoa, babe!" She heard sounds of typing on his end. "Don't talk to anyone else. I'm sure we can make a deal."

"I'm not your 'babe.'"

"Are you going to be home tomorrow afternoon, oh most honorable Ms. Westin? Because I can be on the plane that's landing in Bellingham at five ten p.m. tomorrow. I'll take you out to dinner and we can get totally wasted to celebrate the rebirth of our dynamic duo."

"Trio. You can take Chase out to dinner, too."

"Killjoy. Can we really trust the FBI to keep our secret? I hear those special agents have loose lips. Whereas mine are tight. And plump. And handsome."

"See you tomorrow, Adam." She ended the call.

"Simon," she said, stroking the cat, "I think it's all going to be okay."

Acknowledgments

All authors need the opinions and suggestions of others to improve our work, and I am so grateful that my readers and editors always do that for me. I'd like to express my gratitude to the following people who graciously took the time to read my drafts and share their comments to improve *If Only*: Worldkeeper Diane Garland, Rosie Sundre, Jeanine Clifford, author Sean Dwyer and Alison Malfatti. And I could never publish a book without the careful scrutiny and clever suggestions from super-editor Karen Brown.

And last but never least, thank you to my readers for being willing to go on another adventure with Sam Westin and Neema.

Thank you all!

Books by Pamela Beason

The Sam Westin Wilderness Mysteries
Endangered
Bear Bait
Undercurrents
Backcountry
Borderland
Cascade
If Only

The Neema the Gorilla Mysteries
The Only Witness
The Only Clue
The Only One Left

Romantic Suspense
Shaken
Again
Call of the Jaguar

The Run for Your Life Adventure/Suspense Trilogy
Race with Danger
Race to Truth
Race for Justice

Nonfiction E-books
So You Want to Be a PI?
Traditional vs Indie Publishing: What to Expect
Save Your Money, Your Sanity, and Our Planet

There's always another book in progress.
Keep up with Pam on https://pamelabeason.com

Sign up for my newsletter and download a free copy of
Race with Danger!

About the Author

Pamela Beason is the author of the Sam Westin Wilderness Mysteries, the Neema the Gorilla Mysteries, and the Run for Your Life Adventure Trilogy, as well as several romantic suspense and nonfiction books. She has received the Daphne du Maurier Award and two Chanticleer Book Reviews Grand Prizes for her writing, as well as an award from Library Journal and other romance and mystery awards. Pam is a former private investigator and freelance writer who lives in the Pacific Northwest, where she escapes into the wilderness whenever she can to hike and kayak and scuba dive.

https://pamelabeason.com

Made in United States
Troutdale, OR
01/17/2025

28000602R00210